Acclaim f[or]

# Andrew Vachss

"Vachss [is] in the first ra[nk...] writers."

"Next to Vachss, Chandle[r...] boys."
—*Cleveland Plain Dealer*

"[Vachss] does to pimps, pederasts, snuff film makers and porn industry purveyors what you know he'd like to do in real life, but seldom can. In other words, he decimates them."
—*Detroit News*

"Vachss is a contemporary master." —*Atlanta Journal-Constitution*

"Move over, Hammett and Chandler, you've got company. . . . An absolute original . . . Andrew Vachss has become a cult favorite, and for good reason."
—*Cosmopolitan*

"Vachss' writing is like a dark rollercoaster ride of fear, love and hate."
—*Times Picayune*

"Andrew Vachss, a lawyer who specializes in the problems of child abuse, writes a hypnotically violent prose made up of equal parts of broken concrete block and razor wire."
—*Chicago Sun-Times*

"The best detective fiction being written . . . add a stinging social commentary . . . a Célinesque journey into darkness, and we have an Andrew Vachss, one of our most important writers."
–*Martha Grimes*

# Andrew Vachss
# Born Bad

Andrew Vachss has been a federal investigator in sexually transmitted diseases, a social caseworker, and a labor organizer, and has directed a maximum-security prison for youthful offenders. Now a lawyer in private practice, he represents children and youth exclusively. He is the author of numerous novels, two collections of short stories, three graphic series, and *Another Chance to Get It Right: A Children's Book for Adults*. His work has appeared in *Parade, Esquire, Antaeus, The New York Times,* and many other forums. Born and raised in New York City, he now lives in the Pacific Northwest.

The dedicated Web site for Vachss and his work is www.vachss.com

## Books by Andrew Vachss

Flood

Strega

Blue Belle

Hard Candy

Blossom

Sacrifice

Another Chance to Get It Right:
A Children's Book for Adults

Shella

Down in the Zero

Born Bad

Footsteps of the Hawk

False Allegations

Safe House

Choice of Evil

Everybody Pays

# BORN
## BAD

# BORN
# BAD

stories

# Andrew Vachss

**Vintage Crime / Black Lizard**

Vintage Books · A Division of Random House, Inc. · New York

A VINTAGE CRIME/BLACK LIZARD ORIGINAL, FIRST EDITION
August 1994

Some of the stories in this collection were originally
published in *The Armchair Detective; Borderlands;
Cemetery Dance; Ellery Queen's Mystery Magazine;
Hard Looks; Hardboiled Detective; A Matter of Crime;
New Mystery; Underground; Cold Blood* (Ziesing);
Crossroads Press (chapbook); Dark at Heart (Dark
Harvest); *Invitation to Murder* (Dark Harvest); *Narrow
Houses* (Little, Brown, UK); *New Crimes* (Robinson
Publishing, UK); *The New Mystery* (Dutton); *Ten Tales*
(Cahill Press).

Library of Congress Cataloging-in-Publication Data
Vachss, Andrew H.
[Short stories.    Selections]
Born bad : stories / by Andrew Vachss. — 1st ed.
p.    cm. — (Vintage crime/black lizard)
ISBN 0-679-75336-2
1. Detective and mystery stories, American.    I. Title.
II. Series.
PS3572.A33A6    1994
813'.54—dc20        94-15177
CIP

Manufactured in the United States of America
B9876543

Tortured far apart
Children of the Secret are
Alone until love

# Contents

# Introduction

**W**riting short stories is like fighting in a real small ring: whatever your style, you have to get busy quick. It's easier to make mistakes, and it costs more if you do.

If you're looking for a Chandler clone, save your money. If you think "noir" is French for "dark meaninglessness," move on. If your idea of a good time is vigilante slasher-splatter porn, pass.

Those interested in labels will find justification for everything from hardboiled to horror. Some of the pieces concern a mercenary named Cross, soon, if my plans work out, to invade the paperback market. Some are stage plays, others are works-in-progress. Some have been previously published in a wide variety of forums. Others are original to this collection. Most are first-person narratives, some from ground zero and some—the "Underground" series—from below that.

I'll spare you self-congratulatory adjectives. Writing isn't my work, it's an organic extension of that work. I may not be a good writer, but I write for a good reason. And if that reason isn't apparent by the time you've finished this collection, I didn't get the job done.

# BORN
## BAD

# A Flash of White

The bitch in 24-G is a whore. A real slut. She parades around in front of her bedroom window in her underwear, trying on different outfits. Sometimes she looks right out the window. She knows I'm here.

The highrise has a lot of windows. They all have different coverings: curtains, drapes, Levelor blinds. The bitch in 24-G has curtains, but she never draws them.

I have a diagram of the building that I made myself. I go in and out all the time. I make deliveries for a florist. They got me that job when they let me out.

I really don't need the job. I have the money my mother left me. But the bitch from the Probation Department, she said I have to have employment.

The bitch in 19-E just came home. She's a pig. When she gets home, she throws off all her clothes, right on the floor. When she comes back into the front room, she has a towel wrapped around her. She doesn't even pick up her clothes until she has a drink. I'm sure it's liquor, because she takes so long to put it together.

I wouldn't drink liquor.

**T**here's a blonde in 16-F that I really hate. She's the biggest bitch of them all. She walks like there's a poker stuck up her ass. I'd like to stick a poker up her ass. A red-hot poker.

A thought like that, I'm supposed to snap the rubber band. The one I have to wear around my wrist. I have to remind myself that those are bad thoughts.

**T**hey taught me that inside. Before they let me go.

I never would have gone inside at all except for that bitch. I got caught lots of times. My mother always got me a lawyer. Nothing ever happened. They sent me to counseling twice. The important thing was, I never hurt anybody. I just looked at them, mostly. When I went inside one of their houses, they were never home. I only took panties. That's where bitches keep their secrets, in their panties. If you hold them, you know their secrets. They belong to you.

The last time they caught me was when the bitch got me sent away. The District Attorney. Not the real District Attorney, not the head man. A woman. While I was locked up, she got a search warrant for my room. My lawyer said she was able to get it in the middle of the night because I had my ninja outfit on when they caught me. And the piano-wire garrote.

They almost gave my mother a heart attack, charging in there like that. They found my stuff. My stalker's journal, my magazines, even the straight razor. The bitch D.A. told the judge I was dangerous. A ticking bomb, she said. They wouldn't let me out on bail.

**T**hat's when the bitch tricked me. She had me brought to this room to talk to me. My lawyer was there. He said I didn't have to answer any questions. The bitch said she knew there was a reason why I went prowling. That's what she called it, prowling. It sounded good when she said it. Strong. Not like I was a freak or anything.

She had a theory, she said. About why I did it. If she was right, maybe I wasn't a criminal after all. Maybe I was a sick person. Maybe I needed help.

I started to say something, but my lawyer stopped me. We were just there to listen, he said. Just listen.

The bitch started talking about my mother. I saw what she was doing, so I explained the truth to her. It was all just normal discipline. Children need discipline. She never really hurt me. I love my mother.

My lawyer was shaking his head. Not to stop me, like he was sad or something.

**T**he judge sentenced me to this place. For treatment, he said. I didn't know what it was going to be like.

But I bet the bitch knew.

I had to talk. All the time. Every day. Talk about what was inside my head, what I was feeling. They showed me pictures. Lots of pictures. Different kinds. Movies too. Videotapes. They would ask me, does this make me excited? Was I aroused?

After a few months, they put this cuff on me. Right around my . . . thing. They could tell when I got aroused. From the pictures. They had stories too. On tape. You sit in a chair and close your eyes and put on the earphones and the stories come.

I had to wear the cuff while I heard the stories.

They did something else to me too. Shock. They had this tape of a woman being tied up. And whipped. I watched it. They made me watch it. And when the cuff filled up, I got a shock.

After a while, I didn't get shocked anymore. I didn't get hard when I saw women get hurt.

They made me masturbate. Alone in my room. Over and over again. First I had to masturbate every time I thought about a woman getting hurt. I was the one who got hurt. My . . . thing was all red and raw. I had to have medicine for it. But they made me keep doing it.

After a while, I didn't have those thoughts anymore.

Then they made me masturbate to sex images. Sex with women. Romantic sex, they called it. They had movies of that too. Kissing, holding. Slow moving.

I had to see therapists too. They made me talk about my mother. About the closet. About being tied up. About the time she caught me playing with my . . . thing. And what she made me do. With her panties.

I have to wear a rubber band on my wrist. If I ever get a thought about hurting women, I snap it. It reminds me of the place, and the shocks.

**M**y mother was killed while I was inside. She was mugged. Somebody followed her up in the elevator and pushed in the door right behind her. She got hit over the head with something hard and she died. Whoever killed her took money from her pocketbook and other stuff from the apartment.

I went to the funeral. The therapists said I shouldn't feel guilty because I hadn't been home. It wasn't my fault. I asked if the killer had sex with her after he hit her.

I live in the apartment now.

**T**he woman in 16-F just came in. I could just barely see her in the living room. She walked into the bedroom. She never raises the blinds in any room except the living room. Even there, she only keeps them open a little bit. I can never see much. In the bedroom, the window is open. Just a slit. I saw a flash of white. Maybe her panties, just coming off. I cranked up the zoom on the telescope, aiming right at the slit. Nothing. I waited. Another flash of white. I couldn't tell what it was.

The lousy bitch. A tease is worse than anything.

**I** was only home about an hour when the buzzer rang. I knew who it was. My lousy bitch of a probation officer.

I have to let her in. My lawyer explained it to me. It's part of my probation. Like the treatment center was. If I don't do what they say, they can violate me. That's what my lawyer said: they can violate me.

If they do that, the judge could send me to prison. A real prison. For a long time.

I let her in. She sat down on the couch across from me. She crossed her legs. I could hear the nylon. I didn't look—I know how the bitch watches me.

She asked me about the job. I told her I like flowers. They always smell good. I like bringing them to people.

She asked me about counseling. I told her I still go. Twice a week. And once to the group, too.

She asked me about if it bothered me to have a woman probation officer. I told her no—I like women now.

When I said that, she said she wanted to see my bedroom. I was scared. But she walked in there by herself. When she saw the telescope, she got angry. I was afraid she was going to do something to me for a minute. I told her it was for astronomy. She said she didn't care what it was for, it better not be there the next time she came back.

The bitch. I wonder what's inside her. I'd like to take a look inside her. With the telescope.

After she left, I was very stressed. I was shaking. I tried to be calm. She hadn't found my other stuff. I do a lot of research. I have books. Lock-picking. *Black Dragon Death Grip Techniques. Secrets of the Ninja.*

There's a woman I write to. I never met her, but she sent me pictures. I send her a money order with every letter and she sends me a letter back. She is my slave. She does whatever I tell her to do. She is a bitch too, but a tame bitch. She knows better than to disobey me. I got her name from one of the guys in group therapy. He said it's an outlet, a release thing. So we don't get worked up and maybe hurt somebody for real.

Every time I get a letter from her, I want to hurt some bitch even worse.

**I** looked out the window. The redhead in 18-H was home. She doesn't go out much. She has a man who comes to visit her. I always know when the man is coming. She gets dressed in sexy clothes. When he comes there, she treats him like a king. Brings him drinks, lights his cigar, sits on his lap. He's an old, fat man. Bitches always go for money.

She was just lying on her couch, watching TV. I saw her hand go between her legs. She knows I'm watching.

**I** looked into 16-F. A long time. I couldn't tell if the blonde was home. Then I saw it, the flash of white.

**T**hey are going to come for me soon. Coming to violate me, the bitches. All of them.

I have my list. I have my list of bitches. Everything about them. Some are from my delivery route. Only the ones where I actually got in the house. But I like the ones in the building across from me the best. I'm in their houses all the time, with my telescope.

I may only get one of them before they come for me. I'll get one. I'll have her. And then I'll always have her. In my mind. No matter where they put me, I can always have her. Again and again.

So I have to make a choice.

24-G is a whore. She deserves whatever happens to her.

19-E is a pig, a dirty slob of a bitch.

18-H lets a fat old man do anything he wants to her.

16-F, she's the worst bitch of all. The way she walks. The way she keeps me from seeing her. Just that flash of white.

That's what decided me. I need to know what that white flash is.

**I**'m in the corridor now, right outside 16-F. It's late in the afternoon—she won't be home for another hour or so.

# A Flash of White

This is so easy.

The lock picks really work. I can hear the last tumbler fall. I'm going in now. The bitch isn't home, so there won't be a chain on the door.

I'm going to step inside and wait for her. Teach her a lesson.

The door opens. It's dark in here. But I'll find her secret.

From the back room . . . a flash of white . . .

Teeth.

# Alibi

**I** walked slowly down the corridor, my footsteps soundless against the deep burgundy carpet. The door was an ornate slab of burnished teak gleaming blackly from within its bronze frame. The immaculate surface was broken only by a small mirror set high and centered in the slab, as carefully as a jewel.

I gently touched the tiny pearl button on the door frame, watching my reflection in the mirror, knowing I was being watched from inside.

The mirror wasn't the only observer—I knew there was a video camera concealed somewhere too. I stood quietly, letting my soul radiate patience.

It didn't matter how long they made me wait. It didn't matter how closely they observed me. Nothing would make me impatient now—it had taken me a little more than four years to find that door.

Four years and almost thirty thousand dollars—the time and the money parceled out slowly, much of both wasted.

But now . . . I was close. I kept my mouth expressionless, willing the same emptiness into my eyes. Waiting.

The door opened. The man standing in the doorway was

thick-bodied, competent looking. He made no attempt to conceal the shoulder holster under his suit jacket.

"Can I help you?" he said.

"I hope so," I told him. "I'd like to speak to Mr. Mason."

"Is he expecting you?" the man asked.

"Yes. I made an appointment. My name is—"

"If you'll just step over here and wait a bit," the man said, ushering me through the door, indicating where I was to stand, "I'll see if Mr. Mason is available."

I stood there waiting. Still waiting. Waiting still. *Stop that!* I commanded myself. I took a deep breath in through my nose, expanding my stomach. Then I let it out through my mouth as I snapped my abdominal muscles taut, exhaling the tension from my body. Calm. Calm and centered. Calm and . . .

The man returned. "If you'll just come with me . . ."

I followed him. He walked with a prizefighter's roll to his shoulders, confident in his upper-body strength. I rounded my shoulders, narrowed my silhouette. Radiating calm. Serenity. And safety to all.

The man stepped aside, moving his hand to wave me into the office. The room was huge, big enough for a half-dozen normal offices. The man behind the kidney-shaped glass desk was husky, his body covered with muscle slowly losing the battle to fat. He had a shaved head and a prominent scar on his right cheek.

"Right on time, Mr. Knight," he greeted me, motioning toward a padded leather chair set in front of the desk.

I sat down, slumping to visually reduce my size even more. I waited. Patient. Calm and patient. Quiet. No threat to anyone. So close, now . . .

"I understand you've already spoken to Roger Blue," the man who I guessed was Mr. Mason said.

I didn't answer, waiting.

"Is that right?" he asked, not even a trace of impatience in his silky voice.

"Yes," I told him. "That's right."

"Then you know what our services cost?"

"Fifty thousand dollars," I said. "In cash. No bill bigger than a hundred. No new bills, no consecutive serial numbers."

"Very good." The husky man smiled. "May I assume you have it with you?"

"Yes," I said, moving my right hand slowly so he could see the leather briefcase. "It's all here."

"Raymond will take care of that for you," Mr. Mason said, pointing with a stubby finger. A diamond glittered on his hand.

The man who had let me in took the briefcase out of my hand, then he walked out the door, closing it behind him.

I was alone with the husky man. "This will only take a few minutes," he said. "Can I offer you a drink?"

"No thank you," I told him.

It was almost eight minutes before the man he called Raymond came back. Raymond's hands were empty. He made some gesture I didn't understand. The husky man turned to me. "Are you ready?" he asked.

I nodded yes. The husky man got up from behind the big desk and walked up to me. I stood up too. "What's the name?" he asked me.

"Knight," I told him. "It's my real name."

"Okay," he said. "What do your friends call you? You know, the guys you hang out with?"

"Knight," I told him.

"Knight it is," he said. "Come on."

I followed him out of the office. Down the hall, he opened another door. Inside was a staircase. A staircase down. He went first. I was behind him. I could feel Raymond behind me.

At the bottom, there was a big paneled room. In one corner there was an octagonal table covered with green felt. The border of the table had little round cutouts, one on either side of each chair—I could see what they were for, a place to rest an ashtray and a drink. Five men were seated at the table, playing cards. There were a lot of chips in the middle of the table.

"Have a seat," the husky man said.

I took one of the empty chairs. A girl came over, said "What will you have, sir?" She was a tall girl. She looked even taller in the fishnet stockings and black high heels. She wasn't wearing anything else.

"A glass of water," I told her.

Nobody laughed, the way they do sometimes when I say that. The girl went off and came back with a heavy-bottomed crystal tumbler full of water and ice.

"Meet your poker buddies," the husky man said to me. He went around the table, pointing at each of the five men in turn.

"Indian Pete," the husky man said.

A medium-size man with a dark reddish complexion nodded at me.

"Sammy Belt," the husky man said.

A slender man with a wispy mustache nodded at me.

The husky man did the same for all of them. Then he said, "Boys, this is Knight, okay? He's a semi-regular, plays stud and draw, plays for cash, no markers. He settles up each time. Sometimes he wins, sometimes he loses. Heavy cash player, but not much swing, you all got it?"

The five men nodded again.

"Questions?" the husky man said.

"You smoke?" a black man with a fine-boned face asked. His voice was Caribbean.

"No," I answered.

"Drink anything but water?" a pudgy blond man asked me.

"No." I told him.

"You mind turning around . . . slow?" the man who said he was Sammy Belt asked.

I did that, one full turn. When I faced him again, he nodded an okay.

A tall slender man came over to the table. A couple of the

players nodded at him, but he didn't say anything. The tall man opened a mahogany box and took out a new deck of cards. He slit the wrapper with his thumbnail and dumped the cards out onto the green felt. Then he shuffled the cards, his hands moving in a blur, faster and cleaner than any machine. When he was done, he looked up expectantly.

"We need you to play a few hands," the husky man said. "Take you maybe an hour, an hour and a half, all right? Just so we can get a look at your style."

The tall slender man looked at the pudgy blond guy to his left, raising his eyebrows in a question.

"Draw," the pudgy blond man said.

The tall man tapped the table in front of him. Each player tossed a blue chip into the middle. "The chips are twenty, fifty, and a hundred," the husky man said. "You'll probably need about five grand worth."

"You already—" I started to say.

"This is an honest game," the husky man said. "Dead honest. If you don't play . . . with your own money . . . we can't really get to know you. And you can't get what you're paying for."

I took five thousand dollars out of my jacket and put it on the table. A girl came over. A redhead, shorter than the first one but dressed the same way. She opened a box. It was lined with white velvet. She put three stacks of chips in front of me: red, white, and blue. Then she put my money in the box and walked away.

I tossed a blue chip into the middle of the table like the others, and the tall man dealt the cards. The men were good players. I'm a good player too. After about an hour, the man called Sammy Belt said. "You don't talk much, do you?"

"No," I said.

"That's the way you are? All the time?"

"Yes," I said.

The man they called Indian Pete laughed.

The husky man came back into the room. He tapped me on the shoulder. "How are you doing?" he asked.

"Good," I said.

"Let's count them up," he said. He spread my chips around on the green felt. "You got sixty-one hundred dollars here," he said. "JoJo will cash you out."

I guess the redhead was JoJo because she came over with the velvet-lined box. She put my chips inside, then she counted out the money for me—sixty-one hundred dollar bills.

"Here's the setup," the husky man said to me. "The house cuts every pot five percent. That's all you pay, ever. Anything you want to eat, anything you want to drink, it's on the house. Got rooms upstairs where you can take a nap, take a shower, take one of the girls if she's willing, okay?"

"Okay," I said.

"The house provides the dealer." He pointed at the tall man. "That's Slim," the husky man said. "This is his table. Your table too, all right? This table is only stud and draw—no red dog, no wild cards, nothing fancy. Other tables, they have different rules. The five percent of each pot, that buys you the entire services of the club, understand?"

"Yes," I said.

"Anything else?" the husky man asked, glancing around the men seated at the table. Nobody said anything. The husky man put his hands behind his back. "Knight here comes in around ten," he said, watching me. I nodded. "Leaves around four, five in the morning."

I nodded again.

"What night?" the husky man asked me.

"Tomorrow," I told him.

"You got it," the husky man said. "Remember what Roger Blue told you, right? Tomorrow is what you bought for your fifty large. It don't go down like you expected, you want to do this again, it costs the same."

"I know," I told him.

**I** went out around nine the next night. The doorman saw me leave. He's very alert.

The doorman pushed the call button. A light would go on outside, a signal that a cab was needed. When a taxi pulled up, the doorman opened the back door for me. I thanked him and palmed a dollar bill into his hand.

I told the cab driver where to go. He wrote the destination down on his trip sheet. When he pulled up in front of the club, I thanked him for the ride. I gave him a tip too.

I walked the rest of the way. It was almost midnight before I arrived at his house, a big house in a fancy neighborhood. I went over the back fence. He didn't have a dog. I knew that from watching. I'd been watching a long time.

The back door lock wasn't much. I slipped inside. He lived alone. It was easier for him to be himself that way.

I moved toward the light. He was watching television. On the screen, it showed a little boy. The boy was . . . It wasn't television he was watching, it was a videotape.

The same kind of videotape I knew he made of my son. The police had never found it, but I knew.

I made a little noise so he'd turn around. He saw me then. He sat back in his chair, startled.

"Wha . . . ?"

"You know who I am?" I asked him.

"No. Look, if you want—"

"It's you I want," I said quietly. "For what you did to my son. My son David. Remember?"

Sweat broke out all along his hairline, but his voice was calm. "Look, I . . . I know who you are. I couldn't tell at first . . . in that bad light. I . . . don't blame you. Any father would be enraged if that sort of thing happened to his kid. But I was the wrong man. Come on, you remember—you were at the trial, for God's sake! It wasn't me. You know that. It wasn't me. It's a terrible thing, what happened to your boy. But it wasn't me. They all testified. That whole night, I was—"

"I know where you were," I told him. "I'm there myself. Right now."

# Anytime I Want

She didn't answer my knock. I used the key she gave me to open the door. When I saw her lying on the bare hardwood floor, I knew he'd finally taken her. Like he always told us he would.

I went next door, rang the bell. The people there called the police, like I asked. I didn't scare them, didn't panic. I was polite, like I always am.

Two detectives came. I told them Denise was my sister. My big sister. They were all my big sisters, four of them. Denise was the baby girl, twenty-two years old when he took her.

The cops asked me a lot of questions. It was okay—I'm used to questions. They asked me where I'd been, before it happened. That was the easy part—I work the night shift, plenty of guys at the plant saw me.

I gave them the names: Fiona, Rhonda, Evelyn. And Denise. My four sisters. I have one brother, Frankie. He's sixteen. I wasn't worried about an alibi for him—he was in the last month of a one-year jolt with the state. Frankie's a big kid, and he's got a bad temper.

I'm nineteen. I work nights, go to college in the daytime. Weekends, I'm a thief. A careful, quiet thief.

Denise's face was all swollen, slash marks on her hands, trying to stop the knife before it went in the last time. All her clothes were off, thrown around the room. He left her like that.

"Did you love her?" one of the detectives asked me.

"I still love her," I told him.

I went home, changed my clothes, put on a nice suit. I drove down to Pontiac. The guards like me there. I'm always polite, always respectful.

They brought Frankie out, left us alone.

I told him.

"Don't kill him until I get out," he begged me, looking at me with those big dark eyes.

"Can I count on you?" I asked him.

"Count on me? He's dead, Fal. On my honor, he's dead. You just make sure you got yourself a place where you can be seen, first night I come out of here."

Frankie calls me Fal—short for Falcon. Most of the kids in our club did. Because I was always watching. I leaned over close to him, talking quiet. "You remember, Frankie? Remember how it was . . . before we got out?"

His face was chiseled stone, big hands clenched the table. Scars all across his knuckles.

Our house. A terror zone. No locks anywhere, not even on the bathroom door. The basement, where he'd take the girls. One at a time. The leather strap, the one with the brass studs. I can still feel it across my back.

I was just a baby when he started with Fiona—Frankie wasn't even born. One after the other. His property. Mom tried to stop him once. I remember—I was eight, Evelyn was about thirteen. He made her suck him, right at the kitchen table. He made us all watch. "Anytime I want," is what he said. "My property—anytime I want." I tried to go after him—Denise held me back. It didn't do any good. He beat me so bad I woke up in the hospital.

Mom told them I fell down a flight of stairs. Into the basement, onto the concrete floor.

He never got Denise. She wouldn't do it. He broke her arm once, twisted it hard behind her back. I heard it snap.

I don't know what Denise told the hospital, but some social workers came to the house. The older girls, they all said Denise was a liar . . . she was staying out late, smoking cigarettes, drinking. Messing with boys. The social workers said something to him about counseling.

When they left, he punched me in the face. I lost two teeth. Then he took Rhonda down to the basement.

Denise tried to stab him once. With a kitchen knife, when he was holding my hand in the flame from the stove burner. I threw up on myself but he didn't stop.

The girls moved out, one by one. Fiona is a whore. She works in a club downtown, dancing naked. Rhonda killed herself with drugs. Evelyn went off with a biker.

He still sees Fiona. Anytime he wants.

Denise worked as a typist. For a lawyer. She was the smartest one, Denise. She was going to go to law school herself, someday. He picked her up once. Told her Mom was in the hospital. Drove her into an alley and went after her. Denise fought him to a standstill. She told the cops. They picked him up. He said it never happened—he was home with Mom all night. Mom was never in the hospital. But Denise was. Once before. A psychiatric hospital. When she tried to kill herself.

When the cops found out about that, they closed the case.

He always said he'd take her. She was his. They all were. Fred is his name. The girl's names were his brand. Fiona. Rhonda. Evelyn. Denise.

Frankie's name didn't matter. Neither did mine.

"Can I count on you?" I asked Frankie again.

He got it that time. Reached out his hand. "It has to be right," I told him. "For Denise. Blowing him up, it wouldn't be good enough. You understand?"

He nodded.

"No more nonsense, Frankie. Do the rest of your time, no beefs, got it?"

He nodded again.

I waited and I watched.

Mom said he was with her the night Denise was killed. It's an Unsolved Homicide.

Frankie got out on a Monday. I picked him up. He came to live with me.

Friday night we went in. The locks only took me a couple of minutes.

He never woke up. I left Frankie at the head of the stairs while I went down into the basement. Frankie had a tire iron in his hand. "If he comes downstairs, you can do it," I said.

I know where he keeps his trophies. In this little back room he built in the basement. Under a loose brick in the corner. A red silk scarf, a faded corsage from a dance, a pair of little girl's panties, white. And the pictures: Fiona on her knees, with him in her mouth. Rhonda bent over, something sticking out of her. Evelyn nude, lying down, a mirror between her legs. He didn't have any little-girl pictures of Denise . . . just a Polaroid of her lying on the apartment floor. Naked. A knife between her breasts.

I took everything. Left him a note.

He's a creature. Needs his blood. After the girls left, whenever something went wrong, when he got stressed, he'd go down to his room, take out his trophies, say his prayers.

Saturday morning, I called the house. Mom answered, like she always does.

"Put him on," is all I said.

"What d'you want?" he challenged. Hard, aggressive. The way he told us you had to be . . . to be a man.

"Revenge," I told him, quiet-voice. "Revenge for Denise."

"Hey! I didn't have nothing to do with . . ."

"Yes. Yes, you did. You're going down. Soon. Very soon. Maybe a fire while you sleep. Maybe your car will blow up when you start it. Maybe a rifle shot. There's no place you can go. Nothing you can do. I'm good at it now. Stay there and wait for it, old man. It's coming."

I hung up the phone.

He called the next day. Frankie listened in on the extension. He told me how he was a sick man. How the girls had led him on, how Mom wasn't any good for sex anymore, what with all her plumbing problems. How he was going to see a psychologist, get all better. It wasn't his fault.

I told him I didn't know what he was talking about.

When Frankie called later to tell me the old man went out with Mom, I drove over there.

Frankie and I went in the back door, quick and smooth. I popped the fuse to the basement lights and went downstairs. I opened my briefcase, took out the sheets of clear soft plastic, like cloth. We wrapped the plastic around ourselves and we waited.

It was late when he came downstairs. We heard the click of the light switch. Nothing. He came back with a flashlight. Made his way into the little back room.

We heard the sound of the brick being moved. He made some beast-noise in his throat and ran out. Frankie and I took him before he got to the stairs.

We left him there on the concrete floor. He was just bloody pulp, no face left. A corpse, clutching the suicide note he wrote years ago.

Anytime I Want.

# Born Bad

**T**he man was husky, with a big chest and thick wrists, wearing a tweed jacket over an oxford-cloth white shirt and plain dark tie. His hair was cropped short, eyes alert behind aluminum-framed glasses. He handed his battered leather medical satchel to the guard standing by the metal detector.

"Morning, Jackson," he said.

"Good morning to you, Doc. Carrying any weapons today?"

Doc tapped his head, smiled. The guard looked carefully through the satchel, ran his electronic wand over Doc's body.

"Everybody there?"

"Waiting on you, Doc."

He threw a half-salute at the guard and strolled down the sterile concrete corridor, the bag swinging at his side, taking his time.

He came to an institutional green door with a hand-lettered sign taped on its front: Task Force. He knocked. The door was opened by a heavyset, thick-necked man wearing a shoulder holster. He stepped aside and the man the guard had called Doc entered.

The room was long and narrow. He was facing a row of windows. Barred windows. The wall behind him was covered with corkboard, littered with randomly fastened charts, graphs, maps. A battered wood podium stood at the head of a double-length conference table; behind it, a small movie screen pulled down like a window shade. In the upper corner of the room, a TV set stood on an elevated platform, a VCR on a shelf underneath. Cigarette smoke hung in the air, blue-tinted in the slanting sunlight.

Doc took his seat, looked around. They were all there, waiting.

"How come you're always the last to show up, Doc?" Oscar asked. The slim black investigator pretended an irritation he didn't feel. "We moved the Task Force into this looney bin just 'cause you work here, the least you could do is make the damn meetings on time."

"Sorry, hoss. There was a little problem on one of the wards."

"Never mind that now," a red-haired woman said, the chief prosecutor in the Homicide Bureau. "Tell him what happened."

A tall blond man stepped to the podium, moving with the authority he carried from his long-ago days as a street cop, a sheaf of papers in his hand. He carefully extracted a single sheet, smoothed it flat, flicked on an opaque projector. One page of a neatly typed letter sprang into life on the screen.

"It's from him?" a Hispanic with a duelist's mustache asked. He was the group's forensics expert.

"Yeah," the blond man answered. "We Xeroxed the whole thing. Seven pages. The lab boys went over it with an electron microscope. Typed on a computer, probably that laptop he carries around. It was printed out on a laser printer. Generic paper, standard number ten business envelope. Untraceable. But we know it's him—he left us a perfect thumbprint below the signature."

"Damn!" the black man said.

"Postmark?" the redhead asked.

"Tucson, Arizona. Four days ago," the blond answered. "Central Post Office. He won't be there now."

On the screen, the letter stood out in bold contrast to the darkened room. Justified margins, single-spaced with the paragraphs indented.

"He's always so neat, so precise," the woman said.

"Yeah," the blond agreed. He looked across the table. "Looks like your idea worked, Doc. When you wrote that article about the Surgeon—the one where you said he had to have been an abused child—it made him mad. Smoked him out. Look at this letter—he's boiling over. Slashed at your theory like he's been doing at women all around the country."

Doc nodded, waiting patiently for the recap he knew was coming as soon as he'd spotted new faces in the room.

The blond man swept his eyes around the table, willing everyone to silence. "Mark Anthony Monroe," he began, nodding his head toward a blown-up black-and-white photograph on the wall to his left. "White male, age forty-one last birthday. Five foot eleven, one hundred and sixty pounds. Blond and blue. Undergraduate degree in physics, graduate work in computer technology. No scars, marks, or tattoos. No known associates. Mother and father divorced when he was two. Mother remarried when he was five. Divorced again when he was eight. No contact with either father or stepfather since, whereabouts of both unknown. Mother died when he was in his late twenties. You with me so far?"

Nods and grunts of assent from around the room. Doc drew a series of tiny boxes on his notepad, not looking up.

"First arrest, age thirteen," the blond man continued. "Fire-setting. He convinced the juvie officers it was an accident—dismissed. Next time down, he was fourteen. He put a cat in a shoebox, poured gasoline over it, dropped a match. He got probation, referred for counseling. The counselor said he didn't mean to hurt the cat—some kind of scientific experiment. At sixteen, he was dropped for attempted rape. Attacked a schoolteacher on a stairwell right outside the gym. Cut her too. Sent to a juvenile institution. Did almost five years. After his discharge, he was quiet for a while. We have an admission, voluntary admission to a psychiatric hospital when he was in his mid-twenties. He was treated for depression, signed himself out after a few months. Nothing since.

"He went to college, like I said. Far as we can tell, he's never worked a real job.

"For the last two and a half years, he's been roaming the country. Killing. He kills them different ways. All women. But no matter how he kills them, he always cuts out the heart. Neat, clean cuts. He knows what he's doing. That's why the newspaper guys call him the Surgeon.

"We got thirteen confirmed kills, and a whole bunch of Unsolved that may be his.

"He's smooth and slick. Talks nice, got a lot of employment skills. And a good deal of cash . . . money his mother left him when she died. He don't look like a killer . . . hell, he don't look like much of anything. He could be anywhere."

He looked around the room. "Any questions?"

"You do a profile on him, Marty?" the redhead asked.

"Profile? Yeah, we did a damn profile, Suzanne. Nomadic, prolific driver, rootless, pathological hate for females. Serial killer . . . that's what we got. Big deal."

The Hispanic looked up from his place at the end of the table. "He . . . do anything to the women? Besides kill them?"

"No. At least nothing we can tell. No semen found on or in any of the bodies."

"Why's he do it, then?"

"Because he likes to," Doc said, so softly some of the assembled hunters had to lean forward to hear his voice.

"Yeah, well let's all see what he says about it," the blond man said, stepping to the corner and switching off the overhead lights. He adjusted a dial until the letters on the screen were big enough to read from anywhere in the room.

My dear, ignorant Dr. Ruskin:

I read your fascinatingly stupid "analysis" of my motivations in the June 15 issue of *Parade*. It was so pathetically uninformed, so lacking in insight, so bereft of logic that I felt compelled to provide the education you so obviously neglected in medical school.

It is my understanding that you have been "studying" my case for some months now. How unfortunate that your politics interfere with your judgment—that is highly unprofessional. You are clearly one of those irredeemably ignorant individuals who takes it on faith that nobody is "born bad." You believe there must be some etiology of a monster—some specific cause and effect. I quote from your purple prose:

"There is no biogenetic code for serial killer. There may be some hard-wired personality propensities, but the only way to produce such a monster is early, chronic, systematic child abuse." How I pity your lack of intelligence—and what contempt I have for your cowardice. Like all liberals, you hide your head in the sand of religion, convincing yourself that evil does not exist.

Pay attention, you little worm: I *was* born bad. I came out of the womb evil. My only pleasure is power, and I learned early on that the ultimate power is to possess life. To extinguish it at my will. You know how some men break hearts? Well, I *take* hearts. And I keep them.

Was I an "abused child"? Certainly not. My mother was, if anything, over-indulgent. I was always treated with kindness, love, and respect. And I repaid that investment in blood. I am not insane, and never have been. When I admitted myself to the psychiatric hospital, it was to avoid the consequences of my own act—the rape of a little girl. I was never caught. Never even charged. And I probably never will be.

I am not insane, despite your fervent wish that I be so. The behavior you so carefully chart is not the prodromal phase of psychosis, it is entirely volitional.

Should you be interested in propounding a more accurate, precise diagnosis, you might check your holy DSM-III, your biblical attempt to quantify human behavior. I'll guide your dim brain to the right spot, Doctor: Anti-Social Personality Disorder, 301.70. Such high-flown verbiage to describe what I am. Dangerous. Remorseless. Evil.

By now I am certain you stand in abject awe of my protean grasp of psychiatric jargon. Do not be surprised, I have been studying your ancient tablets for many years—preparing my defense. You see, Doctor, I have none of the grandiosity that characterizes others who have walked my same road. Such subhumans are not of my ilk. Ted Bundy was a contemptible, whining worm—an obsessive-compulsive the media made into a criminal genius simply because he possessed the slightly above-average IQ sufficient to enter law school. Arrogance without intellect personified. And John Wayne Gacy, a repulsive gargoyle. Were the media not so utterly enthralled by high body counts, he would not have merited a line of type. Lust-driven cowards, with not the remotest concept of higher orders. Your pedestrian theories fit such creatures quite well, Doctor—both abused children, screaming in rage against their past.

As I said, I am not grandiose, or narcissistic. I acknowledge that capture is possible. Should such luck (and it will take considerable luck) befall you, I expect to be acquitted at any trial. You will all judge me "insane." Because you fear the truth.

So please spare me your insipid wish fulfillment. I am not a "sexual sadist," I have no "fetish." My rituals are of my own making, designed for my pleasure, not the subject of any compulsion. They are, in fact, private ceremonies—homage to my sociopathic genius. I am capable of modifying my behavior. Indeed, I have done so on many occasions. The unexpected presence of potential witnesses has caused me to forsake my trophies several times. But, if you look closely, you will note unmistakable forensic evidence of my passage even when I have not had the opportunity to take the hearts from my victims. Read the last sentence carefully, you stupid slug: *my* victims. They belong to me, forever.

My many homicides are not a "cry for help." I have no desire to be caught. I have taken great pains to avoid capture. But, should that unlikely event come to pass, I know I can rely on religious cowards such as yourself to leap to my defense, to stridently proclaim my "insanity" to a court. And should a different result emerge, my situation will not change materially. I have no need of sex, and less of human companionship. Serial Killer Chic has infected American consciousness. (Perhaps you should be studying *that* phenomenon instead of wasting your time trying to analyze me.) I will be an object of fascination. Women will offer to marry me. Publishers will clamor for my life story. Wealthy morons will buy my paintings, telling their friends they have seen into my soul.

You are not my nemesis, Doctor, you are my safety net.

Oh, don't you wish I were insane? Don't you pray to your ineffectual gods that I am the product of an abusive home? Doesn't the truth terrify you?

Let me appeal to your scientific mind—if only to that portion not clouded by your so-called "education." You claim to be an environmentalist, a determinist, if you will. I cannot, in your narrow-minded view, be "born" bad. It must be attributable to something in the way I was nurtured, yes? Unfortunately for your indefensible theories, there is irrefutable evidence to the contrary. My mother, despite her impeccable conduct toward me, was no saint. She had her own demons. I was, as I said, raised in an environment of total love. Yet my brother, my half-genetic counterpart (we had different biological fathers), was not. Unlike myself, he was the target of my mother's insanity. Yes, Doctor, my mother was conventionally insane. Bipolar, schizoid, with more than a touch of pedophilia. Ah, wouldn't your liberal heart bleed for my poor brother—locked and chained in a dark basement closet for literally days at a time, beaten with a wide variety of objects, burned with cigarettes. The poor tyke was violated by one of my mother's gentleman friends while my mother held him. A Polaroid camera provided many hours of entertainment for my mother, and, later, a considerable source of income as well. And yet, my brother is a fine, upstanding citizen. He has never committed a transgression against society in his entire life. A credit to the community, welcome anywhere. If your lamentably weak little theories had any basis in fact, my brother would have been a prime candidate for what your stupid article called the "negative fallout" from child abuse: drugs, alcohol, promiscuity, suicide, crime. None of the above ever occurred. Perhaps you should do some research, Doctor. Have you ever read the seminal work of Denis M. Donovan in the field of traumatology? His concept of "inescapable shock syndrome" is most illuminating, although I fear it would be wasted on a man of your distinctly limited scope.

Your theories are lies. I am the living, life-taking proof.

Absent fortuitous circumstance, you will never catch me. I am invisible. People like you make it certain that we don't see evil. I am a shark in a suburban swimming pool. Safe and deadly forever, feeding as I will.

Take my warning, Doctor. So long as you promulgate your explanations for evil, it will flourish. Face the truth. And fear it forever.

The blond man waited patiently until the entire Task Force had finished reading. Then he flicked on the lights and looked across the room at Doc.

"You know, Doc, you and me, we've been having this go-round for years. I always said your theories were nonsense, didn't I? I been a cop too long. I got to hand it to this freak—he told it like it is. I mean, there's your evidence, right? Two brothers, raised in the same household. Look how different they turned out. One's treated like a prince, he turns out to be a monster. The other's tortured all kinds of ways, he turns out to be a decent guy. I think we all learned something today. The freak's right: all the stuff about child abuse causing crime is just so much liberal claptrap. You got anything to say?"

Doc took off his glasses, cleaned them patiently with a handkerchief. The red-haired woman lit a cigarette. Others leaned forward, watching from the sidelines.

"Come on, Doc. You've been studying the Surgeon for years, going over the ground inch by inch," the black man said. "You got any comeback for what Marty said?"

The husky man said, "Yes," very quietly, and got to his feet. He looked into the face of each person in the room, one by one, eyes shining with sadness and with truth.

"He doesn't have a brother," he said.

# Cain

"Look at my Buster . . . look what they did to him."

The old man pointed a shaking finger at the dog, a big German shepherd. The animal was cowering in a corner of the kitchen of the railroad flat—his fine head was lopsided, a piece of his skull missing under the ragged fur. A deep pocket of scar tissue glowed white where one eye had been, the other was cataract-milky, fire-dotted with fear. The dog's tail hung behind him at a demented angle, one front paw hung useless in a plaster cast.

"Who did it?"

The old man wasn't listening, not finished yet. Squeezing the wound to get the pus out. "Buster guards out back, where the chicken wire is. They tormented him, threw stuff at him, made him crazy. Then they cut the lock. Two of them. One had a baseball bat, the other had a piece of pipe. My Buster . . . he wouldn't hurt anyone. They beat on him, over and over, laughing. I ran downstairs to stop them . . . they just slapped me, like I was a fly. They did my Buster so bad, it even hurts him when I try and rub him."

The old man sat crying at his kitchen table.

The dog watched me, a thin whine coming from his open mouth. Half his teeth were missing.

"You know who did it," I said. It wasn't a question. He didn't know, he wouldn't have called me—I'm no private eye.

"I called . . . I called the cops. 911. They never came. I went down to the precinct. The man at the desk, he said to call the ASPCA."

"You know who they are?"

"I don't know their names. Two men, young men. One has big muscles, the other's skinny."

"They're from around here?"

"I don't know. They're always together—I've seen them before. Everybody knows them. They have their heads shaved too."

"Everybody knows them?"

"Everybody. They beat other dogs too. They make the dogs bark at them, then they . . ." He was crying again.

I waited, watching the dog.

"They come back. I see them walking down the alley. Almost every day. I can't leave Buster outside anymore—can't even take him for a walk. I have to clean up after him now."

"What do you want?"

"What do I want?"

"You called me. You got my name from somewhere. You know what I do."

The old man got up, knelt next to his dog. Put his hand gently on the dog's head. "Buster used to be the toughest dog in the world—wasn't afraid of nothing. I had him ever since he was a pup. He won't even look out the back window with me now."

"What do you want?" I asked him again.

They both looked at me. "You know," the old man said.

# 2

**A** freestanding brick building in Red Hook, not far from the waterfront, surrounded by a chain-link fence topped with razor wire. I rang the bell. A dog snarled a warning. I looked into the mirrored glass, knowing they could see me. The steel door opened. A man in a white T-shirt over floppy black trousers opened the door. He was barefoot, dark hair cropped close, body so smooth it might have been extruded from rubber. He bowed slightly. I returned his bow, followed him inside.

A rectangular room, roughened wood floor. A canvas-wrapped heavy bag swung from the ceiling in one corner. In another, a car tire was suspended from a thick rope. A pair of long wood staves hung on hooks.

"I'll get him," the man said.

I waited, standing in one spot.

He returned, leading a dog by a chain. A broad-chested pit bull, all white except for a black patch over one eye. The dog watched me, cobra-calm.

"Here he is," the man said.

"You sure he'll do it?"

"Guaranteed."

"What's his name?"

"Cain."

I squatted down, said the dog's name, scratched him behind his erect ears when he came to me.

"You want to practice with him?"

"Yeah, I'd better. I know the commands you gave me, but . . ."

"Wait here."

I played with Cain, putting him through standard-obedience paces. He was a machine, perfect.

The trainer came back into the room. Two other men with

him, dressed in full agitator's suits, leather-lined and padded. Masks on their faces, like hockey goalies wear.

"Let's do it," he said.

# 3

**I** walked down the alley behind the old man's building, Cain on a thin leather leash, held lightly in my left hand. The dog knew the route by now—it was our fifth straight day.

They turned the corner fifty feet from me. The smaller one had a baseball bat over his shoulder, the muscleman slapped a piece of lead pipe into one palm.

They closed in. I stepped aside to let them pass, pulling Cain close to my leg.

They didn't walk past. The smaller one planted his feet, looking into my eyes.

"Hey, man. That's a pit bull, right? Pretty tough dogs, I heard."

"No, he's not tough," I said, a catch in my voice. "He's just a pet."

"He looks like a bad dog to me," the big guy said, poking the lead pipe into the dog's face, stabbing. Cain stepped out of the way.

"Please don't hurt my dog," I begged them, pulling up on the leash.

Cain leaped into my arms, his face against my chest. I could feel the bunched muscles in his legs, all four paws flat against me.

"Aw, is your dog *scared,* man?" the big one sneered, stepping close to me, slapping the dog's back with the pipe.

"Leave us alone," I said, stepping back as they closed in.

"Put the dog down, faggot!"

I put my mouth close to Cain's ear, whispered "Go!" as I threw open my arms. The pit bull launched himself off my chest without a sound, his alligator teeth locking on the big guy's face. A scream bubbled out. The big man fell to the ground, clawing at Cain's back. Pieces of his face flew off, red and white. He spasmed like he was in the electric chair, but the dog held on, wouldn't drop the bite. The smaller guy stood there, rooted, mouth open, no sound coming out, his pants turning dark at the crotch.

"Out!" I snapped at the dog. Cain stepped away, his mouth foamy with bloody gristle.

"Your turn," I said to the smaller guy. He took off, running for his life. Cain caught him, running right up his spine, locking onto the back of his neck.

I called him off when I heard a snap.

As we turned to walk back down the alley, I glanced up.

The old man was at the window. Buster next to him, the plaster cast on his paw draped over the sill.

# Cough

**T**his business, I know how it goes, the old man thought to himself. He'd been at it a long time. Dead reliable, that's what they always said about him. He kept his thoughts to himself. Nothing showed on his face. The way it was supposed to be. The younger ones come in, take over. In business, you have to make room for new blood. The young ones, they think I don't know that. I know how they think. Cowboys.

He mused to himself, alone in his room. They wouldn't call me in, ask me to retire. I would have done it, they asked me. When you're done, you're done. But they don't know how to ask. No class. It's as if they *like* to do it. Only amateurs like to do it.

I was never one of them. Not a Family man—just a soldier, doing my work. They let *them* retire.

The old man was just back from Miami. The last of the bosses called him down there. The old man thought it was just another job.

"You always done right by us," the boss said.

The old man didn't say anything. He wasn't a talker. That used to be a good thing, he thought to himself, waiting.

## Cough

"Vito, he don't know you like I do. He's a young stallion. Wants his own crew, you know?"

The old man waited. For the boss to tell him about the retirement plan.

"They think you're past it. Spooking at shadows, hearing things—you understand what I'm telling you?" The boss puffed on his cigar. He wouldn't look the old man in the face. The old man got it then.

The old man didn't know anything about running. He had always lived in the same place, done the same things. Kept it nice and quiet. By himself.

When Vito called, they said they had a job for him in Cleveland. He knew it was time to show them he could still do it.

His flight was supposed to leave from La Guardia at nine that night. I've been doing this forever—I know how it's done, he thought. They'll have a man on the plane with me. Take care of business in Cleveland. Sure.

He got to the airport at three in the afternoon. Stashed his carry-on bags in the coin lockers. Checked the schedules. Figured it would take about five trips through the scanners. Bought tickets for Chicago, Detroit, Milwaukee, Pittsburgh. Different airlines. All departing from gates in the same corridor.

He went through the scanner, one of the pieces of the gun buried inside his carry-on. The X-ray machine would show an aerosol can of shaving cream. He left the bag inside, walked back out, patient, taking his time. The old way. The right way. By seven o'clock, he had all the pieces through the scanner. The last time through, he had a garment bag over his shoulder. In the men's room, he put the pieces together and stuffed the soft carry-on bags into the larger case. Then he sat down to wait.

The old man felt the other guy behind him. He didn't look. Smell of some aftershave he didn't recognize—one of those new ones. Like perfume. The old man heard him cough. A dry, hard cough with a liquid center. Like his lungs were getting ready to go. It was better than a photograph.

You have to be sure in this business, it's not a game, you only get one move, the old man repeated to himself. The catechism he learned as a youth. He switched to the no-smoking section on the other side of the departure lounge. The old man didn't catch a glimpse of him, but he heard the cough a few seats down. The young ones, they wouldn't pick up something like that. The old man was a pro.

Eight-fifteen. The old man got up, heading for the men's room. He knew the shooter wouldn't let him out of his sight. They couldn't be sure he'd get on the plane like some tame old sheep.

Some punk was combing his hair at the sink when the old man went inside. He took the last stall, shut it behind him. Waited.

He heard the cough. In the stall right next to him. He stepped out, bent down quickly, checked under the door. The guy's pants were around his ankles. The place was empty. The old man walked out, letting the guy hear him, slipping gloves on his hands. Checked the door to the men's room. Kicked a little wood wedge underneath to give him a couple of seconds. All the time he'd need.

He stepped back into the last stall and stood on the toilet bowl. The guy was reading a newspaper. The old man put two slugs into the top of his head. Pop, pop. The silencer worked perfectly. He left the gun in the stall.

The old man was back in the departure lounge before they had the first call for boarding.

They'd hear about it. They'd know he wasn't past it. Not some old man who couldn't do the job. He lit a cigarette—the way you do when a job is over.

Then he heard the cough.

# Crime Partner

**W**hen I got out of jail one time, I had no place to go. A bunch of guys I came up with . . . from the old neighborhood . . . they had a big apartment out in Queens, invited me to move in with them. My closest pal there was a guy we called Easy Eddie. He was a stand-up dope fiend—not the kind who'd steal from a friend, even when his Jones was down on him hard. But he was stone crazy—never thought past the next couple of minutes. One time he ran out of dope. He calls the pizzeria, tells them to bring over a large pie with everything. Tells them to bring change for a twenty, that's all he's got. And he mugs the deliveryman in the lobby. And once he stuck up an ice cream truck right on the corner. Put a gun in the guy's face and walks away with about eighty bucks worth of change in his pockets."

Diamond giggled. "He sounds like a lunatic."

"He was, but a good lunatic. You understand?"

"Yes," she said, leaning forward, being serious.

"Okay. Now Easy Eddie, he's buying dope. But another guy who lived with us, guy we called Bird, he's selling it. Soft stuff: marijuana, LSD, pills. Doing good for himself, too. He's got this nice apartment, color TV, stereo, new furniture. And he's got this nice old Alfa. A little red roadster.

"One day I have to make a run out to Long Island. I ask Bird, can I borrow his short, be back in a couple of hours? He says sure—he's waiting on a customer anyway.

"Easy Eddie asks if he can go along. Just to ride . . . get outside. I say okay. We go downstairs to the garage. The Alfa's sitting there, top down. Beautiful day outside.

"Then the maniac asks me if he can drive. Fat chance, I say to him. But he says he's clean as new money, hasn't taken a hit in days. Holds out his hands. Steady as rocks.

"Look, I say to him. You're a dope fiend. How'm I going to let you drive?

"Then he really gets on my case. How we came up together, how we're like brothers and all. Why don't I trust him? You know. . . .

"Anyway, I figure, what the fuck, what harm can it do? So he gets behind the wheel and we pull out. We get about three, four blocks and I can see it's not working out. He's going about fifteen miles an hour in third gear and the Alfa's just stumbling along, bucking and backfiring. I'm about to tell him to pull over when we come to a cop directing traffic. The cop holds up his hand like this," I said, holding my palm out in the universal Stop! gesture.

"So what does Easy Eddie do? He holds up his hand the same way to the cop and motors right by. 'Hey, Stop!' the cop screams at us. I say to Eddie, 'Pull over, fool.' 'I can't,' he says, 'I'm holding.'

" 'Nail it,' I say to him. 'Go!' So the lunatic steps on the gas, but he doesn't downshift and we sort of chug away. Meanwhile, the cop is chasing after us, on foot. And we're in a mess of traffic. I look back—the cop has his gun out—he's waving cars to stop.

"I look over at Easy Eddie. He's pulling bags of dope out of every pocket. Ripping open the bags, throwing the powder into the air. The cop grabs a cab from somewhere, comes screaming after us, cuts us off. Sights right down the pistol at us.

"I get out of the car. Easy Eddie just sits there. We're both covered with heroin. Like we had the world's worst case of dandruff. The cop is out of his mind. He says to Eddie, 'I told you to stop!'

"Eddie just looks up at him. 'Oh, man,' he says, 'I thought you were just saying hello.'

"I go over to the cop, brushing the junk off my coat, pulling out these papers I had. Department of Social Services. I tell the cop that I'm Eddie's caseworker. I'm taking him back—he was on a supervised day-pass from Pilgrim State. The looney bin. Sorry about the whole thing. Blah, blah.

"The cop looks at the papers, looks at me. Then he gets a thought. He's a psychiatric patient—you're a social worker, right? Right. So how come *he's* driving?

"I tell the cop it's all part of our advanced rehabilitation program. So the patient gradually reenters society under supervision. I see the look on the cop's face and I immediately agree with him—this guy is not ready for discharge.

"The cop's acting reasonable about this and Easy Eddie's keeping his mouth shut. I think I have it locked. Then the stupid cop decides he's going to make a point. Asks Easy Eddie if he thought he could outrun a bullet. Easy Eddie sits there, like he's considering the whole thing. Then he asks the cop, how much of a head start would he get?

"I thought the cop was going to start whaling on him right there, but I kept talking to him, saying Eddie wasn't being a wise guy—he's just nuts.

"Finally, the cop pulls off in the cab. I get behind the wheel and take off. I'm not even in second gear when Easy Eddie bails out over the side. By the time I turn around to pick him up, find out what's going on . . . he's down there in the street, trying to scrape the heroin off the concrete with a piece of cardboard."

She knew there was a point to the story and she was trying to keep a straight face, but her whole upper body was quivering. Finally she gave it up. "Oh, God! You're standing knee-deep in smack and the cop's got an attitude about going through this stupid signal. . . ."

"Pretty funny story, huh?" I asked her.

She caught my tone. "Well, it is. I mean . . ."

"Girl, everything Easy Eddie said was true. We had come up together. We were as close as brothers. He was a stand-up guy. He didn't mean any harm—never thought about getting me in trouble. If we'd gone down for the dope, he would have taken the whole weight."

"So?"

"So he was really sorry about what happened. And I never rode with him again."

# CROSS

# Bandit

**T**he Group Home was a garbage can. It wasn't as bad as the Institution, that part was true. We lived in rooms, not dorms. And the bathrooms were like real ones, in houses. The windows didn't have bars, and the fence around the house was nothing—just wood, with no razor wire on top. But it was a garbage can anyway . . . a place where you throw things away.

It was a mix inside. Not like the Institution, that was a mix too, but at least everyone in there was bad. In the Group Home, you had bad kids like me, on the way out from the Institution. You had to stay there for a few months before they let you go for real. But they also had other kids, kids who never did nothing, but they locked them up anyway because nobody wanted them.

That was Rodney. He was smaller than most of the kids, although he wasn't the littlest. Rodney had a bad leg, from where his mother's boyfriend beat on him. He had to drag that bad leg behind him when he walked, and he couldn't run at all.

A big black guy ran the place. He was the Director. That's what they call them in the Group Homes, not Superintendent, what they call them in the Institutions. Mr. Allen, that was his name.

When I got there, he told me it was a place where kids got ready to go out on their own. A Halfway House, he called it. Halfass was more like it—just like the joint, only there was more talking.

We mostly talked in Group. We would all sit in this circle and talk. About our feelings. Mr. Allen, he said that was important. To express your feelings.

I never did that lame stuff. You talk about your feelings, people think you're weak.

Mr. Allen, he wasn't weak. He was an ex-con, a big guy with a hard face and heavy muscles. I want to look like him—it's a good way to look when you're inside. He did State time, years ago. Now he works for the State.

**R**odney lived in my room. Just the two of us—the room was real small. I didn't have much stuff, but I had a radio. One day, when I was out looking for a part-time job, three guys from upstairs came into the room after my radio. Rodney walked in while they were doing it. They told him to mind his own business, but he tried to stop them. They rat-packed him, stomped him good. But they left the radio, because they knew from how he fought that he would tell me.

They took Rodney to the hospital. That night, Mr. Allen came into my room. He asked me how come I wasn't playing my radio. I told him I wanted to read. He went over to the radio, turned it on. Nothing happened.

"Where are they?" he asked me.

I gave him the Institution look, but Mr. Allen stared me right back.

"Give it up," he said.

I reached under my bed and gave him one of my thick white socks. Full of batteries from the radio.

"Going for some payback, Marlon?"

I didn't say anything.

"That's not the way it works in here," he said. "I'll take care of it."

The next morning, they shipped the three guys out. Back to the Institution.

When Rodney came back, Mr. Allen told us in Group that the three guys couldn't live by the rules of the Community, so they were expelled.

Everybody nodded, like that was righteous. I could feel Mr. Allen watching me, but I didn't look at him.

One day, in Group, Rodney said he wanted a puppy. He even had a picture of the one he wanted. A black and white puppy. "I would call him Bandit," Rodney said.

Mr. Allen said maybe someday he could have one, if he would take care of it. Rodney got all excited. One of the guys whispered "punk" real quiet, but I heard him. I said I wanted a puppy too, looking the guy in the face. He didn't say anything to me.

Mr. Allen took me aside later. He told me it was good that I watched out for my partner, but not to be stupid.

Rodney cried every night, but I never said anything.

Nobody ever visited him.

Nobody ever visited me either, but that was different. I knew nobody would come, but Rodney, he always thought his mother would come.

The lock on the back door of the pet shop was nothing. I went in like I learned in the Institution.

Rodney cried when I showed him the puppy. "Bandit!" he said. The puppy slept on his bed.

They came for me the next morning. Mr. Allen took me in his office. The cops said it was okay, but they left the hand-cuffs on.

"Will you let Rodney keep the puppy?" I asked him.

He said he would. His face was sad. "I'll pay for the dog, Marlon," he said. "You pay me back when you can."

"I will," I told him. I always pay back.

Those guys who did Rodney . . . I'll see them soon.

# Cripple

**I** worked my way down the long corridor toward the spill of light, antenna out. Ready. The door to the room was standing open, a greenish glow from the computer terminal marking the path. I stepped inside, my rubber-soled shoes soundless on the thick carpet. He was in his wheelchair, facing the screen, huge head wobbling on the thin stalk of his neck, skeletal fingers splayed across the keyboard.

On the screen, the image of a little boy dressed in a sailor suit.

He touched some keys. Another figure entered the screen. Dark, looming in the shadows. The human in the wheelchair tapped more keys and the image crystallized. Into a man. A tall man, neatly dressed.

Faint hum from the computer. The man's breathing changed, went from smooth to ragged.

"How did you get past the dogs?" he asked, not turning around.

"Tranquilizer gun," I told him. "Secobarbital. A grain and a half in each cartridge."

# Cripple

He pushed a button on the wheelchair's console. The motor moved him back, away from the computer, rotating until he faced me across the room.

"You must be very good at what you do," he said. His voice was as atrophied as his body, rusty from neglect.

"Like you are," I replied, just above a whisper.

"What do you want?"

"I want what's in your computer."

"It's not for sale."

"That's why they sent me."

"You don't understand. I'm not a pornographer. I don't hurt children. This is all a game. For entertainment. What I do is create interactive computer modules. Just images on a screen. You push the buttons, and the images do whatever you want them to. It doesn't hurt anybody."

"Whatever you say."

"This isn't even illegal, you know. I've got my rights. The First Amendment, you ever hear of it?"

"Sure."

"No, you wouldn't understand. You're just a mercenary. A man for hire. A common criminal. Well, you tell the people who sent you that they'll never be competition for me. You can steal my computer, but I always have my brain. My intelligence. Whatever you take, I can just make more of it."

"I know."

"Then take whatever you came for and get out. I have work to do."

He spun the wheelchair again, faced the screen. Tapped the keys. I took out the pistol, screwed in the silencer, and shot him in the back of his head. His brains splattered the screen, obscuring the images.

A mind isn't always a terrible thing to waste.

# Mad Dog

**H**ow come you want to give him up? He turn on you or something?"

I shifted my weight in the battered vinyl office chair, scratching the big Doberman behind his ears the way he liked. The fat man sat facing me across an old wooden desk under a painted metal sign. CENTURION GUARD DOGS—*Sales and Rentals*. He held a pencil in one hand, a clipboard in front of him. The sleeves of his graying T-shirt were rolled up, a tattoo of a hula dancer on his right biceps. When the flab had been muscle, the dancer would shake her butt when he flexed.

I snapped a match into flame with my thumbnail, lit my cigarette. The Doberman's ears were flat, corded neck muscles gentle against the choke collar.

"That's a lot of crap," I told the fat man. "Dobermans don't turn on you. They got a bad rep for it, but they don't deserve it. See, what happens, a guy hears all the stories, okay? He gets a Dobie as a puppy, he figures he's going to make sure the dog never turns on *him* when he grows up. So he beats the hell out of the dog every day. Takes control. Dominates. It's easy to make a puppy afraid of you. Makes some people feel tough, you understand? But Dobermans, one way they're different from other dogs, they got good memories. Real good. So, one day, the guy goes to beat up his dog and the dog says, 'Un huh, not today, pal.' And the dog nails him. Like he deserves. Then this guy, this guy who beat his own puppy, he says, "The son of a bitch *turned* on me.' You understand what I'm telling you?"

The fat man's eyes flicked a challenge at me. Dropped it when I tossed it back. His voice was soft, sly-cored. "If he didn't turn on you, how come you're giving him up?"

My expression didn't change. "He's brain-damaged. I had to leave him at a kennel when I went away. He got hold of some virus from the other dogs. Almost died."

"He looks okay to me."

"Oh yeah. He's in great physical shape. But his mind's not right. He'll be just sitting around and all of a sudden he'll go off. He's not safe. You couldn't put him in a home or anything."

"You sure? I mean, he looks so good and all. He should be worth . . ."

I gave the Doberman's chain an imperceptible tug. His ears shot up. A blood-chilling snarl slipped between his flashing teeth. "Stop it!" I yelled at him, tugging again. He lunged at the fat man. I jerked the chain hard. The dog's ears went flat again like nothing had happened.

"What d'I do?" the fat man asked, rubbing his hands together.

"Nothing. You don't have to do anything. He's just nuts. It's not his fault."

"Yeah. Yeah, maybe I could use him for a warehouse job. Or something. But I can't pay much . . . I mean he's not trained or nothing."

"You got a mobile cage?"

"Back of the station wagon."

I walked the Doberman around the back of the joint to the cage. The fat man opened the door. I jerked the chain and the

Doberman jumped inside, quiet as oil in water. The fat man slammed the cage shut. The Doberman looked at me. I reached my hand inside the cage, rubbed the side of his head. Turned my back on him.

The fat man handed me the money. "What's his name?" he asked, pencil poised.

"Devil," I told him.

**T**he concrete processing plant stood alone in the middle of a prairie on a six-acre lot in Brooklyn. Surrounded by a six-foot chain-link fence topped with loops of razor wire. Nothing nearby but abandoned factories. No streetlights. The front gate was wide enough for the sand and gravel trucks to make their daily deliveries. The two sides of the gate were held together by a heavy padlocked chain. A white metal sign was posted on the front. Big red letters: PATROLLED BY ATTACK DOGS. It was 5:50 A.M. early in June. I watched the dogs through the binoculars. A pair of Shepherds, their coats thick and matted with the concrete dust. A barrel-bodied Rottweiler. And a sleek Doberman.

Okay.

**I**t's gotta be an accident. This guy, he's not reasonable. We got no problems with the other partners. They understand the way things are. The way they gotta be. This guy, he's a hardnose. He gets shot or something, maybe the other partners get the message, maybe they spook and run to the *federales*. You know how it works."

"I know."

"You pull this one off, there's a place for you with us. I told you this before."

I kept my face neutral. The way they taught me. In the place where I was raised. The man in the white silk shirt watched me, waiting. I waited too. Another thing they taught me. He shrugged his shoulders. "Half now, half when it's done?" he asked.

"Yeah." I held my hand out for the cash.

• • •

**T**wo days later, I pulled the rented car up to the gate. The sun was just making its move, dawn coming fast. I slipped the leather gloves on my hands. They were lined with a fine chain mesh. I knelt, pointed the Polaroid camera at the plant. Waited.

I heard his car coming. Didn't look up. A squeal of rubber as his white Caddy pulled across the front of my car, blocking any escape. He charged out, waving the tire iron.

"What the hell you think you're doing?"

I tried to hide the camera under my jacket, sneak back toward my car. He cut me off. His face was twisted into frightened hate, white foam on his lips.

"You son of a bitch! You're not taking what's mine. I worked for this! You tell those bastards I'm *never* paying!"

"Hey! I don't know what you're talking about. I just wanted to take a picture of the dogs."

He was past talking. Charged at me, whipping the tire iron at my head. I dropped the camera, caught the first shot with my left hand, spun to face him, my back to the gate. The dogs went mad. The switchblade popped open in my hand. I dropped into a crouch, working my way to him, one hand in front to take his next blow with the tire iron.

He was a big man, block-shouldered. He'd seen knives before. He backed away from me, parallel to the gate. Raised his right hand, bluffed a swing with the tire iron, and rammed his shoulder against the gate, forcing a narrow slot open. "Get him!" he screamed. And the Doberman flowed through the opening past him in one bound, heading for me.

"Devil!" I yelled. "Hit! Hit him, boy!"

The Doberman whirled and turned on the big man like a

tornado swooping up a farmhouse. Buried his teeth deep into the man's upper thigh. The man's scream hit a past-human octave as he raised the tire iron to smash down on the dog's head. I hooked him hard in the belly and he went to his knees. The Doberman ripped at his throat. A chunk of red-and-white flew into the air.

It was over fast. "Devil! Out!" I shouted. The big dog backed away, his muzzle bathed in blood. I opened the back door of my car, gave the dog the signal and he jumped inside. I slammed my shoulder against the gate, shoving the man's body inside, face first. The other dogs tore at the body. I left it where it was.

It's all in the way you raise them.

# Statute of Limitations

## 1

**I** watched her coming down the stairs to the basement pool-room. Watched her in the bank-security mirror the old man keeps just inside the door. All in black, she was—but dressed for mourning, not for style.

She threaded her way through the maze of tables, a dark, slender wraith, not even drawing a glance from the men playing their various games. I was where I said I'd be—back corner, away from the windows. She was wearing a black pillbox hat with a black half-veil. Her face was anemia-pale under the mesh.

"Mister . . . Cross?"

"Sit down," I told her, pointing toward a small round table with the tip of my cue stick.

She took one of the two wooden chairs, took off her gloves, fumbled in her purse for a cigarette. I pocketed the last ball on the table, left my cue on the felt and sat down. Two men detached themselves from the wall and moved into my spot, racking the balls and starting a game. The woman and I were invisible behind their shield.

I took a seat, lit a smoke of my own. Waited.

It took her two more cigarettes to realize I wasn't going to say anything.

She had a chemotherapy voice, juiceless and resigned. "You have to make him stop," she said. "He's never going to stop."

I'd expected a battered wife, from what the old man had told me. But this woman's soul was carrying the scars, not her body.

"Just tell me," I said.

"I can pay. Whatever it costs, I can get it."

"This is part of what it costs."

"I thought . . ."

"I don't know you."

"And you don't trust me."

"That too."

She lit another cigarette with the glowing butt of her last one.

"I could lie to you," she said. Like she knew all about lying.

"No. No, you can't."

"You have a lie detector somewhere around here?"

"I am one," I said, holding her eyes so she'd understand, get down to it.

## 2

**M**y . . . stepfather," she finally said, the last word a mucus-coated maggot. A dangerous, deadly maggot.

"What?"

"He . . . had me. When I was a baby. When I was a girl. When I was a teenager. Now I'm away. But I'll never be free from him. I'll never have a boyfriend, never have a husband. I'll never have a baby—he burned me inside."

"There's people who can fix that. Therapists . . ."

Her eyes were corpses. "He burned me with a soldering iron. Right after I had my first period. He put it inside me and pushed the switch."

"What do you want?"

"I went to the police," she said, like she hadn't heard me. "They told me I came to them too late. Too much time had passed since the last time he had me. The statute of limitations, they said. He can't be prosecuted. So I went to a lawyer. He has money. I thought, if I could sue him, take his money, it would take his power. The lawyer told me I was too late too."

"Okay, so . . . ?"

"The prosecutor, he was very kind. He told me I couldn't even get an Order of Protection. You can only get one if there's an ongoing criminal case. But he said if he . . . my stepfather . . . ever bothered me again, he'd lock him up. He said they know about him . . . from other things. He wouldn't tell me what."

"Would that be enough?"

"Nothing would ever be enough. For him to die, that wouldn't be enough. But if he could lose his power, if he could be in prison, that would . . . I don't know, give me a chance, maybe. To be free."

"What did you think I could do?"

"Hurt him," she whispered.

"Felonious assault, that's a big-time rap in this state. If you've got a record, you could pull twenty years inside."

"He has a record," she said.

"For what?"

"Rape. Before he married my mother. A long time ago. My mother didn't find out about it until much later. He told me first. When I was just a little girl. He raped a girl and he went to prison. He told me he'd never rape a girl again. He hated prison. That's why he married my mother. So he could do what he does and not go to prison again. He was like some kind of . . . gangster, maybe. He'd talk real hard on the phone sometimes. And other times, he'd grovel. Crawl on his knees to whoever was on the other end of the line. I heard him doing it once and he . . . hurt me very ugly that night."

I lit another smoke, watching her. "You want this bad?"

"It's all I want," she said, holding my eyes.

Then I told her what it would cost.

# 3

**H**e lived alone. In a nice house in the suburbs. Neighbors on both sides, but he had a high fence all around the property. Solid cedar. It wouldn't keep out an amateur.

A hard, slanting rain wasn't doing much to break the summer heat as I rang his bell just before midnight. No dog barked. We didn't expect any, not after a week of watching and waiting.

I didn't hear footsteps before he threw the door open. A big man, paunchy, hair combed to one side exaggerating the baldness he was trying to conceal. Wearing a white T-shirt over baggy black pants, barefoot.

I asked his name, holding my wallet open so he could see the police shield. He looked at it closely, eyes narrowing.

"You don't mind waiting outside, Sergeant? So I can just call the precinct, make sure you're who you say you are?"

"No sir," I said, watching his expression change as he felt the pistol in his back.

I stepped inside, pushing him back gently with the palm of my hand. I tilted my hat back on my head, quickly pulling the brim down again as I saw his eyes flash to the dragon tattoo across my forehead. I gestured for him to turn around. Buddha showed him the .357 magnum, close enough so he could see the rounds in the cylinder. Buddha's face was covered with a dark stocking mask.

"Let's go into your study," I told the man.

We walked him down the carpeted hallway in a sandwich, took him over to his glass-topped desk, told him to sit down, make himself comfortable.

"You from Falcone?" he asked me.

I put my fingers to my lips, made a *ssshh*ing gesture.

"Look, you want money? I got . . ."

Buddha ground the tip of the pistol barrel deep into the man's ear. The man let out a yelp, then he was quiet.

I opened my satchel, taking the stuff out one piece at a time, letting him see what was going to happen. A pair of hand-cuffs, a hypodermic, a small bottle full of clear fluid with a flat rubber top, surgical bandages, a Velcro tourniquet, some pressure tape, a mini-blowtorch. And a stainless steel butcher knife.

"Wh . . . what is this?"

"Just a job, pal," I told him. "Just earning my living. Don't worry, it won't hurt a bit . . . once I give you a shot of this stuff."

He watched as I stuck the hypo into the rubber-topped bottle, filled the syringe, pushed the plunger to check it was flowing smoothly. His face was a jelly of terror.

"Please . . ."

"Look, pal, you think I get any kick out of this? I'm not a sadist. Hey, I don't mind telling you the score. Woman comes to see me, says you did her real bad. Paid good money to take a piece out of you, even the score. Only thing, she's not a professional . . . wants me to bring her the proof."

"Proof?" The word slid out of his throat.

"Sure, pal. Proof. Couple a broken legs wouldn't satisfy this lady. She wants your hand. Your right hand."

"Oh god . . ."

"Look, pal, it don't make no difference to me. She paid full price for a body, you understand? She's paying the same for your hand she'd pay for your head. You just relax, do it the easy way. My man Fong's gonna cuff your hand flat to the table, I'm gonna wrap this tourniquet around your arm, find a vein, shoot you up with this happy juice. You go to sleep. You wake up, you got one less hand. All nice and bandaged, better than they'd do it in a hospital." I hit the switch on the blowtorch. The hissing butane was the loudest sound in the room. I cracked a wooden match into life, fired the torch.

"What's that?" He was trembling so hard, it sounded like his mouth was full of pebbles.

"To cauterize the wound, pal. So you don't bleed to death."

"Ca . . . cauterize?"

"Hey, pal, what do you think I should use . . . a soldering iron?"

# 4

**B**y the time he came to, we had him all strapped down and ready to go. Buddha had the tourniquet around his biceps, I was tapping his veins to make them stand out.

"Could I talk to you?" His voice was a practiced weasel-whine, begging, promising.

"Talk quick, pal," I told him.

"Look, you're professionals. Like you said, right? I mean . . . you got paid to do this, I could pay you more not to, okay? I mean, pay you right now. Whatever you want."

"You got thirty large in the house, pal?" I asked, sarcasm lacing my voice.

"I got it . . . I mean, it's not mine, exactly. That's why I thought you were from Falcone. But . . . I'll give it to you, make it right with him tomorrow. I mean, I got equity in the house, my cars . . . I can cover it, easy."

"Thirty large? In cash?"

"Yes!"

"Here? Now?"

"Yeah, yeah. For real. I swear. Just let me. . ."

"Man, I don't know. We already took the broad's money."

"Come on. Please! You're a man. I didn't do anything to the bitch she didn't deserve. I mean . . . cutting off a man's hand, for god's sake . . . Take the money! My money's as good as hers."

I sat back in my chair, thinking it over. Watched the hope in his eyes. Looked over his shoulder at Buddha.

"Where's the money?" I asked him.

He went through a full-body shudder before he whispered "Safe."

He gave me the combination. I dialed it quickly. Half a dozen kilo-sized bags of white powder, shrink-wrapped in clear plastic. And cash. Neatly stacked, all in hundreds. I speed-counted the banded stacks . . . more than sixty grand.

I dropped it in the satchel.

"We'll leave you the powder," I told him.

"Hey! There was. . ."

"Shut up, now. You got a good deal. You paid us to call it off, right? The rest of the cash, we'll do a job for you."

"What job?"

"You think that broad's not going to come after you again, pal? You think this ends it? You bought yourself one safe night, that's all."

"You mean . . . ?"

"Sure. Way I figure it, we owe you a job . . . right, Fong?"

Buddha nodded behind the stocking mask.

I could see him thinking it over.

"When would you do it?" he finally asked.

"Tonight."

"And that's it?"

"Tell her," I said, handing him the phone.

# 5

Toxic waste bubbled out of his mouth, hard, evil ugliness over the phone lines. Telling her that her little scheme backfired. How he had her and he'd always have her.

"You listening to me, cunt? You understand the way things are now? I'm coming to *see* you, bitch. And when I'm done, you'll come back here. On your knees. I'll have my mark on you again, you . . ."

He hung up, bathed in sweat, licking his lips.

I nodded to Buddha. A hard hand clamped down on the back of the man's neck as I slid the hypo home.

# 6

**H**e went out in a minute. I gently taped his right hand into a fist, watched as Buddha took the man's elbow in one hand, held his wrist in the other . . . and slammed it into the glass desk top until the knuckles were bruised and swollen. I took a wax model of a woman's hand out of my satchel, the long false nails with their bright red lacquer gleamed in the light. I held the wax hand, scratched a long, deep gouge in the man's cheek.

# 7

**I**n the car, I used a Handi-wipe to remove the dragon tattoo. Buddha took off the stocking mask, popped the rubber wedges out of his cheeks, took off the bulky jacket and lost fifty pounds. Our prints weren't anywhere.

We were at her house in an hour.

"You get it all?" I asked her.

She nodded, pointed to the tape recorder attached to her phone.

She held out her hands. Stayed perfectly still while I attached the false red nails.

I slapped her in the face, hard. Her eyes flared into life, watching me, focused. Good.

"He came here about an half hour ago. You opened the door, didn't expect him. He punched you in the stomach. You went down. He punched you in the face, over and over again, twisted your arm so hard you felt it snap. You scratched his face . . . You remember doing it, you felt your nails go in. Deep. Then he beat you some more until you passed out."

"Thank you," she said.

Then I went to work.

# Crossfire

## 1

**B**e careful with it," the man told the uniformed parking valet. "It cost me a bundle," he added unnecessarily, the gleaming black Mercedes 600SL coupé making that statement on its own.

"Yes *sir*," the valet responded, throwing a half-salute, palming the ten-dollar bill and sliding behind the wheel all in one smooth motion.

The man entered the Runway Club slowly, his eyes sweeping the main room as he paid the cover charge. The joint sat in the shadow of the airport, but its name came from the long T-shaped platform that bisected the interior, not its location.

The man made his way to a small round table toward the back, a good distance from the end of the runway. It was harder to see the girls from there—early on a Tuesday night, the man was surrounded by pools of shadow.

A blonde waitress approached, wearing a tiny black Spandex skirt over fishnet stockings and spike heels. A fine black mesh blouse did little to conceal her breasts as she bent over to take the man's order.

"Absolut rocks, water on the side," the man told her, not making eye contact.

When the waitress returned with two glasses on a small lac-quered tray, the man pulled a folded sheaf of bills from his shirt pocket and handed her a twenty. "A gambler," the waitress thought to herself, noting where the man carried his money. She returned with a ten-dollar bill and one single, laying them across the tabletop so they were slightly separated. The waitress took one step back, watching, her hands clasped in front of her to squeeze her breasts into deeper cleavage.

The man drew a wider separation between the two bills, this time catching her eyes—his were a bright China blue, star-tling under a Las Vegas tan. Then he took a gold coin from his jacket pocket, turned it in his fingers so the waitress could see both sides—a Queen's head and a maple leaf. The man pointed at the separated bills, bull's-eye tattoo prominent on the back of his hand.

"Feel lucky?" he asked.

"Go for it," the waitress smiled.

The man flicked the coin with his thumb. As it turned gently in the smoky-blue air of the club, the waitress called out "Tails!"

The man caught the coin in a cupped palm, slapped it against the back of his other wrist. He removed his hand to show the waitress the maple leaf.

"You're a winner," he said.

The waitress bent forward, delicately scooped up the saw-buck and blew the man a kiss, switching her hips as she walked away in a good-bye wave.

# 2

The man watched the runway dancers patiently, not reacting as one after another stepped down and continued to dance at vari-ous spots throughout the room. Other men were stuffing bills into garters or G-strings, applauding as the girls danced on table-tops. Occasionally, one of the dancers would perch on a patron's lap, but the man passed up all such offers, sipping at his drink, watching quietly.

The waitress watched too. Watched the man's slouchy-cut black silk suit, the diamond flashing on his left ring finger, the wafer-thin gold watch. She made two more trips to his table, each time opting to risk her tip, each time winning.

"Tails have always been lucky for me," she said to the man, standing hip-shot, "but I like heads too."

"Do you?" the man asked.

"Very much," she said, licking her lips.

"You're a smart girl," the man said. "You pay attention, don't you?"

"When I'm supposed to," she said, her eyes on the gold chain around the man's neck, barely visible under the open collar of his white silk shirt.

The man reached into his shirt pocket, thumbed off a bill without looking, tossed it on the table. A hundred.

"Yours," he said. "For a little favor."

"Tell me," she said, bending forward, reaching.

The man covered her hand with his, the bull's-eye tattoo holding her eyes.

"Tell Reba to come over this way," the man said.

"This isn't her spot," the waitress said. "I could . . ."

"Just tell her," the man said, removing his hand.

The waitress picked up the bill, said, "I'll see what I can do," and walked off, spike heels clicking on the tile floor.

# 3

**T**he brunette was tall, extravagantly built, her hair a thick, wild mane falling past her bare shoulders. Her height was exaggerated by a pair of dark stockings, anchored by thick black bands around the top, flowing out of high spike heels. Her only other article of clothing was a black G-string.

"You asked for me, honey?" she said.

"Yeah," the man replied, his eyes scanning her face, not stopping until they located a tiny scar just past the corner of her right eye.

"Well, I hope it's gonna be worth it, baby. . . . It costs me fifty to switch my spot."

The man reached forward, stuffed a couple of bills into the top of her stocking. The brunette held out a hand, so the man could help her onto the tabletop. But the man pulled her down instead, into his lap. The brunette squirmed, purring "Lap dancing costs—"

"Just do it," the man said quietly, his right hand around her waist. With his left hand, he reached into his shirt pocket, tossed several bills on the table.

The brunette tried to turn so she could throw one leg over the man's lap and face him, but he held her firmly with one hand. She wiggled her buttocks hard against the man's lap, making practiced sounds of pleasure, throwing back her head so she was cheek-to-cheek with the man, facing forward.

As she reached one hand out for the money, the man whispered in her ear, "You wanted to see me?"

She sat up, startled, but the man's hand on her waist held her close. "You told Lucinda you wanted to see me?" he said again.

The brunette relaxed, leaning back again, her mouth close to the man's ear. "You're Cross?" she asked.

"Yeah."

"I thought you'd look . . . I don't know . . . different."

"Tell me what you want," he said, voice flat.

She shifted her weight, still wiggling in time to the music, whispering, "I want a gun. A cold gun. Never used. Lucinda said you could . . ."

"What do you want it for?"

"A fucking paperweight for my coffee table, what do you think?" she snapped.

"I don't sell guns," the man said. "Not individual guns. You want to buy a crate, we can talk. One piece, go visit a pawnshop."

"I'll pay—"

"Tell me what you want," the man said again.

"Not here. Pick me up after work. I'll—"

"Won't the boss—?"

"I don't *have* a boss," the brunette said. "I rent this space. What I do after work is my own business."

"What time do you—?"

"I'll be out front at four."

# 4

She was standing on the apron to the parking lot at 4 A.M. when a white Cadillac sedan pulled up. The driver stepped out, a pudgy man with black hair plastered across his forehead, wearing a voluminous calf-length coat despite the summer heat. The driver walked around behind the Cadillac, opened the back door. Then he stepped close to the woman, said, "Mr. Cross is waiting," and swept his hand toward the opened door in an invitational gesture.

The brunette put one long leg inside the car, saw the man with the bull's-eye tattoo on his hand sitting inside, and climbed in the rest of the way. The door slammed behind her, and the Cadillac pulled away smoothly.

# 5

I have to make a stop first," Reba said. "It's over on Diversity."

If Cross felt any impatience, his face didn't reflect it.

The Cadillac purred through the empty streets, alone except for an anonymous smog-colored sedan trailing a respectful distance behind. If the driver noticed, he gave no sign.

When the white car pulled to the curb, Reba turned in her seat, facing Cross full on. "Come on," she said. "You might as well see the reason for all this."

It was a three-story brownstone, the polished wood door

covered by black wrought-iron grillwork. Reba took out a key, opened the gate, then the door. "Come on," she said again.

Cross followed her up the stairs, reflecting on the wisdom of Keith Gilyard, the ground-zero poet laureate of New York . . . how true it was that walking up stairs exaggerates female hips . . . for good or for bad. The brunette was all good.

On the top floor, she used another key to let herself in. A hefty woman with short-cropped brown hair was sitting on an exercise bike, pumping away. She looked up at the entrance, gasped an incomprehensible greeting, and went back to her silent work. Reba flashed her a smile, walked past the exercise bike down a hall, Cross close behind.

She opened the door to a small bedroom. The walls were a soft pink, decorated with dolls, stuffed animals, a giant poster of some sleek, androgynous individual holding a guitar. A blonde girl was asleep in the single bed, a quilt covering her to her shoulders. Her face, childlike in repose, showed a girl somewhere in that borderland before adolescence. Reba bent at the waist, gently brushed the girl's soft hair from her forehead, kissed her on the cheek. Then she straightened up, took a sweeping look around the little bedroom as though reassuring herself, spun on a spike heel, and walked back into the front room.

The hefty woman was sitting on a futon couch, sipping a greenish-colored liquid from a tall glass.

"You didn't let her watch that damn MTV again, did you, Anna?"

"She did all her homework first," the hefty woman said. "And her yoga too."

"I told you—"

"Come on, Reba," the hefty woman interrupted. "We had a deal. You can't stop her from growing up."

"I can stop her from growing up like I did," the brunette replied.

"Your problem wasn't MTV," the hefty girl said, her voice thick with a shared secret.

"Okay, okay," Reba surrendered. "You're going to bring her by after school, right?"

"She has gymnastics class, remember? How about you come by and watch, take her home yourself."

"You got a deal," Reba said, flashing a smile.

# 6

**T**hat's my Angel," she said to Cross in the backseat.

"She looks—"

"I mean, that's her *name,*" Reba said sharply. "You want to know what she *is,* she's my life. My whole life."

The woman was quiet on the short drive to her apartment building. Again, Cross followed her, this time through the lobby with its half-asleep doorman, all the way up to the twenty-first floor in a silent elevator.

The apartment was two bedrooms, with a balcony and a view of the lake from the living room. "Make yourself comfortable," she said over her shoulder, walking down the carpeted hall. "I'll be back in a minute."

Cross pulled a flat cellular phone from inside his jacket, punched in a number.

"Anything?" he asked the person on the other end. He nodded to himself at the answer, put the phone back inside his jacket.

Cross looked around the living room for a minute. Finally he shrugged his shoulders and lit a cigarette. He was on his second drag when Reba walked back in, barefoot, dressed in a heavy white terry-cloth bathrobe, hair pulled back, face freshly scrubbed.

"There's no smoking in here," she said. "Take it outside," indicating the balcony.

Cross opened the sliding glass doors, stepped out on the balcony, hands on the railing, looking down.

"Sorry about that," Reba said from behind him. "Where I work, everybody smokes. I come home, I have to really scrub the smell out of my hair. I used to smoke, but Angel went crazy with it . . . cancer and all. So I promised her I'd stop. That's why I don't allow it in the house—that girl has a nose like a blood-hound."

"It's okay," he replied, taking another drag.

"What do I call you?" the brunette asked, standing against his shoulder.

"Cross."

"I'm Reba. But I guess you know that."

"Yeah."

"About what I asked you . . . I thought if you could see the reason why, maybe you'd change your mind."

"The kid's the reason?"

"Yes."

"She gonna visit you in the joint?"

"Oh, I'd never let her come in there. Why . . . ?"

"Not the joint where you work. Jail. Prison. You want a cold gun, you want to smoke somebody. You don't know what you're doing, you're gonna go down."

"What do you care?"

"The way it works, you're gonna go down, the Man makes you an offer. Who sold you the gun, girlie? Like that."

"And you think I'd tell them?"

"Sure. If it meant a couple of years off your sentence, a couple of years where you get to be back with your kid, why not?"

"But if I . . . hired you to . . . take care of this problem, why wouldn't it work the same way?"

"I don't get caught," the man called Cross said.

# 7

**A**ngel's eleven," said Reba, sitting at her kitchen table, holding a coffee cup in her hand. "I had her when I was seventeen. The boy who got me pregnant, he got in the wind. Joined the Army or something. I never heard from him."

Cross watched her eyes, not speaking, waiting as a stone waits.

"I was a high-school senior," she said. "And a National Merit Scholar, already accepted to college. I didn't want an abortion. They put me in a group home. It was heaven. When the blood test came back, I was so happy I cried for days. You know why?"

"Because it wasn't your father's baby?"

Two bright red dots bloomed on the woman's pale cheeks. "How could you . . . ?"

"From what you and that girl in the apartment said to each other. From what you're willing to do to protect the kid."

"You . . . Lucinda said you knew things."

"What's important, I *do* things," he said. "You got the money, I can do this."

"You don't even know what 'this' is?"

"Then tell me."

"When I got out of the group home, I tried working. Flipping burgers, waitressing, a 7-Eleven. I could keep Angel away from the damn Welfare people, but I couldn't give her the things I . . .

"Anyway, I tried whoring too. Escort service," she said, looking Cross full in the eye. He stared back, unblinking.

"The money was good. Real good. We moved to a better place, I could pay for the gymnastics lessons, get her a great babysitter. But it got too ugly. Kickbacks to the cops, pimps always trying to move in. Freaks who want to hurt the girls. Then AIDS. So I started private dancing. It's pretty clean, all things considered. You rent some space from the owner, pay the hairdresser and the makeup girl. You don't have to hustle drinks . . . the girls who do that, they do okay too. There's no sex. Unless you want to make some special arrangement for after. You dance on the tables, maybe wiggle around in their laps. You know . . . ?"

"When I was a kid, we called it dry humping."

She flashed a broad smile. "Yeah, only now they call it safe sex. Some of the girls throw in a hand job now and then, but that's it. Anyway, I can't do this forever. I went for the implants," she said, flicking a hand across her breasts. "That's part of the deal. And I work out like a bandit. But, sooner or later, you get too old. I've been saving my money, living small, you understand? Another couple of years, I'm going to open a little place of my own."

"A bar?"

"God forbid. No, a pastry shop. I'm really good at it. Taught myself. Here, wait a minute . . ."

She got up, walked over to the refrigerator, a large side-by-side, gleaming white. She reached inside, took out a small tray of tiny tarts, placed it on the table.

"Try the lemon, they're good, even cold."

Cross took the indicated pastry, chewed it thoughtfully. "It *is* good."

"Don't act so surprised. I love to cook fancy little things. I know I can make a living at it. Anna's going to help me get an SBA loan, and I already know the neighborhood I want to open up in."

"You want an investor, let me know," Cross told her, polishing off the tart and reaching for another.

Reba smiled again. Then her generous mouth turned down. "Everything was fine. Until . . . he showed up."

"He?"

"Wieskoft. Robert James Wieskoft. R.J., his friends call him. He's a gymnastics coach. Really top-rated. He coached three Olympians himself. I checked his references before I let him work with Angel. All the organizations said he was great."

"So?"

"He started out fine. He was really devoted to Angel. Worked overtime without asking for more money. Videotaped her so he could analyze her moves in slow motion. She really liked him too. But then he started getting strange. . . ."

"What?"

"Oh, sending her presents. First, it would be a special pair of gym tights. Or ankle weights. But then it was flowers. Candy. Like you'd send to a date. And he wrote her letters too. About how they'd always be together. How she had to obey him if she really wanted to be the best. When he told me she should drop out of school and work with him full-time . . . he'd get her a tutor and all . . . that's when I fired him."

"Then he threatened you?"

"Threatened? No, he didn't do that. He fought against it. Said he was going to call Child Protective Services, say I was abusing Angel. That's when I told him if he did that, I'd kill him."

"And he did do it?"

"No. What he does, he *stalks* her. Every day, he's outside, watching. Carrying that damn video camera of his, like he's capturing her on tape or something. He calls all the time, sends notes to Angel. Then he . . . ." The brunette put her face in her hands, crying.

Cross watched, not moving. Waiting. Finally, she stopped. When she lifted her face, it was streaked with tears, but her eyes were hard.

"He filed a petition in Family Court. Said I was abusing Angel. That I *beat* her, can you imagine? And he made an application to be her foster parent! The court, they told me that I shouldn't worry about it . . . he's just a lunatic. He can't make his own application to be a foster parent. I *asked* them to come and investigate me. Come right over to the house, talk to my daughter alone, speak to her pediatrician, her teachers . . . *anything*. But they said they wouldn't do that because once he tried to be Angel's foster parent, they could understand what his game was. He wants to own my child, Cross. And he's not going to stop."

"You tell the cops?"

"Sure. A fat lot of good that did. Oh, the detective was nice enough. When he stopped staring at my chest long enough to talk, he said R.J. hadn't broken any laws. It isn't against the law to go the places he goes . . . especially the gym . . . he has a right to be there. It's a free country. Once the detective found out where I worked, he said maybe he could go talk to him . . . but I could see what he wanted in exchange and I told him to go play with himself."

"Good move."

"I don't care. I'm not a piece of meat. I was really angry and I made a complaint about the detective. They told me to speak to this other cop, McNamara. He was really sweet. Explained the whole thing to me. He wasn't putting on the moves either . . . I could see it bothered him, but there was nothing he could do."

"So it wasn't Lucinda who gave you my name, was it?"

"No," she replied, eyes downcast.

"And you don't really want to buy a gun—it's a gunman you're looking for?"

"I can pay—"

"I don't do hits," Cross said. "McNamara would have told you that."

"He said . . . maybe you could . . . fix things."

"Some things. I work for money."

"I know. Me too, right? I want—"

"For this Wieskoft to go away. You don't care *where* he goes, that's not part of the deal."

"Do you guarantee—?"

"Guarantees cost more."

"Don't you care about what he's doing to my Angel . . . even a little bit?"

"If I made this guy go away . . . if he glommed onto another little girl and left yours alone, would *you* care?" Cross asked.

The brunette took a deep breath, lightly scratched one cheek with a bright red fingernail. "Tell me how much it costs," she said.

# 8

**T**he two men in white coveralls with the logo of a cable TV company emblazoned across their backs were working dangerously close to the roof's edge, apparently stringing wire. Physically, they had only their uniforms in common—to a distant observer, one was remarkably small in stature, otherwise featureless, while the other looked fat, wearing a set of eyeglasses so heavy they might have been mini-binoculars. Both men worked with practiced grace, thoroughly professional to any watchers.

"You got him, Rhino?" the small man asked.

The other man grunted an acknowledgment. His huge, formless body weighed in at over 350 pounds. Nominally covered by the voluminous white coveralls, he dwarfed Cross's normal-sized frame. He pointed one gigantic hand in the general direction of a tall, slender man standing across the street from Reba's apartment building—the tip of his right index finger was missing, the scarless stub as smooth as an aluminum cigar tube, and about the same size.

Cross pulled the cellular phone from his pocket, punched a single digit. "Some of us will be around when you stop by gym class," he said. "Something may happen. It's got nothing to do with you—just go about your business."

Cross hit the END button on the phone, punched in another number, waited a few seconds, then handed the instrument to Rhino. The double-wide truck of a man took it delicately, spoke in a high-pitched, squeaky voice:

"Tall. Six foot two, maybe three. Skinny, maybe a hundred and forty, fifty pounds. Dark, wiry hair, combed straight back. Triple-black on the vine, right down to his shoes. Gold watch on his left wrist, carrying a videocam. Driving a dark blue Lincoln Town Car, license 4-Alpha-7-oh-9-X-Ray. Got it?"

The huge man listened for a minute, said, "Yeah, yeah: over and out," and handed the phone back to Cross. "Princess is still doing his Lone Wolf number," the big man laughed.

Cross punched another number, waited for the pickup, then said, "Ready to roll. ETA like we expected. Sit on him tight, all right, brother?"

# 9

If Reba recognized the pudgy man who had been driving the white Cadillac the night before, she gave no sign. She never gave him a second glance—her eyes were riveted to the man standing next to him . . . an outrageously overdeveloped bodybuilder with a shaved skull whose heavily corded, deeply veined muscles seemed to threaten the confines of his skin. The bodybuilder was dressed in a pale pink silk tank top and a pair of Spandex white shorts with a matching pink stripe down the side. But Reba's eyes never left the man's face, marveling at the heavy application of rouge, the dark eyeliner, the lip gloss . . . and the earring that dangled from one ear on a long chain . . . a miniature of a wrecking ball.

"God! You see that?" she whispered to Anna.

"I see it but I don't believe it. You think it's one of those S&M things?"

"I don't know. I thought I'd seen everything at least once, but . . ."

"He's here, you know," Anna said, dropping her voice.

"I know," Reba said, her eyes glancing over to a far corner where the tall man in black lounged, a tiny smile playing across his thin lips. "He won't try anything as long as I'm around, the sonofabitch."

"Just relax," Anna said, patting her friend's forearm. "That's what he wants, for you to make a scene. Did you speak to that man? The one—?"

"That was him. Last night."

"That guy? He didn't look like much."

"It's not a beauty contest, girlfriend."

The youthful performers came out one at a time for floor exercises, mostly tumbling runs set to music. As the pudgy man became more one with his surroundings, the bodybuilder seemed to swell with outrageousness, imitating the tumbling moves, screaming encouragement to the kids, raising enough of a fuss so that he soon had a clear circle of empty space around him, spectators clucking their tongues in disapproval as they gave him room. The man in black was still, only his eyes animated.

"That was Roscoe Holmes!" the announcer said over the P.A. system as a caramel-skinned boy maybe twelve years old bowed deeply at the conclusion of his routine. "Next up, Angel Andrews!"

The little girl bounded onto the mat, gave a brief bow to the audience, waved gaily at her mother, and charged to the far corner, flinging herself into an airborne one-and-a-half gainer before landing lightly on her feet.

"Way to stick it, honey!" Anna shouted.

As the child got deeper into her routine, the man in black pushed himself off the wall, unlimbering his videocam, moving closer. The bodybuilder tracked him like a heat-seeking missile, banging his way through the crowd. Standing just off the man in black's right shoulder, the bodybuilder spoke in an overenthusiastic, booming voice.

"Hey! Is that one of them mini-cameras? Damn, it sure looks like fun."

The man in black looked over his shoulder, shuddered, and moved quickly to his left, slamming into the pudgy man who had quietly taken up that post.

"Please," the man in black said. "She's almost through. I have to—"

"Can I see?" the bodybuilder asked, reaching for the camera.

The man in black snatched it away, but he was too slow. The bodybuilder's hand wrapped around the man's biceps, squeezing it into liquid pain. The videocam slid from the man's hand, and the bodybuilder grabbed it, holding it to his eye. Before the man in black could react, the bodybuilder pointed the camera at his shocked face and pushed the RECORD button.

"You can't *do* this!" the man in black protested. "Give it *back* to me!"

"Oh, calm yourself, Mary," the bodybuilder said, continuing to aim and shoot.

The crowd's attention was pulled away from the gym mat, but the little girl didn't seem to notice, going through her routine with practiced, confident precision.

"Give it to me! Give it to me!" the man in black was screaming.

The pudgy man stepped forward. "I want to apologize for my friend," he said smoothly. "He's just . . . excitable, you know? Tell you what, we'll pay you for the tape he wasted, okay? Give me the camera, Princess."

The bodybuilder sheepishly handed over the camera. The pudgy man expertly popped out the cassette, handed the empty camera back to the man in black together with a fifty-dollar bill. "Keep the extra for your trouble, okay, pal?" he said.

The man in black's face flushed, red, then white. He grabbed the empty camera and walked out of the gym, stiff-legged.

The pudgy man pocketed the cassette, turned to the bodybuilder. "Cross said he needed an hour—Ace did the freak's car, just to be safe."

"Can we watch the rest of the routines?" the bodybuilder asked. "Can we, Buddha?"

"All right, Princess. Just don't get into anything . . ."

# 10

**T**he man in black stalked angrily out to the school parking lot, the videocam in a white-knuckled grip, muttering a string of obscenities to himself. He stopped short when he saw his blue Lincoln kneeling on four neatly-flattened tires. He punched a keypad he removed from a side pocket to unlock the doors, ripped his car phone from its housing and was just preparing to dial when an unmarked police car pulled up. A sandy-haired man with a mustache stepped out of the sedan, moving toward the Lincoln much faster than his gait would appear. The sandy-haired man leaned in through the opened window.

"Detective McNamara, sir. I noticed the condition of your car. . . . Any trouble?"

"Trouble? Yes, I have some trouble, Officer. I know who did this. Her name is Reba, Reba Andrews. I used to coach her daughter—I'm a gymnastics coach . . . maybe you heard of me? R.J. Wieskoft?"

"No sir, I'm sorry. I don't really follow that sport. Why would you think this Mrs. Andrews was responsible?"

"Well, who *else* could it be? I mean . . . she even *threatened* me once."

"Threatened you, sir?"

"Yes, that's what I said—are you hard of hearing?"

"I don't believe so, sir," McNamara said. "If you'll just remain calm, I'm sure we can—"

"Calm? Why should I have to be calm—I'm the one who's being harassed."

"Yes sir. I'm sure. But without some proof . . ."

"Never mind," the man in black snapped, reaching for the car phone again. "I'll just call my garage. If that bitch thinks she's going to . . ."

He was so absorbed in his own anger that he didn't notice McNamara pulling out of the parking lot.

# 11

**T**hat lock was Swiss cheese," the small-boned, fine-featured black man said from a leather easy chair. He looked as relaxed as a man lounging in his own home except for the sawed-off shotgun balanced delicately across his knees. "Whoever this freak is, he ain't no heavy hitter, home."

"We'll see," Cross said over his shoulder, working diligently with a set of lock picks at a gray metal filing cabinet that dominated the studio apartment. "Got it," he finally said.

His gloved hands rifled through a sheaf of papers, moving rapidly but with assurance—just another day at the office for a pro burglar.

Time passed. The black man checked his watch, but Cross's eyes never looked up from his work. "Twenty minutes," the black man said.

"Damn!"

"Z'up, home? Twenty is plenty, what we got to do."

"Look at this, Ace," Cross said, handing over a leather-bound book, diary-sized.

The man called Ace opened the book, his own hands encased in black leather gloves. Each page was meticulously covered in thin block letters.

VITAL STATISTICS—SCHOOL SCHEDULE—BABYSITTER—DUAL MEETS—DOCTOR'S APPOINTMENTS . . . every page devoted to exhaustive data-gathering on Angel Andrews. The back of the book held photos, some posed, some candid. A photocopy of the girl's birth certificate (the space for "Father" was blank). Copies of report cards, even a vaccination record. Every movement was documented: Wieskoft knew when she was scheduled for dental checkups, the date her report card was to be issued, what time she was dropped off at the babysitter's . . .

"This motherfucker's on the job 24-7," Ace said. "I know pimps don't know half this much 'bout they ho's."

"It's more than that," Cross said. "The man has a plan." He was holding a set of leather handcuffs in one hand, pouring through a whole drawer full of restraints: a leather bondage mask, various-length chains, dog collars, ball gags.

Cross stood up, opened the single closet. Inside he found a wooden yoke designed to hold a person in an impossibly uncomfortable position, leather wraps at each end for the victim's hands. Casually stored in a corner of the closet, he found an electronic stun gun, several cans of Mace, and a cattle prod.

He carefully replaced all the items in the exact position he found them, then walked over to a computer standing on a small wooden desk. He removed the dust cover, turned it on.

"Not even passworded," he muttered to himself, calling up a list of documents. He used the cursor to scroll down the list . . . past TAXES, past REAL ESTATE. When he came to MY SLAVE, he hit the keys, opened the document onto the screen.

You will learn to obey me. You will find true happiness through obedience. We were meant to be together, you to serve me. Forever. The pain will be a learning expe-

rience. The path to liberation. Your freedom. The program will take approximately one year. Then I can allow
you some freedom. When you can be trusted. I . . .

Cross exited the document, went back to REAL ESTATE, studied the
screen for several minutes, nodding to himself. "You hear anything
on the phone yet?" he asked Ace, speaking over his shoulder.

"No, man. And I be surprised behind it, to tell you the
truth. Once that monster-mutant starts playing Junior G-man,
there's no turning off his mouth."

"That's it!"

"What, home?"

"You just put it together for me, Ace. Locked and loaded.
Let's get the hell out of here."

# 12

**H**e's going to kidnap the child," Cross told his crew. They were
in the basement of the Red 71 poolroom, as removed from pry-
ing eyes as if they had been on another planet.

"Ransom?" Rhino asked.

"No," Cross said. "Torture. He's got it all laid out. First he
snatches the kid, probably use that stun gun he's got to take her
down. He's got this cabin, way out in the sticks. Owns it outright,
no mortgage. The plan is to bring her up there. And *keep* her,
see? He's got this whole conditioning program worked out. Like
he was a coach. Only it's a POW thing. Pain conditioning. He's
got a library of bondage-torture books. You know how it plays . . .
all those freaks think the same way . . . he's gonna *train* her, right?
Own her the same way he owns the cabin. He's just waiting for
the right time. And he's getting near critical mass."

"We got a plan too, right?" Rhino said.

Cross looked around the room. "Any ideas?" he asked.

"Get the motherfucker and turn off his lights?" Ace offered.

"I got it," Princess said, barely able to contain his excitement. "How about this? I knock on his door, tell him I'm selling high-tech surveillance equipment . . . like night scopes and all, see? That'll get his motor running. So he lets me into his apartment and I wait for the right moment—then I snap his neck like a fucking twig and throw him out the window. Okay? Then I write a suicide note and split. Is that slick or what?"

"What," Ace said sourly.

"Princess," Cross said patiently, "he takes one look at you and he starts screaming. Come on. . . ."

"Hey, that's the beauty of my plan—I'll wear a disguise."

Rhino gazed at the ceiling as if it had some answers.

Buddha said, "Jesus H. Christ." Very quietly.

Cross shot the pudgy man a look.

"How about a car accident?" Buddha asked, trying to divert Princess. "You know . . . drunk driver, leaving the scene of the smash. I could take him out soon as it gets dark."

"How do we get paid, then?" Cross asked.

"I dunno," Rhino replied. "Isn't the woman—?"

"Yeah, she's in for a piece. But we need to score at both ends, cover our nut with this one," Cross told him. "I got an idea. Okay, you guys all have a clear sight picture, right? Just take a look at the video Princess made if you need a refresher. Keep on him like a blanket . . . I don't know when he's gonna blow, but it has to be soon."

# 13

The white telephone buzzed. Wieskoft looked up from his computer, surprised—the number was unlisted—he only used it to make outgoing calls—take-out food and 900 numbers. His favorite was 1-900–LOLITAS.

He reached for the receiver cautiously.

"Hello . . . ?"

"Good evening, sir," a clear, distinct voice came over the line. "My name is Morgan . . . I'm in the private delivery business. I thought you and I could meet, maybe discuss my services."

"I don't want any deliveries. Who gave you my . . . ?"

"Sure you want a delivery, pal. A live one, if you get my meaning. My prices are very reasonable, and I guarantee I'll deliver the package right to your door . . . or any place you say. Remember, it's a guarantee. And no risk to you. None whatever."

"Leave me alone!" Wieskoft screamed, slamming down the phone.

## 14

Cross strolled away from the pay phone and climbed into the passenger seat of the Shark Car. Buddha threw the car into gear and made the vehicle disappear into a clot of city traffic.

"That should do it for the pressure cooker. We mailed him a copy of the video Princess took, too. Maybe he'll move before he was ready to—he'd be easy then."

"What if he just lays there? What's the backup?"

"You still in touch with that researcher? Cheryl?"

"Sure," Buddha replied. "What you need?"

"Tell her everything she can get on the President's kid. The daughter, what's her name, Chelsea or something?"

"Yeah, that's right. What you want to deal with that draft-dodging weasel for?"

"What difference would that make, brother?"

"Hey, come on, Cross. We was both in the Nam—how you feel about guys that slicked their way out of it?"

"I wish *I* had," Cross said, looking out the window.

## 15

Two days later, the cellular phone rang in the basement of Red 71. Cross looked up from a stack of clippings on a door laid across a pair of sawhorses he was using as a desk.

"What?"

"He's in a rental car, parked right across the street." Rhino's voice, even squeakier than usual, lowered to a whisper.

"You got him tight?"

"In a box. He tries it today, he's going down."

"Stay on him," Cross said, breaking the connection.

"What's with all this stuff?" Princess asked, indicating the pile of clippings.

"We're making a bomb," Cross told him. "Want to tell Ace to come downstairs?"

# 16

The delicate-featured black man's hands matched his face. His fingers were long, tapered, the nails immaculately manicured and covered with clear polish. He sat at the makeshift desk under a powerful lamp, working with a straight razor, his hands covered with membrane-thin surgeon's gloves.

"Got it," he finally said, carefully applying a last drop of paste to the back of a piece of newsprint.

Cross laid the artwork out in long row, nodding his head. "You got the touch, brother," he said admiringly. "This'll do it."

# 17

McNamara stood in one corner of the boxing ring, wearing a loose pair of pants and no shirt, modified boxing gloves on his hands, with footguards that left the soles of his feet bare . . . kick-boxing gear. His handler dipped a black rubber mouthpiece in the bucket, started to place it in McNamara's mouth, but the cop shook it off, took one step forward, shaking a fist.

"I'm warning you, Princess. You try and head-butt me this time, I'm gonna stop your goddamned heart!"

Princess stood in the other corner, devoid of makeup and earring, his grotesque torso rippling under a sheen of oil. He shrugged his shoulders in a "Who, me?" gesture, grinning, as Cross kneaded the back of his shoulders, waiting for the bell.

"Fucking fag," one of the watching spectators mumbled.

Buddha nudged the spectator with his shoulder. "Say what?"

"What's it to you?" the spectator challenged.

"That's my brother," Buddha said, an ugly grin on his pudgy face.

"Fags can't fight," the spectator snarled, holding his ground.

"Never stopped me," Rhino squeaked, shoving his massive bulk against the spectator from the other side.

The spectator looked up at Rhino, then rapidly decided he had better things to do.

The bell rang. McNamara glided forward into a cat-stance, one leg pawing the air a foot or so off the ground. Princess stepped to him, firing a jet-stream left hook at the smaller man's midsection. McNamara spun inside the hook so his back was against Princess's chest, whipping an elbow at the bodybuilder's face. Princess locked McNamara's arm, holding him close. He leaned down, whispered urgently into the cop's ear, "Cross says he needs your RI. Tonight, at ten."

McNamara broke the hold, spun away gracefully. They sparred three full rounds, Princess never seeming to fully connect with any of his punches . . . McNamara landing blow after blow without apparent effect.

Cross wrapped a robe around his tired fighter as McNamara bowed to close the match.

# 18

**M**cNamara was at his desk at ten when the call came in on his private line.

"Detective Bureau, McNamara."

"You know who this is," a muffled voice said. "Listen good—I'm not gonna say this again, okay?"

"Go," McNamara said, flicking on a cheap tape recorder he had connected to the phone.

"There's a guy who's gonna do a snatch. He's been stalking, waiting. This ain't no job for you, McNamara, I give you the dope, you better call the *federales*, okay? Now listen up . . ."

The voice went on for a couple of minutes, uninterrupted. Then the line went dead.

McNamara sat for a few minutes, staring at the cigarette-discolored acoustic tile ceiling of his cubicle. Then he stepped away from his desk and shouted down the hall. "Hey, Trikowski, you still got the number of the Secret Service?"

# 19

The next morning, McNamara was in the chambers of Judge Byron Blake, arguing his own case.

"Your Honor, I know this is an extraordinary application, but . . ."

Judge Blake was a large black man with an even larger head of graying curls. His intelligent eyes were a deep, rich chocolate, unwavering. "I know, I know. . . . You have this Reliable Informant, right?"

"He's never been wrong before, Your Honor. And this gentleman—"

"Agent Cooper, Your Honor," the slim man with the blond crewcut introduced himself. "United States Secret Service. We realize this is a federal matter, and we're prepared to execute the warrant ourselves. But we asked Detective McNamara to make the application personally rather than rely on pieces of paper . . . as a matter of respect."

"I'll bet," the judge sighed. "Well, on the facts you've *sworn* to in this affidavit, detective, I don't see where I have much choice," he said, signing the papers on his desk with a flourish.

## 20

**W**ieskoft stepped out the door of his building, video camera in one hand. He walked past a brightly colored florist's van when he heard a voice yell "Hey you!" He turned to see what was going on and walked smack into a homeless man stumbling along, half drunk. He raised one hand to protect his camera when he felt a circle of steel close around the back of his neck. Wieskoft cried out in pain as the bum pushed the button on an aerosol can, discharging a mini-cloud of greenish gas into the dangling man's face.

Wieskoft woke up in the back of the van, bound, gagged and blindfolded. Terror drove him back into unconsciousness.

## 21

**I**t was a long ride. If Wieskoft could have looked out the windows, he would have recognized the route.

They carried the terror-stiffened man inside. When the blindfold came off, he saw two things: three men, each wearing a red ski mask with a white pentagram symbol on the forehead, gloves on their hands . . . and that he was inside his remote rural cabin.

One of them pulled off the gag, a piece of duct tape. Wieskoft shrieked in pain. He knew nobody would hear—that had been part of his own plan.

"Your Lincoln is outside," one of the men told him. "Keys in the ignition. When we're done, you just drive yourself back home."

"Why did you—?"

"Shut up, weasel," another of the men said. "We're just soldiers, doing a job. What we promised, see, is that you wouldn't bother that girl anymore."

"What . . . girl?"

"You know what girl. Angel. Now there's two ways to do

this, okay? One is we kill you and leave you here. That ain't no big thing . . . probably nobody'd even find the body for months. The other thing is, you disappear. Got it? Get in the wind. Get yourself *gone*. That way, we still get paid. What do you say?"

"I'll go! I'll go tonight!"

"Yeah, we kind of figured that. But, see, we got this problem. You know what our problem is, buddy? Our problem is . . . what's in it for us? See, we got paid, and we always keep our word. That's our stock-in-trade. Now we didn't promise to snuff you, but it *is* easier . . . you understand?"

"I have money!"

"Do you now? Okay, two questions. How much? And where is it?"

"It's mostly in mutual funds. I could—"

"There's the phone," the man told him. "And here's your list," another man said, handing Wieskoft a computer printout of all his financial holdings.

## 22

**I**t was late afternoon by the time Wieskoft's Lincoln steamed up to the curb in front of his building. He slammed on the brakes, jumped out of the car and charged for the stairs. "Maybe there's still time . . . stop payment on the currency transfer orders, pack some bags, take Angel, get out of . . ."

"Freeze!" several voices yelled simultaneously. Wieskoft looked around, seeing only a river of handguns pointing at various parts of his body.

## 23

**L**et me get this straight," McNamara was saying. "We find a stalker's journal in your apartment, okay? Detailed plans for kidnapping and torturing a little girl. All kinds of equipment to do the job. Piles and piles of newspaper clippings about the

President's daughter. Magazine articles, photographs . . . even her school records, the name of her cat . . . everything. We know you own this cabin out in the sticks. Nice of you to set the trip odometer before you made the last run . . . the round-trip mileage is just perfect. And pasted over every picture of this little girl, you got the word 'Angel' too. I'll bet when we search the cabin, we find her name all over that place too.

"And your story is you were kidnapped by a gang of devil-worshipers who made you clean out your bank accounts, is that it?"

"I . . ."

"You're a sick bastard, aren't you? Well, you're going down for this one. Down deep. Maybe if you get lucky, you'll end up playing cards with John Hinckley."

"You don't . . . understand," Wieskoft muttered. "I don't even *know* that girl. I never . . ."

"So who's this 'Angel,' then?" McNamara asked.

"I . . . I . . ."

"He's all yours," McNamara told the waiting feds.

# Epilogue

**I** can't believe it," Reba told Cross, sitting at her kitchen table. "All this time, he was after the President's daughter . . . God!"

"His lawyer is pleading him NGI."

"NGI?"

"Not Guilty by reason of Insanity. He's going with a public defender . . . looks like he's broke, too."

"Will he go to prison?"

"A mental hospital, most likely. But, those places, the thing is, they don't let you go until you admit what you did . . . so they can 'cure' you, right? This Wieskoft character, he keeps telling this crazy story . . . they're *never* gonna buy that one."

"I can't buy it myself."

"That's not what you bought," Cross said, holding out his hand.

# Value Received

**I** waited for him in the warehouse, standing back in the shadows.

The midnight-blue Mercedes sedan purred through the open door. He climbed out, adjusted his shirt cuffs so they showed just past the sleeves of his suit coat, patted his hair. Tapped his fingers on the sleek fender.

I stepped out of the shadows.

"I see you're on time."

"Like I said."

"I don't have much time for this. I have a lot to do."

I didn't say anything. The phone in his car chirped. He nodded in its direction, making no move to answer.

"They think I'm already on my way to the Bahamas."

I watched his hands. Waiting.

"I have the money. Right here," tapping his breast pocket. "All in fifties, no sequential serial numbers."

I watched his eyes.

"I know the way you guys work. We have a deal. I'm paying good money for this. It's still a lot cheaper than a divorce, but I still expect value received."

I nodded.

"It has to happen before midnight tonight."

"It will."

"Make it happen slow, okay? I want that fucking little cunt to hurt first."

" I don't do that."

"I'm paying you . . ."

"You're paying me for a body. You'll get a body. On time."

His face played with a sneer. "You're supposed to be the best. Like my car. Like my clothes. I pay for the best."

I watched him.

"You're a machine, right? A death machine. And you work for whoever pays you."

"Whoever pays me first."

# Head Case

## 1

The woman was so impossibly beautiful it hurt to look at her. The old man did it anyway—it was his job.

"Nobody named Cross here, lady," he said, glancing up from behind the counter at the entrance to the basement poolroom.

"Is that right?" the woman challenged. "Then maybe I'll just play some pool."

"There's no tables available," the old man said.

The woman shot a glorious hip, her orange silk sheath rippling in appreciation. She swiveled on spike heels, taking in the scene behind her. Most of the room was in shadow, broken up by low-hanging shaded bulbs over the tables. Only a few of the bulbs were lit, and even those were shrouded in a thick haze of yellowing smoke.

"I see plenty of empties," she said, her voice flat.

"Those ones are broken, lady."

"I guess I'll just wait, then," she said, walking away from the counter to an old-fashioned red-and-white Coke machine. She perched on a nearby stool, crossed her marriage-wrecker legs, and took out a cigarette.

A wooden match flared just past her cheek. She leaned forward, caught the light. She leaned back, took a deep drag, her breasts threatening the silk. She looked up at the man holding the match, veiling her eyes under butterfly lashes. His head was shaved, sitting on a thick, corded neck. The earring in his right ear was a long chain attached to a ball, like a convict's shackles. His upper body was grotesque: so outrageously ripped and heavily veined it looked artificial. The flesh sculpture was barely covered with a pale purple tank top.

"Thank you," the woman whispered, photographing his face with her turquoise eyes, recording the mascara and eyeliner, the thin coating of lip gloss.

"Can I help you with something?" the massive creature asked her.

"You're not femme," the woman said. It wasn't a question. "Why all the makeup?"

"It helps get me into fights," the man said.

The woman nodded like she'd just heard common sense. "I want to see Cross."

"Not here," the bodybuilder said, leaning forward as his voice dropped. The woman cocked her head, listening. Finally, she nodded.

The ivory balls seemed to click along with the rhythm of her hips as she walked out.

# 2

The woman on the street corner was all in black, a deeper, darker shade than the surrounding night. A big sedan slid to a stop—it was gunmetal gray with darkened windows, generic and anonymous. The front door opened and the bodybuilder stepped out, nodded to her, opened the back door like an usher. She climbed inside. The door closed behind her. Another door slammed, and the car was in motion.

"You wanted to talk to me?" A voice from the far recesses of the back seat.

"What I want to do is hire you," the woman said, aiming her voice at a pool of blackness.

"Tell me," the voice said, as the car turned a corner.

# 3

The top floor of the luxury apartment building looked more greenhouse than penthouse—the exterior walls were all glass. Past the glass, a railed balcony ran the length of the apartment, wide enough to accommodate a substantial outdoor garden. Three men sat in the living room, widely separated, on different points of a white horseshoe-shaped sofa. Another occupied a black leather lounger. The fifth man was standing, talking. A computer sat in one corner, its double-width screen a mass of paper-white emptiness. Against the windows, a matched pair of high-power telescopes on tripods, one fitted with a 35mm camera instead of a conventional eyepiece.

In the alley behind the building, a man carefully shaped a claylike substance around the edges of a door marked SERVICE ENTRANCE. When he was done, a string dangled from the lower edge of the substance.

Around the front of the building, a razor-thin black man walked soundlessly across the carpet runner toward the security guard on duty behind a marble-topped desk. The black man was wearing a Zorro hat and a calf-length black leather coat, black gloves on his pianist's hands. The security guard, a burly black man with a round, friendly face, looked up from the bank of video monitors behind him.

"Can I . . . ?" But before he could finish his challenge, the intruder was two feet from his face, the gap bridged by a sawed-off shotgun.

"What's the haps, home?" the slim black man whispered, holding the scattergun as casually as a cigarette.

"Ace . . ."

"You remember me from the 'hood? Good. Let's you and me talk, okay?" The slim black man slid behind the front desk and sat down, slouching so that he was invisible from the front. "Just be calm, brother. Don't be reaching for the piece, okay? You know me, you know what I do. Good news is . . . it ain't you. Understand?"

"I got it."

"Here's the deal. Real simple. Lady's gonna come in. With another guy. You don't know her. You don't say nothing to her. Just watch the little TVs here, do your job, all right? Some time's gonna pass. You and me, we gonna pass it together, see? Talk about old times. When the lady leaves, I'll be right behind her. That's all she wrote. Nothing's gonna happen. Not to you, not to nobody. Unless you gotta be stupid. You gonna be stupid, brother?"

"No."

"Good. We got a contract. Now grab hold of this." The slim black man handed over a thick white envelope. "It was 303 today. Remember it, bro' . . . that's your lucky number from now on. You had a dime on it, straight up. With Spanish Phil's bank, South side, do or die. This here's your payoff, case anybody asks you where it come from. Six grand, ain't that sweet?"

"Sure is."

"Okay. Let's chill, now. Nothing more to do. Ain't gonna be no po-leece in this. No reports, no phone calls, no nothing. But listen up, homey: I got a contract of my own. Contract says you don't do nothing. You try it, I got to leave you here, right?"

"I'm not . . ."

"Right?"

"Right."

"Righteous. Now, which one of these little TV things covers the front door?"

# 4

**T**he woman walked in, the bodybuilder at her side, carrying an attaché case. The man behind the desk didn't look up. They strolled leisurely over to the elevator bank. Their image didn't register on the TV screens, two of which were dark.

The couple got on the elevator. The man took out a small plastic box about the size of a cigarette pack. He pressed a button on the side of the box and a tiny red light glowed next to his finger.

The man in the alley was holding a similar transmitter. When his own red light blinked, he struck a match and held it to the string dangling from the door. There was a brief spark, then a flash followed by a muffled *whoompf!* as the door popped off its hinges, swinging free.

The man stepped through the door. As he did so, the shadow cast by an enormous dumpster moved with him. The shadow was human. Three hundred and fifty pounds of human, moving with a delicacy and grace that belied its bulk.

Both men huddled in the darkness. "Princess is inside with her now, Rhino. I figure we got a clean shot up on the service elevator. If they open the door, that'll mean I got in from the balcony. You roll in behind Princess. If the door doesn't open from the inside, it means I couldn't reach it like we planned. Let the woman ring the bell, then. The people inside, they'll probably crack the door on the chain. Just take it down, then come get me. Got it?"

"Yeah. If Princess don't jump the gun."

"He's not that stupid, Rhino."

"Yeah he is."

The two men boarded the Service Elevator, pushed the button marked 44. The car engaged smoothly, silently.

"Cross?"

"What?"

"You really think the broad's going through with it?"

"We already got paid." Cross shrugged.

# 5

Inside the passenger car, Princess inserted a plastic card into a slot next to PH on the wall of the elevator. The letters lit up in recognition.

The service car stopped on 44. Both men got off. A seamless window was at the end of the corridor. Working quickly, Cross duct-taped the glass, working in an X pattern until it was completely covered. He stepped back. Rhino placed his gigantic hand against the glass, moving it delicately like he was feeling for a pulse. The tip of one finger was missing. The huge man nodded, then he slapped the flat of his hand against the glass. Again and again. Cross peeled the duct tape toward him, pulling the glass along for the ride. He brushed away shards from the window sill and perched, facing Rhino, who held him around the waist.

Cross took a grappling hook from his coat. The hook was heavily taped except for the very tip, attached to a length of black Perlon climbing line.

"I think we got a shot," he said. "Ready?"

"Go," Rhino said.

Cross leaned completely out the window so his back was parallel to the ground below and heaved the grappling hook in an overhand motion. It caught. Cross pulled on it.

"That'll hold," he said. "I must have snagged it right."

Rhino took the line from Cross. "Let me see," he said, giving a mighty pull. "Yeah," he said.

Cross swung out the window, soles of his boots against the building, pulling himself toward the balcony. Rhino watched, looking up.

# 6

**C**ross levered himself over the balcony railing carefully, watching the activity inside. He crouched behind a potted tree, watching. The men were animated, focusing on their conversation. Cross slipped the black ski mask over his face, unslung the Uzi from inside his jumpsuit, took a deep breath, let it out slowly. Then he quietly slid back the glass door to the balcony and stepped into the living room.

"One man screams, everybody dies!" he spat out, sweeping the Uzi in short, menacing circles.

The five men were frozen, mouths open.

"You!" Cross barked, pointing a black gloved finger at the chubby blond man closest to the front door. "Open the door! Now!"

The chubby man got up on shaky legs and did it.

The woman walked in. A sharp intake of breath from the dark-haired man who had been standing when Cross came in. Princess followed, his mask in place, a chrome .44 magnum in his fist. Then Rhino, also masked, turning sideways to get in the door. His hands were empty. He shut the door behind him, gently.

"Everybody on the couch," Cross said, gesturing with the Uzi. The men sat together, hunched, trembling. Cross pointed, and Rhino stepped behind the couch, looming over the seated figures. Princess stood to the left, his feet braced in a shooter's posture. Cross held his place on the right.

The woman stepped into the middle of the V. "You," she whispered, pointing a long, lacquered nail at the man who had been standing. "Look at me. You've been doing it for months—do it now." The man blanched.

Cross nodded at Rhino. The huge man walked out from behind the couch to the other side of the room. He picked up a marble coffee table like it was a book, carried it to a place in front of the couch. Then he picked up a straight-backed chair in each hand, fussily arranged them so that one was on either side of the coffee table. He took his place behind the couch again. The woman took one of the chairs. "Sit," she said to the dark-haired man, pointing at the other. He did.

The woman nodded at Cross.

"Here it is," Cross told the men. "We got paid to do a job. The job is, you all sit quiet. The lady wants to play a game. We got paid to make sure she gets to play it. We were going to kill you, we wouldn't be wearing the masks. You let the lady play her game, then we all leave. That's it. No violence, no robbery. You do something real wrong, you're going to get dead."

The woman took a deep, harsh breath. It was the only sound in the room.

"So this is the Stalkers' Club," she said. "How long have you been doing it?"

Nobody answered.

"Take the one on the end and break his arm," Cross said to Rhino.

"Two years!" the one on the end squeaked. "Two years, this June."

"Don't you talk again," the woman said. "You"—pointing at the dark-haired man—"you do all the talking, understand?"

"Yes," the man said.

"You take pictures?" she asked.

"Yes."

"Video too?"

"Yes."

"You use the computers? Get information from the data banks on the women you stalk?"

"Yes."

"It's all in fun, right?"

"It *is*. We never . . ."

"You're a rapist, aren't you?"

"No!"

"You have me, don't you? All of you? Captured on your dirty little pictures. It's no fun after a while . . . unless they *know*, yes? I could *feel* you on me after a while. You like that, don't you?"

"It doesn't hurt . . ."

"Yes it does. And you know it. And you *like* it."

"I never . . ."

"Sex, it's all in the mind, isn't it? You have me in your minds."

"No!"

"Yes. I can prove it. Here's the game we're going to play. I bet I can make you come. In ten minutes. Without touching you. Just touching your mind. I'll bet a hundred thousand dollars I can do that. You want to bet?"

"What if I don't?" A trace of sulkiness in his reedy voice.

"Then these men take off their masks, understand?"

"Yes."

"You want to bet?"

"Yes."

The woman nodded at Princess. He walked over to the coffee table, opened the attaché case. It was full of money, banded bills, clean and new. He carefully stacked the cash on a corner of the table, stepped back.

"There's my stake. One hundred thousand. You ready to play?"

"I don't have that kind of money. . . ."

"You want to put up something else? Like your right hand—the one you use on me when you're alone with your dirty pictures?"

"Are you crazy! I won't . . ."

"Stop lying," the woman said. "I don't have time. You have a safe here. Go and get it."

The dark-haired man got to his feet. Cross stepped next to him, the Uzi between them. They left the room.

They were back in two minutes. Cross dropped a double

handful of wealth on the coffee table. Unmounted jewels, cash, gold coins, bearer certificates.

"There's more than a hundred . . ." the man said.

"Shut up, liar. What's there is what you're playing for. You ready?"

Princess shifted his weight. "Yes," the man said.

The woman stood up. Took off her coat. Under it she wore black fishnet stockings anchored by thick bands around the top of each perfect thigh. Her long legs ended in black spike heels. She turned slowly. A black silk thong divided her buttocks. She was nude from the waist up. The woman turned again, one full turn. Then she sat down on the straight-backed chair, nodded to Princess again. The bodybuilder holstered his huge pistol, took a pair of handcuffs out of his pocket, and cuffed the woman's hands behind her. Then he wrapped a pair of thin black leather straps across her chest, separating her breasts bandolier style. He pulled the straps under the chair and around her thighs, securing her in place. Princess knelt, quickly wrapping two more straps around the woman's ankles. She squirmed against the bonds, unable to move.

"Ten minutes," the woman said. "Start counting."

Princess held another leather strap. The woman licked her lips, opened her mouth. Princess fitted the gag, tied it at the back of her head. The woman's eyes bored into the man facing her. Then Princess fitted the black blindfold in place.

Breathing was the only sound. The woman writhed under the bonds, an oily sheen popping out across her ivory-cream skin.

Dots of white flowered on the dark-haired man's cheeks.

Cross walked over to the computer, tapped a couple of keys. He inserted a floppy disk, hit the Return key. The screen went crazy. The hard disk whirred.

Nobody's eyes left the woman.

Cross prowled the apartment until he found the video library. He pulled a glass bottle from his coat, poured the clear contents over the stacked videotapes. A faint hissing sound filled the small room as the acid went to work. He stepped back inside. The woman's head was back, a throaty moan bubbling past her lips—her sweat mingled with a heavy perfume, choking the room.

The dark-haired man hadn't moved his eyes. His hands were clenched into fists at his side.

A tiny beep sounded from Cross's watch. "Time," he said.

Princess untied the woman. She put on her coat. Stood over the man, hands in her pockets.

"You get one answer," she said. "Did I prove my point? Did you come?"

"Yes," the man said. Not looking at her.

The woman stepped around the coffee table, holding the man with her eyes. She took a cork-tipped ice pick from the folds of her coat. He was rooted. She snapped the cork tip off the ice pick with a fingernail.

"You can rape with your eyes, can't you?" she whispered.

"I . . ."

"*Can't* you?" Her voice was a whipcrack.

"Yes," he mumbled, not looking up.

"And you never know who's watching—don't forget," she said. The woman nodded to Princess. He scooped everything on the table into the attaché case, popping the sides so it expanded to hold it all. Then he handed her something that looked like a flat disk with elastic straps. She slipped it over her nose and mouth as Rhino sprayed a canister of some greenish gas over the seated men. They all went down, swooning.

Princess opened the door. They all stepped out into the elevator, pulling off the ski masks to reveal the same kind of disk the woman wore underneath.

At the nod from Cross, the disks came off. He pressed a button on a transmitter.

The elevator opened in the lobby. As they walked across the carpet, Ace stepped from behind the security desk and joined them.

The anonymous gray car was waiting at the curb, its motor

idling undetectably. Princess climbed in the front, Cross and the woman in the back. Rhino and Ace disappeared into the night.

The car pulled away. Cross opened the attaché case, rifled through the contents.

"There's something like a quarter mil here, everything included. It's 50-50 over the hundred grand, like we said?"

"Yes."

"I'll take the jewels and the bearer bonds—they'll have to be discounted. You keep the cash and the gold coins, deal?"

"Deal."

The big car moved silently through the night. Cross pushed a button and a partition slid up between the front and back seats. Cross dimmed the interior lights, lit a cigarette, turned to the woman.

"He didn't come," Cross said. "After that, he probably never will."

"I did," the woman said.

# Kidnap

**H**ey, Buddha, you seen Princess?" the giant asked, his three hundred and fifty pounds of flesh blocking the opening to the back room of the Red 71 poolroom. "He didn't come back to the spot last night."

"Maybe he got lucky," the short, pudgy man offered, glancing up from a white tablecloth he had spread out on a desk made from a solid-core door positioned over a pair of sawhorses. On the tablecloth were arranged various parts to an automatic pistol. "Even a maniac like Princess has to score once in a while."

"What's your problem with Princess anyway?" the giant asked. "He doesn't mean any harm—you know that."

"He's like a little kid, Rhino," the pudgy man answered. "A little kid, playing games. I'm a professional—so are you. Fact is, I can't figure out why Cross—"

"You want to know, why don't you ask him?" the giant responded, his voice an incongruous high-pitched squeak.

"Take it easy," Buddha said. "What you so worried about? This can't be the first time he didn't show."

"Yeah, it is," the big man replied. "At least, he always left word."

"Hey, he's a grown man," Buddha said gently.

"No," the big man said, shaking his head sadly. "You're right—he's a big kid." Rhino glanced quickly around the room. "Cross around somewhere?"

"Somewhere," Buddha replied. "Either he's up on the roof playing with those stupid birds of his, or else he's down at the Double X checking out a new shipment."

"I'll go check," the big man said. "Maybe he—"

"You're on duty, right?" Buddha said kindly. "What if someone comes around? I'm not doing nothing—let me go see if I can scare him up."

"Thanks, Buddha," Rhino said, backing out the door.

Buddha quickly reassembled the pistol, slipped it into his shoulder holster, buttoned his khaki army jacket and went out another door.

**B**uddha took the back staircase, using a key to open a heavy-braced steel door. The floors were empty, the building having long since been listed as "unoccupied" in the city's computers—the only one of several just like it to have escaped the developer's wrecking ball. The owner of the apparently empty building was a corporation. Its officers had consistently refused all offers to sell during the mid-to-late 80's. Word on the street was that the corporation had outsmarted itself, holding out for a bigger price during the yuppie boom. A developer had razed the other buildings, cleared the land for new construction and then gone bankrupt—now the building was worthless, surrounded by a huge lot choked with refuse and debris. The owners of the last remaining building had enclosed it with a chain-link fence topped with concertina wire during the construction, but now the fence guarded nothing but junk.

Buddha made his way to the roof, musing that being a part-owner of a city building didn't make you a mogul. The poolroom in the basement was the only source of income, and that barely netted enough to pay the taxes. "We have to own our base," Cross had told the crew years ago. "Own it legit. That's the only way we can protect every square inch." Every member of the crew had chipped in to make the buy, but Buddha owned the whole thing on paper—he was the only one with an above-ground identity, complete with address in the suburbs and employment as a limo driver. He filed a tax return every year. Even collected a twenty-percent disability pension from the government for a wound he suffered in Vietnam. The building would go to his wife and children when he died—he was the only one of the crew with someone to leave anything to.

Buddha opened the door to the roof and stepped out gingerly, scanning the terrain, his eyes sweeping over a wooden box that looked as though it had been dumped carelessly. Buddha moved carefully, showing the box the same respect he had shown jungle trails in Vietnam. A bird's head popped up from the center of the box, it's yellow eyes gleaming with malevolence. "Don't get all excited," Buddha said softly. "I'm just looking for Cross— I'm not messing with you."

The bird's eyes tracked Buddha's every movement. It fluttered its wings briefly as though considering flight. Buddha registered the flash of blue on the wings—the male of the mated pair of kestrels Cross maintained on the roof. The kestrels were small birds, less than a foot in total length, including the long stabilizing tail feathers, but they were fierce, relentless dive-bombers. Other birds ran for cover when the kestrel's shadow darkened the sky. Kestrels are blessed with incredible eyesight and awesome dive-speed—the pit bulls of the air.

Satisfied that Cross wasn't on the roof, Buddha carefully backed up until he was on the stairs, gently closing the overhead hatch after him.

The Double X had the usual LIVE GIRLS! sign, blood-red neon against blacked-out window glass. Buddha opened the door, grateful for the air conditioning. The bouncer greeted Buddha at the door by nodding his head a couple of inches. He knew better than to ask for the cover charge—Buddha was the nominal owner of that joint, too. "We need a place where we can meet with people—a place we can control," Cross had argued.

"You got a thing for topless dancers, that's your problem," Rhino had responded. "How come we gotta chip in, too?"

"It could be a real money-maker," Cross said.

"I'd rather do what we do—steal," Rhino replied. "I don't know anything about running a goddamned strip joint."

"I can get someone to run it," Cross said. "Tell you what . . . if it's not making money in six months, I'll buy you out. Deal?"

"Come on, Rhino. It'd be fun," Princess begged.

The giant reluctantly agreed, shaking his head at his own stupidity. But, after a rocky start, the joint was coining money. Word got around fast—if you danced at the Double X, you didn't have to worry about the patrons getting out of hand. And if you were having trouble with your boyfriend, the joint was an absolute safe harbor. "He started it!" Princess said, explaining to the others why he had fractured the skull of a man who had slapped his girlfriend after a set. Rhino also worked the floor for a few weeks—protecting his investment, he claimed. Bruno, the bouncer they had now, was infamous—a notorious life-taker who'd already served two long sentences for manslaughter. But compared to the Rhino-Princess combo, the patrons considered him a teddy bear.

None of the girls were paid for working the club. They rented "space" from the management and got to keep their "tips." The cover charge and the watered booze kept management in the black. The bartender was a short, thickset Mexican, improbably known as "Gringo" to everyone. An ex-boxer, he was still quick with his hands. He was quicker still with the .357 magnum he kept under the bar, as two would-be holdup men had found out last year. The deal was this: get to the Double X any way you can, and park at your own risk. But once inside, you were as safe as in church. Safer, if the stories about the local archdiocese were to be believed.

Buddha found Cross at his table in a triangulated corner in the bar of the joint, watching an almost-nude brunette table-dance for three guys in business suits.

"What's happening, boss?"

"Same old," Cross replied.

"Rhino says Princess hasn't been around. He's worried out of his mind about that looney-tune—wanted to speak to you. He's on duty, so I volunteered. You seen him?"

"No," Cross said, snubbing out a cigarette in a black glass ashtray. The smoky light in the bar was just bright enough to illuminate the bull's-eye tattoo on the back of Cross's hand.

"Yeah. Well, he's a fucking head case anyway, right? I mean, I don't see why you—"

"That's enough," the medium-sized man said. "Princess is one of us. Yeah, he's a stone fuck-up. But he's *stand*-up, too, don't forget that. Everybody in this crew has a reason to be here."

"So what's his MOS?" Buddha challenged.

"I haven't figured that one out yet," the man called Cross answered. "But I will." He lit another cigarette, took a deep drag and placed it in the ashtray. "There's a new girl working—she goes on in about an hour. I'll be back over to the poolroom after that."

**S**ix hours later, at the battered wood counter standing at the basement entrance to the poolroom, an elderly man reclined with his feet up, watching a small black-and-white TV from under a green eyeshade. A tall, handsome Latino entered, dressed in a flashy pink silk sportcoat over black silk balloon pants. The Latino tapped on the counter with the underside of a heavy gold ring. After a minute, the elderly man put the eyeshade up on his head and swiveled to have a look. "What?" he asked.

"I got a message for Cross," the Latino replied.

"Who?" the elderly man asked, a puzzled look on his face.

"Cross. You know. *El jefe* around here, right?"

"I don't speak Italian," the elderly man replied.

"Hey, old man, I don't have time for your fucking humor, okay? Just give this to him," he said, sliding a folded square of white paper across the counter.

The elderly man made no move to pick it up, readjusting his eyeshade and turning his attention back to the TV. The Latino spun on his heel and walked out.

**C**ross unfolded the white square of paper in the back room. He looked at the writing for a minute, then he said, "Buddha, take a look at this."

The note was in a flowery script, heavily serifed, obviously written with a fountain pen.

> We have El Maricon. We know he is one of yours and we know where you got him from. If you wish to have him returned, you must call 977-456-5588 *tonight* before midnight. If you do not call, the next package will be the head of El Maricon.

"They got Princess," Cross said.

"It don't sound like they know what they're doing, whoever they are," Buddha reflected. "I mean, Princess plays the role and all, but that's just to get into fights—he's about as homosexual as a fucking tomcat."

"If it's the people I think it is, they do. I saw the light go on," he said, nodding his head in the direction of a red bulb hanging from an exposed wire. "And Rhino took off. Maybe he'll be able to tell us something when he comes back."

"What do you think they want, boss?" the pudgy man asked.

"Money or blood," Cross told him, closing his eyes.

"He just rode around," Rhino told Cross later. "Fancy car. Red Ferrari, for chrissakes—I couldn't have lost him if I tried. But all he did was drive. Finally, he pulled into an underground garage . . . a high-rise on the lakefront. No way to tell if he lives there—the garage is open to the public, too."

"How come you came back?" Cross asked.

"Fal's on him. I reached out on the cellular."

"That's probably what the guy in the Ferrari did, too,"

Cross said. "See this note? The number they want me to call, that's a cellular number, too."

"Fuck! If I had known . . ."

"Don't worry about it. It's SOP, follow anyone who comes in here asking for me, right? You were already gone by the time the note got back here to me. Maybe Fal will come up with something."

"I find this boy again, he's gonna tell us. Tell us anything we want to know," the giant muttered.

"If it's who I think it is, this guy in the Ferrari, he's just a fancy errand boy."

"Who do you think it is? Who'd want to snatch Princess, anyway?" Rhino asked.

"It smells like Muñoz," Cross said, lighting a cigarette. "And it smells bad."

Ten o'clock. Cross stepped out on the darkened roof of the Red 71 building. He did a rapid circuit of the roof, ignoring the large wooden box with a round opening on its side. Satisfied, he took a cellular phone from his pocket, punched in a number.

"Yes?" said a voice in Latin-flavored English.

"It's me," Cross said.

"We have your boy. And we have a deal for you."

"I'm listening."

"A job you have to do for us. That's all. One job. You do it, you get your boy back."

"I'm still listening."

"Not on this phone—you know better. We need a land line."

"Say it."

"There's a phone booth. Just off the Drive. You know where Michigan Avenue takes that big curve? Across the Drive, on the other side, there's the phone booth. It has a big red circle painted on the side. Go there, tomorrow morning, daybreak. You'll hear from us then," the Latin voice said, breaking the connection on the last word.

Cross looked at Rhino. "It's Muñoz all right," he said. "I guess it wasn't done the last time."

**5**:45 A.M. The shark car swept along Michigan Avenue, Buddha at the wheel. Cross spotted the open-air phone booth. A few feet away stood a black man in his late teens, dressed in the latest gangstah chic—gleaming white hightops on his feet, an X cap on his head, the brim turned to the side. The black man was walking in tiny circles, glancing down to consult a beeper in his hand. Two members of his posse lounged nearby, leaning against a black Jeep Cherokee.

Cross exited the shark car, walking briskly toward the phone booth.

"Motherfucker, don't even *think* about it," the leader snarled. "That is *my* phone. Go find yourself another one, man—I got business."

Cross turned so his back was to the phone, pulling a black semi-auto pistol from his coat in the same motion. "Me too," he said quietly.

The leader glanced over at his crew, noticing for the first time that their hands were in the air. Buddha stood across from them, the three forming a triangle. The Glock looked comfortable in Buddha's hands.

"This isn't a diss," Cross told the leader quietly. "Like you said, it's your phone. I'm waiting on this important call, okay? Soon as it's over, you got your phone back. Okay?"

"Yeah, all right, man," the leader said, his eye on the pistol. "Only thing, I need privacy for my call, understand?"

"Yeah. Yeah, man. Don't get crazy. We just jet, all right?"

"Thanks," Cross said.

The leader backed away toward the Jeep. He climbed behind the wheel, keeping his hands in sight. The other two climbed in the back. The Jeep took off, scattering gravel.

Cross stood next to the phone booth, visually confirming the large red circle spray-painted on its side. He picked up the phone, listened for a dial tone to confirm it was working and quickly replaced the receiver. Cross lit a cigarette, took a deep drag.

Traffic was still sporadic. The party-goers were all off the street and the commuters hadn't yet made their appearance. Cross took a second pull on his cigarette, then snapped it away.

The sky continued to lighten. Cross and Buddha didn't speak, didn't move from their spots. A lustrous gray-white pigeon swooped down and perched on the top of the phone booth. Cross eyeballed the pigeon—it was different from the winged rats that so thoroughly populated the city—this one had the characteristic small head, short neck, and plump body, but its bearing was almost regal. Cross nodded to himself as he spotted the tiny cylinder anchored to one of the pigeon's legs. He approached cautiously, even though the pigeon showed no signs of spooking. Cross reached up and stroked the pigeon, pulling it gently against his chest. He opened the cylinder, extracting a small roll of paper. The pigeon fluttered its wings once, hopping back onto the phone booth.

Cross unfurled the paper, eyes focusing on the tiny, precise writing.

> We are both professionals. A meeting must be made safe for us both. We will not come to your place, and you do not know where we are. We will meet you at noon tomorrow on State Street, at the outdoor cafe Nostrum's. You know where it is, I am sure. If you are coming, you must come alone. Write your decision on this paper and it will come back to us.

Cross took a felt-tipped pen from his jacket, scrawled the single word "Yes" on the bottom of the note, and replaced the paper inside the pigeon's courier pouch. The bird preened itself for a few seconds then took off, climbing into the sky with powerful thrusts of its wings.

**L**ate that same night, the crew was gathered in the basement of Red 71.

"You went by, right? What's it look like?" Cross asked Buddha.

"I don't like it, boss. The tables are all outside, pretty spread out. It's only set back maybe fifteen, twenty feet from the sidewalk. I don't think they could do a drive-by . . . not without hitting a lot of people. But they could just *walk* it by. You'd never see it coming."

Cross turned to the giant, who was standing against the wall, watching. "Rhino?"

"The roof across the street's even worse. No way to cover it all. Fal says he could get up there easy enough. But he might not be the only player."

Cross drew a series of intersecting lines on the pad in front of him, eyes down. He took two drags from a cigarette before he snubbed it out.

"Here's what it comes down to . . . who's gonna make the meet for their side. If it's Muñoz himself, he's got to know we can take him out if he makes a move. If it's some flunky, he wouldn't care."

"So . . . ?" Buddha queried.

"So this. We get Fal up on one roof, leave him in place. We get Ace to work the sidewalk. I don't think they'll make him for our crew—he wasn't on the bust-out down there. Buddha, you get us a cab from someplace, all right? You cruise by. Short loops, okay? Rhino takes the rear seat."

"But what if they—?"

"Listen, Buddha, that's where you come in. I'm gonna roll up just at noon, like they said. I see Muñoz at the table, I go ahead and sit down. You don't see me take a seat, it means it's me they want—get ready to lay down some cover fire."

"You think it's like that? Personal?" Buddha asked.

"It could be," Cross replied. "Muñoz always was unstable."

**T**he next day, 11:56 A.M., Cross emerged from the underground train station on State Street and headed east. It was 11:59 when he came within sight of Nostrum's, and a few seconds before noon when he spotted a man he recognized at a table by himself. Cross kept his eyes on that man alone as he approached, hands empty at his sides.

Cross sat down across from a copper-complected man who wore his thick hair pulled straight back, tied in a ponytail.

"Cross," the man said, not offering to shake hands.

"Muñoz," Cross replied.

"Good afternoon, gentlemen," a voice said. Both men continued to stare at each other. "My name is Lance. I'll be serving you today," the voice continued. "Our house specials today are a spinach salad with a mild vinaigrette dressing, together with—"

"That sounds perfect," Muñoz said, his English laced with a regal touch of Castilian. "Bring us two of them. But first . . . you have Ron Rico?"

"Yes, we do," the waiter replied. "But if I could perhaps suggest—"

"Bring me a double," Muñoz cut him off again. And for my friend here . . ."

"Water," Cross said.

"We have Evian, Perrier, and also a new—"

"Just water," Cross said.

The waiter flounced off. "I hate them," Muñoz said.

"Who?" Cross asked.

"Maricons. You know what I mean. You must know. After all, one of your own crew—"

"You trying to tell me you took Princess easy?" Cross asked, his face blank.

"Mio dios, no!" Muñoz smiled. "That is one hard man, no matter that he is not *really* a man at all. He took out two of my best men. With his hands. I held a pistol on him, but he only laughed. If Ramon had not shot him, we would still be—"

"You shot him?" Cross asked, soft-voiced.

"With a tranquilizer dart, amigo. Like you would use on a mad dog. Even with the serum in him, he continued to fight. I wonder how such a man—"

"What do you want?" Cross interrupted, no impatience showing in his voice.

"I already told you, hombre. I want you to do a job for us. Then you get your merchandise back."

"What job?"

"You see this?" Muñoz asked, sliding a tiny microchip across the marble tabletop.

Cross didn't touch the chip. "So?"

"So this is what we need. Watch," Muñoz said. He grasped the chip with the thumb and forefinger of each hand and pulled it apart, revealing one male and one female coupling. "We have this one," he said, holding up the male piece. "The other one, the mate, that is in the hands of another."

"Who?"

"Right to the point, yes? You know Humberto Gonzales? He works out of a bunch of connected apartments in the Projects."

"I never met him."

"Okay, sure. We will tell you where he is, and you will take our property from him."

"How can you be sure—"

"It is always with him, Cross. Always on his person. There is no one he could trust with it. But we have very good sources. We know exactly where to look his right arm."

"I don't get it."

"On his right arm, right here," Muñoz said, patting his right biceps. "He has a big tattoo. Of a dancing girl. Very pretty. The chip is somewhere in the tattoo. Implanted. A fine piece of surgery. After you drop him, we need his arm. You bring it to us, your job is done."

"No go."

"What do you mean, no go? Why do you say this?"

"I'm not sending a goddamned arm through the mails—you wouldn't give me an address anyway. And I'm not meeting you to hand it over. Send your carrier pigeon—the chip would fit in his carry-pouch easy enough if it's this size," Cross said, pointing at the microchip lying on the tabletop.

"That is a good plan, hombre. As soon as our bird is home, we will release your man . . . or whatever he is."

"What's on the chip?" Cross asked.

"That is not your business, my friend."

"Then get somebody else to do it."

"I don't think you understand . . ."

"Sure, I understand just fine. What's on the chip?"

Muñoz stroked his chin. Cross lit a cigarette and took a deep drag. A long minute passed. Cross took another drag and snubbed out the cigarette. The waiter approached, a pair of glasses on a tray. "Here you are, gentlemen. Your salads will be along in a few minutes."

Muñoz waved him away, leaning forward so his eyes were locked on Cross. "Herrera had a couple of dozen locations. Where he stashed money. Money and product. He and I were partners. He gave me half of the microchip—it only works with his half. Herrera, he was having a problem. He paid you to retrieve a certain book. I heard nothing after that, until I learned Herrera was blown up. His car, his bodyguard . . . everything blown to pieces. I figure you got paid for that. Paid twice. Now I know Humberto has the chip. He must have been secret partners with Herrera, but partnerships mean nothing to such a savage—I figure he paid you to take Herrera out. Humberto and I, we have been warring for months. Now it is getting too public. The newspapers are nosing around. We each have several dead soldiers, but we have a man in his camp. This is how I know about where he keeps the chip. Each of us is nothing without the other, but our negotiations have proved fruitless. This is where you come in. I want to go back across the border, but, first, I need all the locations."

"What's my piece?" Cross asked.

"Your piece? Your *piece*? I told you . . . you get El Maricon back."

"You got a good sense of humor, Muñoz. You want me to

do all kinds of risky stuff and score something worth millions to you . . . and you want to trade a POW in exchange? Do the math!"

"This . . . Princess. He is your man. We have—"

"What you got is a soldier. A soldier who knew the deal when he signed on. There's no patriotism in our country, pal. I'll take half a million. Cash. And Princess. For that, you get your little chip."

"You will trust me to—"

"Get real. I'll trust you to release Princess—it don't do you any good to dust him. But the cash . . . no way. You send a man. Your man, okay? You tell him what the chip looks like. Don't tell me—that way you'll know you're getting the real goods. Your man puts the chip in the pigeon's bag. The bird takes off, and your man hands over the cash. We hold on to him until we see Princess. Got it?"

"What is to prevent you from killing my man and keeping the money? And the chip?"

"The chip's no good to me. I want the money. And I want you back over the border, too. This strike's gonna draw too much heat anyway."

"Your salads, gentlemen," the waiter said, putting a plate in front of each man. "Will there be anything—?"

"No," Muñoz snapped, eyes still on his opponent. Finally, he slid a folded piece of paper over to Cross. "It's all there. Everything you need. Make it fast."

Cross lit a cigarette, ignoring his salad as he pocketed the paper from Muñoz. Then he leaned forward slightly, dropping his voice a notch. "You're a professional," he said. "So am I. We understand how these things are done. Money's money. Business is business. I'm gonna get you your little chip. You're gonna pay me my money and let my man go, right?"

Muñoz nodded.

"You know how soldiers are," Cross said softly. "In war, you don't look too deep. A guy's good with explosives, another's a top sniper, maybe another's a master tracker, right? It all comes down to what you need. Turns out one of the guys is a little bent, you don't pay much attention to what he does when he's out of the field, you understand what I'm saying?"

Muñoz bent his head slightly forward, waiting.

"Some people, they're in because they *like* it. It's not for the money—they like the action. That's not you—that's not me. But, maybe, you got guys like that. Do something unprofessional . . . just because they like to do it. You can always spot them, right? Guys who volunteer to do interrogations. Rapists. Torch freaks. You always got them, right?"

"So?" Muñoz challenged. "What has this to do with what I—?"

"You got my man, got him locked up. He's your hostage—I understand that. I don't expect you gonna feed him whiskey and steak, send up a hooker if he gets lonely. That's okay. But, maybe, you got guys who like to hurt people. Hurt them for fun. That's not professional."

"Yes," Muñoz said impatiently. "I know all this."

"Herrera, he liked to watch men die. That's why he had those cage fights."

"Herrera is no more, amigo. You above all should know that."

"There's others. Maybe you have some of them. What I want to tell you is this: I got some, too."

"Why do you say all this? What is your meaning?" Muñoz said softly, a titanium thread of menace in his voice.

"Play it for real," Cross said quietly. "It don't make you any money to be stupid. If you hurt Princess, if you hurt him or kill him, that would be a mistake. If we don't get him back the way you found him, it's going to take you a long time to die."

**H**ow much do I owe you?" Rhino asked the waiter from Nostrum's. They were standing near the mouth of an alley that opened into a street in the heart of the gay cruising area.

"You owe me respect," the waiter said. "I don't forget what Princess did for us. I'm a man," he said with quiet force. "I pay my debts."

"I apologize," Rhino squeaked. "If there's ever—"

But the waiter was already walking away.

**I**n the basement of Red 71, Cross was using a laser pointer to illuminate various parts of a crudely drawn street map he had taped to the back wall.

"He's somewhere in here," Cross said, the thin red line of the laser pointer aimed at a cross section of a tall building standing next to three others exactly similar—the Projects. "We don't know what apartment. Hell, we don't even know what floor—he may even switch from time to time."

"He never goes out?" Rhino asked.

"Once a week. To the airport. He meets an international flight on the south concourse. A different guy comes each time. Humberto meets this guy, talks to him for a hour or so, then the guy just turns around and gets back on another plane."

"The courier, he has to clear customs, right?" Buddha asked.

"Yeah. It's a sterile corridor up to that point. No way to get in or out. But he's not bringing product . . . at least not much of it. When he clears customs, he has a conversation with Humberto. That's it."

"Don't make sense," Buddha said. "That's a ton of money and time just to beat a wiretap."

"I don't think that's what it is," Cross said. "I think he's bringing in a chip. Like this one," holding up the chip he got from Muñoz. "The only way to see if it works is to try it . . . they all look alike. The way I got it figured, Herrera was playing both sides. Trying to get Humberto and Muñoz to waste each other, each of them thinking they were partners with him, see?"

"So?" Rhino put in impatiently.

"So Herrera's probably got chips stashed all over the damn place. Maybe Humberto thinks Muñoz hasn't got the only one. Or even the right one. They go through this negotiation dance, but it's really a stall for time."

"He cuts the chip out of his own arm every week?" Fal asked, skepticism in his voice.

"Maybe not. Maybe he's got a dupe. I don't know. This much is for sure: we got to take him at the airport. The deal is for half a million. That's a hundred grand apiece," he said, glancing around the room.

"You want to dust him at the airport, then chop off his fucking arm right there?" Ace asked caustically.

"No. We got to take him out of there. I think I know how to do it. Something I've been working on. But he won't be there alone. I figure we take him when he comes out. Just as he gets into his car. Buddha can get an ambulance real close. What we need is a hideout . . . someplace close to the airport . . . where we can do the rest."

"How you figure a hundred G apiece?" Rhino asked, leaning forward, his bulk imposing on the room.

"Me, you, Ace, Fal, and Buddha," Cross replied. "What's the problem?"

"The way I figure it, Princess is in for a share, too."

"*Princess?*" He's the genius who got us into this mess," Buddha said.

"Right," Rhino responded. "So he's the one who brought us the job, too."

"Give him half of your share," Buddha suggested.

Rhino slowly turned, focusing his small eyes on the short pudgy man, not saying a word. Buddha gazed back, unfazed.

"If we each give up a tenth, he gets a half-share. How about that?" Fal suggested in a mild tone of voice.

"Okay by me," Ace agreed.

Cross nodded.

Buddha waited for a slow count of ten, then said "What the fuck . . . sure."

• • •

**C**ross plucked the cellular phone from his jacket pocket in response to a soft, insistent purr.

"Go!" he said.

"He's in. On schedule," Fal's voice, quiet but clear. The voice of a man accustomed to speaking from cover.

"You have his ride tracked?"

"Black Mercedes. Four door. S class. Driver's still with it, parked on the roof. Probably on call."

"Roger that. How many we looking at?"

"One in the car, one with the man."

"See any backup?"

"Negative."

"We're rolling," Cross said, breaking the connection. He turned to Rhino. "They'll probably call the driver as they get close to the exit. He pulls off the roof, swings around, so he's waiting when they step out. You get the bodyguard, I get Humberto. Ace is riding with Buddha—the driver's their job. We ride crash-car on the getaway, meet back at the spot if we get separated."

Rhino nodded. "You really think that contraption's gonna work?" he asked, pointing the index finger with the missing tip at what looked like a particularly awkward pistol—instead of a butt, the pistol's handle was a long, narrow canister.

"It's freon," Cross said. "Like they use in air conditioners. We should get around five hundred feet per second. And it won't make a sound."

"It only works for one shot."

"One's all we need."

"Why don't we just ice this fuck? What do we need him alive for?"

"Because Muñoz wants him dead," Cross said. "And he only paid us for an arm, not a whole body."

**T**he phone purred again. Cross snapped it to his ear. "What?"

"Moving," Fal's voice said.

"Who?"

"All of them. Me, too. You got two minutes, tops."

"Later," Cross said, pointing a finger at the windshield. Rhino keyed the motor of the shark car, threw it into gear. Cross was punching a number into the phone.

"Go!" is all he said when it was answered at the other end.

Humberto stood on the wide curb, his broad-chested body-guard at his side, tapping his foot impatiently. The bodyguard spotted the Mercedes rolling toward them, stepped forward, reaching for the handle to the back door. Cross moved out of the shadows cast by a thick concrete pillar, the freon gun up. Humberto grabbed at his right hip just before he fell. The body-guard whirled just in time to meet a .22 hollowpoint with the bridge of his nose. Rhino pocketed the silenced pistol and charged forward as the ambulance pulled to the curb. The Mer-cedes driver was trying to stare through the darkened side window, when the back of his head mushroomed into tomato paste. The rear doors of the ambulance popped open. Rhino tossed Humberto inside as easily as if he were a sack of grain, then immediately turned to the bodyguard and did the same thing with his dead body. The ambulance doors closed and it took off for the exit, lights flashing. Rhino ran to the shark car and dived into the open back door, his movements acrobatic de-spite his bulk. Cross mashed the pedal and the shark car chased the ambulance.

By the time the airport police arrived, they found one dead man at the wheel of the Mercedes. And a good many highly con-tradictory accounts from spectators.

The ambulance pulled to a stop in the shadows of a bridge abut-ment, just a few yards off the Freeway. The shark car cruised in a few seconds later, Cross skidding the anonymous vehicle so that it lay parallel to the ambulance. Cross stood watch as Rhino tossed Humberto's limp body over his shoulder and transferred it to the shark car's trunk. Buddha took the wheel of the shark car, Cross the shotgun seat. Ace and Rhino took the back, weapons out, each man covering a different rear window. As the shark car pulled away, Buddha said: "I dusted it down good, boss. But you never know what they're gonna find when they vacuum it out."

Cross pulled a small radio transmitter from his jacket, checked the blinking red LED, and threw a toggle switch. A heavy thumping *whoosh* sounded and the sky behind them was brightened with a red-and-yellow fireball.

"What they're gonna find is some dead meat," Cross said. "Well done."

**A**s the shark car entered a quiet community of tract houses, the phone in Cross's jacket sounded. He picked it up, but didn't say a word.

"I'm out," came Fal's voice.

Cross broke the connection, gave the thumbs-up signal to Rhino.

Buddha pulled into a driveway of packed dirt, nosing the car forward until it was inside a garage that had been standing open. He popped the trunk, and Rhino tossed Humberto's still-limp form over one shoulder.

In another five minutes, Humberto was strapped to a straight chair in the basement of the house. The men waited another half-hour, each watchful and alert against the possibility they had been followed.

Finally, Cross stood up from his post. He slipped a stocking mask over his face, signaled Rhino to do the same. "All clear," he said quietly. "Let's get to it."

**T**his should do it," Rhino said, squeezing the plunger of a hypodermic. He compressed Humberto's arm with one huge hand, tapped a likely looking vein, and drove the needle home with unerring precision.

Cross waited as the adrenaline took hold, watched as Humberto gradually regained consciousness. Cross signaled Rhino to stay where he was—looming over Humberto's back, but not visible.

"Wha . . . What is this?" Humberto mumbled, his eyes struggling for focus.

"It's a job, pal," Cross said. "You do what you're told, that's all it stays. You don't . . . ," he let his voice trail off.

"You're not . . ." Humberto said, his vision gradually clearing.

"What we are is professionals," Cross said. "Just like you. We got paid to do a job."

"What job?"

"Muñoz paid us. For your arm."

Humberto went deathly white under his swarthy skin. "I don't know what—"

"Yeah, you do," Cross interrupted. "You got something Muñoz wants. A microchip. Someplace in your arm. Muñoz, he paid us to bring him that arm."

"Wait! Wait a minute! Look, I can—"

"Don't say anything. Listen to our offer. Then you say Yes, or you say No. That's all. You got it?"

Humberto nodded, his hooded eyes steady on Cross.

"We're *gonna* get that microchip. We know it's somewhere under that tattoo. We can take it gentle," Cross said, "or we can take it hard. Your choice."

"I have no choice," Humberto said, his voice calming as strength flowed back into him.

"Muñoz, he has one of my men, understand? He wants to trade him for that chip," Cross said. "But if we take your whole arm like he wants, he gets you dead, too. He didn't pay us for that."

"I could pay you . . ." Humberto said softly.

"That's right. You could pay us to leave you alive. But then, what would you have? Your bodyguard's gone. So is your driver. With the chip in his hands, Muñoz would vamp on you heavy. Take you longer, but you'd be just as dead."

"What do you suggest?" Humberto asked, more confidence in his voice.

"I suggest you pay us. Pay us to take out Muñoz. The chip,

that's what gets us in the door, see? And once we get in there, we total Muñoz, all right? Costs you a flat million. Cash."

"I can get—"

"No," Cross said. "Just forget the games. You're not making any phone calls. Not writing any notes, either. Here's the way I figure it—you got some money stashed. Serious money. And you don't trust nobody with it, okay? I'm betting you got it nice and accessible. No safe deposit boxes, no passwords . . . nothing like that. You tell us where it is. Tell us right now. One of my crew goes there, picks it up. It's in more than one place, that's okay. My man comes back here. With the cash. And then we do the job for you."

"How do I know you won't just take the money and kill me anyway?"

"If I was gonna do that, what would I need this mask for? This is business, that's all. You didn't fuck with us. It wasn't you who snatched my man. Muñoz has to go—I'm just making sure we get paid, all right?"

"And if I say no?" Humberto asked.

"Then we kill Muñoz anyway. But instead of the chip to get us in the door, we bring him your arm."

A long minute passed. Humberto took a deep breath. "It's right under her butt," he said, flexing his right biceps, sending the tattooed dancer into a bump-and-grind. "Have you got a drink for a man first?"

**H**umberto sat in a comfortable easy chair, feet up on an ottoman. He was bare-chested, a bandage around his right biceps. To his right, a water glass half full of dark liquid sat on an end table. A long cigar smoldered in an ashtray. Humberto's handsome face was relaxed, at peace.

"Listen to me, amigo," he said to Cross. "The key to Muñoz is his pride. Muñoz is . . . muy macho, understand? Years ago, he fought a duel. With machetes. It was a matter of honor. He is very, very good with knives . . . any weapon with an edge. And with his hands, too—very quick, very strong."

"And you tell me this because . . . ?" Cross invited.

"Because I trust you, hombre. And I want to prove it to you."

"You think that does it? Telling me about this guy's ego?"

"No," Humberto said, his dark eyes steady on the stocking mask. "*This* is what does it—I know who you are."

"You sure?"

"Yes. You are the man they call Cross, yes? You hide your face, but you forgot to cover your hands," Humberto said, flicking his glance at the back of Cross's right hand where a bull's-eye tattoo stood out in bold relief. "I hired you once before. To do Herrera. We have never met, face-to-face, but I know your markings."

Cross made a sound of disgust, reached up and pulled off the stocking mask. "Tell me what you know," he said.

"You were the one who attacked Herrera. Years ago. I was not there, but I have heard about it many times. Herrera always claimed that you took product . . . but we always believed you took his stash of jewels instead. I know he converted his product to money—gold, diamonds—always in hard currency."

"What else?"

Humberto's shoulders moved in an eloquent shrug. "There was a fight. Many died. And you escaped. That is all I know. That and the tattoo on your hand. Herrera always said he would pay you back. I heard two more things—he hired you to do something . . . and he had an accident."

"Why tell me all this?" Cross asked.

"Because I paid for him to have that accident. We never met face-to-face, but it was you I paid. You did your work well. Herrera is gone. Soon, Muñoz will be, too. You cannot run a drug network yourself. You do not have the contacts down south. You and me, I think we're going to be partners."

"Sounds good to me," Cross responded.

**I**t's done," Cross said into the mouthpiece of the cellular phone.

"I know, amigo." Muñoz replied. "I watch the news on television."

"Let's finish it," Cross said.

"You know the King Hotel? On Wabash, near—"

"I know it."

"My man will be standing in front, on the sidewalk, at midnight. You take him wherever you want. Once you are satisfied that we have not followed you, send the chip."

"How are you gonna know where to send the bird?"

"My man will have the bird with him. In a cage."

"And my money."

"Yes. And your money."

This ain't nothing," Ace said, facing the assembled crew. "I got a half-dozen people in that hotel. It's nothing but a crack house. Low-class dive. I be inside hours before they show, cover you from the top floor."

"Righteous," Cross said. "Buddha and Rhino, you guys make the pick-up, all right? Me and Fal, we'll transport Humberto. Everybody get to work wiping things down—we can't have another fire so soon."

From inside the front door of the King Hotel, all the watchful desk clerk could see was the back of a tall man in a long black coat. The tall man looked as if he was waiting for a bus, smoking a cigarette. Only two discordant notes sounded: at the man's feet was a large cage draped in black with a ring handle at the top. And a bright red dot of light holding steady right between the man's shoulder blades. The red dot tracked the man, moving as he moved.

The shark car pulled to the curb. The back door opened. Some words were exchanged. And the tall man climbed into the car, pulling the cage behind him. The car took off.

A few minutes later, the desk clerk saw a slim, fine-featured black man coming down the stairs, an all-black rifle with a complicated-looking scope in his hand. The desk clerk looked away, not meeting the man's eyes. When he looked up, the man was gone, almost as if he had never been there. The desk clerk didn't react. But it wasn't the two hundred dollars in his pocket that earned his silence—the desk clerk knew what the red dot on the tall man's back meant, and he didn't want one on his own. Ever.

**T**he shark car worked its way through the badlands, heading for Red 71 as unerringly as the homing pigeon it carried in its backseat. The phone on the seat next to Buddha chirped. The pudgy man picked it up, flicking a switch with his thumb. "Go," he said. "All clear here." Fal's voice.

"Coming in," Buddha replied. "ETA ten minus."

"Roger that. You clear behind?"

"Affirmative."

Buddha clicked off the phone, his eyes flicking back and forth between the road and the rear view mirror. He pulled the shark car through a fresh gap in the chain-link fence, parking just behind the back door to Red 71. He slapped the back door three times with the flat of his hand. It opened immediately. Cross stepped to one side, covering the area with an Uzi. Buddha entered first. Then the man they had picked up. Rhino was last inside, blocking the doorway with his bulk.

In the basement, Rhino hand-searched the courier, his touch delicate and sensitive. When he nodded an OK, Cross stepped forward and ran an electronic wand over the courier's body. "Relax," he said to the man. "Have a seat."

The man seated himself in an overstuffed chair, reaching into his pocket to light a cigarette.

"What do they call you?" Cross asked.

"I am Ramón."

"Okay, Ramón. *¿Donde está el dinero?*"

Ramón's lips twisted into a thin smile, not showing his teeth. "In the cage, hombre. In the bottom of the cage. If you will permit me . . ."

Cross nodded, and the man got to his feet. He walked over to the cage and gently flicked the black cover off. Inside was a big-chested pigeon. "This is *el bailador del cielo*," Ramón said, stroking the pigeon's chest. He reached inside and removed the pigeon, cradling it softly. "Pick up the floor," he said to Cross.

Cross studied the cage for a long minute, then he removed the newspaper from the cage floor to reveal a flat metal plate with a ring in the center. He pulled the ring and the floor came off. Underneath there was money. Greenbacks shrink-wrapped in plastic.

"What the hell does Muñoz think I'm gonna do with thousand-dollar bills?" he asked Ramón. "All this has to be washed—I can't just spend it."

"Smaller bills would not fit, hombre," Ramón replied. "I am sure you have . . . resources."

Cross nodded, his fingers stroking the scar on his cheekbone. "Okay, how do you want to do this?"

"First, I check the chip. With this . . ." Ramón said, taking a mate of the chip from his shirt pocket. "You could not duplicate the chip so quickly. If it plugs into this one, we will know you have done your part of the bargain."

"Do it," Cross said, taking the chip from his jacket.

Ramón carefully aligned the two chips. They came together with an audible snapping sound. "*¡Bueno!*" Ramón said. "This is the one."

"And now . . . ?" Cross asked.

"Now you put the chip right here," Ramón said, tapping the tiny cylinder on the bird's right foot, just above the talon. "Then he flies home. Straight home. You will see . . . if you look . . . that you cannot fit a transmitter in the pouch. And if you attach one anywhere else, *el bailador* will not fly. You understand?"

"Yeah," Cross said, still stroking the scar. After a few moments, he left the room.

**W**e're ready to go," Cross said into the cellular phone.

"When will you—"

"I gotta talk to him first."

"Talk to who?"

"My man. The one you got."

"I told you—"

"I don't give a fuck what you told me," Cross said quietly. "We're in the end game now. You want to talk to your man, I can do that. You want to play, you gotta do the same."

"Call back in one hour," Muñoz said. "And have Ramón with you.

**I**t's me," Cross said into the phone. "You want to speak to your man?"

"Put him on."

"Yes, I am here, *jefe*," Ramón said. "Everything is as it should be." Ramón said "Yes" twice, rapidly, then he handed the phone to Cross.

"Okay?" Cross said into the mouthpiece.

"*Momentito*," Muñoz said.

Another minute passed, then Cross heard the unmistakable voice of Princess. "I'm good," the bodybuilder said. "These pussies got me trussed up like a fucking turkey, but they haven't done nothing."

"They feeding you?" Cross asked.

"Hell, I'm probably down to two-thirty with all this crap. They don't even have my vitamin supplements. And—"

"Okay, Princess, just calm down, all right? They'll be cutting you loose soon."

"Are you satisfied?" Muñoz's voice cut in. "Are you ready to release our bird?"

"Tomorrow," Cross said. "Tomorrow at first light."

"Why not now, hombre? Our bird can fly at night."

"I need a few hours to make sure you guys are playing it straight. First light. When Princess shows up, we'll let your man go."

"Adios," Muñoz said, hanging up.

**H**e's okay?" Rhino asked, anxiety making his voice even squeakier than usual.

"He said 'vitamins,' " Cross replied. "You know what that means . . . he's all right, but he doesn't see a way out of there. If he said 'minerals,' he'd have an exit spotted. I don't think they messed with him."

"You think they'd actually let him go?" Buddha asked.

"I was them, I wouldn't," Cross said.

The next morning, dawn slowly breaking through a blue-black night sky. Ramón stood on the roof of Red 71, the pigeon in his hands.

"Do it," Buddha told him.

"*¡Volar!*" Ramón called, tossing the pigeon into the air. The bird took off, climbed, then banked, wings working smoothly.

A few seconds later, a tiny bird took off from Cross's leather-gloved hand, its blue-gray wings a blur in the sky, a distinctive *killy-killy-killy* trilling from its beak. The bird climbed like an F-16, a blur in the vision of the watchers on the roof who were tracking the bird by its rust-colored tail feathers. Cross picked up his cellular phone.

"Launched," is all he said.

"Let's go," Cross said to Buddha. As Buddha turned to follow Cross downstairs, Rhino's huge hand curled around the back of Ramón's neck.

I don't get it, boss," Buddha said. "I know we got a transmitter on that hawk of yours . . . but I've seen that bastard fly. There's no way the pigeon's gonna make it back home before it gets taken out."

"East," Cross said into the cellular phone, watching a small round blue screen set into an electronic box he held between his legs. "Holding steady. You on it?"

"Roger," came back Fal's voice.

"It's not a hawk," Cross told Buddha absently. "It's a kestrel. A falcon, okay? I got a mated pair up there. The female's sitting on some eggs. The male brings food. I haven't fed them for days—

wouldn't let them loose to get food for themselves, either. And I've got the male trained to hit pigeons—he fucking loves them."

"Yeah, but . . ."

"What?"

"You got the bird all stoked up, right? So he's gonna knock that pigeon right out of the sky. How in hell are we gonna—?"

"Kestrels only take prey on the ground," Cross said. "He'll wait until the pigeon touches down. Then its Kaddish for him."

Urban scenery flew past the windows of the shark car as Cross continued to give directions to Buddha in person and to Fal over the phone.

"What's his name?" Buddha asked.

"Who?"

"The bird, chief. The . . . kestrel or whatever you call it."

"Name?" Cross asked, puzzled. "It's a bird."

Buddha shrugged, tracking the big car expertly.

**H**e's heading for the flats," Cross said into the phone. "No place else he could be going. You got visual?"

"Locked on," Fal said. "He's sitting right above the pigeon. Just hovering. Ready to dive."

"When he drops, that's it," Cross said. "Stay tight."

**I** got him," Fal's voice barked. "It's a three-story, bar on the first floor. Says *Los Amigos* on the door. Right on the waterfront, at the end of Pine Street."

"You sure?" Cross asked.

"Dead sure. The pigeon's dropping down, heading for home. And your bird, he's just waiting."

"Cars in front?"

"Just one. A white . . . Lincoln it looks like. I can see . . . yeah! There's a coop on the roof. Whole bunch of birds up there. It's gotta be—"

"Move in," Cross said, breaking the connection.

The shark car's nose shot into the air from the sudden acceleration as Buddha mashed the pedal. The target building came into view as they saw Fal's blue Montero heading toward the back. "Here he comes!" Rhino squeaked as the kestrel went into a power-dive. The pigeon may have seen the kestrel's shadow or it may have been alerted by its primitive sensors—it fluttered its wings rapidly, seeking the shelter of the coop. As the pigeon touched down, the kestrel struck, its tiny talons balled into fists, stunning the pigeon, which staggered away, wings flapping. Muñoz ran toward the pigeon, waving his arms to scare off the intruder, but the kestrel calmly mounted its prey, tearing at the flesh of the pigeon's chest. Muñoz slashed at the kestrel with a machete, but the kestrel danced away, its baleful unblinking eyes trained on the new enemy. Muñoz thrust his body between the pigeon and the kestrel, frantically clawing at the pigeon's courier pouch. A series of explosions sounded below—flash grenades thrown through the glass windows of the bar. Muñoz heard machine-gun fire. A thin smile crossed his lips. With one mighty swipe of the machete, he chopped off the lower portion of the pigeon, scrambling on his hands and knees to recover the courier pouch as the kestrel tore the other half of the pigeon apart—a pair of professional predators, each doing his work.

Downstairs, Rhino swept the ground floor with a long blast from his Uzi, screaming "Princess!" at the top of his lungs. Two men charged down the stairs—they were immediately cut down by a blast from Ace's shotgun. Fal pointed at Buddha, who was working his way along the wall, his Glock out and ready. When Buddha nodded, Fal pointed at an open door. As soon as Buddha started to move, Fal started to climb up the stairs, chest flat against the wall, gun arm extended as a probe.

Buddha stepped carefully down the darkened stairway. He saw Princess in a far corner, the bodybuilder's chest crossed with heavy chains like bandoliers. Princess's head lolled against his chest—Buddha could only see the top of his shaven skull. Buddha holstered his pistol, his eyes sweeping the room for any sign of a key to the chains. A shot rang out, catching Buddha in the left shoulder. The pudgy man went down, whipping out his pistol and returning fire in the same smooth motion. He heard a muffled grunt of pain from the deep recesses of the basement and kept crawling until he was next to Princess. Then he stood up suddenly, firing a burst from his Glock at the same time. With all his remaining strength, Buddha braced one foot against the chair Princess was strapped into and shoved, toppling the bodybuilder to the floor just as more shots peppered the wall behind him.

Buddha crawled until his body was covering most of the fallen Princess, then he calmly ejected the clip from his Glock and snapped in another, waiting.

Muñoz pocketed the microchip and started down the stairs, machete at the ready. On the third floor landing, Muñoz catfooted his way toward the rearmost room. He stepped inside, satisfied himself that the escape rope was still anchored to the floor. Muñoz had a car waiting below—he could be gone in minutes if his luck held. As he gathered the rope in two hands, Cross stepped into the room, a .45 in his fist.

Muñoz turned to face his enemy, legs spread apart, the machete back in his hand. Cross held the .45 in two hands, aimed at Muñoz's chest.

For a few seconds there was silence.

"So, hombre," Muñoz said. "I guess it always comes to this, yes?" He fired the machete at the floor where it stuck, quivering. Then he moved toward Cross, fists clenched. "I guess you always wanted to see who is the better man, didn't you?" he snarled, crouching.

Cross fired the .45—the bullet took Muñoz in the stomach, knocking him to his knees. "No," Cross said, standing over Muñoz. He pulled the trigger twice more, one for the head, one for the chest.

In the basement of Red 71, Buddha lay on a cot, an IV running into his arm. He blinked his eyes rapidly a few times, finally recognizing Cross.

"Everybody made it out?" the pudgy man asked.

"You were the only one who took a hit," Cross said.

"Where's Humberto?" Buddha asked.

"He's with Muñoz. Ramón, too," Cross said. "It's done."

"You're a real man, Buddha," Rhino squeaked. "The way you covered Princess . . ."

"I still don't see why that crazy fuck should get a share," Buddha mumbled as he drifted back to sleep.

# Date Rape

There is a wire twirled in my head. A coil of razor wire. I can feel it. I have to be very quiet or it will tear my brain.

I have to decide. Even though my sister is older than me, I am the man. Ever since I was a little kid, my father explained this to me. He knows everything about the way to do things. The right way.

He's a policeman. He was a patrolman, back in the days when you had to be a man just to put on the badge. He walked around by himself in neighborhoods where they patrol in two-man cars today. He was shot twice, on the job. After the last time, he was made a detective.

Everybody lies, my father says. He explained it to me. Everybody lies if lying makes it better for them. You have to get the facts. You have to get things straight before you act.

There's ways to tell, my father told me. If a nigger is lying, you can tell by the way he breathes . . . his stomach kind of shakes. And a Jew, when a Jew lies, he always rubs his hands together. Like he's washing them, but with no soap.

You can't always tell who's a Jew, though, because they look white.

## Date Rape

He caught me when I lied to him. Down the street, one of our neighbors, a big blonde woman, she told my father she caught me peeking in her window. At night, when she was getting ready for bed. He punched me in the stomach, very hard. I didn't cry. I told him it wasn't me. He smiled then, told me he was proud of me. You couldn't tell if a real man was lying by beating on him, he said. He made me feel good. He told me about women. How they trick you, lead you on, tease you. Like that blonde woman, parading around in her bra and panties with the shades up, just asking for it. I told him it was worse than that— she didn't even have a bra on . . . and then I realized what I said. He just smiled. He told me, there's always a way to tell if a man's lying.

I can't make a mistake now. Or the wire will rip through my head and make my brain scream and bleed.

My sister says she was raped. She came right over here and told me. It was a date, just the two of them. They had dinner together. Afterwards, he drove her to this spot outside of town. It's a restricted area. No Trespassing. So they could have a private talk. He kissed her. But when the kiss got hard, she pushed him away. He slapped her and made her cry. She felt bad, like she wasn't being fair. But then he came at her again, pulling up her skirt. She yelled, but nobody heard her. He dragged her out of the car and ripped her clothes. He raped her in the woods. Then he drove her to where she lives.

I interrogated her. When she cried, I waited for her to stop. I made her tell me her story again and again. I made her tell me backwards, to see if I could catch her in a lie. I asked her if she liked it, once she got into it. She screamed at me and called me all kinds of filthy names, but she had to sit there and listen to me. I had her handcuffed to the chair.

My sister doesn't live at home anymore. I didn't think she'd come back here just to tell me what she did, about what happened, but I guess she knew I'd find her anyway. I was suspicious. I wished I had a lie detector, like in the police station.

"You're a freak, Junior," she told me. "A sorry little freak. I wish I'd never told you."

When I said she had to tell me again, she started cursing. She has a nasty mouth, my sister. She always did.

Finally it was done. It took a long time, and she didn't smell so good. But she still had a nasty mouth.

"Well, what are you going to do now?"

When I told her I was going to ask him the same questions I asked her, she started cursing so loud I had to put a gag in her mouth.

I captured him easily. It was no problem—he didn't expect it, I guess. I took him down to the basement. It's all sound-proofed down there, so you could practice with guns and not disturb the people next door.

I made him sit in a straight chair and then I locked his hands behind him with the handcuffs. At first he didn't want to answer my questions, but I showed him that I had to know the answers. I had to know them.

He said it was a date. She had asked him to take her to dinner, so they could talk. But it was hard to talk in the restaurant, so he took her out to that place, where they would have privacy.

She kissed him. Wiggled against him. Let him know she was ready. Then, when he almost got there, she started putting on a show, like she changed her mind. He said he'd had her a lot of times—sometimes she asks for it, sometimes she acts like she doesn't want it at all. But it always ends the same way. She's a bitch. A cock-teasing bitch. Slap her in the mouth, she starts to tell the truth, that's what he said. He said he'd have her again. If she was so angry, how come she hadn't called the cops?

I left him in the basement. I walked back upstairs very careful, so the wire wouldn't tear in my head. I told her to tell me the truth. The whole damn truth. She started crying again. So I asked her, was it true, that she'd had sex with him before? Plenty of times? She didn't say anything, so I slapped her hard across the mouth.

Then she told me the truth.

She admitted it. He had her lots and lots of times. And she wanted to call it off. So the last time, she asked him to dinner to tell him. And it was true, they couldn't talk about it in the restaurant. So they drove out to that spot.

When she told him it was finally over, that's when he got nasty. Hard and nasty.

A date was a rape. A rape was a date. Date rape. Rape date. I couldn't make the words rhyme.

The wire is burning in my head. I know the truth. I know the right thing to do.

I got the pistol out of the drawer. A Smith & Wesson .38 Special. Police Special. Regulation.

My sister was screaming at me when I walked out of the door. I could hear her screaming all the way downstairs. It doesn't matter if anyone hears her now.

It's hard what I have to do.

Everybody told the truth.

The wire is burning like a fuse. I have to do this first.

I'm going down to the basement to kill the rapist.

He's waiting down there for me.

My father.

# Dead Game

**I**'m no good until I get hit the first time.

Tony says I'm a slow starter.

But once I get going, nothing can stop me.

I never quit. Never.

I looked across the ring. I'm fighting a black guy tonight. Bosco, I think his name is.

It doesn't matter what his name is.

This is the first time I saw him. They don't let me face the other guy at the weigh-ins anymore. Sometimes, I go after them right there. I have to save it for the fight.

He's a little bigger than me, but he's still inside the weight limit.

He's younger than me, too.

But I've been around a lot longer. You can see it on my face. And all over my body. Experience counts for a lot in these fights. You can't tell if a fighter's any good until he gets nailed the first time, that's what Tony says. Then you find out about his heart.

They say it's in my blood, fighting.

But I really only do it for Tony.

I love him.

He's been with me since I was real little. He gives me everything.

I train the old way. Special food. No sex before a fight.

They say that's why we started fighting. For sex. To have our pick of the bitches.

But I could have sex even if I didn't fight. I fight for Tony.

I work out all the time. Tony even built a special treadmill for me, to build up my endurance.

If you get tired in these fights, you lose.

I never get tired.

I watched the black guy across from me, waiting for the signal to start. I watched his eyes. He wasn't afraid.

They never are.

Down here, the purse is nothing . . . all the money comes from betting.

Tony always bets on me.

I'd never let him down.

I'd die first.

I'm not afraid of dying. It's just sleep. And you don't wake up.

I faced the black guy. Tony rubbed the back of my neck, getting it loose.

The crowd screamed.

We bumped once and the black guy came at me.

He was quicker than me. I took his first shot right in the chest. The fire exploded in me and I tried to tear his head off.

He went down, but he got right back up.

The referee separated us a couple of times when we locked together, but they never stop these fights.

It was a long time before I took him out.

Tony carried me out of the ring.

I couldn't see Tony, my eyes were torn.

The other guy hurt me real deep.

I was going to sleep.

I heard Tony crying.

I felt his hand on my head.

Patting my bloody fur for the last time.

# Dialogue

**D**on't be afraid—I promise I won't hurt you. I'm sorry about tying you up, but I wouldn't want you to go away. I want you to listen. Will you listen to me? Just nod your head yes if you will.

Thank you. That's very nice. I'm sorry about the gag too, but we're real close to people here. See, if you look up . . . over there . . . see the windows? It's a basement, this apartment. If you look, you can see people's feet when they walk past.

Don't worry—they can't see in here. I got this stuff out of a catalog. You kind of paint it on the windows and it makes them one-way, like those trick mirrors? We can look out, but they can't look in.

But they're still very close, see? If you were to scream, then maybe somebody would come. And I wouldn't get to finish talking to you.

I'm sorry about that. I know . . . I say that a lot. But only when it's appropriate—it's not a compulsive habit or anything. I just am a polite person.

I know what you think—you think I'm that Call Girl Killer, don't you? The one the newspapers are making all that fuss about. The newspapers lie, you know. They don't tell the truth.

Most of those girls, they weren't real call girls at all. Just common prostitutes. Whores. But "call girl" sounds better in the press.

I can always tell when a woman's a whore. Those are the only ones I take. You can tell. Always. Some of them, they just stand out in the street and *scream* at you—they're not ashamed at all. Some of them are secret whores, though. Like undercover cops. In disguise.

Are you warm in here? Do you want me to . . . No? Okay, that's okay. Just relax. I won't do anything.

What was I . . . oh, yes, undercover cops. They have them out there. I saw them. One, I see her all the time now. But she's not a whore. Not a sex-whore, anyway. But she's still trying to trap me.

I'm too smart for them.

In fact, they were the ones who gave me the idea. The first ones, they were street trash. All I needed was a car. That's what they do, they get in your car. It's easy after that. But they said they were call girls. The papers said that. Or maybe it was the cops. So what I did, I called one myself. They have the numbers in the Yellow Pages. Escort services, some of them are called. Or in the personals . . . role playing, they call it. I just called them up and they sent one over. Every time. I have to move afterwards, but that's no big deal—I just put everything in my car.

I would never order one of the call girls to this place. My basement. I would never want to move from here.

I'm sorry about the ropes. And the tape. I know it's uncomfortable. I'm actually a very nice person. That's what people say about me . . . that I'm a nice person. And it's true—it's not a lie.

I'm really truly sorry. When I saw you, walking alone in that neighborhood, that time of night, I was sure you were one of them.

I'm really sorry, Colleen. That's your name, isn't it? Yes? I thought so. I knew you wouldn't be the type of girl to have a phony ID. You're a student, aren't you? At the University? That's what it says . . . I'm sorry about that, going through your purse and all. I didn't take anything. I'm not a thief.

I guess you work at that diner to pay for school, right? Yes, I thought so. That's very good, to make your own way in the world. That's what I do too. I don't have any family. Do you have a family? Yes? Brothers and sisters and all? No? You're an only child? That's too bad. I was an only child too. It would have been nice to have brothers and sisters.

I'm sorry about . . . looking. I mean, you were dressed in that little skirt and all. . . . I didn't know it was a waitress outfit. I mean, it *looked* like it could be one, but some of the whores, they dress up different ways. That's why I had to look . . . under there. I'm sorry, I really am. I didn't touch you or anything. I wouldn't do that.

Please don't be afraid. It's all right. Look, I'll prove it to you. I take pictures of them. I'll always have the pictures. Even after they're gone. I always take pictures of them. Wait, just sit there . . . oh, I didn't mean anything. I wasn't being sarcastic. I hate it when people are sarcastic . . . they can really hurt you with their words. I'll be right back.

See? See the pictures? Polaroids. I couldn't send film out to be developed. See them? Look—she was the first one. But I never took a picture of you, even when you were . . . out. I know you're not like the others.

I'm really sorry. I know you're innocent. An innocent girl. Do you have a boyfriend? No? Gee, a pretty girl like you . . . you're too busy with school and work and all that, huh?

You don't have a boyfriend. Gee, do you think if I . . . ? No, that's too stupid. I mean, if you met me . . . maybe in the restaurant, we could . . . ?

Yes?

Oh, I know you don't mean it. I'm not mad. I know you're just trying to be nice. Nice to a stranger. That's very sweet. I'm not mad at all.

I'm really so sorry. If I knew, I never would have . . . do you understand?

Good. Once I found out what kind of girl you were, I wanted you to understand. I wanted to talk to you.

# Dialogue

I know this wasn't your fault, Colleen. It wasn't my fault either, not really. If only I could explain it to you. But . . .

It doesn't matter. I know you're really a nice girl. I just wanted to tell you that I'm sorry.

You taught me a lesson, Colleen. People aren't always what they seem. I guess I'm not either.

So I'm done with all this.

I'm really, really sorry. I'm sorry about everything. Maybe this won't help that much, but I wanted you to know.

I promise. I'm sorry and I promise.

You're the last one.

# Drive-by

It was a diss what got me my shot.

I was on the corner in my new jacket, stylin' and profilin' for my homeboys. The jacket was a little big on me but it was a real bad boy—all soft, fine leather, maroon panel on front, white over the shoulders, with this big black 8 Ball in the middle of a triangle on the back. I got it a couple nights ago, when me and my crew went rustling on the subway. You gotta get paid in this life, make motherfuckers give up they gold. This young boy was wearing my jacket, on the J train, comin' home from a party with his girlfriend. The fuckin' coolie didn't even have a ride, takin' the train like a wage slave. Maurice yoked him while I put the box cutter right against his face, sliced a little piece of his cheek to let him know his life wasn't worth that jacket.

Peoples like that, they gotta expect a little vic comin' down on them, they go out on the street.

You don't got the right gear, you ain't shit out here. Motherfuckers be wearin' old raggedy hightops, yesterday's stuff, they don't get over. Bitches don't want a man who don't sport the gold.

My birthday's Saturday night—I'm gettin' too old to be foolin' with this rookie shit. I need to hook up, get somethin' sweet for me.

I'm ready. Man, I *been* ready. Last time I was busted, went down to the fuckin' Youth House, I carved a name for myself, you understand what I'm sayin'?

I saw the posse car pull over across the street. An all-black Jeep. The windows was black too—a very def ride. Everybody knows whose ride that be.

The front window slides down. Big guy in the seat. "Yo! Tyrone!" he calls out.

I cruise over to the car, proud in front of my homeboys. Posse don't be callin' on you for nothin'. A big guy gets out, opens the back door for me. Like a star climbing in a limo. Everybody on the corner saw it.

The car slides off. I'm sitting next to Luther Beauchamp. The Man himself. He got houses all over the 'hood.

Luther don't say nothin' to me at first. The guy driving takes off slow. Smooth. Very chilly. Nice.

Luther, he got a Mercedes hood ornament on a chain around his neck. Solid fucking gold. Black leather gloves on his hands. Thin black gloves.

We go up Buffalo Avenue, turn down behind the Projects.

"Z'up?" I ask him, like I go in his ride all the time. I'm with it, whatever it is.

"You know the house I got over by the Flats?" Luther asks me.

"Sho," I tell him. It's over in East New York. The Badlands. Big house, all empty upstairs, got no windows. There's a steel door with a slot in it. You slide the cash through, the crack come back.

"I'm needin' another man, work the front. Been hearin' about some young dumb motherfuckers, thinkin' about takin' what's mine. I don't play that. Five bills a day, you watch the front. Dust any motherfucker acts stupid. I been hearin' about you. Hear you got a lotta heart. That you?"

"That's me, man."

"You got your shit with you?"

I go in my waistband, pull out my piece. Luther opens his palm—I hand it to him.

"You see this trash?" he says, handing it to the big guy in the passenger seat up front.

"Chinese, man. Probably blow up in your dumbass face, you pull the trigger. How much this cost you, youngblood . . . a half yard?"

"Seventy-five," I tell him.

The driver don't say nothin' just keeps rolling.

"Give my man Tyrone somethin' good," Luther says.

The big guy hands me a brand new piece. Bigger'n mine. He wearin' black gloves too. I got to get some.

"This here's a Glock, homeboy," Luther says. "Smoothest thing they make. You got sixteen rounds in there. Super Nine. Come out fast as you pull the trigger. You know how to work it?"

"Yeah, well, I . . ."

He takes the piece from me, pushes on a button. The clip comes out the butt. He slams it back in, jacks the slide forward. "There ain't no safety on this sucker. It's locked and loaded now . . . all you do is pull. Got it?"

"I got it."

"I got dissed the other night," he said. "Dissed bad. I park my ride over the other side of Atlantic, do one of the clubs. I come out and some foul little motherfucker scraped a key all along the side. Took the paint right off. You know what that mean, boy?"

"Mean somebody got to pay."

"Righteous. Nobody works one of my houses 'less he shows his heart. You ready to go the other half?"

I knew what he meant, the other half. I got a baby. By this girl Sarita. A little boy. He named for me. I can *make* a life. The Man wants to know . . . can I *take* a life?

"Fuck, yeah." I says to him. Icy, the way you suppose to say it. Be for real. That's me. Real. 24–7, real.

He gives me a long, cool look. Nods his head. "We goin' round the block, homeboy. Right past the corner where I got dissed, okay? We just go'n' drive by. They be standin' on the corner, doin' what they do. You push this switch here, the window goes down. Then you *do* some motherfuckers, understand? Take 'em out. Many as you can, got it?"

"I'm down," I tell him.

This is where it shows, the heart of a man.

The Jeep makes the turn, slows down, rolling near the curb.

There's a righteous rap on the speakers inside the ride. Chug-a-chug. Like a train.

"Hit the window, Tyrone," the man up front tells me.

I push the switch. I don't feel nothin'.

People all over the corner, sittin' on the stoops, couple a girls dancin' to the music from a big box sittin' on a car. Hot weather brings 'em out.

I stick the piece out the window, start pulling the trigger. *Blam! Blam!* People screamin', runnin'. I keep pullin' till I hear a click in my head. No more.

The Jeep turns the corner, rollin' fast now. I hand the piece back to Luther.

We make it back to the block. Luther, he dukes five yards on me, all in hundreds. New bills. Clean and green.

"You my man, Tyrone. You did the thing. The piece is yours now—be waitin' for you at the house tomorrow. You musta dropped half a dozen of those fuckin' Jakes . . . teach those Rasta motherfuckers they don't be downin' me—it don't fuckin' pay. Come by the house tomorrow, ask for Dice, he run the joint. He'll show you where you work. You in the crew now."

I slap him five, hit the pavement.

I'm out there a long time that night. Tellin' my homeboys the score. Tyrone's movin' up. Movin' out. Go'n' be somebody. I flashed the cash. No more rustlin' for me—I'm a shooter now.

Women come over, give me the eye. Bitches, they always the first to know who's the man.

We did some smoke, did some wine. Went down to the basement, did me a bitch too. Fine little young bitch. I give her one of the new bills, tell her, next time I see her, she be wearing somethin' nice. For me. Her eyes get big behind that. They all ho' in they heart anyway.

Like my momma, and that's the truth.

Almost light when I roll back to my crib. Climb the stairs, smell them nasty smells. Elevator don't ever fuckin' work in this place. Even the Welfare don't come around no more. Soon's I get the bread, I get me a place. Giant color TV, white shag carpet.

Maybe I get me a ride like Luther's too.

I get to my floor, open the staircase door. Two Jakes standin' there, dreadlocks down to they shoulders—got sawed-off shotguns in they hands.

I guess I never get to be sixteen.

# Dumping Ground

**S**odium lights burned islands of orange on the dark wet streets. Sunburst patches. Hard-bright centers tapering off to soft rays around the edges. Black splotches between the islands. Prowler's footprints.

A maroon sedan cruised the streets, a string of police lights across its roof. SAFEGUARD SECURITY SERVICES between two broad white stripes on each side. The factory district was deserted after dark.

Two men in the front seat. Gray uniforms, police caps, gun belts. The radio on the console between them crackled. The man in the passenger seat picked up the microphone, thumbed it open.

"We're swinging past Ajax, then we're checking the freight yards."

"Dead zone," the dispatcher's voice chuckled.

"We're on the job," the guard said, a hurt tone in his voice. "Ten-four."

The sedan's tires hissed on the greasy streets. The guard looked out his window.

"I don't like this part," he said.

The driver was a tall, slightly built man in his forties. Dark hair, long, hollow-cheeked face. His eyes had a yellowish cast in the streetlights. He glanced over at his partner. "You like the other part."

The passenger lit a cigarette. "You think maybe we should find another spot?"

The driver's lips moved, showing his teeth. "It's perfect. Everybody knows the wiseguys use the back end of that wrecking yard to dump toxic waste. Nobody's going to go poking around in there."

"You really think . . . you think the ground is poison and all?"

"How could it be? The dogs are always there."

The passenger dragged on his cigarette, watching the empty factory buildings as the cruiser sliced through the night.

The car circled the dump at the edge of the district. On patrol.

"Quiet as a grave," the driver said.

"Tommy, the last time we were here . . . the dogs tore the bag open."

"So what? They're animals. They get a taste of something, they want more."

The passenger's face was sweat-sheened. He stubbed out his cigarette. His hands shook.

"Like us," he whispered.

The driver wheeled the patrol car onto a dirt road, running parallel to the pit. He killed the headlights. "Last stop," he said, turning off the ignition.

They climbed out. The driver opened the trunk. It was lined with green plastic garbage bags. Industrial strength. A heavy white canvas sack was inside, dark stains running across its surface like marbled fat. They each took an end of the canvas sack, wrapping the garbage bags around their hands. Pulled it free from the trunk. They made their way down the embankment in the dark, balancing the weight of the sack between them.

"She was the best one yet," the driver said.

At the bottom of the slope, they swung the bag back and forth. "One, two, *three!*" the driver grunted as they flung the bag into the pit.

Fire-dots of light shone from below. The passenger was breathing hard. "Fucking dogs. They always know we're here."

"They're the only ones who do," the driver said, starting back up the slope.

The patrol car waited for them as they climbed toward the dirt road.

"Tommy, maybe we shouldn't do it for a while. Maybe—"

"Shut up!"

"What?"

The soft wet ground around the car was a pool of shadows. The shadows moved. Low throaty sounds, gleaming eyes. A river of dogs, rushing.

# Exit

**T**he black Corvette glided into a waiting spot behind the smog-gray windowless building. Gene turned off the ignition. Sat listening to the quiet. He took a rectangular leather case from the compartment behind the seats, climbed out, flicking the door closed behind him. He didn't lock the car.

Gene walked slowly through the rat-maze corridors. The door at the end was unmarked. A heavyset man in an army jacket watched him approach, eyes never leaving Gene's hands.

"I want to see Monroe."

"Sorry, kid. He's backing a game now."

"I'm the one."

The heavyset man's eyes shifted to Gene's face. "He's been waiting over an hour for you."

Gene walked past the guard into a long, narrow room. One green felt pool table under a string of hanging lights. Men on benches lining the walls. He could see the sign on the far wall: the large arrow—EXIT—was just beyond Monroe. They were all there: Irish, nervously stroking balls around the green felt surface, waiting. And Monroe. A grossly corpulent thing, parasite-surrounded. Boneless. Only his eyes betrayed life. They glittered greedily from deep within the fleshy rolls of his face. His eight-hundred-dollar black suit fluttered against his body like it didn't want to touch his flesh. His thin hair was flat-black enameled patent-leather, plastered onto a low forehead with a veneer of sweat. His large head rested on the puddle of his neck. His hands were mounds of doughy pink flesh at the tips of his short arms. His smile was a scar and the fear-aura coming off him was jail-house-sharp.

"You were almost too late, kid."

"I'm here now."

"I'll let it go, Gene. You don't get a cut this time." The watchers grinned, taking their cue. "Three large when you win," Monroe said.

They advanced to the low, clean table. Gene ran his hand gently over the tightly woven surface, feeling the calm come into him the way it always did. He opened his leather case, assembled his cue.

Irish won the lag. Gene carefully roughened the tip of his cue, applied the blue chalk. Stepped to the table, holding the white cue ball in his left hand, bouncing it softly, waiting.

"Don't even think about losing." Monroe's voice, strangely thin.

Gene broke perfectly, leaving nothing. Irish walked once around the table, seeing what wasn't there. He played safe. The room was still.

"Seven ball in the corner."

Gene broke with that shot and quickly ran off the remaining balls. He watched Monroe's face gleaming wetly in the dimness as the balls were racked. He slammed the break-ball home, shattering the rack. And he sent the rest of the balls into pockets gaping their eagerness to serve him. The brightly colored balls were his: he nursed some along the rail, sliced others laser-thin, finessed combinations. Brought them home.

Irish watched for a while. Then he sat down and looked at the floor. Lit a cigarette.

The room darkened. Gene smiled and missed his next shot. Irish sprang to the table. He worked slowly and too carefully for a long time. When he was finished, he was twelve balls ahead with twenty-five to go. But it was Gene's turn.

And Gene smiled again, deep into Monroe's face. Watched the man neatly place a cigarette into the precise center of his mouth, waving away a weasel-in-attendance who leaped to light it for him. And missed again . . . by a wider margin.

Irish blasted the balls off the table, waited impatiently for the rack. He smelled the pressure and didn't want to lose the wave. Irish broke correctly, ran the remaining balls and finished the game. EXIT was glowing in the background. As the last ball went down, he turned:

"You owe me money, Monroe."

His voice trembled. One of Monroe's men put money in his hand. The fat man spoke, soft and cold: "Would you like to play again?"

"No, I won't play again. I must of been crazy. You would of gone through with it. Yes. You fat, dirty, evil sonofabitch . . ."

One of the calmly waiting men hit him sharply under the heart. Others stepped forward to drag him from the room.

"Let him keep the money," Monroe told them.

Gene turned to gaze silently at the fat man. Almost home . . .

"You going to kill me, Monroe?"

"No, Gene. I don't want to kill you."

"Then I'm leaving."

A man grabbed Gene from each side and walked him toward the fat man's chair.

"You won't do anything like that. Ever again."

Monroe ground the hungry tip of his bright-red cigarette deep into the boy's face, directly beneath the eye. Just before he lost consciousness, Gene remembered that Monroe didn't smoke.

He awoke in a grassy plain, facedown. He started to rise and the earth stuck to his torn face.

His screams were triumph.

# Family Resemblance

**I**t's easy to find a parking place in the Garment District on a Sunday morning. I locked the Hertzmobile sedan, sweeping the street with my eyes. Empty. A cold, hard wind hawked in off the Hudson. I adjusted the black-wool watch cap until it rested against the bridge of my dark glasses, slipped my gloved hands into the side pockets of my gray arctic coat, and started my march.

The back alley was clogged with trash, already picked clean by the army of homeless looking for returnable bottles. A wino was sprawled half out of a packing crate, frozen fluid around his open mouth. Working on being biodegradable.

I found the rust-colored back door. Worked the numbered buttons in the right sequence, checked behind me, and slipped inside. Staircase to my right. One flight down to the basement, four up to the top floor, where they'd be.

My rubber-soled boots were soundless on the metal stairs. I tested each one before I moved up. No hurry.

I heard their voices behind the door. Just murmurs, couldn't make out the words.

I pulled off the watch cap, pocketed the dark glasses, fitted the dark nylon stocking over my face, the big knot at the top making me look taller. Like the lifts in my boots.

I unsnapped the coat. The Franchi LAW-12 semi-automatic shotgun hung against my stomach, suspended from a rawhide loop around my neck. The barrel was sawed off to four-teen inches, the stock chopped down to a pistol grip. Twelve-gauge magnum, double-0 buckshot—four in the clip, one in the chamber. The safety was off. I checked the heavy Velcro brace on my right wrist—the cut-down scattergun kicks hard.

The door wasn't locked. I stepped inside. The voices went silent.

I was in a small room, facing three men, one directly in front of me, one to each side, ledger books open on the small table between them. Their eyes locked on the shotgun like it was the answer to all their questions.

The far tip of the triangle was a fat man with a suety face. White shirt, black suspenders, half-glasses pushed down on his nose. The man on my right was barrel-chested, wearing a red sweatsuit zipped open to show a hairy chest and some gold chains. On my left was a younger guy dressed in one of those slouchy Italian jackets, a pastel T-shirt underneath.

"Put your hands on the table," I told them. The stocking mask pressed against my lips, changing my voice, but they heard me clear enough. Hands went on the table. The guy on my right sported a heavy diamond on his ring finger. The young guy had a wafer-thin watch on his wrist.

I let the scattergun drift in a soft arc, covering them all, let-ting them feel the calm.

"There's no money here today," the fat guy said, just a slight tremor in his voice. It wasn't his first stickup.

"Shut up," I told him, not raising my voice.

"What is this?" the heavyset one asked.

"I ask the questions, you answer them," I told him.

"And then?"

"And then I kill one of you."

"Why?" the young guy squeaked.

"That little girl, the one they found strangled in the base-ment a couple of months ago. They found her when this joint opened up on a Monday morning. You three meet here every Sunday. To cook the books, play games with the IRS, whatever. It doesn't matter. One of you killed her."

"The cops already checked that out," the fat man said.

"I'm not the cops."

"Look, pal—" the guy to my right said.

"I'm not your pal. Here's the deal. One of you killed her, period—I got no time to argue about it. I don't find out who did it, now, in this room, I blow you all away. Then I'm sure."

"That's not fair," the young guy whined.

"It'll be fair," I said. "If I wanted to kill you all, I wouldn't be wearing this mask. Now, who likes little girls?" I asked all three of them.

No answer.

"Last chance," I said, not moving.

The fat guy's eyes shifted to his left. Just a flicker. I pinned the guy with the gold chains. "You keep magazines in a desk drawer?" I asked him.

His face went white. "It's not what you think. I'm straight—you ask anyone."

I watched his face shake, waiting.

"It's not me! Ask Markie—ask him about where he was a couple a years ago!"

"That wasn't for anything violent!" the young guy yelled, sweat popping out on his face. "I just liked to look."

"In windows?" I asked him.

"I was—sick. But I'm okay now. I see a therapist and everything. Right, Uncle Manny? Tell him!"

Manny nodded. "Markie wouldn't hurt anyone." Veins of contempt in his fat voice.

"How about you?"

"Me! What do I want with little girls? I take a nice massage right here in the office twice a week, you know what I mean?"

"You tell the cops about that?"

"You think it's a big deal to them? They're all on the pad—they know how it goes."

I turned to the young guy. "You like to look, Markie. Did she scream when you wanted to look too close?"

"It wasn't me! I didn't see her until—"

"It's okay, Markie. Until when?"

"Louie did it!" he shouted, pointing at the guy with the gold chains. "He showed me. He made me help him take her down to the basement—"

"You lying little punk!" Louie muttered, nodding at Manny. "He always wanted me outa here. Never wanted a partner." Then he turned to face me. "Yeah, okay. I took her downstairs. But *after* this freak finished with her. It wasn't me. The cops know. Manny pays them regular."

"He said she came here looking for a job," Markie said, indicating Louie. "I guess she needed some money and—"

The fat man smiled, watching my eyes under the mask. "Look, you're a professional, right? Somebody paid you to do a job. Okay, I understand. Business is business. Markie's a relative. A nephew, you know what that means? The kid's a peeper, but he never killed anyone. Louie's the one you want. You got paid for a body, do what you have to do. Everybody's happy."

"Markie don't look like a relative of yours," I told the fat man.

"You look real close, you can always see the family resemblance," he said, the smile leaving his face, knowing how it was going to end.

I tightened my finger on the trigger. Reached up and pulled the mask off my face.

# Hostage

**I**'ve got a gun! Aimed right at her head. See? Take a look for yourselves. You make one move to come in here, I'll blow her away!"

The man was on the top story of a three-family frame building in a middle-class section of Brooklyn. Standing at the front window, looking down at us. He was visible from the waist up, the silver revolver clear in his hand. We could only see the old lady's head and chest, the small body framed by the handles of the wheelchair. I felt a crowd surging behind us, held back by the uniformed cops. A TV camera crew was setting up to my left.

"I guess this one's yours, Walker."

I nodded agreement at the big detective. I'd seen him around before, at scenes like this one. Never could remember his name.

"How long's he been like that?" I asked.

"We got a call about six this morning, just around daybreak. Prowler. Radio car took it, found the kid in an alley, peeking in windows. They chased him, he made it to the back door of that house there. They start up the stairs after him, that's when he flashed the piece. He's been up there for hours."

"That's his house?"

"Yeah. How did you know?"

"He was just running in panic, he wouldn't have gone all the way to the top floor. I'll bet the gun was in the house all the time, probably didn't have it with him when he was outside."

"Yeah. He's even got a permit for it, all registered, nice and legal."

"What else you got?"

"His name's Mark Weston. Age twenty-three. Got two priors, indecent exposure and attempted B&E. Got probation both times. Sees a psychiatrist. Lives off his mother's Social Security check—that's her up there in the wheelchair."

"You think he'd blast his mother?"

The detective shrugged. "You're the expert," he said, just the trace of contempt in his voice.

I'd been a cop a long time. Ever since I came home from the killing floor in Southeast Asia. It seemed like the natural thing to do. My first assignment was vice, but I got kicked back into uniform when some dirtbag pimp complained I'd roughed him up during a bust. Then I worked narcotics. The first week on the job I killed a dealer in a gunfight. He was shot in the back. The Review Team cleared me—he'd shot first and I nailed him going for the window.

I got a commendation, but they put me back on the beat. That was okay for a while. The people in the community knew me, we got along. I caught two guys coming out of a bodega, stocking masks over their heads, one had a shotgun. I cut them both down. Turned out one was thirteen years old. How was I supposed to know?

They sent me to the department shrink. Nice guy. Gave me a lot of tests, asked a lot of questions. Never said much.

The shrink's office was in Manhattan. The locks were a joke. I went back there one night and pulled my file. It made interesting reading. Post-Traumatic Stress Disorder, fundamental lack of empathy, blunted affect, addicted risk-taker.

I'd been a sniper in Nam, so they tried me on the SWAT Team. When I did what they hired me to do, they pulled me off the job. Took away my gun.

Then they gave me a choice. I could take early retirement, go out on disability. Emotionally unsuited to law enforcement, that kind of thing. Or I could learn hostage negotiation work. Go to this special school they have. The boss said I'd be real good at it—I always stayed calm, and I could talk pretty sweet when I wanted to.

But I couldn't carry a gun. My job was to talk. The boss said if I proved myself, I could go back on a regular job someday.

Okay.

I lit a cigarette, thinking it through. "You got a telephone link?" I asked.

"There's a number listed. We haven't tried it yet. Waiting on you. You can try it from the truck."

I walked over to the blue-and-white truck, introduced myself. Sat down at the console and dialed the number.

It rang a half-dozen times before he picked it up.

"Who is this?"

"My name is Walker, Mark. I want to talk to you. About this situation, see if we can't work something out, okay?"

"Are you a cop?"

"No," I said, my voice soft, starting the lies. "I'm a psychologist. The police figured you'd rather talk to me. Is that okay?"

"Make them go away!"

"Okay, Mark. Take it easy, son. There's nothing to get upset about. You didn't do anything."

"Make them go away, I said! I'll kill her, I swear I will."

"Sure, I understand. Give me a few minutes, okay? You'll do that, won't you Mark. I can't just snap my fingers, make them disappear. I have to talk to them. Like I'm talking to you, okay?"

"I . . ."

"I'll call you back. In a few minutes, okay? Just relax, I'm going to fix everything."

I stepped out of the truck, feeling his eyes on me. The big detective was rooted to the same spot.

"Can we move everyone back? Just out of the sight-line from his window?"

"Procedure . . ."

"Procedure is we don't let him walk away, we don't give him weapons, and we don't set him off, right? Just pull back, okay? What's the big deal? You can keep the perimeter tight. Anyway, it's a good idea to clear the area . . . what if he starts firing out the window?"

The big detective gave me a steady gaze, not giving anything away. "It's your show, pal," he said.

In five minutes, the street was empty. I went back to the truck, made my call.

"Okay, Mark? Just like I promised. Nobody's going to hurt you."

"I'm sorry for what I did. Can't I . . ."

"Mark, I did something for you, right? Now it's time for you to do something for me. Like good faith, okay?"

"Wha . . . what do you want?"

"What I want is to talk to you, Mark. Face-to-face."

"I'm not coming out!"

"Of course not, Mark. I wouldn't want you to do that. I'll come in, okay? And we'll talk."

"If this is a trick . . ."

"It's no trick, Mark. Why would I trick you? I'm on your side. We're working together on this. Tell you what: I'll take off my shirt, so you can see I'm not carrying a gun, okay? I'll walk up the stairs, you can watch every step. And you can keep your gun on me all the time. Fair enough?"

"I'll think about it."

"There isn't much time, Mark. The cops, you know how they are. I got them to listen to me because I told them we had a relationship. That we could get along, you and me. If they think we can't talk, you know what they'll do."

"I'll kill her!"

"Why would they care, Mark? You know how the cops are. Another old lady gets killed in New York, so what? Besides, if I come up there, you'd have *two* hostages, right? Even more insurance."

"How come . . ."

"Mark, I'm coming up now. I want you to watch me, okay. Watch what I do. You'll see I'm on your side, son."

I hung up the phone, stepped out of the truck. I saw him at the window, watching. I waved. Took off my jacket, laid it on the ground like a blanket. I dropped my shirt on top. Took of my undershirt and added it to the pile. I unlaced my shoes, took them off, peeled off my socks and put them inside. Rolled up the cuffs of my pants to mid-calf. Turned one complete spin, my hands high in the air.

Then I started for the stairs. On the second flight, I heard a door open.

"It's me, Mark," I called out.

The door was open at the top of the stairs. I stepped inside. He was standing next to his mother, the gun leveled at my chest.

"Hello, Mark," I said, reaching out to shake hands.

He didn't go for it, the pistol trembling in his hands.

"Okay if I sit down?" I asked, not waiting for an answer.

He stood silent, watching me. The old lady's eyes were ugly and evil, measuring me. She didn't look afraid.

"Mark, do you smoke?"

"Why?"

"I didn't want to bring my cigarettes with me. Didn't want you to be suspicious. But I'd sure like one now."

"She doesn't let me smoke in the house," he said.

The old lady's expression didn't change, but her eyes flickered triumph. The pistol wasn't cocked.

"Okay, no big deal. Let's talk now, you and me."

"About what?"

"About how you're going to get out of this, okay?"

"The probation officer, she said if I messed up again, I was going to jail. I can't go to jail."

"You're not going to jail, Mark. Why should you go to jail? Your mother, she's not going to press charges against you, right?"

He looked down at her. She nodded agreement.

"See?" I told him. "What we have to do, now, is *bargain* with them. Make a deal, you know?"

"What kind of deal?"

"The only trouble you're in, near as I can see, is maybe running away the cops this morning. That's nothing, that's not even a crime. But you know how judges are . . . so we have to give them something, make you look good. Like a hero, okay?"

"A hero?"

"Sure! What we do is, we let your mother go. We let her go outside. You still have me as a hostage. But first, I call the cops. And I make them promise, if you let her go, then they'll drop the charges. Then, you and me, we walk out of here together. Okay?"

"What if . . . ?"

"How does your mother get around, Mark? I mean, how does that wheelchair get outside?"

"She can walk. If she had some help. I used to . . ."

"Okay, here's how we'll do it. I'll help your mother downstairs, right to the door, okay? That wheelchair, it folds up, right?"

"Yes."

"Okay. I'll help her downstairs. You're right behind me, with the gun. Then you and me, we'll go back upstairs and talk. After a while, we walk out. And that's it."

"You promise?"

"Just watch me," I said, reaching for the phone. I dialed the truck. "This is Walker," I told them. "Mark and I have had a discussion about this situation and here's what we have to offer. He's going to let his mother come out, okay? In exchange, we want you to drop the charges against him. You do that, and he and I will come out together. But remember, the deal has to be no jail for Mark, you understand?"

Mark stood next to me, the pistol inches from my face. I held the receiver so he could hear the cop in the truck tell me they agreed to my terms, no problem. So long as he sent the old lady out first.

It took a long time to wrestle the old lady down the stairs, her gnarled hands on my arm. I wasn't surprised at the strength of her grip. I snapped the wheelchair open and she sat down. I gently pushed her out into the sunlight. Climbed back the stairs, Mark right behind me.

We both sat down. "You can smoke now," I told him. "She's gone."

His smile was tentative, but he produced a pack. Handed it to me. We lit up, smoked in silence.

Then he told me his story. They all have a story. He was a change-of-life baby. His father left soon after his birth, and the old lady raised him alone. Hard. He showed me the discolored skin on his right hand where she'd burned him when she caught him with dirty magazines. The whip marks on his back. From an electrical cord. He dropped out of school when he was a teenager. Never had a friend. Lonely, scared, sad. Scarred.

In another hour he was crying

I got up, went to him. Put my arms around him. Took the gun gently from his hand. Patted his back, talking softly to him. Telling him he was gong to a better place. Where nobody could ever hurt him again.

I stepped away from him. Turned and brought up the pistol. His face froze. I put two rounds into his chest. Footsteps pounded on the stairs.

Self-defense.

Maybe now they'll give me my gun back.

# It's a Hard World

**I** pulled into the parking lot at La Guardia around noon and sat in the car running my fingers over the newly tightened skin on my face, trying to think through my next move. I couldn't count on the plastic surgery to do the job. I had to get out of New York at least long enough to see if DellaCroce's people still were looking for me.

I sat there for an hour or so thinking it through, but nothing came to me. Time to move. I left the car where it was—let Hertz pick it up in a week or so when I didn't turn it in.

The Delta terminal was all by itself in a corner of the airport. I had a ticket for Augusta, Georgia, by way of Atlanta. Canada was where I had to go if I wanted to get out of the country, but Atlanta gave me a lot of options. The airport there is the size of a small city; it picks up traffic from all over the country.

I waited until the last minute to board, but it was quiet and peaceful. They didn't have anybody on the plane with me. Plenty of time to think; maybe too much time. A running man sticks out too much. I had to find a way out of this soon or DellaCroce would nail me when I ran out of places to hide.

Atlanta Airport was the usual mess: travelers running through the tunnels, locals selling everything from shoeshines to salvation. I had a couple of hours until the connecting flight to Augusta, so I found a pay phone and called the Blind Man in New York.

"What's the story?" I asked, not identifying myself.

"Good news and bad news, pal," came back the Blind Man's harsh whisper. He'd spent so much time in solitary back when we did time together that his eyes were bad and his voice had rusted from lack of practice. "They got the name that's on your ticket, but no pictures."

"Damn! How did they get on the ticket so fast?"

"What's the difference, pal? Dump the ticket and get the hell out of there."

"And do what?"

"You got me, brother. But be quick or be dead," said the Blind Man, breaking the connection.

The first thing I did was get out of the Delta area. I went to the United counter and booked a flight to Chicago, leaving in three hours. You have to stay away from borders when you're paying cash for an airline ticket, but I didn't see any obvious DEA agents lurking around and, anyway, I wasn't carrying luggage.

With the Chicago ticket tucked safely away in my pocket, I drifted slowly back toward the boarding area for the Augusta flight. It was getting near to departure time. I found myself a seat in the waiting area, lit a cigarette, and kept an eye on the people at the ticketing desk. There was a short walkway to the plane, with a pretty little blonde standing there checking off the boarding passes. Still peaceful, the silence routinely interrupted by the usual airport announcements, but no tension. It felt right to me. Maybe I'd try for Augusta after all; I hate Chicago when it's cold.

And then I spotted the hunters: two flat-faced men sitting in a corner of the waiting area. Sitting so close their shoulders were touching, they both had their eyes pinned on the little blonde, not sweeping the room like I would have expected. But I knew who they were. You don't survive a dozen years behind the walls if you can't tell the hunters from the herd.

They wouldn't be carrying; bringing handguns into an airport was too much of a risk. Besides, their job was to point the finger, not pull the trigger. I saw how they planned to work it; they had the walkway boxed in. But I didn't see what good it would do them if they couldn't put a face on their target.

The desk man announced the boarding of Flight 884 to Augusta. I sat there like it was none of my business, not moving. One by one, the passengers filed into the narrow area. The sweet Southern voice of the blonde piped up, "Pleased to have you with us today, Mr. Wilson," and my eyes flashed over to the hunters. Sure enough, they were riveted to the blonde's voice. She called off the name of each male passenger as he filed past her. If the women passengers felt slighted at the lack of recognition, they kept quiet about it. A perfect trap: if I put my body through that walkway, the little blonde would brand the name they already had to my new face, and I'd be dead meat as soon as the plane landed.

I got up to get away from there just as the desk man called out, "Last call for Flight 884." They couldn't have watchers at all the boarding areas. I'd just have to get to Chicago, call the Blind Man, and try and work something out. As I walked past the desk, a guy slammed into me. He bounced back a few feet, put a nasty expression on his face, and then dropped it when he saw mine. A clown in his late thirties, trying to pass for a much younger guy: hair carefully styled forward to cover a receding hairline, silk shirt open to mid-chest, fancy sunglasses dangling from a gold chain around his neck. I moved away slowly and watched as he approached the desk.

"I got a ticket for this flight," he barked out, like he was used to being obeyed.

"Of course, sir. May I see your boarding pass?"

"I don't have a goddamn pass. Can't I get one here?"

"I'm sorry, sir," the desk man told him, "the flight is all boarded at this time. We have four more boarding passes outstanding. We can certainly issue one to you, but it has to be on what we call the 'modified standby' basis. If the people holding boarding passes don't show up five minutes before flight time, we will call your name and give you the pass."

"What kind of crap is this?" the clown demanded. "I paid good money for this ticket."

"I'm sure you did, sir. But that's the procedure. I'm sure you won't have any trouble boarding. This happens all the time on these short flights. Just give us your ticket, and we'll call you by name just before the flight leaves, all right?"

I guess it wasn't all right, but the clown had no choice. He slammed his ticket down on the counter, tossed his leather jacket casually over one shoulder, and took a seat near the desk.

It wasn't a great shot, but it was the best one I'd had in a while. I waited a couple of heartbeats and followed the clown to the desk. I listened patiently to their explanation, left my ticket, and was told that they would call me by name when my turn came.

I didn't have much time. I walked over to where the clown was sitting, smoking a cigarette like he'd invented it. "Look," I told him, "I need to get on that flight to Augusta. It's important to me. Business reasons."

"So what's that to me?" he smirked, shrugging his shoulders.

"I know you got ahead of me on the list, okay? It's worth a hundred to me to change places with you. Let me go when your name is called, and you can go when they call mine, if they do," I told him, taking out a pair of fifties and holding them out to him.

His eyes lit up. I could see the wheels turning in his head. He knew a sucker when he saw one. "What if we both get on?" he wanted to know.

"That's my tough luck," I said. "I need to do everything possible to get on the flight. It's important to me."

He appeared to hesitate, but it was no contest. "My name's Morrison," he said, taking the fifties from my hand. "Steele," I said, and walked toward the desk.

The watchers hadn't looked at us. A couple of minutes

passed. I gently worked myself away from the clown, watching the watchers. The desk man piped up: "Mr. Morrison, Mr. Albert Morrison, we have your boarding pass." I shot up from my seat, grabbed the pass, and hit the walkway. The little blonde sang out, "Have a pleasant flight, Mr. Morrison," as I passed. I could feel the heat of the hunters' eyes on my back.

I wasn't fifty feet into the runway when I heard, "Mr. Steele, Mr. Henry Steele, we have your boarding pass." I kept going and found my seat in the front of the plane.

I watched the aisle and, sure enough, the clown passed me by, heading for the smoking section in the rear. I thought he winked at me, but I couldn't be sure.

The flight to Augusta was only half an hour, but the plane couldn't outrun a phone call. The airport was a tiny thing, just one building, with a short walk to the cabs outside. The clown passed by me as I was heading outside, bumped me with his shoulder, held up my two fifties in his hand, and gave me a greasy smile. "It's a hard world," he said, moving out ahead of me.

I watched as two men swung in behind him. One was carrying a golf bag; the other had his hands free.

# Joyride

Just past midnight on the Old Motor Parkway, outside of town where there used to be factories. They closed the road down years ago—when they closed the mills. Nobody uses it anymore.

My car was standing at the beginning of the two-lane crumbling blacktop road. Me looking straight ahead through the narrow slit of windshield on the chopped-down '49 Ford coupe, Wendy next to me in the passenger seat, her left hand on the inside of my right thigh, smoking. To her right, a new guy. In a snarling Mopar, giant rear tires raking the nose almost down to the pavement.

I didn't know him, an outsider, invading. He'd cruised into the drive-in, looking for me. Offered me out to the highway. Cash, pink slips, anything I wanted to play for.

People were watching. They always watch. I upped the stakes—first man over the bridge takes it. His girl was a busty little brunette with a slashy red mouth, draping her heavy breasts over the windowsill of his shiny car, watching us lay it out in the parking lot.

"Do it!" she told him.

Wendy just watched her. Arched her back. Nodded okay to me.

The road turns to dirt after the first bend and ends with a sharp hook-turn just before the abandoned wood bridge. There's no water under that bridge anymore. My little car was hunched over, waiting. Growling, ticking. I felt what it wanted to do.

Velvet-ink out there but I knew the road. I'd done this before. Slower, in daylight. Practicing my moves.

I pulled the switch for the cut-outs. The motor crackled now, unmuffled. We'd only have a few minutes before the Highway Patrol heard the noise and came after us. I'd be long gone.

They'd chased me before, knew who I was. But they'd have to catch me to hold me.

We don't use a flagman for these runs—Wendy shouts out the count, a white silk scarf in her right hand. We go on Three. I'd feel her quick, sharp squeeze on my thigh just before she dropped the scarf—that was my edge.

I blipped the throttle, looked past Wendy's profile to the other guy. He gave me the thumbs-up, grinning. She gave me a quick kiss—as wet under her jeans as I was hard under mine.

I pressed down the heavy clutch, shrieked the potent engine, grabbed the floor shift and slipped it toward me and down. First gear. I telescoped my eyes down to the little bridge, spit my chewed cigarette out the window.

Wendy squeezed my thigh a split second before *Three!* as I dropped the clutch. The rear wheels clawed for a foothold and the Ford got burning sideways . . . straightened out and launched.

I was off first but he was closing. Couldn't see the tach needle—I power-shifted into second, grabbed half a length on him. The bridge: I saw the hook coming, pumped the brake with my left foot, squatting for the turn. The beast screamed on . . . ignoring me. It was too close. All by myself. One long second left. I gambled: clutch in, tromp the gas, ram the lever back into first. No time now . . . I popped the clutch, heard the vicious *crack!* as the transmission dropped and we went freewheeling . . . no traction. Lost. The shift knob came off in my fist. I crouched low and whipped the wheels inside the opening to the bridge but it was no good—the rear end slid out and hit the wall. We started to roll—I dove for the floor, Wendy's blond hair flying ahead of me. The icy metal of the shift lever stabbed into my mouth, shattering teeth and coming out my ripped cheek just as we went over.

I heard the sirens. Couldn't move. When the law came I was still pinned by the long stick, an insect on their spreading board. Everything in flames.

The young cop was crying when I came to and some white-coated liar was telling me how all right things were going to be.

# Lynch Law

**May 1959**

The predator slouched against the soft leather seat, eyes half-closed. Parked near the edge of a drive-in hamburger joint on a thick summer night, listening to the frightened voices swirl like fog around his open windows. The little weasels were whining about a story they thought only their pitiful little town knew. But the predator knew better—he heard the same story everywhere he traveled: some ancient black madman living in the swamp out past the abandoned factories and mill works; a monster with the strength of a dozen men, escaped from a chain gang years ago and never brought to justice. And he waited out there every night, living on human flesh. You don't give Fear a Christian name in the Bible Belt, so they called him "The Nigger." Those who claimed to have seen him said he had a hideous scarred face and only one hand—the other stump ended in a hooked spike.

The Nigger only lived to make people die.

A stupid myth—the predator had used it before.

And this time, he couldn't miss. Last Saturday night, two of the town's bright little stars hadn't returned from their date. They found them the next morning on the edge of the swamp. Both heads hacked off—not cleanly. The boy's wallet had been torn open and his mouth stuffed with dollar bills. The girl's body was naked except for her underpants, but the investigators couldn't tell who took her that far.

The kids knew. Everybody had known about Rob and Sally for quite a while. Rob talked a lot because it was his first, and Sally didn't care if he did because it wasn't. Or so people said.

The church people got hard around the eyes when they heard the stories. Punishment for sin was one thing, but God wouldn't pick a nigger to do his work.

Frightened wisps of talk floated past the predator's window:

"It was a tramp—some hobo who got thrown off the train. Probably camping out there when he saw them . . ."

"He didn't take the money."

"An escaped convict . . . run off from the prison farm."

"It was the Nigger . . . *had* to be the Nigger!"

"There *is* no goddamned Nigger out there."

"Lots of folks saw him."

"Yeah, well, whatever it is, I'm not going out there again without a gun."

"I suppose you'd go even with a gun, huh?"

"I might . . ."

The predator listened carefully. He was a good listener. Patient, doing his work. Teenagers gathered around his new Coupe de Ville, sat on the hood, lit their cigarettes with the lighter from his dashboard. The predator blended in easily—a professional stranger with soft ways about him. He was twenty-four years old—could look seventeen or thirty, depending on what he needed.

The predator added nothing to the conversation unless someone pushed him. His smile never got near his eyes.

That was his way—stand close, but apart. A wolf watching the campfire. He remembered one night in Chicago. A crap game behind a car wash where he'd been working to build up a stake after they let him out the last time. He faded the shooter all night long, never touching the dice. But finally they passed cubes to him, telling him he had to roll. He refused again. Politely. One of the men patiently explained to him that the odds were always a little bit against the shooter, so it wasn't fair to hang back like he was. The predator listened to the explanation, no expression on his young face. He knew all about the odds. But he didn't touch the dice. They crowded in around him, telling him to roll or walk . . . and leave his winnings behind. With a frozen face and a crackling thunderstorm in his chest he grabbed the dice and threw eight straight passes. He walked away from the car wash with four hundred dollars of their rent money. Miserable slugs didn't know how lucky they'd been—if he'd had a gun instead of the straight-edged razor in his jacket pocket . . .

An old man who had been in the game caught up with the predator at the end of the alley.

"I hope you learned something, son," he said.

The predator looked at the old man. "I'm not your fucking son."

The old man knew it was the truth.

But this was way south of Chicago. And young people never knew the truth. He got Joanne's phone number from one of the grinning boys at the drive-in. He knew why they were smiling—any number they gave up so easily had to be a girl they hadn't gotten to. The kind he wanted.

Three nights later, they were coming back from the movies. Driving in the Cadillac an old woman had bought for him in Phoenix. There had been a newsreel about the lynching of Mack Charles Parker in nearby Mississippi. A mob had stormed the jail where Parker had been waiting trial for rape—his body had never been found. Joanne had been horrified. She kept saying, "It's not right—he didn't do it."

The predator knew she would have sacrificed the black bastard in a minute if he had. Knowing things—that's how you got on in this world. Patience. He drove out past the old factories, watching the quick pulse throb in her neck.

"Where're you going?"

"I thought we'd park the car and talk for a bit. I can't handle the drive-in and all those silly kids."

Joanne responded to the implied threat to her sophistication. "Anything's better than that," she agreed.

The predator parked near the edge of the swamp, fitting his car inside the sulfurous mist. He left the engine running—windows up, air conditioner on. Started his work in the dead-quiet night.

"I can't believe those punks were really serious about some nigger living out here and slicing people up. . . . You can tell when a kid's never left home."

"Well," she said, "they really are pretty immature. I never go out with any of the boys around here anymore, not since I got back from college. . . ."

"Christ, you can't see a thing out there, huh?"

"This is the first time I've ever been out here. None of the town boys come out here now. You know, ever since . . ."

The predator lit a cigarette, watching her face over his cupped hands. "Doesn't bother *you*, right?"

The old factories shifting on their rotten foundations made a moaning sound that seemed to blossom from the ground around the car. A tiny red light appeared in the distance. The predator glanced at the glowing tip of his cigarette—just a reflection in the windshield. He smiled his smile.

Joanne shuddered in the chill of the air conditioner. "I know a much better place, out by the lake. It's really beautiful in the summer . . ."

"Ah, let's stay here. Besides. I thought you liked niggers, the way you were carrying on in the movies and all. . . ."

The predator pumped the gas pedal, listening to the engine roar against the swamp-sounds. The Caddy rocked in its place, a frightened beast chained by the predator's foot.

"No," the girl said. "I don't want to stay here. I don't . . . please . . ."

"Come on, what's the big deal? Wouldn't you like to have some big black gorilla get hold of you? You might like it."

Joanne opened her mouth, trying for indignation, but nothing came out. The predator reached for her with his right hand, flicking away the hem of her full skirt, shoving his hand roughly between her legs. He grabbed the soft flesh of her inner thigh, pulling her around to face him, holding tight.

"It's getting pretty stuffy in here; I think I'll just open this window and . . ."

"No!"

"What's your problem?" he whispered, still holding her. "I've got this." The predator pulled a shiny little automatic from under the dash, holding it up so she could see it gleam in the darkness.

"Please . . . please. I want to go home. . . ."

"I got something to do first," he told her, watching the dice bounce on the blanket and thinking "natural" in his mind. It was a word he liked.

Joanne's head whipped back and forth on her neck, no longer feeling the pain in her thigh. "No, no, no . . . no, please, take me home . . . I'm so afraid . . . god, please!"

The predator twisted his hand, making her see his face. The swamp-sounds tightened around the car, but the predator was calm within himself. The key was knowing when to move—picking your time. He made her look until she understood.

"Take me home and I'll do whatever you want," Joanne said, her voice quiet now.

"Sure. With Mommy and Daddy watching, huh? You must think I'm a fucking idiot."

"No! I think you're wonderful . . . so strong. My parents are up north on vacation . . . we'd be all alone. Please?"

The predator's teeth flashed. He had known all about the vacation before he'd called Joanne.

"I don't believe you," he said. "How do I know you wouldn't just run in the house and call the cops?"

"Oh, I wouldn't. I never would. Just take me home . . . to my house . . . and . . ."

"You do something for me first. Just so I'm sure."

"Wh . . . what?"

The predator took his left hand off the wheel. He stepped on the gas, hearing the engine scream as he unzipped his slacks. He backed off the engine, letting the car idle down. "Show me," he told her.

Joanne reached uncertainly toward him—his *slap!* was a whipcrack in the quiet night.

"Not with your hand."

"No! I can't . . . I never . . ."

The predator took his hand from her thigh and moved it to the back of her neck. He slowly forced her head down and held her against him, the pistol in his left hand tapping a steady rhythm against the driver's window. When he was sure she was going to do the right thing, he took his hand away from her neck and let it rest across the top of the seat.

When she finished he jerked her back by the short hair at the base of her neck.

She looked at the predator, her eyes milky, unreadable.

"Do you believe me now?"

He nodded, waiting.

"I love you," Joanne told him. "I swear I do. Take me home now. Please . . . hurry! We have to leave, honey . . . I will, oh . . . anything! Just take me home."

The predator stomped the gas, shoving the Caddy into gear—it fishtailed on the soft ground, clawing for a grip. The predator flicked the wheel expertly, guiding the big car out of the dying swamp. He released the girl, shoving her against the passenger door.

The predator drove straight to her house. He didn't need directions. When they pulled up, he pushed her out her side of the car, following close behind, never taking his hand off her.

An hour later the predator remembered he'd left his pistol in plain view inside the car, but the doors were locked, so he went back to what he was doing. He kept asking Joanne, "Isn't this better?" and she didn't know what he meant but knew enough to say "Yes" every time.

It was still dark when the predator left the house. He was going to the furnished room he'd rented and sleep until the next night. Then he'd finish with Joanne and move on, doing his work.

He walked around to the driver's door, keys in hand, like walking out of that alley in Chicago.

A heavy, hook-twisted steel spike was dangling from the door handle, swaying gently in the night breeze. Its thick base was crusted with flesh, torn off bloody at the root.

# Man to Man

**Y**ou wait for an obvious score, man. They are not hard to spot after a while but I'll show you a few from the next bunch that pass by. You have no trouble . . . since you so well-dressed for the role. And make sure you get it straight in front: how much and what you gonna do. There's a lot of studs on this street who'll do any fucking thing for half a C-note, but the real men here, we just let the goddamned queers swing on our joints and that's all! Don't *ever* come on to a score. Say *nothin'* to them. Don't talk. Just nod your head if you want to make it and walk away if you don't. The Law around here really don't care so long as you not soliciting . . . you know, like the hookers do, screaming at the cars and all. And there are some faggot cops who will make it with you and *then* bust you, man . . . some motherfucking heat *that* is! Stay out of the toilets and the movie balconies . . . 'specially on this street 'cause then you become too well-known and it will not take long for the fags to look for a new face and the price drops on you. That's the way they are.

Best deal is to set a goal for yourself each day; like, say, a yard. And not to panic or press if you not goin' to make this right away and bein' sure to quit when you got this because that way the pressure is not on you.

Trouble is, man, you look too much like one of those motorcycle studs and you gonna get all kinds of action from freaks who want you to whale on them for bread. Not that there is anythin' wrong with working over a fucking queer but you got to go someplace to do it . . . like a room . . .

In the summer we make it to one of the queer beaches, but you got to have body for that stuff. I work out regularly and don't smoke or drink . . . only sometimes the queers expect you to smoke while they copping your joint because that is cool and removed . . . but you look wasted, man. Maybe you want to come along with some of the guys next time we hit the gym. Good bucks to be made from the camera freaks too . . . if you got the body. You got to have a partner to work out with you. You know, hold your legs while you kick and spot weights for you and stuff like that. . . . I'll go with you sometime.

And don't be talking like some fuckin' intellectual all the time . . . the scores don't dig that shit. Tell them you a truck driver or a serviceman or something like that. I tell 'em I'm a professional athlete . . . you better not try that, though. In fact, just tell them you a hustler and let it go like that. That will clear the air and you won't get beat out of bread by some freak thinking you for free.

Lots of goddamned size-queens too. Like to measure the meat *before* they buy. I got no trouble like that so I make extra bucks sometimes. You, uh . . . hung pretty good? Better let me check you out first so I can tell you if you should show it to 'em first. . . .

Oh, look, *okay*, man . . . that is your choice. I *personally* don't give a shit. . . . I am just trying to give you a picture of this street so you last and live out here like me. I have been hustling this block for two seasons now and have only one time been busted. You just got to know how.

Listen, man, don't look at me like that. I know all about this "if you'll pitch, you'll catch" shit, but, dig, I don't do nothing! Even in the House, I don't do a fuckin' thing. The *House*, man . . . the fucking *jail!*

## Man to Man

That was for somethin' else, not hustling.

Listen, man, you want to make it up to my room, just around the block? I got some beer on ice and we could talk more about this scene. . . . I mean, this fucking street is a drag sometimes.

# Plan B

**I** call myself a gambler, but that's not what I am—a gambler wins sometimes. Me, I'm a loser, that's the right word for it.

In all my gambling life, I only had one piece of luck. And like they always say, luck is a lady. That's my Penny. My Lucky Penny, I used to call her . . . back when I was keeping at least some of my promises.

The guy who said "for better or for worse" must have had me and Penny on his mind. Yeah. She was the better, I was the worse.

When I first knew her, when I was taking her out on the town, she was such a beauty guys would just bite their hands when she walked down the street.

That was more than twenty years ago, but even all those years of hash-house waitressing haven't made it all go away. She's still gorgeous, and not just to me. Yeah, she's put on a few pounds. And being on your feet all day don't do much for your legs. And having to eat most of her meals at that greasy spoon joint don't help your waistline either. They give her free meals at the joint— that's so they don't have to pay minimum wage. Penny could of made a lot more cash working in one of those joints where letting the customers grab your ass is part of the deal, but she wouldn't do that. I mean, I wouldn't of *wanted* her to do that, but I couldn't have stopped her. I mean, I was never enough of a man to take care of her like she deserved. How was I gonna tell her I want her to quit her job, when I wasn't bringing home the cash?

It wasn't that I didn't try—I'm a gambler, not a pimp. Truth is, I get ideas . . . good ideas . . . but I'm no good at carrying them out.

I mean, I don't drink or nothing. Never touched dope except for when I was in the Army. Everybody smoked in the Nam. Or did something heavier. I hated it over there, but I don't blame nobody but myself. I mean, I was a stone bust-out gambler before I ever got drafted.

Before I ever met my Penny.

Anyway, I always worked steady. Gamblers don't miss work the way drunks do. I got damn near twenty in on my job. At least, I *did* have until they laid me off. Hell, they about laid *everybody* off. Some of the guys said it's a bluff. They said they're trying to bust the union. Near as I can tell, the union's *already* busted. All I got to show for all those years is I get to keep my health plan for another year or so. Of course, I got to pay for it myself—the only thing management kept up was the lousy life insurance . . . twenty-five grand if I croak, big deal.

And, anyway, the truth is, I'm not keeping up the health insurance—Penny's doing that.

She always has faith in me. No matter how many times I screw up, no matter how many times I lie. Every time I get in a hole because I did something stupid, I always tell her I got another move. "I'll just go to Plan B, little girl." That's what I used to tell her when it started. But Penny ain't no little girl anymore. And me . . . me, I'm nothing but a liar. A promiser and a liar—for me, they're just the damn same.

Only one promise I ever kept to Penny. The one she told me she'd leave me for, if I broke it. "I'm not waiting around for you if you're in jail," she told me. And I knew she meant it—

Penny is real strict about that kind of thing. So I never went to the sharks. Yeah, I was a *good* gambler, you understand?—I only lost the money I had on me at the time.

*All* the goddamned money.

*Every* single time.

If it wasn't for the house, I would of probably gone on like I was forever. This house, it was right across the street from the one we lived in. Rented in, I mean. A little house, but real nice. Penny loved it. She always said it was her dream house. The old couple that lived there, they decided to sell out and move down to Florida—the winters here are cold as hell. Penny was always doing things for them—baking them some cookies, even helping the old lady clean when her arthritis got too bad—so they told her she could have first shot at the house. They told her she could have it for fifty-five thousand if she could buy it before they put it on the market. The broker told them to list it for seventy-five, and be prepared to come down to sixty-five. But, the way they figured it, with the broker's commission and all, they could do a nice thing for Penny and still come out just about the same.

When Penny told me about it, she was so excited her face got all red, like when she was a kid. Like how she was when she still believed some of my lies.

All we needed was ten percent down, she said. She already talked to a man at the bank. She didn't make much, but she sure was steady. Hell, before I got laid off, I was, too. All we needed was about six grand, she said. For the down payments and the points or whatever. And all the crap the bank sticks you with when you're up against the wall.

Six grand. Where were we gonna get that? She told me she had almost two grand socked away. She put her face down when she said it—like she was ashamed for holding out on me. You see what I mean about her?

If you counted all the money I wasted chasing horses that wouldn't run and opportunities that did, I probably could have bought Penny the whole house in cash.

# Plan B

The payments would be four hundred and eighty-seven dollars and twenty-six cents a month, Penny told me. "And we're already paying four-fifty, honey," she said.

I hated myself so much that I tried to talk her out of it. I told her we would have to pay our own heat and hot water and taxes and stuff, so it would be a lot more, really. But she said the mortgage, it would always be the same—but the landlord was gonna raise the rent eventually. All landlords do that. So, in the long run, we'd be ahead.

And when we were done working, we'd have a place of our own. The only thing that really scared Penny was being homeless. When she saw a homeless person on the street, she would get so scared. . . like the person was her in a few more years.

And Penny wanted a garden. The guy who rented the house to us, he wouldn't allow it, don't ask me why.

I never deserved Penny. She should be wearing silk. I get depressed every time I see her dabbing at her stockings with clear nail polish so the runs don't get lower down, where they would show. When I get depressed, I gamble more, that's the kind of real man I am.

I made her old. I made her scared of being homeless. And she never complained.

The only truth I ever told Penny was that I loved her. I was never as big as my own lies—I never caught up to them.

It had to be cash. At least four grand in cash.

All I had was health insurance that was running out and life insurance on a worthless life.

It had to be cash. So I had to break the one promise I always kept. "I can get the money," I told her. "I swear it on my love for you."

"Don't you dare—"

I cut her off. "I won't," I told her. "It's too complicated to explain, girl. But I—"

"Plan B?" she said. But with her sweet smile. Like she still believed in me.

Jesus.

"You just wait and see," I said. I knew I had six days. Six days and five nights. It couldn't be anything big, like a bank. You need partners for that and I didn't know anyone who could handle it. I mean, you're a gambler, you meet all kinds of guys say they do all kinds of things. But, the way I always figured it, if they were hanging out with a lying loser like me, how smart could *they* be? And because I never went near the loan sharks, I didn't know any, like, *organized* guys.

I had to do it alone.

First I needed a gun. That was so easy. I mean, I didn't have to do nothing illegal. I just went into a gun store and told them I wanted a pistol. What kind, they asked me. Cheap, I told them.

They had a bunch of them. I had to fill out a form. They asked questions like: was I a felon and was I crazy? I mean, they expect a escaped con or a drooling lunatic to admit it, *they* were the ones who were crazy. I had to wait three days, then I could come and pick up the gun.

I found where I wanted to do it. It's a club. Not like a nightclub or anything, although it was only open at night. A gambling club. Dice and cards only—none of that silly roulette or slot machines—*real* games, where a man has a chance. The club was protected. Protected from getting busted, that is—they paid off the cops. They had a guy at the door. Big huge fat guy, probably kill you if he fell on you. But I wasn't going to challenge him, anyway. I mean, he *knows* me. And I promised Penny I would never go to jail. No, I needed a stranger. A new guy. They were always coming in and out. I needed one coming in—when he still had money. It would be big money, too—there was no penny ante stuff inside—you had to have coin to sit in. That's why I only went there once in a while . . . when I was ahead from gambling someplace else. Naturally, I always lost. But I don't think the games were rigged—I'm just a loser.

When I went to the gun shop they had the pistol ready for me. "Don't you want some ammunition?" they asked me. "I got some at home," I told them.

## Plan B

On the second night, the right guy came along. I saw him park a smoke-gray Lincoln Town Car across the street. That's a classy ride, runs about thirty grand. He was sharp-dressed, too. Not flashy, more like a businessman. I could see the strong way he walked. Confident-like. Not the old gangster swagger, like a man who was in control of himself.

In a couple of minutes, Penny's dream was going to come true. I knew it. I was sure of it. Not like when I had a sure thing at the track, but *sure* . . . like nothing else could be.

Just as soon as he walked into the alley where the door to the club was, I stepped out from behind a dumpster and stuck the pistol in his face. "Give it up!" I told him.

He was real calm, real professional—just like I thought he'd be. "Do you know who I am?" he asked.

"Give me the money!" I said, cocking the pistol like I was gonna shoot him.

He took a shiny wallet out from under his coat. Real, real slow, so I wouldn't think he was reaching for a gun. He opened the wallet and took out a thick wad of bills—I could see they was all hundreds. "I'm sure you don't want my credit cards, right?" he said, a thin smile on his face.

I snatched the money out of his hand and backed away. He just stood there. "Don't try to come after me," I said. I turned around and ran. I heard footsteps behind me and I whipped around. It was the guy, holding something in his hand, some black thing, near his mouth. I turned around again and started to run. Three more corners and I'd get to where the car was waiting. Three more corners and . . . then I saw them across the street. Two of them. Cops. They were standing with their feet wide apart, guns in their hands.

"Freeze!" one of them yelled, and I knew I was never going to hand the money to Penny. I pulled out the pistol and I pointed it right at the cops.

I never heard the shots, but I felt them rip into me. One, two, three of them. In my chest and in my gut. I closed my eyes and went to Plan B.

# REPLAY

# Replay

*A Play in Three Acts*

## Scene 1

**Bordertown, Illinois-Indiana: Summer, 1992**

*The scene opens on the front room of a large office. There are no windows—the sense is that it's underground or just below first-floor level. There is a long couch against one wall, a desk and swivel chair just to the right side of a doorway. It has a large, multi-line telephone console as well as several other, free-standing phones, a rectangular digital timer with a row of buttons along the top—it reads: 0:00.00. A small computer screen sits over a keyboard. Over the desk is a bulletin board with various pieces of paper tacked up. The walls are covered with color posters of motorcycles, surf scenes—resembling the room of a teenage boy, but no pin-ups. There is a small refrigerator in another corner, a hot plate next to it. Over the couch (set so it is in view of the audience) is a huge cross-hatched chart. Across the top are various girls' names: Monique, Barbie, Jennifer, Candy, Kitty ... down the left-hand margin are code letter combinations: B&D, S&M, H/S, F-D, S-R, and at the bottom, SCREENER.*

*The cross-hatching is marked with an X in various squares . . .
so that Barbie is matched with H/S, Kitty with S-R, and so on.
A big clock stands over the charts: it reads 7:50.* [NOTE
TO DIRECTOR: THIS CLOCK RUNS IN "REAL TIME"
THROUGHOUT, BUT IS RESET BETWEEN ACTS.]

*A tall well-muscled man is seated at the desk chair, legs up on
the desk. He's wearing a tank top over baggies and running shoes.
He's in his thirties, with long hair . . . an aging surfer, a good-time
boy, not a bodybuilder. This is* BOLO. *He's got a bottle of beer in
one hand, reading a motorcycle magazine with something less
than intense concentration.*

*A bell sounds. He pushes a button on an intercom.*

BOLO:  AYW Enterprises. Can I help you?

LYZA:  I'm here about the job interview. I called earlier?

BOLO:  Oh yeah. Okay, come on through.

*(He hits a switch. A buzzer sounds . . . sound of a heavy lock
releasing. A girl walks into the room through the doorway. She's
small: long, dark hair, with a slim, curvy build. She's wearing a red leather miniskirt over fishnet stockings and black spike
heels, topped off by a black silk blouse. Heavy makeup, like
Central Casting for "hooker."* [NOTE TO DIRECTOR: THIS
MAKEUP GRADUALLY DECREASES AS THE PLAY PRO-
GRESSES, SO THAT SHE IS FRESH-SCRUBBED BY THE
END OF ACT I.] *She looks like she's in her mid-twenties, but it's
hard to tell. She's carrying a small suitcase, about the size of a
hatbox.)*

LYZA:  Hi! You must be Mr. Monroe, the man I spoke with on
the phone. You said to come in anytime after eight.

BOLO:  No, I'm Bolo. You musta spoken to Johnny earlier on,
right? It don't matter: any of us coordinators can do the interview.

LYZA:  Bolo?

BOLO: *(Laughs)* Yeah. Where I come from, it stands for Be On the Lookout. What the cops broadcast over the radio when they're lookin' for somebody. When I was younger, I liked to play pretty hard, you know? *(Making fun of himself)* Held the South Florida Bar Fighting Championship two years in a row.

LYZA: *(Walking over, sitting on the desk, crossing her legs, mildly flirtatious)* And now?

BOLO: Now I just want to hang out. Do some waves, ride my bike. Take it as it comes.

LYZA: And you work here?

BOLO: Yeah. It's perfect for me. Eight at night to four in the morning, five times a week. Like the night manager, I guess. This way, I'm off the streets when it gets dark, see? I mean, this ain't no career, okay? I'm just saving my money. I get enough saved up, I'm off. To Australia. Soon as I get there, I'm buying a touring bike—a monster Kawasaki. I heard there's some great waves over there and I figure on seeing most of them. *(Pause.)*

LYZA: Well, I'm here for the interview.

BOLO: Okay, here's how it works. It's real simple. Guys call, they want to talk to a girl. They want . . . different stuff . . . depending on the guy, you understand? It's all a game, like acting. Fantasy stuff. You get to be one of the *regular* girls. . . See the chart over there? *(Indicating the wall chart)* Each girl does a different thing. We get some regulars, they always ask for the same girl, once they find one they like. That's why we keep the chart—so we can know who played what girl every day. Most of the time, they don't much care. I do this little spiel, find out kinda what they want. Sometimes, they don't want to tell me . . . then it'd be *your* job to find out, see?

LYZA: The ad said twenty-five dollars an hour . . . ?

BOLO: Yeah, right. That's one way. Or you can work on straight commission. We bill them by the minute—they give me their credit card, I run it on the computer over there *(Indicating)* and if the card's good, they're off to the races. The longer you keep them on the phone, the more money you make.

LYZA: How much do you charge them?

BOLO: We tell 'em it's a buck ninety-five a minute, but this timer we got, it comes out to more than two and a quarter.

LYZA: A *minute*?

BOLO: *(Laughs)* Yeah! You work on commission, you can figure about sixty bucks an hour just for your end.

LYZA: Wow!

BOLO: And we pay in cash, too. End of each shift, you get your money. I keep track of it on this timer here . . . It's not for the other calls, just for the ones coming in here, understand?

LYZA: Don't all the calls come in here?

BOLO: No way! Some nights, I'm the only one here. Most of the time, we just use this call-forwarding deal—I switch them right into the girls' homes. You work tonight, you'll be the only one.

LYZA: I just talk to them on the phone?

BOLO: Well . . . yeah. But . . . look, I don't mean to get in your business or anything, but . . . I mean, you look like an actress made up for a part or something, okay? I mean, some of these callers, they're not looking for romance, you understand what I'm saying. Hard core is what we sell here. Even over the phone, it can get kind of ugly. Have you ever . . . ?

LYZA: Look, I *am* an actress.

BOLO: Oh, yeah, we get a lot of actresses working here. . . .

LYZA: Okay, never mind the sarcasm. It's not that you would have seen me in the movies or anything, but I'm an actress. That's what I do. I sing, I dance . . . light comedy, Shakespeare . . . everything. I had lessons from the time I was just a baby. My Daddy paid for them . . . I was an only child and I guess he kind of spoiled me. I used to put on concerts for him, do little plays, dress up like a fairy princess. He's a doctor, over in Winnetka. I came to Chicago to work. And it's hard. I mean, if you were in the business, you'd *know* that. It's real hard to get a break, get a chance to show people what you can do. The thing is, I'm short of money. Daddy wanted me to stay in a nice place, and I promised him I would. What with the rent and clothes and going to auditions all the time, it adds up. I could just pick up the phone and ask Daddy for money and he'd send it right down to me. In fact, I was just thinking about it when I saw your ad. The phone, see? Kind of like Kismet. So I thought I'd come down here and audition for you instead.

BOLO: You mean like for a play or something? That's why you're dressed like this?

LYZA: Well, it *is* that, isn't it? Come on, give me a chance. Everything I told you was the truth. This is just a job. An acting job.

BOLO: Yeah, I know, but . . .

LYZA: Come on. Go sit over on the couch. Drink your beer, pretend you're an audience, okay?
(BOLO *makes a rueful face, shrugs, and walks over to the couch.* LYZA *leaps lightly from the floor to the desk, seated, her legs dangling over the side, clasps her hands in front of her, takes a deep breath. She plows through her bag, pulls out a small tape recorder, plugs in a cassette. A musical intro flows out. Then she launches into a sweet version of "You Made Me Love You," switching to a bawdier tone nearer the climax.*)

BOLO: All right! (*Claps, not faking it*) Girl, you can *sing.*
(LYZA *luxuriates in the applause . . . the applause she lives for.*

*Bows, does a little curtsy as though she were wearing a full dress, then pulls a natural segue into a dance number, using most of the office as a stage. Ends up back on the desk, blows* BOLO *a kiss.)*

BOLO: *(Claps again)* Okay, okay. Anybody asks me, you got what it takes. *(Getting up from the couch and returning to the desk chair)* But listen to me a minute, okay? There's only one way you can do this job, see? You got to tell yourself, you're like an . . . outlet, you know what I mean? Some of these guys who call, they sound like real freaks, real sickos. But it's all in their head. I mean, let's face it, they're getting off on it—that's why they call, spend their money. But it's not *real,* understand? Some of them, they want . . . things . . . if it scares you, it's okay. Just give me the signal . . . You can see me from where you work, see that window right through there *(Indicating)* . . . and I'll call it off. It's really funny, you look at it the right way. You see the chart? See the name Kitty? Under *S-R.* That's short for Sexy Romance. Soft stuff. She talks so sweet it sounds like honey on ice cream . . . got a whole flock of regulars love to hear her talk dirty to them. Well, her real name's Bertha, and she weighs about three hundred goddamned pounds. Sits there on her fat ass in her house over in Hegwisch, plopped on her sofa, stuffing bonbons into her piggy face. These guys who call, if they could ever see her, they'd have a fit. It's all a game. . . . I know you're an actress and all, but you gotta remember . . . it's not for real.

LYZA: I understand.

BOLO: Maybe you do, maybe you don't. We'll give it a spin, okay? You want the hourly rate, or take a shot on commission?

LYZA: How would I make more?

BOLO: Look . . . what's your name, anyway?

LYZA: Lyza. Lyza with a *y,* not an *i.* L-Y-Z-A.

BOLO: That's a pretty name.

LYZA: It's a stage name. I picked it myself. When I was just a little girl. Lyza Langtree. I always knew what I wanted to be. It has a nice ring, doesn't it?

BOLO: Yeah. Lyza. Well, as far as how you'd make more, it's all the luck of the draw, you know? The way it works, if there's a girl working inside, here with me, I try and throw all the business I can her way . . . unless they ask for one of the regulars. And even if they do, sometimes I tell them that girl's not working tonight, you know? It gets pretty busy sometimes, but, this is a Tuesday and all. Probably our slowest night. Friday's the best. And it's early yet . . . they really don't get rolling until just before midnight. It's up to you.

LYZA: Well . . . I think I'll try the commission thing. What do I do, just wait around for the phone to ring?

BOLO: That's about it.

LYZA: Well, *that's* sure as hell like the acting business too!

BOLO: I'll bet. Me, I never worry. There's always something. I just let it happen. Come on, I'll show you where you work.
   (BOLO *leads* LYZA *into the second room set up next to the first, equally open to the audience. There's a leather psychiatrist's couch, a straight chair, a recliner, some pillows thrown around, and a single Princess phone, white, with an extra-long cord.* BOLO *demonstrates how you can walk around the entire room still talking into the instrument.*)

BOLO: Bathroom's in the back. I keep a few snacks in the refrigerator. You need to take a break, just let me know.

LYZA: What are these? (*Holding up a sheaf of magazines*)

BOLO: (*Mildly embarrassed*) Porno stuff. They got pictures and like . . . letters and stuff. Some of the girls, they read them while they're on the phone . . . so they know what to say. But we got it better organized than that . . . see? (*Pointing to a red*

*plastic milk crate full of file folders. He takes one folder out . . .
just a plain manila folder, like you'd find in a law office.)* This
is the B&D folder, okay?

LYZA: B&D?

BOLO: Uh, Bondage and Discipline. You know, handcuffs, whips,
like that. See, there's a script in each folder, okay? I find out
what the guy wants or, like I said, he tells you. Then you pull
out the folder and you got sort of . . . guidelines . . . you know?

LYZA: *(Thumbing through the pages)* "Ohh, baby, that *hurts*—!"
*(Laughs)* How's that for delivery?

BOLO: *(Chuckles)* Okay. You convinced *me*.

LYZA: Then I'm hired?

BOLO: Sure. We get a call, then it's rock 'n' roll. You want a cup
of coffee or something?

LYZA: A glass of water?

BOLO: You got it. *(Goes to the water cooler,* LYZA *trailing behind
him. He pushes the tap, hands her a paper cup.* LYZA *sips it like
it was champagne, legs crossed.* BOLO *picks up a grip exerciser,
squeezes it rhythmically, a magazine on his lap, watching her.
The phone rings.)*

BOLO: *(Going over to the desk, picking up the phone.* LYZA *is still
perched on the desk, doesn't move.)* AYW Enterprises, how
can I help you? *(Pause)* Yes, Kitty is working this evening, sir.
May I have your credit card information for verification
please? *(Pause)* Thank you, sir—I'll be back on line with you
in just a moment. *(Hits some keys on the computer, watches
the screen, nods. Picks up another phone.)* . . . Bertha? It's
Bolo. I got this Jacobs character on the main line. Okay to send
him over? Right. *(Pushes a button on the phone. A light starts
blinking. Picks up the first phone.)* All right, sir, I'm connect-

ing you right now—have a good evening. *(Pushes one of the buttons on the main phone, watches the lights, nods to himself. BOLO gets up, makes a notation on the wall chart, rubs his hands together in an "all done" gesture.)*

LYZA: That's it?

BOLO: Sure. When it's a regular, all we do is hook them up. The timer runs internally, sucking money off his credit card. When the light stops blinking, it means Bertha's done with him.

LYZA: You don't pay *her* in cash every night, do you?

BOLO: No way—it'd be impossible. See, all the girls, they start out here first. Like a trial period. If it works out, they work right outta their houses. They come in once a week, see the boss, and get their money.

LYZA: Still in cash?

BOLO: No, we give them a check, just like in a regular business. For the tax man, you know? Of course, if they earned, say, five hundred, we'd give them a check for two, pay them the rest under the table.

LYZA: Oh.

BOLO: Hey, come on, everybody does it. We ain't no more illegitimate than your everyday business, right? Your father, the doctor, you think he reports every dime he gets to the authorities?

LYZA: He does! You don't know him.

BOLO: Well that's just fine, Miss Priss—but it ain't the way it works down this end of town. Everybody plays the game. You think these guys who call, they want some sex service on their credit card bill? That's why the boss calls it AYW Enterprises . . . can't tell what *that* is, right?

LYZA: What *does* it stand for? Anything?

BOLO: *(Smiles)* Yeah, it stands for Anything You Want. That's our specialty here: anything you want . . . only it's all in their heads.

LYZA: How come . . . ? *(The phone rings.)*

BOLO: AYW Enterprises, how can I help you? *(Pause)* Yes sir, we have exactly what you want. Candy's here tonight. *(Pointing at* LYZA, *gesturing that she's to go into the next room)* In fact, she's all alone, just kind of pacing around the bedroom. . . . You know how girls get, right? If you'll just give me some credit card information for verification . . . (BOLO *types some numbers into the keyboard, watches the screen.)* Well, now that's just fine, sir. If you'll hold a moment, I'll connect you to Candy. *(Gets up, walks briskly into the next room.* LYZA *is sitting by the Princess phone, back straight, breathing through her nose.)* You gonna be all right?

LYZA: Sure. I'm just centering, getting ready for the role.

BOLO: Okay. What this guy wants, it's almost like a date. Soft stuff, least that's what he told me. Use this script. . . . *(Handing her a folder from the milk crate)* It'll kind of give you the guidelines. He wants a big, busty blonde, got it? You ready?

LYZA: Yes!

BOLO: *(Goes back to his desk. Pushes a button.)* All right, sir. I'm connecting you to Candy right now. Have a good evening. *(Pushes a button, hits the timer. The digital timer starts counting.)* [NOTE TO DIRECTOR: THIS CLOCK SHOULD COUNT FASTER THAN "REAL TIME."] *(Calling across to* LYZA) You're on.

LYZA: *(Picking up the phone)* Hello. *(Double-syllable, sultry-voiced)* Who is this? *(Pause)* Oh Sam, I'm so glad you called. I was getting so lonely, here, all by myself. *(Pause)* Oh, okay . . . well, I don't know where to start. I'm blonde, about five foot seven. I have big blue eyes. . . . *(Pause)* Well, a girl doesn't like to talk about that but, since you asked so nicely, I'm about 38–24–37. *(Pause)* Well, I was just getting dressed when you called. I just have my stockings and garter belt on. I was just trying to stuff myself into this little bra when the phone rang. Just give me minute to get it hooked.... *(Miming the gesture of fastening a bra, holding the phone against her neck. Pause.)* Oh! Okay, baby, if that's what you want. *(Gestures like she's letting the bra fall to the ground.)* Uhmmm ... that's sweet. Yes, I really like that. *(Arching her back, eyes closed. She's still murmuring into the phone. Blackout.)*

## Scene 2

LYZA *is once again perched on the telephone desk, munching on a carrot stick. She's wearing a set of baggy sweats, heavy socks on her feet, hair down, reading a copy of* Variety. BOLO *is facing her. There is a sense of passage of time: the big clock over the charts now reads 2:05.*

BOLO: You're getting pretty good at this, huh? That last guy, I thought he was going to stay on the line till dawn.

LYZA: I told you, didn't I? I'm just getting into it. Before you know, they'll *all* be asking for me.

BOLO: I believe it, girl. But remember what I told you, the later it gets, the more they come out from under the rocks.

LYZA: I know. I know. It doesn't matter. It's a job, like you said. An *acting* job. And I'm good at it. Go on, admit it ... haven't I done better than anyone else, my first night?

BOLO: You have, that's a fact. And they all say, the girls, the first one's the hardest. This is what's happening now. You know, all that safe sex stuff . . . AIDS and all. What some people say, in the nineties, phone sex is going to be how people get off.

LYZA: Poor sorry bastards. They must really be lonely, to spend this kind of money just to have someone talk to them on the phone.

BOLO: I don't think they're so different, really. I read in this magazine once . . . you get to do a lot of reading on a job like this . . . I read that therapy is nothing more than the purchase of friendship.

LYZA: What's that supposed to mean?

BOLO: Well, what the writer was saying, it's like, if you had a real good friend, you could tell them your problems, you understand? Tell them your secrets. You got nobody to listen to you, you tell a therapist. And *they* charge by the hour too.

LYZA: But a therapist isn't just supposed to listen—he's supposed to help you, right?

BOLO: I think this stuff *does* help them. I mean, a lot of hookers, that's what they call themselves now. Therapists, right? Surrogate therapy, role playing . . . all the stuff they advertise for . . . that's just fancy names for sex. And it helps, sometimes. Sex, I mean. Gives the blues a real kick in the ass if you're down.

LYZA: But they know . . . I mean, they know I wouldn't be talking to them if they didn't pay.

BOLO: It's fantasy, like I told you. That's part of the fantasy, see? That you're really their girlfriend or whatever. It doesn't hurt anyone.

(*The phone rings.* BOLO *picks it up. Goes through his spiel.* LYZA *is already heading into her room.* BOLO *tells the caller to hang on. Goes over to the chart, checks S&M with a Magic Marker, walks into* LYZA's *room.*)

BOLO: I know this guy. He wants a different girl every time. One of those "let's meet and beat" freaks. He wants a hard-core fem-dom. It's this script *(Handing her a folder)* And you'll probably have to use this too. *(Handing her a leather belt)* You up for it?

LYZA: Sure. Let's play.

BOLO: *(Returns to his office, picks up phone)* All right sir, Mistress Tanya has agreed to speak with you. Hold on just a second, now.

LYZA: *(Picks up the phone)* Who is this? *(Poring over the script, speed-reading, moving her finger along the page. Hard, cold, domineering voice.)* You want a lesson, do you? Well, you came to the right place. This is Mistress Tanya. Now get on your knees and tell me what you did to deserve discipline. (BOLO *makes a gesture of approval.* LYZA *acknowledges it, but brushes him off, concentrating on her lines. Pause.)* Is that right? I can't hear you, you miserable little creature, speak up! *(Pause)* That's right . . . that's right. Tell me the whole thing. Don't you dare leave anything out.

(BOLO, *satisfied she has it under control, and proud of her speed-reading, gives her a high-five, walks out of the room. The audience sees* LYZA *whispering into the phone.* BOLO *goes into his office, picks up a magazine, starts to read.* LYZA *keeps talking on the phone. Phone rings.)*

BOLO: AYW Enterprises, how can I help you? *(Pause)* Sure. No problem. Absolutely. You don't find any of the girls here drawing those kinds of lines, sir. I mean, people have a right to express themselves, don't they? Sure. All I need is a credit card number and you're in business. Yes sir, okay. Now if you'll just stay on the line while I run that through . . .

(Focus shifts back and forth between BOLO *and* LYZA, *emphasized by lighting and by who is speaking most audibly.* BOLO *occasionally answers a call, switches the lines, taps into his computer.* LYZA *slips off her sweatpants. She's wearing the fishnet stockings and a garter belt under them. She puts on her spike heels, all the while talking into the phone.* LYZA *stalks around the room, obviously speaking in a commanding voice. Finally, she picks up the leather belt.)*

LYZA: *(Slapping the belt hard against the desk)* You want some more of that? Yeah, well you're going to get it anyway. Here! *(More slaps)* Now get back on your knees and lick my boots, you piece of garbage. Do it!
(BOLO *shakes his head good-naturedly. Blackout.)*

### Scene 3

*They're both back in* BOLO's *office. The big clock now reads 3:15.* LYZA *has a sweatshirt on over her stockings and heels, pacing back and forth, a little pumped, but still under control.*
LYZA: I can't believe there's guys like that.

BOLO: You're here long enough, you'll see it all. Funny, we get more calls from guys who want the fem-dom stuff than the other way.

LYZA: Why is that funny?

BOLO: Not funny ha-ha, just . . . weird, you know what I mean?

LYZA: It's just sex . . . different strokes *(She giggles.)* and all that. The hardest thing is not laughing. I mean, it's so silly. Silly and sad. You think they're married, most of these guys?

BOLO: No way to tell. This ain't no survey we're running here, right? I mean, all of them, they got to have some kind of money . . . or credit, anyway. Otherwise, we don't take the calls. When you think about it, it's crazy. I mean, for what they spend for an hour on the phone, they could buy the real thing.

LYZA: Well, maybe they don't want the real thing. You know

how they say nothing's as good as your imagination? Maybe *that's* it.

BOLO: Marcy, one of the girls that was here the longest, she would come in sometimes, work over where you are. She always said she didn't mind any of it . . . like she was working a suicide hot line or something. Only thing she didn't like was when they were mean.

LYZA: Like that guy who wanted to spank me?

BOLO: No. I can't explain what she meant. Some of them, they're just ugly . . . like they really want to hurt the girls. Marcy, she used to get them a lot. I don't know why.

LYZA: What does she do, Marcy? In real life, I mean.

BOLO: I don't know. She quit a few weeks ago. Some of them do. Listen, you get one of those calls, like we were talking about, you just give me the high sign and we'll cut it off. It's no problem . . . he calls back, I'll switch him to one of the others.

LYZA: You're sweet. (*Bending down, giving him a quick kiss on the cheek*) But you don't have to worry about me. I'm a pro.

BOLO: (*Looking at her closely*) Sure.

(*The phone rings.* BOLO *goes through his routine, but this caller obviously doesn't want to reveal his preferences to the screener.* BOLO *insists on checking his credit card before he can talk to a woman, any woman, but promises him he can speak to Caroline.* BOLO *walks over to the chart (the phone has a long cord), points to the word* SCREENER *in capital letters, points to her.* LYZA *nods, goes back to the perch on the desk, takes a long yellow pad and pen, nods the "go ahead" to* BOLO. *But* BOLO *is not satisfied. He walks over to where she's sitting, leaving the phone on hold.*)

BOLO: Look, I've heard this guy's voice before. Can't remember exactly, but he's a freak. Don't use any of the names on the chart. First you're Caroline, that's the screener. After that, he'll tell you want he wants, just make up a name, okay?

LYZA: *Okay,* baby. Stop fussing.

(BOLO *punches a button, pointing to her again. He kicks the digital counter into life.*)

LYZA: Hi! I'm Caroline. How can I help you? *(Pause)* I see. Why of course, sir. I think little . . . ah, *Melissa* is just the girl for you. She's only eleven years . . . *(Pause)* Why, you're right, now that I look more closely, she's only nine. Such a pretty little girl too. How would that be? Would you like to be with her? She's a really lovely little girl, and very, very sweet. How would that be? *(Pause)* Well, okay, then, I'll just go in the back and get her ready for you. I won't be a minute, you just hang on.

(LYZA *bounces off the desk, offers another high-five to* BOLO, *who ignores it.*)

BOLO: I know this guy. He's called before. He'll never talk to me.

LYZA: Oh, he's just shy.

BOLO: You can handle it?

LYZA: In my sleep, baby. It's a role, playing a role.

BOLO: Yeah.

(LYZA *walks off into the next room, swinging her hips in an exaggerated fashion, tossing her head.*)

LYZA: *(Breathless, little-girl voice.)* Hi. I'm Melissa. *(Pause)* I'm nine years old, on my last birthday. *(Pause)* Yes, Daddy. *(Pause)* Yes, I *love* to play games. *(Pause)* I have on a pretty little pinafore. It's all white and starched, with a petticoat. And white socks and little black shoes with straps. And a white ribbon in my hair. *(Pause)* No, silly, little girls don't wear bras *(Giggles)* I don't have a bra. *(Pause)* Why they're white too,

Daddy. White cotton, with little red hearts on them. They're so pretty. (*Pause*) Oh, Daddy, that's naughty. I shouldn't show you my panties. (*Pause*) Oh yes, Daddy. I'll be good. I'm your good little girl. (LYZA *is on the couch now, in a little-girl posture. She makes a shy gesture like lifting her skirt, bows her head like she's blushing.*) Oh yes! Daddy. I love to sit on your lap. (*Pause*) Yes, Daddy. You want me to dance for you, Daddy? Dance and sing? (*Pause*) I'm sorry, Daddy. I'll be good. Melissa will be the best little girl in the world, you'll see. I'll do just what you tell me. (*Pause.* LYZA *sits sidesaddle on the couch, wiggling like she's finding a place on a lap.*) Oh, Daddy, don't make me do that. (*Pause*) No, Daddy! That's bad! Melissa doesn't *like* that. That's a *bad* game. Please, please, Daddy. (*Crying now*) I don't *want* a nice dress. I'll tell. . . . (*Pause*) No, Daddy, no, please. I didn't mean it. I won't tell. It's our secret, Daddy. I do love you, Lyza loves you, I swear. (BOLO *whips his head around at the change of name.*) I'll be good. So good. (*Pause*) Daddy, I don't want to do that . . . it tastes . . . Daddy, that hurts. Not Melissa . . . Please, please, don't . . . (*Loses it, slams down the phone. Rolls over on the couch, crying.*)

(BOLO *comes running in, looking confused and angry.* LYZA *is on her knees now, face on the couch.* BOLO *awkwardly pats her, coaxes her to her feet. He walks her into the other room, as though taking her out of the zone of danger. She slumps against him. He has to half-carry her out.*)

BOLO: (*Laying* LYZA *down on the couch in the front room. A long minute of comforting, with appropriate* BOLO *ad libs here. Finally . . .*) You okay?

LYZA: It . . . happened. Flash. Flash. Flashback. My Daddy . . .

BOLO: It's just a . . .

LYZA: Daddy! (*She whirls and slams her fist into the wall.*) Daddy! Daddy! Daddy! (*Now she's wrecking the place, sweeping things off the desk, screaming without words. She tries to say something, but gags on the words . . . like something too ugly to swallow is stuck in her throat.* BOLO *hauls her away, lifting her right off the ground, wraps his arms around her, crooning into her ear, being comforting, not knowing how to do it. Finally . . .)*

BOLO: Well, I guess that's one freak who won't be calling back. It's fantasy they want, everything going the way they want . . . the way you went off on him . . . Jesus . . . it's like it was really happening.

LYZA: I . . . remember.

BOLO: It's okay. It's over. Just a game, right, baby? A game that got out of hand. I . . . *(*LYZA *doubles over, likes she's going to throw up. Then goes rigid, near-catatonic as . . . the phone rings.)*

BOLO: AYW Enterprises. How can I help you? Yes sir. You want *(*BOLO *looks at* LYZA, *getting it for the first time, sharing it.)* . . . Melissa?

*(Freeze. Hold. Blackout.)*

# Bridge

## Scene 1

*Interior of a Solarium, an open, well-lit area furnished in
"conversation-pit" style. The placement of chairs, small tables,
and a single sofa suggests the ability to have private conversations. The room is clean, with cheery posters along the back wall,
ranging from the standard "Today is The First Day of the Rest of
Your Life" to New Age photos of soaring sea gulls with "Freedom" lettered across the bottom. The front of the stage is per-
ceived as all glass by the actors—a gradually varying broad spot
is the afternoon sun. The back wall has windows too, much
smaller ones. The presence of bars suggests maybe this isn't a
convalescent home.*

*LYZA is stage right, seated in a straight chair at a small round
table, across from a matching, empty chair. She is wearing a
shapeless hospital shift, gazing out at the grounds (directly at the
audience). She wears no jewelry other than a distinctive hospital
band around her left wrist. Her face is strangely expressionless.
Other conversation areas are filled with various individuals, who
converse in pantomime throughout this scene, including entering*

*and leaving. Their age, race, sex, et al., are irrelevant, but the patients must all be adult. A* NURSE *enters stage left,* BOLO *slightly behind her.* BOLO *is wearing a suit, hair neatly combed. The* NURSE *is saying something—*BOLO *is not listening, his eyes sweeping around the room. The* NURSE *leads* BOLO *over to* LYZA's *area.*

NURSE: Edith, look who's here! (NURSE *indicates* BOLO *with her right hand as she walks behind* LYZA, *putting her left hand on* LYZA's *shoulder.*)

LYZA: Bolo? Is that you? (*Her voice is strained, weak from lack of practice. Her affect is flattened . . . her speech is a question, not an expression of delight.*)

BOLO: (*Starts toward her, perhaps as if to give her a kiss. Seeing her lack of response, he plays with the back of the empty chair, finally sits down across from her.*) Yeah, it's me. How are you doing, girl?

NURSE: She's doing just fine, aren't you, honey?

LYZA: Yes.

NURSE: Well, I'll just leave you two alone for a bit. Remember, Edith, there's no smoking in here. If you want to smoke—

LYZA: (*Interrupting*) My name is Lyza. And I don't smoke.

NURSE: (*Patting* LYZA's *shoulder before walking away*) Okay, honey. (*She gives* BOLO *a meaningful look behind* LYZA's *back.*)

BOLO: Sorry I couldn't come before this. They said no visitors until—

LYZA: (*Interrupting*) I know.

BOLO: I was at the trial too. A few times. I stayed back in the—

LYZA: (*Interrupting*) I know. I saw you there.

BOLO: Your lawyer was real good.

LYZA: *(Runs both hands through her hair, shifts her body posture to one more focused and alert. This is subtle, not melodramatic.)* He had to be. The way it works, if the jury found me guilty, I couldn't inherit any of his money. Then *he* wouldn't get paid.

BOLO: Yeah . . . I didn't really get that part.

LYZA: It's really not so complicated. They said I was NGI. Not Guilty by Reason of Insanity. Isn't *that* insane? I mean, think about it. How could insanity have a reason?

BOLO: *(Uncomfortable)* Yeah, right.

LYZA: It wasn't any mystery what happened. I mean, when the police came, I was still there. With him. I called them myself. If you murder somebody, you go to prison. My lawyer said if that happened, I wouldn't get any money. Because you can't profit from murder, or something like that. I was the only person in Daddy's will. All the money was supposed to be mine. But I couldn't get it unless the jury said I was crazy when I . . . did it.

BOLO: Everybody goes crazy once in a while. I've seen people—

LYZA: *(Interrupting)* Thank God for the pictures.

BOLO: Huh?

LYZA: I told them . . . the police . . . I told them I didn't know why I did it. I didn't remember doing it. Just . . . kind of waking up and seeing him there. They were very nice to me. The police are always nice.

BOLO: Maybe in *your* neighborhood.

LYZA: They found the pictures. They didn't have to look around so much like they did, in the basement and his den and all. They found the pictures and that's what saved me.

BOLO: What pictures, baby?

LYZA: Of . . . me. When I was little. With my Daddy. He took *pictures* of it. He had . . . other ones too. Other little girls. The detective said he would . . . trade them. The pictures. When my lawyer showed the pictures to the jury, you could see them . . . change. They were different after that. They believed me.

BOLO: So how come you—?

LYZA: *(Interrupting)* He had a video too. Of me . . . doing things. He was like the director. I was the performer. I always wanted to be in a movie.

BOLO: Hey, look girl, you don't have to—

LYZA: *(Interrupting)* You believe me, don't you, Bolo?

BOLO: Yeah. Sure. I saw it myself. When you—

LYZA: *(Interrupting)* Not . . . then. That was . . . I don't really remember it. But . . . now. You believe me now, don't you?

BOLO: Believe what? You said—

LYZA: *(Interrupting)* That I was crazy when I . . . did it?

BOLO: Sure. That doctor, the one who testified, he said something about a "fugue state." I looked it up in this book. I really didn't understand it all, but he was saying you just went out of your mind. From the flashbacks and all. It could happen to anyone. I had this partner, he served with me. In Vietnam. One time he just—

LYZA: *(Interrupting)* I told you. Remember, a long time ago? In that place where you work? I told you then. When I auditioned.

BOLO: I don't work there anymore. After you, I—

LYZA: *(With an impatient gesture, childlike)* I *told* you.

BOLO: Okay, okay . . . told me what?

LYZA: That I'm a good actress. *(Standing up)* Come on, let's walk a little bit. It's hard for me to get exercise in here. I'm going to get grounds privileges next week. I could have gotten them quicker, but I didn't want to recover too soon.

BOLO: *(Holding out his hand, which* LYZA *takes, wrapping one arm around her as they slowly stroll across the stage)* You mean you—?

LYZA: *(Interrupting)* Survived? Yes, that's what I did. That's what they call themselves, the ones who went through it. Survivors. Daddy taught me a lot.

BOLO: You never were—?

LYZA: Crazy? Sure I was. After that . . . thing happened. On the phone. Where you work. Where you *used* to work, all right? I guess I was crazy then. I went to a therapist. She brought it all out. It took a while, but it all came out.

BOLO: And that helped you, right?

LYZA: I guess. But it just went on and on. The therapist, she helped me with some things. Like, now I understand why I can't stand vanilla. Anything vanilla. Ice cream, milk shakes . . . But she wanted me to do things, and I couldn't. I just couldn't.

BOLO: What things?

LYZA: Heal. She said, you can't heal until you forgive. She wanted Daddy to go into counseling. With me. So I could forgive him and he could heal.

BOLO: Did you—?

LYZA: I went to see him. Alone. He didn't deny it. Denial, isn't that a funny word. Therapists love their funny words. It's not "denial" when they say they didn't do it . . . they're just . . . liars. But not Daddy. He said I wanted to do it. That I liked it.

He said it *helped* me. There was a knife in the kitchen. I don't remember much after that. Except looking down at him and thinking that he wouldn't heal.

BOLO: Jesus!

LYZA: It doesn't matter. It's over now. I'm fine. Real fine. I've been off the Suicide Watch for a couple of months now. Soon they'll even stop the medication. I perform now. In group. And when I get out, I'm going to act again. I'm a good actress. A real good actress. And I can sing too. Sing and dance. Remember?

BOLO: Yeah.

LYZA: I'm glad you came, Bolo. You're a nice man. But I don't want you to come again, okay? I have to be a different person soon, and you'd just remind me of . . . well, you know.

BOLO: Lyza . . .

LYZA: Mary. I'm going to be Mary soon. And then I won't know you.

BOLO: Look, maybe we could—

LYZA: (*Gently*) No, *we* can't do anything. I'm going to do things by myself. You have things to do too. By yourself.

BOLO: I could, maybe fix it, Lyza. Help you fix it, anyway. If you—

LYZA: I won't. And you can't fix this, Bolo—you don't know how it works. Just forget it, all right? You should maybe get that motorcycle you were talking about. Go west, ride some waves or whatever.

BOLO: Lyza, I—

LYZA: (*Interrupting*) Listen, Bolo. I'm going to tell you the truth. A truth I learned. It's very, very important. Always keep your house safe. No matter what, always keep your house safe.

## Bridge

A home has to be safe, do you understand? A home has to be safe. A safe place. There has to be one . . .

NURSE: *(Entering)* Visiting hours are over, honey. It's time to—

LYZA: *(Interrupting)* I know. *(Turning to* BOLO*)* Goodbye, Bolo. Remember what I said.

BOLO: I will.

LYZA: Promise?

BOLO: I swear it.

(LYZA *stands on tiptoe and kisses* BOLO *goodbye. It's a childish kiss, promising nothing. A dismissal.*

NURSE *leads* LYZA *offstage as* BOLO *stands, watching. When the next scene opens, an older, hard-faced* BOLO *is standing in the exact same spot, in front of a different set.*)

# Placebo

**I** know how to fix things. I know how they work. When they don't work like they're supposed to, I know how to make them right.

I don't always get it right the first time, but I keep working until I do.

I've been a lot of places. Some of them pretty bad—some of them where I didn't want to be.

I did a lot of things in my life in some of those places. In the bad places, I did some bad things.

I paid a lot for what I know, but I don't talk about it. Talking doesn't get things fixed.

People call me a lot of different things now. Janitor. Custodian. Repairman. Lots of names for the same thing.

I live in the basement. I take care of the whole building. Something gets broke, they call me. I'm always here.

I live by myself. A dog lives with me. A big Doberman. I heard a noise behind my building one night—it sounded like a kid crying. I found the Doberman. He was a puppy then. Some freak was carving him up for the fun of it. Blood all over the place. I took care of the freak, then I brought the puppy down to my basement and fixed him up. I know all about knife wounds.

## Placebo

The freak cut his throat pretty deep. When the stitches came out, he was okay, but he can't bark. He still works, though.

I don't mix much with the people. They pay me to fix things—I fix things. I don't try and fix things for the whole world. I don't care about the whole world. Just what's mine. I just care about doing my work.

People ask me to fix all kinds of things—not just the boiler or a stopped-up toilet. One of the gangs in the neighborhood used to hang out in front of my building, give the people a hard time, scare them, break into the mailboxes, petty stuff like that. I went upstairs and talked to the gang. I had the dog with me. The gang went away. I don't know where they went. It doesn't matter.

Mrs. Barnes lives in the building. She has a kid, Tommy. He's a sweet-natured boy, maybe ten years old. Tommy's a little slow in the head, goes to a special school and all. Other kids in the building used to bother him. I fixed that.

Maybe that's why Mrs. Barnes told me about the monsters. Tommy was waking up in the night screaming. He told his mother monsters lived in the room and they came after him when he went to sleep.

I told her she should talk to someone who knows how to fix what's wrong with the kid. She told me he had somebody. A therapist at his special school—an older guy. Dr. English. Mrs. Barnes couldn't say enough about this guy. He was like a father to the boy, she said. Took him places, bought him stuff. A real distinguished-looking man. She showed me a picture of him standing next to Tommy. He had his hand on the boy's shoulder.

The boy comes down to the basement himself. Mostly after school. The dog likes him. Tommy watches me do my work. Never says much, just pats the dog and hands me a tool once in a while. One day he told me about the monsters himself. Asked me to fix it. I thought about it. Finally I told him I could do it.

I went up to his room. Nice big room, painted a pretty blue color. Faces out the back of the building. Lots of light comes in his window. There's a fire escape right off the window. Tommy tells me he likes to sit out there on nice days and watch the other kids play down below. It's only on the second floor, so he can see them good.

I checked the room for monsters. He told me they only came at night. I told him I could fix it but it would take me a few days. The boy was real happy. You could see it.

I did some reading, and I thought I had it all figured out. The monsters were in his head. I made a machine in the basement—just a metal box with a row of lights on the top and a toggle switch. I showed him how to turn it on. The lights flashed in a random sequence. The boy stared at it for a long time.

I told him this was a machine for monsters. As long as the machine was turned on, monsters couldn't come in his room. I never saw a kid smile like he did.

His mother tried to slip me a few bucks when I was leaving. I didn't take it. I never do. Fixing things is my job.

She winked at me, said she'd tell Dr. English about my machine. Maybe he'd use it for all the kids. I told her I only fixed things in my building.

I saw the boy every day after that. He stopped being scared. His mother told me she had a talk with Dr. English. He told her the machine I made was a placebo, and Tommy would always need therapy.

I go to the library a lot to learn more about how things work. I looked up "placebo" in the big dictionary they have there. It means a fake, but a fake that somebody believes in. Like giving a sugar pill to a guy in a lot of pain and telling him it's morphine. It doesn't really work by itself—it's all in your mind.

One night Tommy woke up screaming and he didn't stop. His mother rang my buzzer and I went up to the apartment. The kid was shaking all over, covered with sweat.

He saw me. He said my machine didn't work anymore.

He wasn't mad at me, but he said he couldn't go back to sleep. Ever.

Some guys in white jackets came in an ambulance. They took the boy away. I saw him in the hospital the next day.

They gave him something to sleep the night before and he looked dopey.

The day after that he said he wasn't afraid any more. The pills worked. No monsters came in the night. But he said he could never go home. He asked if I could build him a stronger machine.

I told him I'd work on it.

His mother said she called Dr. English at the special school, but they said he was out for a few days. Hurt himself on a ski trip or something. She couldn't wait to tell Dr. English about the special medicine they were giving the boy and ask if it was all right with him.

I called the school. Said I was with the State Disability Commission. The lady who answered told me Dr. English was at home, recuperating from a broken arm. I got her to tell me his full name, got her to talk. I know how things work.

She told me they were lucky to have Dr. English. He used to work at some school way up north—in Toronto, Canada—but he left because he hated the cold weather.

I thought about it a long time. Broken arm. Ski trip. Cold weather.

The librarian knows me. She says I'm her best customer because I never check books out. I always read them right there. I never write stuff down. I keep it in my head.

I asked the librarian some questions and she showed me how to use the newspaper index. I checked all the Toronto papers until I found it. A big scandal at a special school for slow kids. Some of the staff were indicted. Dr. English was one of the people they questioned, but he was never charged with anything. Four of the staff people went to prison. A few more were acquitted. Dr. English, he resigned.

Dr. English was listed in the phone book. He lives in a real nice neighborhood.

I waited a couple of more days, working it all out in my head.

Mrs. Barnes told me Dr. English was coming back to the school next week. She was going to talk to him about Tommy, maybe get him to do some of his therapy in the hospital until the boy was ready to come home.

I told Tommy I knew how to stop the monsters for sure now. I told him I was building a new machine—I'd have it ready for him next week. I told him when he got home I wanted him to walk the dog for me. Out in the back where the other kids played. I told him I'd teach him how.

Tommy really liked that. He said he'd try and come home if I was sure the new machine would work. I gave him my word.

I'm working on the new machine in my basement now. I put a hard rubber ball into a vise and clamped it tight. I drilled a tiny hole right through the center. Then I threaded it with a strand of piano wire until about six inches poked through the end. I knotted it real carefully and pulled back against the knot with all my strength. It held. I did the same thing with another ball the same way. Now I have a three-foot piece of piano wire anchored with a little rubber ball at each end. The rubber balls fit perfectly, one in each hand.

I know how to fix things.

When it gets dark tonight, I'll show Dr. English a machine that works.

# Rules of the Road

**I** made a mistake with the first two. I didn't think about them being black until the papers said a racist murderer was on the loose. Because they matched the slugs they took out of them, they figured it had to be from the same killer. And because they were black, they did what the media always does.

I mean, they could have said they were both men. Or both married. Or both employed. Or maybe a hundred other different things the two had in common. But they picked the easiest thing, color.

Everybody wants to be P.C. Politically correct. They all want to say the right things.

But they don't *do* the right things.

People won't do the right things by themselves. They have to be shown how to act. We have rules. Laws, regulations, codes of conduct. And we have the Scripture.

But people just won't obey unless you make them.

That's why we have prisons, to make people obey. But it doesn't make them obey. If you don't believe me, look at all the men on parole who commit crimes.

I have been thinking about this for a long time. What happens in prison, I think, is that the people learn to obey, but they obey the wrong things.

Everybody obeys something—if you make them. What happens, after a while, the rules change. The higher laws—the ones made by God—they tell people how to act. But the lower laws—the ones people make up as they go along—they take over.

It's like pollution. You can make all the laws about it, but it still gets into the air. And we have to breathe it no matter how obedient we are to the real laws. We all have to breathe.

See, the *big* laws, everybody agrees about them. You're not supposed to kill. Or steal. Or commit rapes and stuff like that. But it's the *little* laws that start the unraveling.

And pretty soon, it's just threads. Not connected to anything. Just floating in the wind.

The Bible tells the truth. It says not to spare the rod. This has nothing to do with hitting kids, the way some of those people do.

I know all about that stuff.

All of it. The Bible too.

The rod is the Shepherd's Rod. The staff to guide the flock.

People are sheep.

Sheep need guidance.

I know I'm not God. I can't make the sheep stop the ugly things they do. Like killing. Or stealing. Or sex stuff.

My job is smaller—I'm just a messenger.

One of the ways you can see the threads unravel is the way people talk to you when you ask them a polite question.

"Drop dead!"

"Shut up!"

"Fuck you!"

Maybe they don't realize how much that hurts. Or maybe they don't care. I tried to ask someone once, but he raised his hand to me. He was going to hurt me just because I wanted to ask him a question.

You can see the threads unravel. Because the sheep have no rod to guide them, they all follow the herd.

That's where I got the idea. I was driving in my car. I am a very good driver. I always yield the right-of-way, always stop at stop signs. I never cut people off in traffic. I'm always very careful, a good citizen behind the wheel. I obey the rules of the road.

But, what happened, this man cut me off. Right in front of me. If I hadn't slammed on the brakes, I would have smashed right into him. There was no point to it—he couldn't get where he was going any faster for treating me like that. When he stopped at a red light, I looked over at him. I shook my head. Not to admonish him, just to show I was sad at his impolite behavior. He shook his fist at me. He was so angry that he got spit all over the inside of his window. His face was bright red. Then he jumped out of his car and ran toward me. I had to go through the red light to get away from him. Sometimes you have to break the law, but only if there's a really good reason for it.

Anyway, that's what gave me the idea. The sheep are even worse in their cars. They don't act correctly. So what I wanted was to help them. With a message.

I know all about guns. My father taught me. He was a hunter, my father. And a soldier before that. He said you weren't a man unless you knew all about guns.

He taught me himself. So I'd understand. When I didn't get it right, he would tell me I was stupid. That hurt worse than the other stuff. Words can really hurt you.

Most people don't know that.

The first problem I had to solve was the noise. It's easy enough to make a silencer for a pistol, but they only work on semi-automatics. If you use them on a revolver, they don't work very well. That's because the cartridges are exposed and the gas escapes—that's what makes the bang. But if you use a semi-automatic, the cartridges don't stay in the gun like with a re-volver—they fly out all over the place.

So what I decided was I had to shoot from inside my car. Deep inside, so the cartridges didn't get on the ground.

But I didn't think about ballistics. I thought the bullets would get all deformed once they went inside the sheep. But I guess they didn't.

So I use a different gun each time now.

I have plenty of them.

I have a very good car for this work. It's a Lexus. A gray Lexus 400 sedan. It looks like every other car, nothing special. But it's very quiet and very fast. And it doesn't make the sheep nervous.

I have taken eleven sheep so far, but the police still don't get it. Neither does the press. Not the newspapers, not the radio, not even TV.

I have been very careful. I take people of different races, different ages. Once I even took a woman, but that was a mistake—it will make it even harder for the sheep to understand.

I only take sheep when they are impolite in their cars. When they cut me off, or make obscene gestures, or run through red lights.

So far, they don't understand. The press talks about a Highway Killer. And they have all this speculation about why it happens.

Some of them even think the killer is crazy.

It's hard, because I only take them when they're alone. The car usually crashes after I take them, and I wouldn't want an innocent sheep to die. I never shoot when there are passengers. So there's nobody left to tell why I took the driver . . . how impolite he was.

I wish they would make the connection soon. Once they understand, the rules will change. And people will start to be polite in their cars.

But it really doesn't matter.

I have the patience of Job, like in the Bible.

And plenty of guns and bullets.

# Step on a Crack

## 1

**W**hen we were all little kids together, Bobby was the bravest. He was the first to go from one end of the Projects to the other over the rooftops. I remember following him, all of us in a line. The last jump was the worst—the wind was blowing hard and there wasn't room to get a long running start. Bobby lit a cigarette and took a drag. Then he threw the pack over to the other side. He took another drag and snapped the cigarette over the side of the building.

"I'll have a smoke wherever I land," he said to us.

"It's too far, Bobby," Rodney said.

"I don't care," Bobby laughed.

You could see he didn't. He went over the gap between the rooftops like it was nothing, soaring.

Everybody cheered. Nobody followed.

If I knew how to voice such things then, I would have said that I loved him.

## 2

**M**e and Bobby were ten then. We were born almost on the same day. Bobby would stay at my house sometimes. Sometimes he would even tell other kids we were brothers.

He was very brave, but he was cruel and ugly too. He threw a cat off the roof once. He liked to set fires too.

Even when we were real little kids, he was like that. You know how kids have their games . . . their superstitions? Step on a crack, break your mother's back? Bobby saw Joey skipping down the sidewalk one day and he called him a girl for it. Joey got mad, but he didn't want to fight Bobby. Nobody did. Anyway, he explained it to Bobby . . . he wasn't skipping like a goddamned girl, he was just making sure his mother was safe.

Bobby said it was okay. He even said he was sorry for calling Joey a girl.

## 3

**M**y mother was giving me cocoa the next morning like she always does when it's cold.

"I saw your pal Bobby early this morning, Jason, when I first got up. He was practicing."

"Practicing what, Mom?"

"I don't exactly know. . . . It looked like hopscotch to me."

Bobby hadn't said anything to me about practicing. I knew he wouldn't play hopscotch. . . . Only girls did that.

I couldn't sleep that night. I know Mom always got up real early. It wasn't even light outside sometimes. She had to do everything in the house before she went to work.

I was up even before Mom the next morning. I looked out the window but we were up too high to see much of anything. I put on my coat and went downstairs. Bobby was there, all right, just like Mom said. He was running down the sidewalk back and forth, but he was running funny, like he was drunk.

"What are you doing, Bobby?" I asked him, stepping out.

His face got all red. For a minute, I thought he was going to come at me.

"It's a secret, Jason."

I walked over to him. "Tell me, Bobby. You know I'd never tell. You're my pal."

"You'd tell," he said.

I didn't say anything—I just walked away. The wind was cold—it made my eyes water.

I heard him coming after me but I didn't even turn around. I felt his hand on my shoulder.

"I'm sorry, Jace."

"I never told, Bobby. Not about anything. Not even about the cat . . ."

"Shut up. I know. I said I was sorry, didn't I? Stop crying."

"I'm not crying!"

"You are!"

I punched him in the face and then he did come at me. I was doing good for a while but he was stronger and finally he got me down.

"You give?" He held his fist right over my face.

"No!"

But the punch never came. He got off me. After a while, I got up.

"It was a tie," Bobby said. "Even up. Okay?"

"Okay," I said. "You want to come up for some cocoa?"

# 4

**U**pstairs, my mother looked at my clothes and asked me what happened. Bobby told her some other kids jumped us and we fought them.

"I don't like you to fight, Jason," Mom said. "But it's good you and Bobby stick up for each other."

She washed my face and put orange stuff on the cuts. She washed Bobby's face too. He didn't try to stop her.

After Mom went to work, we had some cookies and then we went in my room so I could put on my school clothes.

"Jason . . ."

"What?"

"You know what I was doing this morning?"

"You don't have to . . ."

"I want you to know. I want somebody to know. You're my pal, like you said. You know what I was doing out there? Trying to step on every single fucking crack in the sidewalk."

It was the meanest thing I ever heard anyone say.

# 5

Later, I asked my mother. She told me it was just a stupid superstition—it didn't mean anything. "Bobby could step on every sidewalk in the city, honey," she told me, "and it wouldn't break his mother's back. It's just a saying, not a truth."

Me and Mom lived alone together. My Dad was killed. In the war. The stupid war, my Mom always called it. Bobby used to tell the other kids that his father was killed in the war too. Right next to mine. But he told me that he didn't know who his father was. His mother always had men living with her. One after the other. I asked Mom once, why she didn't have boyfriends like Bobby's mother. Mom said maybe she would, someday. Right now, she didn't have time for that stuff.

# 6

Bobby started to hate queers about the same time I knew I was one.

There was a place near the Projects, right near the river. We called it the Pier, but no boats came there anymore.

Fags would meet down there. There were some buildings, empty now. Sometimes they even did it outdoors. If you snuck up real quiet, you could see them.

Bobby and I were watching one night.

"I hate them," he whispered. Like a snake's hiss.

I said I did too, but I could feel things in me and I knew I didn't. I couldn't.

I was scared, but I knew I would try someday.

# 7

**I**t was just past our fourteenth birthdays when Bobby came over to my place one night. He said he had something real good for us to do. In the basement, we all got together. Seven of us. Bobby passed out the stuff we had stored down there: bicycle chains, tire irons, a couple of sawed off baseball bats.

We thought it was the Uptown Tigers coming down here again, but Bobby said no, it wasn't that. We were going to drive the fags out of our turf. Stomp them down to the Village, where they belonged.

We marched over to the Pier like an army. They ran when they saw us but it was too late for a couple of them. We busted them up good.

# 8

**J**oey told on us. He didn't mean to, but he was talking to his girl. The police came to the block and they took us all in.

My mother got me alone in the station house and she asked me if it was true. I tried to lie to her but it was no good. She didn't hit me or anything. She sat down and lit a cigarette. Her hands were shaking.

"I am so ashamed of you," she said.

I didn't care what happened to me after that.

# 9

**W**e all went to court. My lawyer had long hair. Bobby said he was a fag. Everybody said they were there, at the Pier, but they didn't do anything. Except Bobby. He said he bashed the queers himself. Both of them. He told the judge, they didn't belong in his neighborhood . . . they made him sick.

We all got Probation, except Bobby. They sent him away, upstate. I took a bus up to see him once. He was happy to see me, but he said not to come again.

"It don't look good, Jason," he said. "Having a man visit you, you understand?"

I didn't understand, but I told him I'd do what he wanted.

# 10

**I**t was almost two years before he came back. He was the same, I guess, but quieter.

Bobby never came back to school. I finished up, finally. Mom wanted me to go to college, so I enrolled at City. But I never liked it much.

Bobby went to prison for stabbing a man. The next week, I came out. I told Mom first. She was like I knew she would be. She gave me a kiss. My lover was outside, waiting downstairs. He said he wanted to go with me. In case Mom didn't take it like I meant it. But Mom said to bring him up. We all talked together.

# 11

**I** kind of staggered through college, passing my courses, but none of the things my friends wanted to do were for me. I could tell that things just didn't feel right.

I was walking up Christopher Street with Dave when I saw Bobby the next time. He was bigger, huge in his upper body, wearing a red T-shirt. He had tattoos all over his arms. Bobby walked right up to us, taking away all the air like he always did. He looked ready to spring.

"I'll see you later," I told Dave, so he'd leave us alone. Dave's small, kind of delicate-built, but he's got a heart like a pit bull. He looked Bobby right in the eye. "Maybe I'd better stay," he said.

"It's okay," I told him.

Finally, he turned and walked away. He looked mad. I couldn't tell at who.

"This is you now?" Bobby asked, reaching one hand out to touch the earring in my right ear.

"Yes."

"Why, Jason?"

"It's in the genes, Bobby. It's how I was born."

"Bullshit! I seen guys come in the joint straight, and come out faggots. They can turn you into a woman in there real quick."

"It's not the same."

"Sure. I never figured you for this, Jason. We came up together."

"I'm the same man, Bobby."

"You ain't a man at all, punk. Better check your equipment again."

I tried to explain it to him, but Bobby wasn't listening. Finally, he put a hand on my chest, pushing me back a little bit.

"You remember the time we had the fight?" he asked.

"Yes."

"Still think you could come out even?"

"No, but . . ."

"But what, pussy?"

"But I'd still try."

He made a move with his lips like a kiss but the sound was a snarl. Then he was gone.

## 12

**D**ave was at the café, waiting.

"Well, what did Mr. Macho want?"

"An old friend . . ."

"And now he's a hustler, I see."

"He's not a hustler, Dave."

"What then?"

I didn't know.

## 13

**I**t was Dave who convinced me to join the police force. I didn't believe there were any gay cops in the city until he introduced me to one at a party. The man was out, too. Right in the open. "They'll test you," he said. "And some are stone freaks. Fag bashers themselves off-duty. But you'll have brothers inside, I promise."

The written test was easy. The physical stuff wasn't much either. And there wasn't that much trouble on the job. Two fights, one pretty serious . . . but I always try and I never quit. Once they saw that, it was all right.

## 14

**O**ne night in Brooklyn, I was working a radio car with a big fat Irishman named Peters. Everybody called him Sarge. He'd been on the job since forever—he was too much a brawler and not enough of an ass-kisser to get out of uniform and into plain-clothes—that was my ambition, but I didn't discuss it with any-one. We went up four flights of stairs to answer a Domestic Dispute call—the worst kind, Peters said.

He was right. The woman was beaten half to death, but she wouldn't make a complaint. There wasn't anything we could do.

"Reminds me of home," Peters said on the way down the stairs. "Your people ever brawl like that?"

"My dad was killed in the war," I told him.

"There's some who'd count you lucky," he said, lighting one of his stubby cigars.

I only got three blocks before he told me to pull over to the curb. There was an after-hours joint on the corner.

"I need a drink," he said.

"Maybe we should wait till we're out of this neighbor-hood . . . ?"

"Ah, don't be such a fucking sissy—the monkeys make any noise, I'll throw them a banana."

"Sarge, you know what the Watch Command said about staying out of the clubs. Come on, we'll . . ."

"Keep the motor running, sonny," he said and stepped out the door.

I sat there waiting. I smoked a cigarette almost to the end when I heard the shot. I hit the front door. Sarge was on the ground, facedown, blood all over the back of his uniform. I went right over his body into three of them. One had a machete—I shot him in the chest. Something ripped at my left arm. They kept coming. I backed up until I was right against Sarge's body, firing at the far wall where they hid behind tables. Somebody shot back. I ran out of bullets. I was pulling my nightstick when I felt Sarge moving next to me. He forced himself onto his el-bows, tugged his pistol free. I snatched it from him, kept blast-ing away while Sarge barked 10–13's into his walkie-talkie.

By the time the precinct cops came charging in the door, I had one bullet left in Sarge's pistol.

## 15

**I** woke up in the hospital, a red haze all around me. After a while, it faded to pink, and I could see the tubes running into me. I knew I would live.

Sarge was sitting there, next to the bed, white bandages wrapped all around his head. He had a "little fracture" of the skull, he told me, and he needed some stitches across his chest. He held up two lumps of metal.

"They took these out, my boy. Out of you. One from the arm, one from the thigh. You wasn't wearing your vest like a good little soldier, you'd be in the meat locker right this very minute."

I didn't say anything—there was a plastic thing in my mouth.

## 16

**O**ther cops came in. Some people sent flowers. The mayor came by long enough to get his picture taken.

They moved me to a big, private room with a window and I got better. One day, Dave came in. The room was full of people. He leaned over the bed and kissed me on the mouth. One of the cops made a snickering nose. Dave turned red.

"You got something to say, you better say it outside. Say it to me, you think you're tough enough."

It was Sarge, shoving his fat finger in the chest of the cop who had made the noise. I didn't even know he was there.

I made Detective Third from that. I didn't feel much like a detective—I got to wear nicer clothes, that was really about all. But Mom was real proud at the ceremony where I got my gold shield. Dave was too.

# 17

They found the first body at the bottom of an elevator shaft, nude. The coroner couldn't tell if it was the fall that killed him, or the beating. There wasn't any doubt about the next one—his throat was cut.

When the body count got up to five, the mayor appointed a task force. But they kept dying. Gay males, all of them.

That's when the Commissioner called me in. I went under-cover, working in the bars, but it didn't help. People recognized me—it isn't every day one of us gets his picture in the paper for a shootout with criminals. Nobody even tried to pick me up.

# 18

I talked it over with Dave. The killer wasn't working the bars—he went one-on-one for his pickups, got the victims alone, and did what he did.

There were no letters to the newspapers, no phone calls. We set up a hot line for tips and we got a lot of leads . . . but they didn't amount to anything.

Mom still lives at the same place. With rent control and all, it wouldn't pay to move. Besides, she knows all the neighbors—she feels safe there. I go over every Thursday night, never fail. Sometimes Dave comes with me.

I was there when the phone rang. When Mom said, "It's for you, Jason," I knew who it was.

Maybe I knew all along.

"What's up?" he asked, like it was me who called him.

"You know," I told him.

"I'm tired," Bobby said. "I'm real tired."

"You want to come in?"

"No. I don't want to come in. I want it to be over."

"Just tell me where you are."

"You gonna play it straight, Jason? Just you and me?"

"Just you and me, Bobby," I promised him.

"At the Pier, then. Tomorrow midnight."

"Where it started."

"That's not where it started," he said. Then the phone went dead.

# 19

**F**irst Dave didn't want me to go. When he saw that wasn't going to work, he wanted to go with me. I wouldn't let him. I didn't say anything to anybody on the job.

A few minutes before midnight, I stepped onto the Pier. It was empty now, deserted. The killer had scared everyone off. . . . Nobody was cruising—they stayed inside the clubs. Safety in numbers.

One of the pilings was spray-painted with a swastika in white, the number 9 big above it. Nine bodies so far. Whoever the killer was, the skinheads loved him.

I walked toward the back building, sitting all by itself way out to the edge of the Pier. It was so quiet I could hear the water lapping beneath my feet. The boards creaked, some of the space between them big enough to fall through.

Step on a crack . . .

# 20

**T**he door was slightly open. I could see a flickering light inside. A candle, it turned out to be. A squat white candle on a table, burning. Standing next to it, a brown shoebox.

"Just stand there a minute, Jason."

Bobby's voice. I kept my hands at my sides, waiting.

"Just wanted to see if you really came alone," he said, stepping out of the shadows.

"Like I promised."

"You got the place surrounded?"

"No."

He lit a cigarette, handed me the pack. I lit one too.

"Big hero. I read about you in the papers while I was up-state. Think you could take me now?"

"No, Bobby. Not then, not now."

"I bought you a present, Jason. Look in the box."

I took off the cover. A couple of watches, a signet ring, an ID bracelet, a wedding band, some pieces of paper. I held it close and read it . . . a driver's license. A Social Security card. Something that looked like a little, gnarled piece of sausage.

"What is this stuff?"

"Trophies. One from each of the queers I took out. The lit-tle thing you're holding up, that's a finger—the miserable fag didn't have a thing on him when I wasted him."

"Jesus, Bobby."

"They oughta make you chief behind this, right?"

"I don't know."

He drew on his cigarette. The tip glowed. His face was all lines and angles, a skull painted in fleshtones. "Why'd you do it, Jason?"

"Do what?"

"Turn queer. Why'd you turn out like them?"

"Bobby, it wasn't a choice. . . . It's just the way it happened."

He stood still as a rock. I could feel him watching, but I couldn't see his eyes.

"You ever fuck boys, Jason?"

"What!"

"Boys. Little boys. You ever do that?"

Vomit boiled up into my mouth at the thought—it was the ugliest thing I'd ever heard a person say. "Are you crazy, Bobby? Where'd that come from?"

"That's what you do, right? That's what happens."

"Bobby . . ."

"When I was a boy. A little boy, real small, one of my fucking whore mother's boyfriends, he did it to me. It hurt. Like fire inside me. I was bleeding. I told my mother, when she came home. You know what I got, Jason? A slap in the mouth. From my mother. She knew. When I still believed in God, I prayed for her to die. It didn't happen to me, you know. I never got queer. I'm a man. Ask anybody about my rep. The jailhouse or the alley, it's all the same. Bobby Trainor, that's a man."

"You always were, Bobby."

"Yeah. Well, now I'm done. Almost done, anyway."

He walked around in a little circle, hands at his side. And then I saw the gun. A silver automatic. He held it up, so I could see it in the candlelight.

"I was always jealous of you, Jason," he said.

"Me? Why?"

"I wished I had your mother."

"Bobby . . ."

"Shut up. We're all done now. Here's the deal. Let's find out. You and me. You got a gun with you, right?"

"Yes."

"Take it out. Slow."

I unholstered my revolver, pointed it at the ground the way he had his.

"I'm gonna count to three, Jason. Just like in the movies. When I get to three, I'm coming up blasting. I kill you, I'm picking up my shoebox and walking out of here. You got a ring, Jason? Something I can take with me. Maybe I'll take your badge. Your pretty cop badge."

"Bobby . . ."

"I'm not playing, Jason. You know I never play. You get me first, it's all yours. You don't . . . well, another dead queer ain't gonna change things much."

"There's another—"

"One!"

"Bobby, don't be a—"

"Two!"

I tightened my hand on the gun.

"Three!"

My first shot took him low in the stomach. He went down to one knee, brought the pistol up and I fired again, twice. He hit the floor, the gun rolling out of his hand.

I dropped down next to him, my hand feeling for a pulse in his neck.

"You're a real man, Jace," he said. And then he died.

I waited for the sirens, holding Bobby's cold hand.

# 21

**M**uch, much later, Dave stood next to me on our balcony, looking out at the city.

"Good thing you were wearing your vest," my lover said to me.

I didn't say anything to him, just held his hand. Thinking about Bobby. About our last fight. About what he said. About how I picked his gun off the floor. That deadly silver automatic . . . with the safety locked on.

# Stone Magic

## 1

**I** watched her through the one-way glass. A frail little blonde girl in pink overalls and a white T-shirt, sitting next to a tall Jamaican woman with long, silky hair. The little girl's voice was as fragile as spun glass, but I could hear everything over the speaker set into the wall where I was standing.

"I'm . . . afraid," the little girl whispered. "He has magic. He said if I told, Mommy would die. He would make her die."

"He has no magic," the Jamaican woman told her, a diamond core to the rich black coal of her voice. "He lies, child. All evil creatures lie. And a lie can harm you only if you believe it."

It came out slowly—like pus gently squeezed from a wound. A new man in Mommy's life. Not like the father she'd never met, a rogue who planted his seed one night and moved on without looking back. This new man was warm. Sensitive. Caring.

Mommy met the man in church. In a holy place.

He came into their lives, moved into their house. He took them wonderful places: the zoo, the park for picnics, into the country for a pony ride. She loved him. She was his little princess.

It started when Mommy was out working. Mommy worked nights. She was a waitress.

It started as a game. First she liked it. Warm and gentle and sweet. But then the secrets came. Ugly, dark secrets.

The pressure got too strong for her little-girl heart. She started wetting the bed, her grades fell way off in school. Then the night terrors came.

She told a friend at school. Her friend told her mother. And the evil came to the surface.

The man was in jail, awaiting trial. Her mother had thrown him out, called the police.

And every night, mother and daughter huddled together, afraid of his magic.

It went on a long time but I never moved. I'm good at it. I learned in all the right places. Reform school. Prison. In Africa, where a quiet man in a rich suit I met in a Houston hotel room sent me.

The Jamaican woman was talking urgently to the little girl now, one hand on the child's shoulders, the red-lacquered nails like talons, guarding.

# 2

I s it magic you want, my child? I have magic. True magic. Magic I learned from my mother, who learned from her mother. Look in my garden, see?"

The child's face turned. "It's all stones," she said.

And it was. A rock garden, set into a long slab of polished butcher's block. On a miniature scale, the boulders no bigger than my fist, the pebbles as tiny as grains of sand.

"Magic stones, child. Each has great power. But the power comes from *choice*, you understand? Let your soul guide you. Close your eyes, now. Take a stone from the garden. It will always protect you, I know this."

The little girl hesitated. I felt the waves of encouragement even outside the room. Finally, she closed her eyes and reached out a tiny hand, feeling her way, guided by trust. Her hand closed on a small stone . . . it looked like rose quartz.

"Look at it," the Jamaican woman told her. "Hold it in your hand. Feel how warm it is? That is the power. All you will need. And you can keep it with you, child. When you testify in court, hold it in your hand. It *is* magic, true magic."

The little girl's smile was fragile, holding the stone.

## 3

**I**t took almost another hour before they were done. I watched as a police matron came for the little girl. The guard at the desk nodded his head curtly at me.

"Go on, you waited long enough."

I stepped inside the playroom. The Jamaican woman stood, held out her hand for me to shake. Her grip was strong, dry. Like her eyes.

"Mister . . . ah, Cross, is it?"

"Yes."

"How can I help you?"

"I'm the child's father."

Her eyes hardened, black fires in her mahogany face. "The child's *biological* father, you mean."

"Yeah."

"You've never met her?"

"No."

"But you know she's yours?"

"I sent money. . . ."

"Yes, so you did," she said, waving a sheaf of papers in her hand. "For a little more than three years, and then the payments stopped."

"I was inside."

"I know. It's all here. Five years. A payroll robbery, wasn't it?"

"That's what the court said."

"Are you saying you were innocent?"

"No. I'm not saying anything. A little rat said it all, and got a walk-away out of it. I did my time, paid what I owed."

"And now you've returned to your . . . profession?"

"I'm out of work. Just looking around."

She waved the sheaf of papers in my face again, like a talisman to ward off evil spirits. "According to this information, work isn't something you do very often, Mr. Cross."

"Check those papers of yours—I've never been on Welfare."

"No, you've not, have you? Let's see, now . . . two convictions for armed robbery, one for assault with intent to murder. And you've worked as a mercenary, too." She said the word mercenary like it was coated with maggots.

"I didn't come here for this."

"What *do* you want?"

"To see if there's anything I can do . . . to help."

"A bit late for that, isn't it?"

"Not for justice."

"Oh, it's justice you want? Seems to me you're a bit ill-equipped to play at that game."

"Maybe better than giving the child a voodoo story about magic stones."

"You fight the Devil *with* the Devil, Mr. Cross. And it will work. Watch and see."

# 4

**I** did watch. Watched the little girl testify in court, her tiny hand clutching the magic stone. The defense attorney hammered away at her, like a sweating, fat pig, boring for truffles. But she stuck it out—he couldn't change the truth. I was proud of her.

I saw her mother across the courtroom, but I didn't move toward her. Saw her take my daughter's hand and lead her away after it was over.

They looked so alike in my eyes.


# 5

**W**hen it came time for sentencing, the courtroom was near-empty. The case hadn't made the papers—I guess it was no big deal.

The defense attorney put an expert on the stand. This expert, he was a doctor of some kind. He told the court the man was sick. A pedophile, that's what he called him. Said he'd done a couple of dozen children the way he'd done little Mary. A sickness in him, couldn't be helped. But they had this program he could go into, fix him right up. So he'd be okay.

The D.A. wanted him to go to prison, but the judge said a lot of stuff about mental illness and let him off with probation. Said he had to attend this special program. He could barely keep the smile off his face when he thanked the judge.


# 6

**I** can't make up for it, I know. There's only so much I know about life—I'm a thief.

Two weeks later I went into the building where they interview the abused kids. The ladder was in my pocket—a couple of hundred yards of dental floss, woven into a rope. I went up the side of the building like it was a staircase.

They don't even lock the windows on the fourth floor. I found the Jamaican woman's playroom with my pencil flash. The lock yielded in an eye-blink.

I filled my pocket with stones from her garden.

# 7

It took me another five days to find the man's address, watch his movements, get the timing right.

It's almost midnight now. Dark inside his apartment building too—I unscrewed the light bulbs in the hallway. I'm waiting on the landing just outside his door. Waiting for him to come home from his therapy group.

Waiting with a sock full of magic stones.

# The Promise

**I** got a Legal Aid lawyer. Just like the last time. Young dude. White. Nice suit.

He told me I was busted 'cause this is a racist society.

The Probation Officer is this old man. Maybe forty. Tired old white man. Losing his hair in front. Sorry old suit, don't even fit him right.

I told him the girl was riding through the park on her bicycle. She said something nasty to me, so I threw this bottle at her. Didn't even hit her. She called the cops. I was right there when they came.

PO said the girl said she didn't say nothing to me. I told him she was a lying cunt.

PO didn't say nothing after that.

Girl was riding through the park on her pretty red bicycle. Never even looked at me with her eyes but I know she was laughing inside. I said hello to her, and she went past like I wasn't there. Bent over the handlebars, her ass bouncing in the air like she was telling me to kiss it. I threw the bottle as hard as I could. Right at her fucking head.

Women laugh at me like that all the time.

## The Promise

I got to see the judge tomorrow. Some old man in a black robe. Won't even look at me.

I'll tell him I never meant nothing. Say I'm sorry about the whole thing. It won't take long.

They'll probably send me to counseling again.

One night I'll catch one of those bitches alone.

# The Unwritten Law

**S**ometimes it's easy, but this time Joanne didn't even have her clothes off. I sprayed a lot of shots around the plush private office, making sure the first one got him in the back of the head. Then I dropped the pistol, slumped in a chair like my life was over.

Joanne stripped real fast, tossing her clothes on the leather couch, the black garter belt and push-up bra floating on top of the conservative gray business suit. Still in her black stockings, she took care of the other guy, leaving only his calf-height argyle socks.

Head wounds don't bleed much. She stuck her finger in the opening, painted a little splatter on one cheek. Then she crawled over in a corner, wrapped herself in his suit jacket.

By the time the cops came in the door, she was trembling.

"Oh Christ!" the first cop said, looking at the body. "That's Gerald Lee Ransom."

At the police station, they took me and my wife into separate rooms. Read me my rights. I kept mumbling how I didn't care anymore. My wife would be telling them how I turned the gun on myself when I was finished, held it right against my

**252**

temple, pulled the trigger over and over again on the empty cylinder.

The cops let me smoke, asked me if I wanted anything to eat. If I wanted a lawyer.

I told them it didn't matter now. I'd suspected Joanne for weeks. Whispered conversations on the phone, hang-ups when I answered it myself some nights. A motel key in her purse. Expensive jewelry we couldn't afford—I'm a commission salesman and I wasn't making that much. One day I was so discouraged, I came home early. The back bedroom smelled like sex. I slapped her around then, I admitted that. But she never confessed, never told me the truth. The night it happened, I told her I had to go to a sales meeting, but it wasn't true. I waited down the block. When I saw her car leave, I followed. Right to the big office tower. I knew where she was going. She's an interior decorator— I'd heard her talk about "Gerry" before . . . how she was going to redo his whole office, give him a giant discount, get him to talk about her work to all his big business pals. I knew it was a lie.

Was I going to kill her too? the cops wanted to know. I told them I didn't know what I was going to do, maybe just throw a scare into him, tell him to stay away from my wife. But when I saw them together, her bent over his big desk, her butt in the air like that, him plunging into her from behind like a dog . . . the noises she was making . . . it all went red.

I was in jail almost six months before the trial started. Pleaded Not Guilty. Temporary Insanity. Ransom's wife said she knew he'd been sneaking around, just not with who. My wife admitted the affair. Admitted others too. She cried on the witness stand, said she didn't know what was wrong with her—she'd always been like that.

There were three women on the jury. They watched as Joanne crossed her legs, flashing her round thighs for everyone to see. They didn't believe her, the slut.

My lawyer never mentioned The Unwritten Law, just told the jury I was a good man, unhinged by a cheating, scheming whore of a wife. I'd never been in trouble before. They acquitted me of murder, found me guilty of manslaughter.

The judge gave me three years in the state pen. Ransom's wife got all his money. Joanne left town

She'll be waiting for me when I get out. A million dollars isn't bad pay for three years at hard labor. Ransom's wife will pay the money as soon as the estate is settled and she can convert some of it into cash.

And if she balks, Joanne will play the tapes for her.

# Treatment

## I

The prosecutor was a youngish man, better dressed than his government salary would warrant, ambition shining on his clean-shaven face. He held a sheaf of papers in his hand, waving them for emphasis as though the jury were still in the courtroom.

"Doctor, are you trying to tell this court that it should leave a convicted child molester free in the community? Is that what you're saying?"

I took a shallow breath through my nose, centering myself, reaching for calm. "No, Mr. Montgomery, that is what *you* are saying. The defendant suffers from pedophilia. That is, he is subject to intense, recurrent sexual urges and sexually arousing fantasies involving sexual activity with prepubescent children."

"Fancy words, doctor, but they all come down to the same thing, don't they? The defendant is a homosexual who preys on little boys . . . isn't that right?"

"No, it is *not* right. In fact, your statement is rather typical of the ignorance of the law enforcement community when it comes to any of the paraphilias. A homosexual is an individual whose sexual preference is for those of his or her own gender.

Such a preference is not a disorder, unless such feelings are dystonic to the individual . . . and that is relatively rare. You would not call a man who engaged in sexual activity with young girls a *heterosexual* offender, would you? Of course not. The root of much of the hostility against pedophiles is, actually, nothing more than thinly veiled homophobia."

The prosecutor's face flushed angrily. "Are you saying the State has prosecuted this offender because of *homophobia,* doctor?"

"It is surely a factor in the equation. Isn't it true that you personally believe homosexuals are 'sick,' sir?"

"They are! I . . . I'll ask the questions here, if you don't mind."

"I don't mind. I was trying to answer your questions more fully, to give the court a better understanding of the phenomena involved. If you check the Diagnostic and Statistical Manual of the American Psychiatric Association, you will see that homosexuality is not listed as a disorder. Pedophilia is. The specific code, for your information, is 302.20. Homosexuality is present at birth. Hard-wired, if you will. Sexual activity with children is, on the other hand, volitional conduct."

"And they're not born that way?"

"No. There is no biogenetic code for pedophilia. The essential etiology is an early sexual experience—those you would call perpetrators began as those you would call victims. Once infected, the victim learns to wear a mask. They are capable of the most complex planning, often with great patience."

"So every child who is molested becomes a molester?"

"Certainly not. Some do, some don't. As I explained, it essentially comes down to a matter of choice. No matter what a person's circumstances, he always owns his own behavior."

"So, then . . . what does this manual of yours say about recidivism, doctor?"

"That's a good question. The course of the disorder is usually chronic, especially among pedophiles fixated upon the same

sex. Recidivism, however, fluctuates with psychosocial stress—
the more intense the stress, the more likely there will be a re-
currence."

"So you admit offenders like Mr. Wilson here are more
likely to commit new crimes?"

"All things being equal, yes. However, we don't treat such
individuals with conventional psychotherapy. We understand the
chronicity of their behavior, and it is the goal of treatment to in-
terdict that behavior. To control their conduct, not their
thoughts. I am completing my research for a journal entry now,
but all the preliminary data indicate an extremely high rate of
success. That is, with proper treatment."

"This 'treatment' of yours, doctor . . . it doesn't include
prison, does it?"

"No, it does not. Incarceration is counterindicated for pedophiles. The sentences, as you know, are relatively short. And
the degree of psychosocial stress in prison for such individuals is
incalculable. In fact, studies show the recidivism rate for previously incarcerated pedophiles is extraordinarily high."

"But he wouldn't be molesting children in prison, would
he?"

"I understand your question to be rhetorical, sir, but the real
issue is long-term protection of the community, not temporary in-
capacitation. Even when therapy is offered in prison, and it rarely
is, it is an axiom of our profession that coercive therapy is doomed
to failure. No treatment is perfect, but we know this: the patient
must be a participant in treatment, not a mere recipient of it."

The judge leaned down from the bench. With his thick
mane of white hair and rimless glasses, he looked like Central
Casting for the part.

"Doctor, so what you're saying is that motivation is the
key?"

"Yes I am, your honor. And Mr. Wilson has displayed a high
level of such motivation. In fact, he consulted our program before he was ever arrested, much less convicted."

The prosecutor slapped the table in front of him. "Sure! But he knew he was about to be indicted, didn't he, doctor?"

"I have no way of knowing what was in his mind," I replied mildly. "And the source of the motivation is far less significant that its presence."

"So what's this 'cure,' doctor? What's this wonderful 'treatment' of yours?"

"The treatment is multimodality. Not all pedophiles respond to the same inputs. We use groupwork, confrontation, aversive therapy, insight-orientation, conditioning, even libido-reducing drugs when indicated."

"How much were you paid for your testimony today, doctor?"

The defense attorney leaped to his feet. "Objection! That isn't relevant."

"Oh, I think I'll allow it," the judge said. "You may answer the question, doctor."

"I was paid nothing for my testimony today, sir. I evaluated Mr. Wilson, provided a report to his attorney, a copy of which has been furnished to you. I charge my time at seventy-five dollars an hour. I haven't sent in a bill yet, but I imagine the total will come to around fifteen hundred dollars."

"No further questions," the prosecutor snarled.

# II

**Y**ou're as good as they say you are," the defense attorney told me, shaking my hand in his paneled office. "Nobody knows those people like you do."

I nodded, waiting patiently

"It's just amazing . . . the way you predicted everything the prosecution would do. Hell, I thought we were dead in the water on this one. Told Wilson he could expect to do about five years in the pen. And here the judge hands him probation on a platter."

"Psychiatric probation," I reminded him.

"Yeah, I know. He has to stay in treatment with you for the full term or he goes inside. But so what? It's a better deal than he would have gotten in the joint."

"I kept my word?" watching him carefully.

"You surely did, my friend. And don't think I've forgotten about our arrangement, either. Here you are, just like I promised."

The check was drawn on his escrow account. Fifteen hundred dollars. I put it in my attaché case along with the ten thousand in cash lying next to it on his teakwood desk. As agreed.

# III

**W**ilson sat across from me in my private office, his face a study in eager anticipation.

"This won't be easy," I told him. "We have to remake you, start from the beginning. And we begin with honesty, all right?"

"Yes, that's what I want. Honesty. I didn't see much of it during my trial."

"Tell me about that."

"Well, the boys lied. I don't mean about . . . what we did. But about how they felt about it. You know what I'm saying? I didn't force them . . . *any* of them. It was love. A special love. All I wanted to do was be something special to them. A loving, special friend. That D.A., he turned it into something ugly. The jury never heard my side of it."

"How did it start?"

"With that boy Wesley . . . the first one to testify. When I first met him, he was eight years old. And you never met a more seductive little boy, always wanting to be cuddled. He doesn't have a father, you know. I mean, it's natural for a boy to seek love."

"I know."

"And I loved him. Why should that be a crime? I never used force, never hurt him even once."

"How do you feel . . . about being prosecuted?"

"I feel like *I'm* the victim. I did nothing wrong—it's the laws that are wrong. And, someday, you'll see, the laws will change. I mean, kids have rights too, don't they? What good is the right to say 'no' if they don't have the right to say 'yes'?"

"The law says they're too young to consent to sex."

"That's a lot of crap. Kids know what they want. You know how willful they can get, how demanding. I've been around kids all my life. That's the way they are."

"Okay, look. Your problem is a simple one, isn't it?"

"What do you mean?"

"You got caught."

"But . . ."

"That's your problem, Mr. Wilson. You got caught. And our treatment here, it's to guarantee it doesn't happen again."

Suspicion glazed his eyes. "How could you do that?"

"First of all, we set the stage. You'll get therapy for a while, learn how to talk the talk. Then, eventually, you'll be relocated. You'll never be able to live around here after what happened. Never get a job working around kids. But, after a while, you'll be able to move to a new town. And start over."

"Is this a trick?"

"No trick. I know my business. And I'm smart enough to know it's all a matter of packaging. This is America. Whatever we *call* things, that's what they become. And what they're going to call you is 'cured,' understand?"

He nodded, dry-washing his hands, still apprehensive. "You said something in court . . . about drugs . . ."

"Don't worry about it. Sometimes a court insists on Depo-Provera . . . so-called 'chemical castration.' But that's not a problem here. And even if it were, we could give you one of the androgen group, reverse it almost instantly."

"My lawyer said it would be real expensive."

"Oh yes. We're the only clinic in the country that provides this range of services, but look what you're getting for your money . . . no victim confrontation, no shock treatments, no encounter groups, no drugs. Just preparation for how you're going to . . . successfully . . . live the rest of your life. And you don't spend a day in jail. Pretty good, isn't it?"

"How did you . . . ?"

"Get into this? It's easy enough to understand. While I was still in medical school, I realized that pedophile treatment is the growth industry of the nineties. The money's great, the malpractice premiums are low, and there are other benefits too."

"Like being paid in cash," he said, smiling the sociopath's smile.

"Like that," I said, holding out my hand for the money.

# IV

**O**kay, Mr. Wilson, you're about ready for discharge. Our records will show you've completed intensive individual psychotherapy, participated in group, undergone aversive conditioning. All satisfactory. I can truthfully say you're ready to live without probation supervision. Have you made plans?"

"I sure have. In fact, I've been corresponding with a few boys in an orphanage in Florida. You know, counseling them about their problems. I've been offered a job down there, and I'll be leaving as soon as my lawyer gets me released from probation."

"Good. There's just one more thing. You've never really apologized to the boys, and most therapists think that's a key element in treatment."

"I don't want to . . ."

"No, of course you won't have to see them. What would really help persuade the court is a letter from you to the boys . . . just telling them you understand what you did, how you take full responsibility. Like we taught you, remember? Urge them to go on with their lives, and promise they'll never see you again, okay?"

"You think it'll work?"

"I'm sure it will work. I know these people. Write me out a couple of drafts, and I'll stop by tonight when I'm done with the last group and look them over. Then we'll pick the best one."

"Thanks, doc. You saved my life again."

# V

**W**ilson lived in a modern highrise right near the city line. I rang his bell around 11:30. He buzzed me in. The lobby was deserted—the place is mostly a retirement community. I insisted he move from his old address to a place where there were few children around. To reduce the temptation.

I took the steps to the twenty-sixth floor, not even breathing hard. I don't get to work out at the dojo anymore, but I like to stay in shape.

Wilson had a half-dozen samples ready for me, all in his educated handwriting on personalized light blue stationery. He stepped out onto the balcony to smoke a cigarette while I read them through. Finally, I found one that was suitable.

> I'm sorry for everything I did. I know now that no excuse, no rationalization will ever make things right. I've been learning about myself, and now I know the truth. You are the victims, not me. I know why I did what I did, and I'm sorry for all the pain I caused. It's better this way. You will never see me again. I hope you grow up to be good citizens, and always stay true to yourselves. Goodbye.

His signature was strong, self-assured. I left the letter I selected on his desk. Then I went outside to join him on the balcony.

The night was warm, velvety dark. City lights winked below, quiet and peaceful.

"Was that what you wanted, doc?" he asked.

## Treatment

"Perfect," I said, patting him gently on the back. "Look out there, Mr. Wilson . . . see your future."

He leaned over the balcony. I knife-edged my right-hand, swept it into a perfect power-arc to the back of his neck, followed through with the blow, spinning on my right foot and sweeping him over the side with my left hand.

He didn't scream on the way down.

I stepped back inside, dialed 911, told them he had jumped. While I waited, I tore the other letters into small bits and flushed them down the toilet.

Treatment works.

# UNDERGROUND

# Bum's Rush

**I**t all started when one of them spilled wine on Rajah. We were all together when it happened—Game Boys, out on the stalk. We all had our ID jackets, blue and white Celex. Every jacket cost more than two months' tokens, but we wear only the very finest. You can't be a Game Boy unless you can style. Rajah is the leader. He was then, anyway.

We were coming from the Arcade, where we play. Game Boys play video games. Every crew plays something. You are what you do. The Scooter Boys all ride. The Magic Girls do potions. I even heard about a crew out in Brooklyn, the Cricket Boys. West Indians, I think they are.

Anyway, this bum was staggering down the platform. We were waiting on the Uptown Conveyor—we saw him coming. Just a bum. In a long, floppy coat. Bums have no style. We spread out in a fan, the way we do with outsiders. The bum had to walk real close to the tracks to get past us. Rajah was the closest. The bum turned kind of sideways to get past. His hands were shaking. He had a bottle in a paper bag. Some of the wine bubbled out. Red wine. It splattered on Rajah's jacket, right on the white sleeve with the four Tron-marks branded in blue.

Everybody went quiet then. Nobody can touch our jackets. Rajah just looked at the bum with his mouth open. Like it couldn't be happening.

I took out my blaster. It's really just a pistol, a little .25 caliber automatic. Chrome, with a pearl handle. From the old days. We all have them. You have to have one to be a Game Boy. We call them blasters, like in the video games.

I never shot it before. The Conveyor was coming. I pointed it at the bum and pulled the trigger. It didn't make much noise, like a little pop, but the bum grabbed his chest like he'd been stabbed. I kept pulling the trigger, thinking *"Zap!"* in my head, like I was wasting a whole army of Trons. I felt the rush you get from wasting, running right through me. A perfect score means a free game.

The bum fell down. Rajah kicked him until he went over the side, onto the tracks.

We walked away, smooth. Game Boys don't run.

The next day, it was on the Info-Board in every station. The bum who got done. The sensors light up in the Sanitation Tunnel, and the Squad goes out, finds the dead ones. They had the bum's number on the Info-Board. A low number—he must have been a real old one.

Merlin gave me the idea for the mark. Like we do for Trons. Rajah had four. On his sleeve, where you wear them. You get a Tron-mark for a perfect game. Rajah had four—it was the most of any of us, so he was the leader. Anyway, Merlin said I should have a mark . . . for blasting the bum.

Rajah said that was bogus. Only Trons counted. Merlin said a bum was like a Tron, only harder, maybe. Some of the Game Boys went with Rajah, some went with me. It was a true dispute.

We went to the Arcade to settle it. Game Boys don't fight each other, it's the rules. None of the crews fight each other. I heard they used to, years ago, before the Terror. Before everybody lived underground.

The thing about bums, they don't have crews.

If they catch you fighting now, they put you on the Hydro-

Farm for a year. A whole year, and you don't get any tokens for it.

If you kill someone in a crew, they put you Outside. The crews never fight each other anymore.

In the Arcade, Rajah always wins. He's sharper than me. Faster, with better eyes. But that night I was better. I beat him right at the end, when I fired a laser-combo into the Tron breeding center.

So I got to wear the mark.

For a couple of weeks, I was the only one.

Then Turbo came to the Arcade and said he got one too. A bum. Turbo said he shot him in the back near a Feeding Station.

It was on the Info-Board, but the Dead Score never says *how* they die—they just put the number up. So we didn't know, not for sure. Some of the Game Boys didn't believe him, but Turbo wanted a mark anyway.

He had to play me for the mark, and I beat him, so he didn't get one.

Merlin said we had to have new Rules. My mark was okay, because all the Game Boys saw me earn it. We have to have Rules, like the game, so everyone has the same chance.

When we went out on the stalk, everybody knew what Turbo would do. He blasted a bum right in front of us. He got his mark.

After a while, Rajah got one too. Then he got another one. He was the leader again.

The next time we were in a fan and we saw a bum, four Game Boys blasted him at the same time.

Merlin said we had to have new Rules again.

The bums started to hide, deeper in the tunnels.

We got off the Conveyor and walked right into a fan of Music Boys. They all had their boom boxes. The leader, Mohawk, he had his on his shoulder. He had three yellow X's on it. Rajah asked him what they meant. He pointed to Rajah's sleeve. Same thing, he said.

That's how we knew. Everybody was doing it.

In the Sex Tunnel, we saw the leader of the Dancing Girls, Charm. She had four red slashes on the thigh of her shiny black Dorban pants. It looked like lipstick, but we knew by then.

The Dancing Girls all carry razors. The one I got that night told me they don't have to blast bums in front of the others. They use their razors, take a piece of the bum back to show the score.

I told Merlin, and we changed the Rules again.

We didn't video so much after a while. In the Sex Tunnels, it wasn't so much how you styled anymore—it was your marks. The crews split up. People worked alone. It was easier that way . . . the bums would run if they saw a crew coming.

I was the leader. Not just the Game Boys' leader, everyone. I had the most marks.

They all hunted bums. The Deaf Boys, the Muscle Boys, even the Love Boys . . . the ones who sell in the Sex Tunnels.

Everyone wanted to know my secret. I didn't tell them. But what I did, I just went deeper into the tunnels. At first, the Medical Tunnel was the best. All the bums have to go there, sooner or later. I used to take fingers, they were the easiest. But Merlin said it was *too* easy . . . you could take more than one finger from a bum, and we wouldn't be able to tell . . . it wasn't easy to keep count, like with the Arcade.

Ears were the easiest.

Sometimes we hunted in packs. "There's one of them," the scout would whisper, and we'd get close and do him. But when we started to have arguments over the ears, everyone decided to work alone.

Like the bums.

Soon the bums would run if they saw a crew jacket. That made some of the Game Boys feel good, but I saw they were dumb.

The bums couldn't go into the Safety Tunnels where most of the old ones stay. You have to have tokens to stay there. Bums don't have tokens—they can't get them. They can't even sell their blood.

I went deeper into the open tunnels. And I left my jacket at home.

After a while, I could tell when a bum was close, even with-out looking.

Sometimes I went in so deep, I didn't come out for a week.

But I always had the ears, I was always the leader. The Book Boys kept score. They write on the walls. Every day, something new. With spray cans, they tell the story. That's how we would know if someone got put Outside—it would be on the walls.

When I went deep, I looked like a bum now. Smelled like one. I always carried a paper bag with a bottle of wine in it. And my blaster. And a knife, for taking trophies.

One time, I heard footsteps. People coming. The Cricket Boys, running toward me, holding their bats high over their heads. If I had my jacket, they wouldn't bother me. I could have told them the truth—they wouldn't hurt a Game Boy. But I didn't want them to know my secret, so I ran.

I ran hard, them chasing me, screaming. I heard a whisper-hiss: "In here!" I ducked into a side tunnel. A bum was hiding there. He pushed me down, under a pile of garbage. The Cricket Boys ran on by.

"They're everywhere now," the bum said. "They're trying to kill us all." He looked like a bum all right, but he didn't have any wine. I offered him some of mine.

"Thanks," I told him.

He took a drink. "We have to stick together," he said.

I took his ears.

I pretty much live in the tunnels now. But when I come back, I am the leader. It's on the walls. In the Sex Tunnels, I have my pick. They all know me.

Everybody hunts now. I get spotted a lot by different crews, but they can never catch me. I know the deep tunnels better than anyone.

I used to pop Zoners when I went out, but now I don't need them. Rush-rush-rush. More marks. I'm the best of them all now. I don't need Zoners.

I was lying down with my back against the wall, having a cigarette, when I heard someone call out, "There's one of them!"

It didn't even make me nervous. I got up slow, peeked around the corner to see who was coming. I could always slip away.

They came closer. I couldn't make out their jackets.

Time to run for the deep tunnels. They were real close, charging at me hard.

I took one more look.

It was a crew of bums.

# Tunnel of Love

**B**efore the Terror, there used to be what they called Agencies. I only know part of this—it was a long time ago. I know about it from the Book Boys—what they write on the walls. The Book Boys are the only ones who know where to find the Sages. The Sages are so old that they were born Outside. Born before the Terror. There aren't many of them left. The Book Boys, they used to write what the Sages told them. That was when there were a lot of the Sages, but there aren't so many now.

This is complicated. I know it is complicated. But I have to make a record, so I will try. These Agencies, they were part of the Rulers. Not like the Rulers down here. Outside, before the Terror, the Rulers went back and forth. I mean, the Rulers changed—different ones all the time. Not like down here. Outside, the Rulers had many, many smaller Rulers. Little Rulers. They were called Agencies.

One Agency would be for health. It would rule everything about health. Another Agency would be for war. It would rule the wars.

We don't have wars anymore. We have Warlocks, but that's just a name that sounds the same. Down here, the Warlocks are potioners—they make stuff you can drink. The stuff lets you see the Outside. You can go Outside in your head if the potions work.

They don't work for everyone. I bought a potion once. When I was very sad. It cost me one hundred credits. Open credits, too—the kind you can use in any of the Tunnels. I wanted to see Outside, so I could see the Agency—the Agency that protected the children.

But I never saw it, not really. What I saw, it was like a big blob, spawning. Spawning little blobs. Like what women do, to make babies.

I asked a Messenger what it meant, my vision. Messengers don't really know anything. What they do, you ask them a question, and they find the answer. It costs credits to do that. The Messenger said she could find one of the Sages. So I could get an answer. The Book Boys, they don't answer your questions—they just write stuff on the walls. If the stuff is the answer to one of your questions, then you know. But you can never be sure.

I get very confused sometimes. I mean, I used to get confused. Before I started my work.

Anyway, the Messenger said she found one of the Sages. In a secret Tunnel, away from the Charted Zone. Nobody is allowed outside of the Charted Zone. The Rulers do not permit that. But everyone knows that some people go there anyway. Not Outside . . . nobody does that. Just out of the Charted Zone.

You can buy and sell a lot of things outside the Charted Zone, if you can find the places. It's called the Black Market—I guess that's because there are no overhead lights there, only little ones.

I know this is taking a long time. I'm sorry. Making a record is hard. I have to explain everything. They say there is a way to get things Outside. Not people, but things. That's why I need to make this record. For Outside. If there is anyone there. We don't know. I wouldn't have to explain things if I made this record for here. But if anyone from here finds my record, they will tell the Rulers.

I want my record to go Outside. I don't want to go there myself. So I have to make sure nobody finds my record before it's ready.

The Messenger, she told me what the Sage said. The Sage said that Agencies before the Terror were very, very big. And they gave birth. There would be like a super Agency, and it would have many, many littler Agencies coming from it.

It was a big, big Agency that gave birth to the Agency that protected children.

I wonder if it worked. If it really protected the children. That is called a Judgment Question. Asking if there was an Agency, that is a Truth Question. A Truth Question costs a hundred credits. But a Judgment Question, that costs a thousand. A thousand credits. Actually, it is three thousand, because a Judgment Question has to be asked three times. Each time to a different Sage.

I would never have that many credits.

I cannot bear the crying of a child—that thin, bitter sadness that tells me the child already knows the future. That crying is a prayer, I think. But there is no God down here. Just the Rulers.

I cannot bear it. Every time I hear it, I have to stop it.

I was a Charter when I was younger. The Rulers say we have to chart all the tunnels. When a tunnel is charted, the Rulers give it a name, so it has a purpose. Once the tunnel has a name, it's in the Charted Zone. Some of them have always been here, like the Sex Tunnels. Some are pretty new, like the Sanitation Tunnels. That's where the Conveyor takes people who have died.

A Charter makes a record. And he gives the record to the Rulers, so whatever the Charter finds can go into the Charted Zone. I am not going to give this record to the Rulers—I know what they would do.

When I was younger, before I became wise, I thought I could stop the crying by taking the heart that was closed. If I took the heart, the crying would stop.

When I would take a heart, the Conveyor would take what was left.

But I could never be sure. Not certain-sure. The Settlers would always come and take the child after I took the closed heart—the Settlers work the Hydro-Farms. That's where they send criminals too, the Hydro-Farms. I couldn't tell what they did with the children when they took them.

I went there once, to look for one of the children. But I couldn't find him—the Hydro-Farms are so big. And they would get new names there too. The Rulers call this Adoption.

The Info-Board would always tell it—the hearts I took. Sometimes I would see a picture on the Info-Board. One of the Enforcers would be holding the child and the child would be crying.

But I would never know. I could never really be sure that it was a different crying after I took the heart. I tried and I tried, but you can't listen to the Info-Boards—all they show is pictures.

I couldn't really tell.

I had to be sure. So I stopped taking hearts. Now I take the children.

I never take little-little babies. If they can't talk, they can't tell me the truth.

After I take them, I ask them. I ask them myself. If they stop crying when I am nice to them, then I know.

Then I go back and take the hearts that were closed to them. Sometimes it's only one heart—sometimes it's both. Both parents.

But if they don't stop crying even when I'm nice, I work very hard. Sometimes they cry because they are good-sad, not bitter-sad. Because they miss their parents.

I always bring those children back. If they have a home, I bring them back.

The other children, I keep with me. After I take the closed hearts, I keep the children.

I keep them in a tunnel outside the Charted Zone. I found it a long time ago. I never reported it, so the Rulers don't know it's there.

Sometimes, another Charter comes close. The rats always warn me. They start squeaking—they get very excited. They are excited because they will have food. Special food, not the food I always give them. If the Enforcers would find a body, they would take it away. That's what they do with the parents when I take their hearts. I can't let the Enforcers find a body, so I give the Charters to the rats.

Charters are out a long time. Sometimes years. They are supposed to leave a trail, but they don't always do that. I am careful to take them early, out on the perimeter. The rats live on the perimeter—I don't allow them to live close to us.

I move through the tunnels. I don't need a map. That's why they picked me in the first place. They gave me a test when I was a child. After they took me away. I can find my way always, even in the dark. The tunnels outside the Charted Zone, they never have any light.

I keep all the children. The older children take care of the littler ones. When any of our children cry, it is for good reason. And we can always, always fix it. So they are never sad.

This is a Tunnel of Love.

It's safe where I take them. Nobody ever comes here. Even when I am not around, the dogs would stop them. The children love the dogs. The dogs love the children. The children feed the dogs. The dogs protect the children. If the rats get too close, the dogs fix them too.

When the first children get old enough, I will teach them to do what I do. Some will be Charters, but Charters for us, not the Rulers. Some will be Enforcers, but Enforcers for us, not the Rulers.

The closed hearts will never stop making children cry— there will always be children for us.

We will live forever. Even after I am gone, the children will take the closed hearts.

Someday, there will be many of us.

And then the Rulers will meet us.

# Bad Babies

**F**irst came the Bad Babies—that's what the Book Boys wrote.

That was a long time ago—nobody knows exactly how long. The Book Boys write what happens on the walls, but the writing doesn't always stay there. They have different colors for different places—silver for the dark walls and red for the light ones. Blue is what they use on Forever stuff. You don't see so much of the blue, but it goes on all the walls. It stays there too.

The Guardians protect what the Book Boys write on the walls. They protect the truth. The Guardians are a mixed crew— every way mixed. Most crews have only Boys or Girls. Some of them even have only one skin/shade band—the Turf crews are the strictest for that.

The Guardians don't stop anyone from writing on the walls. There's only two things you can't do: you can't mess up what the Book Boys write, and you can't sign their tag to anything you write yourself.

The Guardians are a crew. So they're not from the Rulers. Which means they can't punish you the way the Rulers can. The Guardians can't send you to the Hydro-Farm. They can't send you Outside, either.

If you mess up what the Book Boys write, they hurt you.

If you sign the Book Boys tag, they kill you.

The Rulers don't allow any fighting between the crews. So what the Guardians do is against the Rules. They get caught too—every once in a while, you would see it. On the Info-Board. That's where they announce the Crimes and Punishments.

Everybody knows the Crimes.

Everybody knows the Punishments.

But nobody knows who the Guardians are. And the Rulers never name a crew—all they do is give the person's Index Number and say what they did and what happened to them. If you know them, if you know them by their number, then you might know their crew. But that's the only way you could know.

But even if you know, you are not allowed to say—that's against the Rules, to acknowledge a crew. That's what the Book Boys do that makes the Rulers hate them so much—when the Book Boys write on the walls, they use a person's name, not their Index Number. And when they name someone, they name their crew too.

Nobody knows why they are called the Book Boys. Everybody knows some of them are girls. But not *which* girls, of course. The Book Boys are invisible. That's how they gather the news. Whatever they write is the truth, so they have to be everywhere the truth is.

Whispers say that some of the Book Boys are Outside—the Rulers sent so many of them Outside that there's a whole colony of them. When the Book Boys write something about Outside on the walls, maybe that's where they get it.

That's probably bogus—nobody ever came back from Outside, so how would they know?

But nobody *really* knows—not for sure.

The Turf crews are always writing on the walls. They don't give you the news, like the Book Boys. They just write their names, or the name of their crews, or stupid stuff . . . like saying they *own* one of the Tunnels. No crew could ever own a Tunnel. Not in the Charted Zone anyway. And outside the Charted Zone, no one would care.

Even their crew names are stupid—the names don't tell you anything about them the way other crew names do. Like the Golden Dragons . . . that's one crew's name. It doesn't tell you anything, that name. It doesn't mean they are all skin/shade band 70, like some people are. And they're not giant lizards either—everyone knows the giant lizards can only live Outside, where there is light coming down on you even without the generators. At least that's the way it was before the Terror—that's what the Book Boys say. In blue. If it's written in blue, it has to be true . . . everybody knows that.

The Turf crews fight each other. That's what they do. All the time. You can watch it happening . . . not the fighting so much, but the score . . . you can see it on the walls. One Turf crew will say they own something. Another crew will cross out what they wrote. That goes on for a while, one crew slashing over what another crew writes. On and on. Until, finally, one crew writes something and it stays there.

But it never stays there too long.

People say the Turf crews did the same thing before. Outside, before the Terror. But that's too stupid to believe. I mean, why would they kill each other over something they could never have? That's as stupid as them saying they own a Tunnel.

Everybody learns the Big Rules first. That's because if you break one of the Big Rules, you go to the Hydro-Farm . . . if you're lucky. There are other Rules too. So many Rules, you could never learn them all. You're supposed to ask if you don't know. You can't ask the Rulers—nobody has ever seen one of the Rulers. But in every Tunnel there are little pockets all along the walls. Just little indentations, not deep enough to be caves. Inside there is a person and a desk. On the desk is a computer. You ask the person if there's a Rule about something. They check the computer, and they tell you the Rule. Then they give you a piece of paper. The paper says the Rule was just explained to you. You have to sign the paper with your Index Number. Then your Index Number goes into the computer and the Rulers know you asked.

# Bad Babies

It's funny, the way they do it. If you have a Truth Question, you have to pay for the answer. You have to ask a Messenger, and they ask one of the Sages. You have to pay for that. I think it's a hundred credits, but I don't know for sure—I never asked a Truth Question. But if you ask a Rules Question, *you* get paid. Every time you ask a Rules question, you get two credits. Not open credits—you have to tell them which tunnel you want the credits for. But, still, for each question, you get that much. They pay you, right after they put your Index Number into the computer.

The people who explain the Rules to you are called Bureaucrats. There are lots of them. They come in every skin/shade, but they all look alike. No, I don't mean that . . . they really don't. They all have the same *look*, that's what I mean.

The Bad Babies were babies against the Rules. They were born against the Rules. There is a Rule about sex. You can't have sex until Year 13 if you are a boy. And not until Year 17 if you are a girl. There are reasons for this, I know. There are reasons for every Rule. That's the first Rule—that there are reasons for every Rule. *Good* reasons. Reasons for our own good.

I asked a Bureaucrat about the reason for a Rule once. He told me that was against the Rules, asking for reasons. But he gave me the two credits after I signed the paper, because even though I didn't ask a Rules question, I got a Rules answer.

Anyway, the Bad Babies came from girls under Year 17—so they must have had sex when it was against the Rules, before they were allowed.

At first, the Rulers would punish the girls. If a girl had a Bad Baby, she would have to go into one of the Medical Tunnels and get fixed. After that, they couldn't have any more babies, not even good ones.

The Book Boys wrote that fixing the girls didn't make them stop. They had sex even when they couldn't have babies. The Book Boys wrote it in blue, so it had to be true.

But they couldn't have sex by themselves. I mean, they could . . . but it wouldn't make babies. For a while, the Rulers had no one to punish for that. If a boy was in his Year 15 and a girl was too, and if they had sex, only the girl would be breaking the Rules.

So the Rulers changed the Rules. They are allowed to do that—it's for our own good. After that, if you helped someone break a Rule, it was the same as if you broke it yourself.

But the Bad Babies kept happening.

You can't keep the truth from the Rulers. If they want to know something, they send you to one of the Synapse Squads. They put this metal band around your head and ask you the questions. Then they just look at the pictures and they know the truth.

But everybody knows this doesn't work on girls.

So when a girl would get pregnant before she was allowed, the Rulers would make every boy she knew go to a Synapse Squad. And they would find out the truth.

But sometimes, they couldn't find the father of the Bad Baby. No matter how far they looked, they couldn't find the boy who was guilty.

The Rulers never give up. They couldn't find the answer Out, so they looked In. They checked the Bad Baby's own spray. And that's when they found out that, sometimes, the father of the girl was also the father of the girl's baby. The father was the father, that's what the Book Boys wrote. In blue.

This was a dilemma. The fathers were old enough to have sex, but the daughters were not. And after they changed the Rules, the fathers would be guilty too. But children belong to their parents—they own them. Everybody knows that.

So they made an Exception. An Exception is when the Rules don't apply. So when a girl had a Bad Baby, they would take it from her and put her on the Hydro-Farm. After she did her punishment time, they would send her back to her own spray.

That didn't solve the whole problem though. While a girl was pregnant, she wasn't much good to her owners. Pregnant girls eat more, and they work less. And nobody wanted them in the Sex Tunnels either. It wasn't fair to the owners: the girl broke the Rules, not them.

But the Rulers are very, very smart—they always figure out what to do. The Book Boys said they made another Rule, a Rule to stop all the Bad Babies. If you were an owner of a girl, when she reached Year 11, you had to bring her to one of the Medical Tunnels. They would give her an implant there, a little fan-shaped thing, five lines with a star at the base—it would always be on the outside of the right thigh, where anyone could see it.

The implants work for six years, so there would be no more Bad Babies.

If it wasn't for the Book Boys, no one would ever know that the Rules used to be different. If you ask a Bureaucrat about an old Rule, you would be in trouble. Everybody knows that asking about an old Rule is against the Rules.

No wonder so many of the Book Boys are Outside.

My name is Hexon. Even though a Warlock named me, I am a Merchant Boy. That's not because we buy and sell stuff. Lots of people buy and sell stuff, especially in the Open Tunnels. The Merchant Boys are different. We sell in the Black Market, outside the Charted Zone. We sell anything. And we share everything we get with each other.

I was the one who heard the whisper first—that someone wanted to buy the Bad Babies. It didn't make sense. With the implants, there couldn't *be* any more of the Bad Babies.

I went in the Open Tunnels to check it out. That's what Merchant Boys do—we scout for new opportunities. New frontiers, we call them.

You have to be careful in the Open Tunnels. There's a No-Name crew in some of them. They went in there to hide. The Book Boys wrote that it was the Game Boys who started it. Then the Dancing Girls too. Killing. But not for money, for marks. Marks on their crew-clothes. It was like a contest. They only killed No-Names—"bums" they called them. They don't play that game anymore, but you still have to be careful in the Open

Tunnels—some of the No-Names never came out, even after the killing stopped. And if they think you're hunting them, you wouldn't come out either.

Everybody knows there's a market for baby parts—hearts and kidneys are worth a lot of credits. That's what the Rulers always used the Bad Babies for: parts for transplants. The Rulers stopped doing it because the parts were no good—every time they used a Bad Baby's organs for a transplant the good baby would die. The Book Boys wrote that on the walls. A big sign—in blue.

## THERE ARE NO BAD BABIES!

It's against the Rules to sell a baby for parts, but some people do it because baby parts are worth so many credits. Some mothers and fathers, they will pay anything to keep their babies alive. Some mothers and fathers will kill their babies if you offer them enough credits. It doesn't make sense—I could never understand why.

I spent thirteen days in the Open Tunnels, but I couldn't pick up a clue. Some of the traders had heard the whisper too, but they thought it was crazy.

I don't know why, but I wanted to know. The longer I stayed out, the more I needed to find the answer. If the Book Boys said there are no Bad Babies, it must be true. So how could there be a price on them?

I went out past the Open Tunnels, past the Black Market. Deep into whatever was out there past the Charted Zone. Looking for the crew that wanted the Bad Babies.

I was out there for another three days. I didn't find anything except rats. I'd seen rats before, plenty of times. But these rats were different. The noise they made was different—I can't explain how it was different, but I knew it was, the first time I heard it.

It's really dark outside the Charted Zone except for the little pools of light where one of the traders had set up shop. That's why it's called the Black Market, I guess—it's mostly black, with just little spots of light. I kept moving, using my crystal-flash only once in a while, to preserve the charge. Once I thought I saw a dog . . . just a flash of fur, I guess, but too big to be a rat. Or maybe I just didn't want to think about how a rat could be that big.

I was on my way back when I stopped into a provisions stand near the Rim. A provisions stand only sells maintenance food, like water or freeze-dry. Some of them sell Zoners too— some of the prospectors won't go outside the Charted Zone without them. When I first saw her, I thought she was one of the girls from the Sex Tunnels—some of them work in other tunnels, but I never heard of one working out around the Rim. She was a short girl, only up to my chest. Kind of slim, but real muscular— you could see it in her arms. I couldn't tell her Year—it's harder to do that with girls—but I could see she was a skin/shade 39— lighter than me, but not real pale like some. You don't offer to buy a girl a drink in a provisions stand, so I asked her if she wanted a cigarette. She said No, but she smiled real sweet when she said it, so I started talking to her.

You can't hang around in a provisions stand—they're too small. You're supposed to buy what you need and move on. She went out ahead of me. I was admiring the way her hips moved when I realized what I was looking at. Black Dorban pants, skin-tight—she was a Dancing Girl.

We found a place to sit, just a little past the halo of light from the provisions stand. She said her name was Fyyah. She spelled it for me, because you say it different from how it's spelled.

Inside the Charted Zone, there are clocks everywhere. Digital clocks, all the same. They are all the same, right down to the exact second no matter where you are. In the Black Market, there are no clocks. But even so, I knew we had talked for a long time. Not because it felt like that—it only felt like maybe a half-hour or something—but because we both said so much. I didn't want to go, and I could see Fyyah didn't want to either, but she had to find a place to sleep.

I told her she could have the sleep-tube I carry in my pack. My sleep-tube is a 33-Z, the very best, one hundred percent Raytell, with a heat exchanger and bubble visor. It only weighs about 12 ounces, so I always carry it in my pack when I'm scouting.

"I couldn't do that," she said. "It wouldn't be fair."

"It's okay," I told her. "I want you to." And I wasn't lying.

We found a flat spot a little bit off the ground. I opened it up and she climbed in. I took off my jacket and laid it flat. Then I put her jacket on top of mine and sat down on them. It gets cold in the open tunnels past the Charted Zone, but if you can keep something between your body and the ground you'll be all right—I slept in the Open Tunnels plenty of times before I got enough credits to buy the sleep-tube.

"Are you sure?" she asked me.

"I'll be fine," I told her.

She shifted her hips inside the sleep-tube, moving right against me. It was nice like that. She didn't kick in the heat exchanger, so the outside of the sleep-tube was warm. She left the visor up too, so we could talk.

"Have you been out here long?" she asked.

I knew she wasn't asking me about being outside the Charted Zone—"out here" means away . . . away from your spray. "Eleven years," I told her.

"You don't look that old," she said.

"I have my Year 19 soon," I answered. "You've been out . . . ?"

"Just about two years."

"Did you run from . . . ?" I let the question trail off. Some sprays sell the children as soon as they're old enough to work— that's what mine did. If you run from a work-site, the buyers can stop the payments. Sometimes a kid's spray will look for him to bring him back, but usually they don't—the crews hate any spray that sells, and a lot of them are dangerous.

"My spray," she said, saying it all.

I dragged on my cigarette. It made a little red dot in the darkness. I watched, looking for other red dots. Red dots in pairs—the eyes of rats.

It was like I was talking to her and thinking inside my mind at the same time. They used to have a different name for sprays once. Families, they were called. The Book Boys wrote that in blue. Families were supposed to really want kids for themselves—to keep, not to sell. They were supposed to love children. And protect them. But after a while, they all stopped doing that. Or most of them, anyway. That was the Terror. I don't really understand it all. The Book Boys wrote it in blue.

## TOO LATE TO WARN
## THE FABRIC WAS TORN
## FAMILY WAS DEAD—SPRAY WAS BORN

*Spray* means genetic connection. When people have sex, sometimes a baby comes. The mother and father are not the baby's only spray—sometimes it goes back a long, long way. The Rulers can always tell your spray. From your blood, that's how they tell.

I look down at Fyyah. Her eyes were closed. Her breathing was quiet. It felt good to look at her. If I was there by myself, I would have gone to sleep. Rats can't get into the sleep-tube, not with the visor down. But she had the visor up. I had to keep watch, so nothing would hurt her.

It felt funny, doing that.

I talked to her. Real soft, so it wouldn't wake her up. I told her about the stuff I had to do when I ran off from the work-site. The first two times, they caught me. They know how to hurt you without crippling you. So after they hurt me, I had to go back to work. The last time, I made it. I had to do a lot of things after that. It got easier after a while. And once I found a crew that would have me, once I became a Merchant Boy, I knew they would never get me back into a work-site.

"You didn't have any choice," she said.

"When did you wake up?" I asked her.

"I never went to sleep. I was just . . . lying here. Feeling safe. I loved that feeling. I didn't go to sleep because I didn't want it to end."

I felt something strange when she said that. Not scary-strange, just . . . new, I guess.

"We can take turns," Fyyah told me. "Sleeping. You watch me for a while, then wake me up and I'll watch for you. Okay?"

"I'm not sleepy," I told her.

"Me neither. Why are you out here, Hexon? Are you scouting for trade?"

"I'm . . . looking for someone," I said. "Someone who wants to buy Bad Babies. I caught it off the whisper-stream and I . . . just wanted to see if it was true."

"It *is* true," Fyyah said, opening the sleep-tube's zipper so she could sit up. "That's where I'm going."

"How do you know?" I asked her. "Why would anyone want to—?"

"It's the same crew that *takes* the babies," she said. "It has to be. You know about them too, don't you?"

"I thought it was sellers," I said. "Stealing the babies to sell."

"No, you can't do that," Fyyah told me. "It's against the Rules. You can only sell babies from your own spray. The Rulers can tell. The crew that's taking the babies, it's taking them to *keep.*"

"The Book Boys didn't—"

"Maybe not *yet*," she interrupted, "but they will. You'll see."

"Do you know where—?"

"No," she said, "but I know it must be outside the Charted Zone. That's the only place the Rulers don't have sensors."

"It's . . . rough out there."

"Have you been there before? Deep?"

"Yes. A few times, but . . ."

"Hexon," she said, "I have to go. I think my little sister is there."

"A sister-for-real? From your own spray?"

"Yes! After I ran, I could still keep watch. My baby sister, Fiona, she's still with them. I knew . . . as soon as she got old enough, my father would . . ."

"How old is she?" I asked. I didn't want to hear about what her father would do.

"She is almost Year 4. Next month, in fact."

"Too young to sell to a work-site," I said.

"Yes! That's right. And it was on the Info-Board too. You know where they list kids gone missing? They don't do that if the kid is sold, you know that."

"But if they didn't sell her, they might know where she is. Couldn't we—?"

"They're dead," Fyyah said. "Both dead. There's other people dead too. First the children get taken, then, after a while, the people are killed. Some crew is doing it . . . they *must* be doing it. Fiona is with them. I know it. And I'm going to find her."

Dancing Girls are all tough. They have to be—when they say "dance," they mean fight. All Dancing Girls carry razors. Some of them work in the Sex Tunnels, but most of them don't work. They steal, mostly. But going outside the Charted Zone takes more than being tough. I know. A few of the Merchant Boys have gone out but not come back. Me, I've come back every time. So far.

"I'll help you find her," I said.

She held my hand after I told her that. It was strange. A Merchant Boy isn't allowed to do anything unless he gets something back. And Dancing Girls, they sometimes trade sex for what they want. But in that dark tunnel, we both knew: I didn't want anything in trade. And she didn't trade sex.

We were out a long time before we found them. They found us, really. The rats were bad, but the dogs were worse.

When they charged, I thought it was over. I had my blaster out, a real good one, but I only had four bullets for it. I tried to push Fyyah behind me, but she wouldn't go. She didn't take out her razor either—she kind of squatted down and held out her hand. The dogs sniffed her. Then they ran around like they were confused. They wouldn't let us go forward, but they didn't hurt us.

We didn't know what to do. Then a kid came. He was about Year 6, I guess—it was hard to tell with all the shadows.

"I want Fiona," Fyyah yelled to him. "I want my sister."

The kid went away. We waited. We knew we were close.

A man came back. A tall, thin man with eyes set real deep in his head. He said something to the dogs and they moved like a gate opening. We walked for a while. The man didn't say anything.

He took us to a cave. A whole bunch of caves, it turned out. There was plenty of light. It was warm and dry. And there must have been a couple of dozen kids there. The oldest was the boy who had come to us first. Some of them were only tiny babies.

The man didn't say anything. Fyyah went to all the children, one by one. "Fiona!" she yelled, scooping up a chubby little girl, hugging the kid to her chest.

Fyyah backed toward me, holding the kid with one arm. She pulled her razor free, crouching. I took out my blaster. "We're going," Fyyah said to the tall, thin man. "Don't try to stop us."

"No!" the kid screamed. "No go!"

"It's okay, baby," Fyyah said. "We're going to take you out of here."

"No! No! No!" the little girl screamed, waving her arms. Nobody moved. Nobody tried to stop us. I turned around, but the way out was blocked by a river of dogs. This time, the gate didn't open.

"You can take her," the tall man said. "But you have to pay."

I stepped forward—this was something I knew about. "You want credits, barter, or task?" I asked.

"Tasks," he said.

"Time tasks or results task?"

"Time tasks."

"How much, then?"

"One cycle."

"Cycle? What does that—?"

"One woman's cycle," he said.

"About twenty-four days," Fyyah whispered to me, still holding her sister.

"Done," I told him. I walked toward him, holding out my wrists for the handcuffs.

"Hexon! You can't—"

"Shut up," I told her. "Take your sister and go. I'll be out in twenty-four days. Give me another ten, maybe twelve to get back out. Take the sleep-tube and the freeze-dry. There's almost forty credits in the tube. Bring the kid to the West-Orange Medical Tunnel, get her a checkup. Then come back, in forty days. I'll be somewhere near the entrance—I'll find you."

I moved away before she could argue, but the tall man held up his hand, palm out, telling me to stop. "Both of you," he said.

I took out my blaster, pointed it at him. "Let them go," I said. "Both of them."

"I am not ready to die yet," he said. "And if you kill me, you will never leave." He pointed a long bony finger at the furry mass behind us. "You can't scare animals with weapons," he said quietly.

"Hexon, he's right!" Fyyah whispered in my ear.

"Both of you," the tall man said again.

That was about a year ago. We learned the truth in those caves. This is a family, not a spray. The tall man never told us his name. He didn't talk much. But some of the little ones called him Father, and we kind of got into the habit too.

Father knows the outlaw tunnels better than anyone. He showed me, a little at a time. Some of them run so close to the Charted Zone that you can just *step* across.

This is a family, not a spray. I go back into the Charted Zone once in a while. To get things we need. Sometimes I trade, sometimes I steal. It doesn't matter. It's *my* family.

After a while, Father showed us how he gets the babies. It's easy. Real easy.

Father said he used to buy the Bad Babies. They were real cheap. But now, when the fathers can't make babies with their own daughters, there aren't any Bad Babies to buy. That's when Father started to take them.

When I go back into the Charted Zone, I always come back with a lot of credits. I know many ways to do that, ways I never dreamed of when I was a Merchant Boy. Soon we are going to buy children . . . the ones in Year 8 that their parents want to sell to the work-sites. We'll just pay more, that's easy.

Fyyah wanted to cut the implant out of her thigh, but I wouldn't let her do that. It is only about twenty months until Year 17. Then we'll have our babies.

Fyyah says she knows three Dancing Girls who would be with us. I only know one Merchant Boy. But there have to be others. We'll find them. They'll find others.

By the time the Book Boys get to write about it on the walls, we'll be too strong.

And too many.

Then we'll see what's Outside.

# Into the Light

**D**ear Logan:

I hope you get this. The cyber-link up here is real old, maybe two or even three spans, and we don't have generators like you do. We have panels that store energy. Big ones, too. Most of them were broken, but there's quite a few good ones left. Besides, there aren't many people up here.

If you're listening to this, you know I made it.

Nobody thinks much about Outside. I mean, not really. It was too many spans ago. They say that some of the ancients were born Outside, but I never believed it—people just don't live that long.

It was the Terror that brought us down. Brought us to the Underground, I mean. That's what they say, the Rulers. It was impossible to stay Outside. But it took a few spans before everything was set up. I guess most of the Originals died trying to do it. That's what the Rulers say.

Do you ever think about Outside, Logan? I always did. When I was being schooled, they didn't say much about it. And I got up to Learn-Rite/Seven before I had to go to work, so I had plenty of chances. All the programs ever said was that the Terror was Outside so we all had to go Underground. The programs never said what the Terror *was*, you know? They kind of let you believe it was something in the air. Like chemicals, or even radioactive stuff. They all say something like that—I was only in Learn-Rite/Two when I first heard it.

It's a lie, sister-of-my-spray. The air is fine up here—at least where I am it is.

After I was up here for a while, I figured it out. There is no Outside. I mean, there isn't only one—there's a lot of Outsides. Travelers come through here and they tell us. They come to trade. Some of them trade stories. In some places, it's warm all the time. And in others, believe it or not, it's *cold* all the time. And where I am, it's both. Not at the same time, but at different times. It's about three slice-cycles for each change. When I got here, it was very warm. Hot, sometimes. Then it got cooler. Then *real* cold. Then warmer a bit. Then it was back to where it was when I got here.

The slice is in the sky. You can see it when it gets dark. It gets dark, and then it gets light. Not like home . . . I mean, not like Underground. Anyway, sometimes the slice is round, like a ball. And sometimes it's so skinny you can barely see it.

Things . . . *change* up here, Logan. The Rulers don't act the same way all the time. One traveler even told us there *aren't* any Rulers up here. Nothing happened to him when he said that, so maybe . . . maybe it's true. I'll wait until I see him again. If I see him again, then I'll know for sure he was telling the truth.

I always wondered about Outside. I guess most people do, right? I mean, people *talk* . . . that's one of the things people do.

Talking isn't the same as thinking. I know that now. It isn't the same as doing, either.

There's only two things that could be true, I guess. Because the Rulers put people Outside. They do it all the time. So either all of the people they put Outside died because the air was so bad . . . or they didn't die at all.

If you think about it, *really* think about it, it *couldn't* be all bad air Outside. I mean, why would the Rulers go through all that just to make somebody dead? People die all the time.

First I thought it was a lie. To scare people. Not because of the air, but because the Terror was still there, Outside.

But then I realized . . . maybe the Rulers aren't lying—maybe they just don't know the truth.

Because you can breathe the air Outside, Logan. I know. I'm here.

When they took Cain, I knew I'd have to find out. He broke a Rule. A Major Violation, so they put him Outside. When the Drover came to our sector, he said I had to go to the Sex Tunnels. I was just in my Year 14, Cain told the Drover—they can't make you go until you're Year 16, that was the Rule.

The Drover told Cain the Rule had been changed. Cain stabbed him and the Drover died.

You remember what happened then, right? Cain had to go in front of the Video-Counsel. It turned out the Rule really hadn't changed—the Drover was lying. But killing is against the Rules, so they still put Cain Outside.

The way I figured it, if I just stayed around and waited until my Year 16 to go into the Sex Tunnels, then it was all for nothing. That's when I decided . . . well, you know what I decided—if they can *put* you Outside, there had to be a way to *get* to the Outside too.

I couldn't go out the way they took Cain. That way is guarded . . . because of all the people standing around, waiting to see if anyone comes back. They all want the first person to come back to be theirs. Nobody came back yet. The crowd is big, really, really *big*. I saw it for myself—I went there when they took Cain. Some of the people *live* there now. Just waiting.

I knew there could be more than one way to get Outside. Outside is too big for it to have only one way there. That's when I left the Charted Zone.

I can't tell you where I went after that. Or who I stayed with. I hope you get this, my sister. I hope you are the only one hearing it. But if it's the Rulers listening, then . . . oh, you will never learn the channel from me.

The Rulers lie.

Cain wasn't dead. I found him.

You know what we have, Logan? A baby. Our own baby.

Other people have babies too. They protect the babies. They learned that from the animals, that's what the Travelers said. The Terror only took the humans, not the animals. I mean, sure, a lot of animals died. But their *ways* didn't die.

There are no Rules here. But there are things you can't do. Everybody teaches those things, because if we didn't have those things, we would all die. Like, you can't take somebody's tools. If you get caught doing that, you have to pay it back *double*.

The big change is about children. You can't hurt children. It's not like Underground, even though the Rule sounds the same. In Underground, you can't hurt children either, unless they are your own. Unless they belong to you. But here, you can't hurt *any* children, even your own. You can't have sex with them either, no matter how many credits you have. Not that we have credits up here like you do, but you understand what I'm telling you.

You can't hurt children. If they catch you doing that, you have to go away. You have to leave the child you hurt, and go away. Away from the group, that's all. In the beginning, people say that there was a lot of that. The people that had to leave, the Wanderers, they kept moving. From place to place. But nobody wanted them.

They tried to form a group of their own, but then they started fighting with each other.

You can feel them sometimes. At night, by the fire, you can feel them looking down at us.

Every group has its own code. That's what it's called up here, Logan . . . a Code. A Moral Code. That means, you live a certain way because it's right. Even if there are no Rules to make you.

Some of the groups are called Families. Not spray, like you have in the Underground—it doesn't have anything to do with your blood. Our Family is called the Warriors. We guard other

Families, like the Weavers and the Builders, and they give us what they do. It's not a trade, not like the Exchanges. We do our best, and they do their best.

And I have a name now, Logan. A real name. My own birth-name, and a Family name. So I'm not Rachel/X/188 anymore— I am Rachel Guardian.

One of the old Travelers told us that Outside just means Starting Over. We are Beginning Again, he said.

It's not like Underground, my sister. Sometimes it's cold and sometimes it's hot. There are animals. Big ones, so big they are scary. And some of the groups hunt too. Hunt us. It's not quiet and clean and safe like the Underground.

If our Codes win, it will be a better place than Underground ever was. And if we lose, we just die, that's all.

But we will die trying.

The people who get put Outside are the people who broke the Rules. The Rulers are sending the best to us. Not all are the best, I know. But plenty of them. Plenty.

I wanted to go back down into the tunnels and show people the way out, but Cain said if too many people came out at once, it would be an overload—it would stop our Code from growing.

But Cain's a man, sister—he's my man, but he's still a man. My heart doesn't have a brain, but it knows what's right. That's easy now, to know what's right.

The tape is almost done. Listen, my sister . . . sister-of-my-spray, sister-for-real, sister of my Family, sister of my Code. Listen now: when we were very small we had a game—a game of counting. I pray you remember. You could do any calculations in your head, remember? Please remember, Logan. Listen: remember the time I counted the most cargo-crates on the Conveyor. The most anyone had *ever* counted. Take that number, the number I counted, all right? Take thirty-one and a quarter percent of that number, and round it off to the nearest hundredth. Go back to the tunnel where you last saw me. Then walk that many steps times twelve out of the Charted Zone. No more, no less. When you get there, *stop!* Just wait. It may take a while, a long while even. But someone will come. They will ask your name. When you tell them, they'll lead you to the tunnel to the Outside. They're a Family too. My Family. My first Family. But they're not coming Outside for a while—they have work to do where they are and they need to stay.

Come Outside, sister. Come into the light. We're starting over.

# Warlord

*The only light in the basement of the abandoned tenement is a heavy wax candle, comfortably seated in an inverted hubcap.*

*A radio is tuned low—only the throbbing bass line from a streetcorner a cappella group comes through. Six boys in the basement, sprawled on ragged armchairs, sitting on boxes, lying on a tattered carpet. Except for their leader, who is pacing before them, talking urgently.*

TONY: Summer's comin'. We got to do somethin' soon or we go under. Just like that. We can't keep tryin' to operate by ourselves out on these streets. The Counts gonna be the damn *no*-counts soon.

RIX: So what we suppose to do, bright boy? Tell the Golden Dragons we all ready to let them join *us?*

TONY: Man, shut the fuck up! I told you before, Rix. The only reason we still alive at all is 'cause of my brains, not your mouth.

RIX: You act like you King Shit or somethin' just 'cause we stayed safe so far. Just keep talkin' . . . I'll show you who's King Shit.

MANNY: Rix! Shut up, punk, or I shut you up.

BILLY: Don't fight, Tony. We not suppose to fight each other, right? Ain't that what you always say?

TONY: *(Wearily)* Yeah, you right, Billy. You said the right thing.

BILLY: Thanks, Tony!

POET: My people tole me today they was gonna move away from the block. 'Cause it's too mean around here now. So mebbe I won't have this problem soon anyway.

MANNY: Listen, motherfucker, you with us from jump, you with us all the way.

POET: Oh yeah, man. I mean, I wasn't talkin' about punking out or nothin'. Just if my people move, then what I'm suppose to do?

TONY: You worry about that if they do move . . . *if* they do. You know they can't go no place without the fuckin' Welfare says it's okay.

POET: I know.

TONY: We can't keep this up. We can't be the only club in this fuckin' city with only six men. We got no protection from the Black Barons this way . . . we be sittin' ducks if they go down on us. And we live too damn close to their turf. We got to figure a way to join up with the Golden Dragons before school is finished for the year. Otherwise, this summer, we be finished.

RIX: We could do just fuckin' fine, I had me some fire sticks. Niggers roll on us, I could blow them to the moon.

MANNY: That's right, punk. You a real mean hombre. You gonna blow eighty men away all by yourself, right?

RIX: (*Resentfully, but out of steam*) I got the balls.

MANNY: Better keep your mouth shut, man. I not playin' like Big Brain here (*indicating* TONY) and I cut you open for one more fuckin' word.
(*Silence*)

TONY: That Peace Treaty I signed with the Dragons ain't good enough. They willin' not to jump on us 'cause they got trouble with the niggers . . . but they won't do nothin' to help us out if the Barons fuck with us, see? And we can't even hold the debs this way . . . no women, no power, not even a fuckin' clubhouse 'cause we afraid of a raid!

RIX: We got to do somethin', make 'em see we got lotta heart, make 'em know we alive.

TONY: For once you right, man. We got to make it like the Dragons think it good policy to let us join. Okay, so I don't be President and you don't be Warlord and shit . . . but we be safe . . . and mebbe we move up inside the organization . . . you know, play it cool and stick together even when we inside. And I know just what we can do to put us on the map.

BILLY: Tell me what it is, Tony. Tell me what it is and I do it for us.

TONY: You a good man, Billy. The fuckin' best! But this is somethin' for the whole club . . . for all of us together. We gonna take off that fat fuckin' cop who thinks he's a social worker. Anderson the cop, man. We gonna burn him right in this alley and burn him so the whole fuckin' neighborhood knows the Counts have the most heart of anyone out here.

POET: You fuckin' crazy, man? Burn a cop and we don't even got a real gun . . . just a couple of lousy zips what don't even work and not even a bullet for them!

PRINCE: It's a good idea, Tony, but the Poet-man is right. How we gonna do somethin' like that and not go down behind it ourselves?

TONY: Manny, you said you put one of the niggers on the other side down for good one time, right? When we went to the institution?

MANNY: (*As if expecting a challenge*) That's right!

TONY: That's the answer right there. Manny's blade and Billy and Prince for the pipes. Rix can use the one good zip—I got a bullet from The Dealer yesterday.

RIX: You mean just burn him when he walks by the alley at night?

TONY: No good, man. That's nothin' but a fuckin' ambush and that means we still ain't nothin'. Just a Jap outfit. No good. We gonna do this before it gets dark. Face to face. I want to watch that cocksucker die.

BILLY: What if we get caught?

TONY: I never lie to you, right, Billy? And I swear we don't get caught if we stick together and do like I say.

BILLY: Okay.

TONY: Listen. I got a plan worked out in my mind and I tell you and then we take a vote. . . .

CHORUS: Let's fuckin' hear it. Run it, man.

TONY: You know how the alley makes a kinda T? Dead-end on three sides? Okay, we set up there like usual and Poet brings his portable radio. We put it on top of one of those old packing crates. Pile 'em up real high at the back of the alley. Now Anderson usually rolls up around nine, right? So we set up back in the alley, just jivin' around, and we keep turning the radio up real loud so people scream down at us to cool it. So they all get the idea we gonna be doing this all night and don't get surprised when the radio gets real loud again. Manny and Billy and Prince all lay up in the back.

Me and Rix be up in the front and we get Anderson rappin' about how we wished we had us a Youth Board worker all our own instead of that faggot Bernstein who only comes 'round once in a while. Then we act like we scared . . . like we boosted something too big for us to fence and we wanna turn it into him so's we don't get in no trouble, see? Rix has the zip. We walk Anderson to the back. Prince turns up the radio. Loud. And we walk past the big crate. Manny shanks him in the back and Billy smashes his fuckin' head with the pipe. And then Rix . . . burns him.

Nobody hear the zip over the radio and if they do they don't do nothin' anyway. We shove him under the crate and then we split. Poet is all the time watchin' the front and he yells back to cool it if anyone rolls up. Then we walk out the front like nothin' happen and the zip goes through the window into the basement here. Then the word gets around fast! The Counts burned a fuckin' headbreaker.

See, first we use a couple a days . . . spread the word around school that Anderson is fuckin' with us . . . messing in our business you know? Then, when he goes down, the Counts go up. We have a rep. A *name*. The Dragons fuckin' *beg* us to join them. We be the first in the neighborhood to burn a cop. Nobody sees, but everybody knows. Now I say we vote.

RIX: It's still pretty dangerous . . .

MANNY: Pussy!

RIX: I got as much heart as you, spic!

MANNY: I guess so—you willin' to die for your mouth. (*Reaching in his jacket pocket*).

TONY: Manny, no! Come on, brother. We all need each other right now. Rix didn't mean nothin'. We don't stick together, we get stuck. Now, vote, motherfuckers!

MANNY: I'm in.

RIX: Yeah, me too. I was only . . .

BILLY: If you say so, I do it, Tony.

POET: All right.

PRINCE: I go with the President.

TONY: (*Looking around*) Okay that's it. Now we go to school tomorrow. All of us. And we spread the word, cool. *Cool,* Rix! But we let the Dragons know that the Counts be ready to make their big move real soon.
*Three nights later. The boys have been in the alley since seven* P.M. *Waiting.*

POET: What if he don't show?

TONY: He'll show. The stinkin' headbreaker never miss his chance to be a motherfucking preacher.

RIX: I'm ready. The whole street knows he's gonna die. I hope nobody tip him off.

TONY: You crazy? 'Round here, even the niggers want a cop to die.
PATROLMAN ANDERSON *approaches the alley, swinging his nightstick. He is tall and confident, with a hearty manner too old for his years.*

ANDERSON: How's things, men?

TONY: How they suppose to be? You want to do us a favor, give us some police cannons so's we can protect ourselves from the Black Barons.

ANDERSON: (*Snide*) There hasn't been any trouble between the *big* clubs for a long time now.

TONY: Yeah, we know we ain't no big club, man. And we got nothin' goin' for us when the niggers make they move.

ANDERSON: Maybe you boys want to join up with the Golden Dragons? They got a full-time Youth Board worker now and a clubhouse. They don't even bop so much anymore. They got a basketball team, they put on dances and everything.

(POET's *eyes flash hope. It dies when* RIX *speaks.*)

RIX: Oh yeah, man. Where do we get an application?

ANDERSON: (*Seriously*) I can speak with Lacey. He's even getting a salary now from the anti-poverty people and I think he'd let you all join . . . except maybe Manny.

RIX: What's wrong with Manny? He's got heart, man.

ANDERSON: All he's got is a switchblade. Take that away from him and he's a punk without an ounce of guts to his name.

TONY: Yeah, well, listen, Anderson. We got other troubles, man. The boys copped something and we don't know what to do with it. I mean, we can't just peddle this stuff, you know what I mean?

ANDERSON: (*Interested*) Where is it?

TONY: We got it stashed behind a crate in the back, man. Come on, I'll show you.

ANDERSON: (*Confidently*) I'm sure we can work this out.
(*They walk toward the back:* TONY *leading the way,* ANDERSON *following,* RIX *close behind.* POET *stays at the alley's mouth.* TONY *whirls to face* ANDERSON.)

TONY: Okay, cop. Here's somethin' I wanted to tell you, but I didn't want to shout it out up front.

ANDERSON: (*Impatiently*) Well, what is it?

*(The radio is turned up full blast.* MANNY *steps from behind the crates and rams his blade into* ANDERSON's *back as* BILLY *brings his lead pipe down on the cop's skull.* ANDERSON *goes down without a sound.* PRINCE *drops to his knees, holding his own lead pipe in two hands, clubbing* ANDERSON *across the chest.* RIX's *hands are shaking—he shoves the zip gun into* ANDERSON's *mouth and jerks the trigger. There is a soft* pop! *and* ANDERSON's *head jerks in a final spasm.* BILLY *and* RIX *grab the cop's legs and drag him deeper into the alley as* MANNY *tips over the largest crate. They shove him underneath.* RIX *is still holding the bloody zip gun.* TONY *grabs it from his hands and throws it through the opened basement window. The radio blasts. The killing-sounds remain trapped in the alley.* TONY *runs to the front, calling to* POET.*)*

TONY:   We gonna split, man. It's done. Go back and pick up the zip, like we said. Later!

*(*POET *is already moving toward the back of the alley, bringing his radio.* MANNY *has faded into the basement shadows.* PRINCE, BILLY, RIX, *and* TONY *walk together to the corner, where they go their separate ways.)*

*The next morning.*

*All the boys except* MANNY *and* BILLY *are still pumped up on last night's blood.*

TONY:   We don't want to walk into school together, but we get together inside, right? Rix, stash that weed, man . . . I can smell it from here. You don't need to be nervous man, it went perfect.

RIX:  I ain't nervous, man. Just a little smoke to celebrate.

TONY:   Billy, you stay by me today. See the rest of you men in the shop later.

*Shop Class. The word has spread and* TONY *is waiting for the approach.*

*(*LACEY, *the leader of the Golden Dragons, slides in next to him.)*

# Warlord

LACEY: Hey, brother, is it true what I been hearing?

TONY: Yeah, man. The Counts took too much shit from that roller. And you can't take shit when you small or the other clubs . . . you know, the nigger clubs . . . man, they go down on us and we get blown out.

LACEY: Mebbe you thinkin' about joining us?

TONY: Well, we did, man. But we heard you all was going a bit sporty, like no more boppin' when the Youth Board faggot says and all like that . . .

LACEY: (*Quietly*) Watch your mouth, man.

TONY: Brother, I'm glad to hear you talk like that. Sure, we all knew it was a bullshit rep they was layin' on you. Man, we proud to join a true fighting club. We get together, straighten the niggers right out, right?

LACEY: (*Mollified*) Yeah, baby. Where's your boys now?

TONY: Manny is out of school, man. Billy and Poet are over near the printing press, and Prince is on my right hand here.

LACEY: Give me skin, Poet, you all right!

POET: My pleasure, President.

LACEY: Hey! You swift, baby. Looks like you got prime boys, Tony.

TONY: The best. Rix just rolled in. He's by the tool chest. Hey! Isn't that Priest of the Black Barons?

LACEY: Yeah. The fuckin' nigger thinks he's bad shit. Only reason we don't jump him before this is 'cause we don't waste our time with nothing less than an all-out. Anyway, boppin' in school is no fuckin' good—we lose that anti-poverty green behind shit like that . . .

(PRIEST *is cleaning a linoleum-block print with a white rag, singing softly to himself.* RIX *walks past and brushes against him.* PRIEST *looks up, catches* RIX's *eye, says nothing.* RIX *wheels around, loud.)*

RIX:  Motherfucker, watch where you put your feet!

PRIEST:  You talkin' to me, paddy?

RIX:  You heard me, nigger!

PRIEST:  *(Not raising his voice, flat-toned)* Outside. After school. You and me.

RIX:  *(Contemptuous)* I'll be there, punk.
   PRIEST's *boys move in fast and* RIX *is quickly surrounded. He backs against the printing press, watching hands reach into pockets. The scene freezes.*

LACEY:  Dragons!
   *Other boys drop their work and move toward the printing press, reaching for the kind of instant weapons you find in shop class. About thirty boys are milling around, waiting for the match to hit the gasoline, when the* SHOP TEACHER *jumps in the middle.*

TEACHER:  Get back where you came from you punk bastards! I'm warning you, one fucking move and I call the cops. This is the last damn time I'm telling you . . . move!

   *The groups part. Hands return to pockets.* PRIEST *walks up to* LACEY.

PRIEST:  That paddy-punk one of your boys, huh? Want to make it an all-out tonight?

LACEY:  Whatsamatter, boy? Afraid to go up against the man who burned the heat?

PRIEST:  Be outside after school. We see who burns who. And maybe I see you afterward.

LACEY: I'll be there.

*The schoolyard looks like the recreation yard in any maximum-security prison: high fence, blacktop, slit-window buildings. About seventy boys are on each side of the yard, waiting for the gladiators.*

LACEY: How you want it, fair one?

PRIEST: Okay by me. I don't need a blade for that punk.

MANNY *and* RIX *are off to one side, whispering.*

MANNY: Take this, man. (*He shows a steel can-opener, flattened at one end and sharpened so that it glints in the faint light*). I tape this to your wrist—you slice him when you get in close.

RIX: Man, I don't need that. I kill the nigger with my bare hands. Kill him like I killed that fuckin' cop.

MANNY: Rix, that is Priest of the Black Barons! He is a stone vicious killer, brother. I know for a fact he's killed four men. You take this, man, or you're dead.

RIX: Yeah. Yeah, okay . . . just for insurance.

TONY: Happy nigger-hunting, man!

LACEY: You take Priest and you next Warlord of the Golden Dragons!

POET: Go, man. Kill the motherfucker!

(*They circle slowly,* PRIEST *the confident veteran of a hundred such battles. The Dragons scream encouragement at* RIX—*the Barons beat a heavy silent tattoo with their minds, disciplined.* PRIEST *feints with a left hook and catches* RIX *with a kick to the groin.* RIX *hits the ground and* PRIEST *dropkicks him in the face.* RIX *rolls away and comes up throwing a handful of pebbles and dirt.* PRIEST *fakes backing off, then suddenly moves in, drops his shoulder and drives a straight right hand to* RIX's *head.*

RIX *throws up his hands to protect his face and* PRIEST *is all over him with heavy, driving punches.* RIX *gives ground, not returning the fire. His nose is squashed flat on his face and his eyes are glazed.*

PRIEST *slams a fist into* RIX's *stomach, watches him double over, and steps back like an artist admiring his work.* RIX *feels the slippery steel at his wrist and lets it fall into his cupped hand. He pulls back his right foot, drops to one knee.)*

PRIEST: You down on your knees for me, paddy-boy? You wanna suck some good black cock?

RIX: *(A dead man's voice)* Come on, nigger. Just come on.
*(*PRIEST *charges and the steel spike whips like a jet from around* RIX's *knees . . . catches* PRIEST *full in the face and slices his cheek off like raw meat. A slab of flesh flies away and lands at the feet of the assembled Dragons.* PRIEST *is down on the ground rolling with his face in the dirt, screaming. Blood and white muscle tissue foam up between his clenched hands. The Barons all reach for their weapons.* RIX *stares fixated at* PRIEST *on the ground before him. He slowly climbs to his feet.* PRIEST *struggles to his knees to face him. He pulls his hands from his face with an effort of will. One eye lies on the blacktop next to him. His voice comes from the grave.)*

PRIEST: You dead.
*(Police sirens split the air and the gangs turn to run.* MANNY *bends and picks up* PRIEST's *eyeball. He walks over to* RIX.*)*

MANNY: This is yours, man. You earned it. I told you you needed the blade, right, baby?

RIX: *(Dazed, pocketing the eyeball)* Yeah, Manny. Thanks. You all right, brother.

LACEY: Tony, come to our clubhouse tonight . . . and bring your boys. And Rix, man, you got heart to spare. You my man. Later!

*That night. The clubhouse of the Golden Dragons, a seven-room apartment on the sixth (top) floor.*

(TONY *and* BILLY *are the first to arrive from the Counts.* LACEY *motions him over to a quiet corner.*)

LACEY: Listen, Tony, you want to be with us permanent, right?

TONY: Yeah, man. We proved that, I think.

LACEY: You surely did, brother. You a natural leader. But I got to talk somethin' over with you. The Black Barons sent The Messenger over to see us. Earlier. Before you got here. They not fuckin' around this time. They got the Egyptian Kings and the Harlem Raiders, plus a brother club, the Devil's Disciples. They got more than four hundred and fifty men, Tony, and they fixing to burn us all for what Rix did to Priest.

TONY: Holy shit, man! Can't you go to the Youth Board? Get them to cool it?

LACEY: Man, everyone knows the Youth Board ain't really for niggers. Besides, those Egyptian Kings, they just rumble, man . . . they ain't no social club. They even called off their war with the spic crews just to get at us. They got fuckin' guys in there must be thirty years old. I mean real gangsters, man. The Messenger said they emptied the treasuries of all the nigger clubs just to buy some death for us.

TONY: But first they got to call a War Council . . .

LACEY: They don't got to do shit! They say all the rules is gone for this one because they got to have the boy who blinded Priest. Man, they gonna go down without warning and they gonna jump guys in neutral turf and in school and even in they homes, man. They say vengeance by fire, man, you understand?

Nobody safe until they get Rix.

TONY: What . . .

LACEY: Yeah, that's like it is. The Messenger say they call the whole thing off if we give them Rix.

TONY: They want Rix to fight another one of their boys?

LACEY: Oh, man . . . they want to torture the cat. The Messenger says they have to cut off his balls and watch him bleed to death, pull out his eyes with pliers. They say he got to pay!

TONY: You mean like . . . fuckin' *deliver* him? Hand him over? What if we hip him and he cuts out . . . splits the neighborhood for good?

LACEY: Don't be crazy, man. They will know how he knew and we will all pay the fuckin' price. The niggers are crazy behind this one. Anyway, with all the shit on the street, the cops must know one of you guys burned that cop. Somebody got to pay for that, too.

TONY: I got to make a decision.

LACEY: I been talkin' to you like a brother, man. But the only decision you got to make is if Rix dies by himself, dig?

RIX *arrives at the clubhouse to a party in progress. He is greeted like a conquering hero by the Dragons. Representatives from white gangs from all over the city are there. At 2:30 A.M.,* LACEY *goes over to* RIX, *puts his arm around his shoulders.*

LACEY: How's it feel, man? To be the baddest cat of all?

RIX: I'm feelin' no pain, man. I shoulda killed the fuckin' nigger.

LACEY: Listen, Rix. We got a pound of smoke and an ounce of snow stashed over near the border, in spic territory. And you know that fine spic whore, the one they call Rondella? Well, she wants to meet you, man. She heard what you did, baby, and she thinks she be safe from niggers, she was your woman. We always keep the stuff over at her home 'cause her mother works this night shift at the hospital. We called, man, and she wants you to pick up the stuff personally. She waitin' on you.

Don't worry about the turf, either. I have ten good men go with you, like an escort for a king, man. They watch the house while you inside with her. And they be fully heeled, with *pistols*, man. Nothing but the best for my new Warlord.

RIX: Hey, beautiful, man. I don't need no escort, but if you want . . .
*(The phone rings. One of the Dragons says it's for* LACEY.*)*

LACEY: Man, I told you I will deliver and I will. Just hold tight for an hour or less. Yeah. . . .
*(*RIX *is putting on his new club jacket. Beneath the embroidered golden dragon is the red legend* WARLORD.*)*

LACEY: Rix, man, you gettin' ready to go?

RIX: Man, I gettin' ready to *come!*
*(Laughter chases him out the door.)*

# Warrior

**T**he Golden Boy was black. Twenty-one and O, with seventeen KOs. He was as sleek as an otter—all smooth, rubbery muscle under glistening chocolate skin. He wore royal purple trunks with a white stripe under an ankle-length robe in matching colors, his name blazing across the back: Cleophus "Cobra" Carr.

Tonight he *was* the main event, a ten-rounder. Middleweights, they were supposed to be, but they called Carr's weight out at one sixty-four.

There was a lot of betting in the mid-priced seats just past ringside—betting how long the fight would go before Carr stopped the other guy.

Nobody knew the opponent—he was the last-minute replacement for the guy Carr was supposed to fight. He walked to the ring by himself, wearing a thin white terry-cloth robe. His trunks were black.

The announcer pointed to the opponent's corner first. Manuel Ortiz. Dragging the last name out way past two syllables—*Orrrr-Teeese!* Ortiz was fifty-six and sixteen, with thirty-two KOs. Originally a welterweight, he'd go up or down . . . wherever there was work. They had him at one fifty-nine tonight.

Maybe he had dreams for this once—now it was a part-time job.

I knew his story like it was printed in a book. He got the call the day before, finished his shift at the car wash, got on the Greyhound and rode until he got to the arena—I could see it in his face, all of that.

Carr was twenty-two. He'd gone all the way to the finals at the Olympic Trials before turning pro two years ago. They said Ortiz was thirty, shading it at least a half dozen. The guy who managed him worked out of a phone booth in a gym somewhere near the Cal-Mex border. His boxers always gave good value—they wouldn't go down easy, didn't quit, played their role.

The fighters stepped to the center of the ring for their instructions. Carr had three men standing with him, one to each side, the third gently kneading the muscles at the back of the middleweight's neck. Ortiz stood alone—the cornerman they supplied him with stayed outside the ring, bored.

Carr gave Ortiz a gunfighter's stare. Ortiz never met his eyes. That was for younger men—Ortiz was working. I could feel the Pachuco cross tattoo under the glove on his right hand. . . . I knew it would be there.

The referee nodded to the fighters. Ortiz held out his gloves, just doing as he was told. Carr slammed his right fist down against them. The crowd cheered, starting early.

The bell sounded. Carr snake-hipped out of his corner, firing a quick series of jackhammer jabs. Ortiz walked forward like a man in slow motion, catching the jabs on his gloves and forearms, pressing.

Carr danced out of his way, grinning. I dropped my eyes to the canvas, watching parallel as Carr's white leather boxing shoes ice-skated over the ring, purple tassels bouncing as Ortiz's black lace-ups plodded in pursuit.

Deep into the first round, Ortiz hadn't landed more than a half-dozen punches. He kept swarming forward, smothering Carr's crisp shots, his face a mask of patience. Suddenly, Carr stopped back-pedaling, stepped to the side, hooked off his jab and followed with a smoking right cross, catching Ortiz on the lower jaw. Ortiz shook his head—then he stifled the crowd's cheers with a left hook to Carr's ribs.

The bell sounded. Carr raised his hands, took a quick lap around the ring, like he'd already won. Ortiz walked over and sat on his stool. His cornerman held out his hand to take the mouth-piece, splashed some water in the fighter's face, leaned close to say something. Ortiz didn't change expression, looking straight ahead—maybe the cornerman didn't speak Spanish.

Over in Carr's corner, all three of his people were talking at once. Carr was grinning.

A girl in a gold bikini wiggled the perimeter, holding up the round-number card. The crowd applauded. She blew a kiss.

Carr was off his stool before the bell sounded, already glid-ing across the ring. Ortiz stepped toward Carr, as excited as a gardener. Carr drove him against the ropes, firing with both hands, overdosing on the crowd's adrenaline. Ortiz unleashed the left hook to the body again. Carr stepped back, drew a breath, and came on again, working close. Ortiz launched a short uppercut. Carr's head snapped back. Ortiz bulled his way for-ward, throwing short, clubbing blows. Carr grabbed him, clutch-ing the other fighter close, smothering the punches. The referee broke them.

Carr stepped away, flicking his jab, using his feet. The crowd applauded.

The ring girl put something extra into her wiggle between the rounds, probably figuring it was her last chance to strut her stuff.

Halfway through the next round, the crowd was getting im-patient—they came to see Carr extend his KO record, not watch a mismatch crawling to a decision.

"Shoeshine, Cleo!" a caramel-colored woman in a big white hat screamed. As though tuned in to her voice, Carr cranked it up, unleashing a rapid-fire eight-punch combo. The crowd went wild. Carr stepped back to admire his handiwork. And Ortiz walked forward.

By the sixth round, Carr was a mile ahead. He would dance until Ortiz caught him, then use his superior hand speed to flash his way free, scoring all the while. When he went back to his corner at the bell, the crowd roared its displeasure—this wasn't what they came to see.

A slashing right hand opened a cut over Ortiz's eye to start the next round. An accidental head-butt halfway through turned the cut into a river. The referee brought him over to the ring apron. The house doctor took a look, signaled he could go on. The crowd screamed, finally getting its money's worth.

Carr snapped at the cut like a terrier with a rat. Ortiz kept playing his role.

Between rounds, Carr's handlers yelled into both his ears, urging him to go and get it. Ortiz's cornerman sponged his cut, covered it with Vaseline.

The ring girl was really energized now, hips pumping harder than Carr was hitting.

Carr came out to finish it, driving Ortiz to the ropes, firing a quick burst of unanswered punches. Ortiz came back with his trademark left hook, but Carr was too wired to get off-tracked, smelling the end. A right hand landed flush on Ortiz's nose, a bubble-burst of blood. Ortiz spit out his mouthpiece, hauled in a ragged breath and rallied with both hands. A quick look of surprise crossed Carr's face. He stepped back, measuring. Ortiz waved him in. Carr took the challenge, supercharged now, doubling up with each hand, piston-punching. Ortiz's face was all bone and blood.

The referee jumped in and stopped it, wrapping his arms around Ortiz.

Carr took a lap around the ring, waving to the crowd.

Ortiz walked over and sat on his stool.

The announcer grabbed the microphone. "Ladies and gentleman! The referee has stopped this contest at two minutes and thirty-three seconds of the eighth round. The winner by TKO, and *still* undefeated . . . Cleophus . . . Cobra . . . *Caaaarrrr!*"

The crowd stood and applauded. Carr did a back flip in the center of the ring.

Ortiz's cornerman draped the white robe over the fighter's shoulders.

Ortiz walked back to the dressing room alone.

"That's a real warrior," Frankie said to me.

"Carr? He's nothing but a—"

"Not him," Frankie said. "The Spanish guy."

That's when I knew for sure that Frankie was a fighter.

# White Alligator

**T**he alligators were tiny, perfectly-formed predators. They shone a ghostly white in the swampy darkness of the big tank.

"You never saw white ones before, did you?" The curator was a plump young woman, thick glossy hair piled carelessly on top of her head, soft tendrils curling on her cheeks. Wearing a white smock, no rings on her fingers, nails square-cut. A pretty, bouncy woman, full of life, in love with her work.

I shook my head, waiting. I hate this part of the business. They always have a reason for what they want done—I don't need to hear it.

"Actually, white alligators aren't all that rare. It's just that when they're born in the wild, they don't have much chance of survival. A grown alligator is a fearsome thing—it really has no natural enemies. But the mother alligators don't protect the babies once the eggs hatch. One old legend says that a baby alligator who actually manages to survive all its enemies and grow to full size spends the rest of its life getting even. That's why they're so dangerous to man."

I nodded again.

"You don't talk much, do you?"

"That's part of the service," I said. Catching her dark eyes, letting her feel the edges of the chill.

We walked past the bear pit. Grizzlies, Kodiaks, brown bears, black bears, all kinds. But the polar bear was in a separate area just around a sharp corner in the path. Prowling in circles, watching.

"How come the polar bear can't be with the others? He needs colder water or something?"

"She. That's a mama bear. Polar bears are solitary animals. They don't mix well. And when they have cubs, they attack anything that approaches."

"Show me where it's been happening."

We strolled over to the African Plains enclosure. Somebody had been sneaking into the zoo at night. It started with stoning a herd of deer. Then they shot one of the impalas with a crossbow. The animals didn't die. Whoever did it came back again. And a cape buffalo lost an eye.

"It's just a matter of time before he kills one of our animals," the curator said.

"He doesn't want to kill them. He wants them to hurt. Wants to hear them scream."

White dots blossomed on her cheeks. "How do you know?"

"I know them."

"Them?"

"Humans who do this."

Her hands were shaking.

"Nature can be hard, but it's never cruel. Survival of the fittest—that's how a species grows and protects itself. But animals never kill for fun."

"Neither do I," I said. Reminding her.

She reached in her pocketbook and handed me a thick envelope. "This is my own money. I couldn't go to the Board for help. They tried hiring security guards, but it kept happening. I can't have the animals tortured like this."

"I'll take care of it."

She fumbled in her purse. "You'll need a key. To get in after dark."

I waved it away. "Whoever's doing this didn't need a key."

The curator took a deep breath. Making up her mind, getting it under control. "I believe there have to be laws. Nature has its laws, we're supposed to have ours, too. But I don't want—I mean, you promised."

"I told you the truth," I said. . . .

**H**e didn't come until the fourth night. I was waiting in the shadows cast by the Reptile House. The African Plains enclosure was to my left, the bear pits just past that. He was wearing sneakers, but the animals let me know he was coming. Restless stirring. A nightbird screamed.

I circled behind him to the bear pit. As soon as he walked past, I took the five cans of industrial-strength Teflon spray out of my pack and went to work. It wouldn't last more than a half hour—the concrete absorbs it real fast.

When I caught up with him again, he was standing at the fence, watching the herd of antelope, picking a target. Wearing some store-bought ninja outfit. Stalking, he thought.

I stepped out of the dark, the pistol in my hand. He didn't turn around.

"Drop the toy, punk," I whispered, giving him a choice.

It fell from his hands.

"Hands up," I said, calm and quiet, moving closer.

"Wha—what do you want?"

"What do I want? I want you. I've been waiting for you, maggot. We're going to take a little ride. To a nice hospital. Where they'll *talk* to you, boy. Maybe find out what else you've been doing when it gets dark. Understand?"

Standing maybe fifteen feet away. Giving him another choice.

"No!" he screamed, turning and running from me, sneakers slapping hard on the concrete.

I chased after him, letting him feel me coming. He was doing fine until he got to the curve just before the pit where the polar bear guarded her cubs.

Maybe he screamed.

# Witch Hunt

## 1

The first time I heard a message, I couldn't obey. I could hear it, but I was distant from it, the way I am from people talking. They think I can't hear them, but I can—I just can't get close enough to say anything.

The messages don't come from inside my head, no matter what the doctors say.

I was small when I first heard them. I couldn't do anything to stop them. Any of them. The people, I mean, not the messages. I can stop people, sometimes, but I would never stop the messages.

## 2

No matter how much I screamed, my parents would still leave me with her. They acted like they didn't understand, because I couldn't talk then.

By the time I could talk, I was too scared.

# 3

**E**llen burned me. Just to show me she could do it. My babysitter. She was in charge when my parents would go out. Sometimes she would beat me. Spanking, she called it. She would do it real hard until I would cry. Then she would tell me I was a good boy.

She showed me how to do what she wanted. If I didn't do it, she would hurt me. Sometimes she hurt me anyway. She liked to do it. She would get all sweaty and close her eyes. Later she would laugh.

# 4

**M**y parents liked her. My mother told my father he only liked her because she wore her blue jeans so tight you could see her panties right through them. My father got all red in the face and said how reliable she was. My mother said how hard it was to get anyone to watch me.

Ellen made me lick her. And she put things inside me too. When I got older, she took pictures of me.

She said if I ever told, they wouldn't believe me. And then she'd get me good the next time.

Cut out my heart and eat it.

Sometimes Ellen wore a mask. Sometimes she burned things that smelled funny.

Her eyes could cut me and make me bleed.

She had a tattoo inside her leg. On the high, fat part where her legs came together. A red tattoo of a cross, like in church. The cross was upside down. Where it would go into the ground, it went inside of her.

## 5

**I** told on her. One night, just before my parents were going to go out. I was five years old and I could talk. I was so scared I wet all over myself, but I told.

They looked at each other—I've seen them do that a lot, ever since I started watching them. But when Ellen came over, they told her they weren't going out that night and she could go back to her house.

Ellen looked right at them. Right in the eye. "Is Mark telling his crazy stories again?"

"What stories?" my mother asked her.

"His Devil stories, I call them. He told me his kindergarten teacher was a monster. How she wore this mask and carried fire in her hand. It must be that cable TV. My Dad won't let me watch it."

I could see it happening. I screamed so loud something broke in my eyes. Then I couldn't see anything.

## 6

**T**hey put me in a hospital. A lady came to see me. She was very nice. She smelled nice too. She came a lot of times. Every day.

After a while, I could see again.

I wouldn't talk to the nice lady at first, but she promised me Ellen could never get me. I was safe.

So I told her. I told her everything. She said she would fix it. Everything would be all right.

When they came back a couple of weeks later, they had the nice lady with them. She sat down on the bed next to me and held my hand. She said they looked at Ellen. Without her clothes on. And there was no red tattoo like I said. It must be my imagination, the lady said. She had a sad face when she said it.

I knew it then. She was with Ellen.

I was already screaming when they showed me that first needle.

## 7

**I** was in the hospital a long time. Sometimes my parents would come in there with the lady I thought was nice. After I took my pills I would get dreamy. But I wouldn't sleep, not really. Just lie there with my eyes closed and listen to them.

"We could get sued," my father said. "Ellen's father hired a lawyer. He said false allegations happen all the time. A witch hunt, he called it."

It scared me, the way he said it. I didn't look.

## 8

**T**hey tested me, to see if I was stupid. When they found out I wasn't, then they said I was crazy. I had to talk to a doctor. I told him about the messages. He was the first one. He said they came from inside my head. I told him "No!" and he pushed a button and some big men in white coats came in.

Later, they started the drugs. Haldol. Thorazine. All kinds of things. I learned to take the pills. Otherwise, it was the needle.

Some of the attendants, they gave you the needle anyway, even if you were good. They liked to do it. But it was the nurse who gave the orders. She was with Ellen.

## 9

**T**hey let me go home sometimes. My mother would make me take the medication. I got older and older, but it didn't make any difference. I still had to do what they said.

I cost a lot of money. I heard them talking. A lot of money.

"Paranoid schizophrenic," my mother would say. What the doctors told her, like a religion.

Ellen's picture was in the paper. Her father was arrested for having sex with his daughter. A little girl. Nine years old. I was eleven then, and I could read good. Ellen's picture was in the paper because she told on her father.

In the paper, they said Ellen was a hero. For saving her sister.

When I asked my mother about Ellen, she slapped me. Then she started crying. She said it wasn't my fault—I was born this way. I knew she meant the messages. Then she called the hospital and they came and took me away.

# 10

**T**he medication has side effects. I know what they call it. Tardive dyskinesia. My face jumps around. My whole body twitches. My mouth is so dry and it's like it is stuffed with cotton. My hands shake. I'm dizzy. My stomach is upset. I hate it.

When I stop taking the pills, they give me the needles.

They never catch me not taking the pills. It's just that I act different without them. And they can tell.

Act. That was a message I got all the time. *Act!*

# 11

**I**'m an out-patient now. I live in a room. My parents moved away. I don't know where. I'm an adult now. Twenty-three years old.

I get a check. From the Government. Every month. It comes to where I stay. I pay my room rent. I eat in restaurants, but I don't eat that much. I'm not hungry much.

There is a television set in my room. I always leave it on. Messages come through it for me.

I don't take the medication very often, but I act like I am. Nobody looks that close.

# 12

They send you cues. That's the message, to watch for the cues. I go out, looking. The subways are the best. There's all kinds of crazy people in the subways. People never look at me that way. I look right. I'm careful.

I look carefully. At everything, I look. There's a third rail. It's death to touch it. If you look down, down into the pit, you can see the other tracks. Water runs between the tracks, like a river. You can see the things people throw there. Sometimes you can see a rat, watching up at the people.

The messages are everywhere, but they are never spoken. Not out loud. They come through things.

You have to watch them from behind because their eyes can burn you.

The first time, in the subway, the train came through the tunnel. Shoving through, too tight for the tunnel, like Ellen did to me. When the train screamed, I knew I was in the right place.

From behind, they look alike unless you look close. If you can see their panties, the outline of their panties, under their skirts or their slacks, then that's them. That's how you know them.

The first time I saw that, the train was screaming in. I was jammed in behind her in the crowd. When I pushed her, she went right under the wheels. Then everybody screamed like the train.

Nobody ever said anything to me.

# 13

The message comes to me anytime. Especially in my room, where the medication doesn't block the signals. When I hear the message clear, I go out. To do my work.

I'm on a witch hunt.

# Working Roots

**S**hawn knelt at the door to his tiny closet, worshipfully regarding a red shoebox. He slowly removed the lid and carefully removed his prize. Air Jordans, Nike's very best. The Rolls-Royce of sneakers, gleaming in pristine white with artful black accents. He turned one gently in his hands, admiring the intricate pattern of the soles, the huge padded tongue, the plastic window in the heel through which he could see the air cushions. No matter how closely he looked, Shawn could not find a single blemish to mar their perfection.

Almost two hundred dollars for a pair of sneakers. Granny would never understand. All they had to live on was her miserable little Disability check. If Granny wasn't able to make a little extra selling potions and charms to other people in the Projects, they wouldn't make it at all. It got harder and harder to sell her spells every year, Granny told him—younger people just didn't believe in the old ways.

Granny might not understand, Shawn knew, but she would never get mad at him. Old people were supposed to be mean, but Granny never was. She never punished him, even when he deserved it. Other kids got a whipping for nothing at all, sometimes. He'd heard them talk about it, at school.

Yeah, Granny was old, and she was kind of strange. And, sure, there was that back room, where he was never allowed to go. But she was always home, always had food for him. Always cared for him when he was sick or hurt. So maybe they didn't have a color TV like everyone else. Maybe he couldn't play Nintendo, couldn't have his friends over either. He had complained about the old lady's ways to his running partner Rufus one day.

"Shut up, fool!" Rufus replied.

Shawn saw the pain in his best friend's eyes—he felt ashamed again. Granny never got drunk, didn't take drugs, didn't have strange men living with her, different ones all the time. Rufus was right.

Shawn had worked for his special sneakers. Worked hard. There was easy money to be made around the Projects, inside and out. The drug dealers were always looking for new runners, the numbers man could always use a smart kid who could keep records in his head. Stealing and hustling were a way of life . . . sometimes a way of death, too. Shawn didn't touch any of that. All summer long, he had worked . . . hauling the monster bundles of newspapers the trucks dropped on the streets at dawn to the individual newsstands. Afternoons, he helped out in a car wash. He didn't spend his money, although the temptations were great. . . . Shawn was fifteen.

Now it was September, and school was starting. Shawn bought his own clothes this year, with the money he'd earned. Granny was proud of him for that, but she didn't know about the sneakers.

When he'd gotten his first money from the newspaper driver, he bought Granny a gold necklace. Twenty dollars, the young man in the long black coat told him . . . for gen-u-ine eighteen-karat gold. Shawn thought how pretty it would look on Granny. He showed it to Rufus, but his friend said it wasn't gold at all.

"You been hustled, chump. That ain't nothin' but brass . . . turn green right around your neck."

Shawn gave the necklace to Granny anyway. But because he had been taught not to lie, he told her what Rufus had said.

"Sometimes, people believe thinkin' the worst means they smart. It ain't always so, son," Granny told him. And she told him the necklace was real gold too. Gave him one of her dry kisses.

She always wore the necklace. And it never turned green.

Shawn couldn't really remember a time when he hadn't been with Granny. He knew his mother was dead, killed in a drive-by shooting while she was standing on the corner, just talking with a friend. They never caught the night riders who so casually blew her away. The police told Granny the shooters were really trying for a dope dealer standing on the same corner, like that would comfort her.

There was an "Unk" written in the space for his father's name on his birth certificate. Rufus explained that to him.

"Jus' means yo' momma didn't tell them yo' daddy's name at the hospital, that's all."

"Why wouldn't she tell them?"

"'Cause the Welfare go after him for the support money, see?"

Shawn nodded like he understood, but he was confused. Granny didn't collect Welfare—her Government money came from working all her life. As a maid. In Louisiana, where she was from. Where his Momma was from too, she told him. But Momma had come north when she was only a young girl.

"Came for the party, stayed for the funeral," Granny told him.

Sometimes, people would come to the apartment to see Granny when they had a problem. A lover who jilted them, a job they were hoping to get . . . stuff like that. Granny always seemed to know what they wanted before they even asked. She would speak a foreign language while she was working . . . sort of like French, Shawn thought, but he couldn't tell for sure. He knew it wasn't Spanish—he heard that every day in school and this wasn't the same. And she worked with roots. Special roots she got from someplace. Dried old things, all twisted and ugly. But

Granny could make things happen with them, folks said. Some folks, anyway.

Other folks, they said she was crazy.

School was tomorrow, and Shawn couldn't decide. His beloved sneakers wouldn't change his status sitting in his closet, but if he wore them outside . . . there was a risk. The Projects were full of roving ratpack gangs. They'd take your best clothes in a second, leave you bleeding on the ground if you tried to stop them. School was close by, but it was a long, long walk.

"I'm going downstairs to hang out, Granny. You want anything from the store?"

"No, son. Just watch out for yourself, hear?"

"Yes ma'am."

Shawn took the stairs. It was only seven flights, and the elevator scared him. You got trapped in one of the cars, there was no place to go.

He spotted Mr. Bart on the third floor landing. Mr. Bart was a monster of a man, over six and a half feet tall, more than three hundred pounds of muscle. But his mind wasn't right and he could be vicious, rip your head off with one hand, easy as pie. He could never catch anyone, though—his legs didn't work. Mr. Bart supported his huge body with a steel cage that went from his waist all the way to the ground. It had four rubber legs, like a walker. The hospital had to make it up special for him. Mr. Bart would pick it up, stick his arms straight out, slam it down, then swing his legs forward, supporting all his weight on his massive forearms. His hands were the size of telephone books . . . the Yellow Pages. You could hear him coming a mile away . . . like an elephant thumping.

"Good evening, Mr. Bart," Shawn called out.

"My money!" the giant grunted, touching a leather bag he had looped over a hook on the front of his walker.

"Sure is, Mr. Bart. Your money."

The monster smiled. Kids were always snatching his little bag, just to be doing it, show how brave they were flirting with disaster. They would grab the bag and run, stand down the corridor and empty it of its few coins, then drop the bag and run away. Mr. Bart could never catch them. He would thump over and drop himself on the floor to pick up his leather bag. Then he'd pull himself upright again, making horrible noises.

Everybody said if he ever caught one of those kids, he'd pull them apart like wet Kleenex.

Shawn hit the front steps running, spotted Rufus across the street and waved.

"What's up, home?" Rufus greeted him.

"You know."

"Yeah, you still fussin' about them shoes, wearin' 'em to school tomorrow?"

"Yeah."

"You got to do it, homeboy. The ladies ain't goin' to see what you worked so hard for they be sittin' in your house, right?"

"Right."

They exchanged a high five, Shawn drawing strength from his friend.

A young man of about nineteen turned the corner, wearing a multicolored leather 8-Ball jacket, black leather sneakers on his feet displaying the distinctive red ball for Reebok Pumps. He hard-eyed the two friends, then dismissed them with a sneer, moving away in a shambling, practiced mugger's gait.

"That mope, he think he bad, doin' the strut like that?" Shawn said.

"Brother, he *be* bad. That is Marcus Brown, man. You see that jacket? Cost you a thousand damn dollars, you buy it in a store."

"So what'd he do, rip it off someone?"

"You don't know 'bout that jacket? That jacket *famous,* man. Marcus, he roll up on this boy from the Jefferson Houses, throw down on him, point the piece in his face. Marcus, he don't go nowhere without his nine. Marcus say, give up the jacket. This boy, he don't play that . . . worked his butt off for that jacket, he ain't givin' it up. Marcus, he just squeezes one off. Right in the boy's chest. Ices him right in front of everybody. You look at that jacket close, you see a hole right over the heart. *Bullet* hole, man. Marcus, he one cold dude. Got *everybody's* respect."

"He don't have mine," Shawn said, his voice laced with bitterness. Marcus wouldn't worry about wearing *his* fresh sneakers on the street.

That night, Shawn couldn't sleep. He got up and went into the kitchen for a glass of water. Granny was there, cooking something in a big black cast iron pot she brought with her from down home.

"What troublin' you, son?"

It took a long time, but Shawn finally told her about the sneakers. Granny sat at the kitchen table, watching the love of her life struggle with more weight than he could carry.

"What do I do, Granny?"

The old woman looked around the kitchen, brought her eyes back to rest on Shawn. "Go get them shoes for me."

Shawn brought the shoebox into the kitchen. Slowly took out his prizes, laid them on the table like an offering on an altar. Granny held one in each hand, eyes closed. Words came out of her, but her mouth never moved. Then her eyes snapped open, but they looked someplace else. Some other place. Shawn didn't move. Finally, Granny focused on her child.

"Shawn, here is what be. What be the truth. The spirits can't protect *things,* you understand? Ain't nothing they can do, keep those special shoes on your feet. But I got a spell . . . an old, old spell that I never used in all my life. What it can do is make those shoes do good, you see?"

"No, Gran."

"I can't swear you keep the shoes on your feet, but, with this spell, whoever wear the shoes got to do the right thing, or . . ."

"So if somebody take them . . . ?"

"Somebody take them, he have to walk right the rest of his days. Like when you run off from a chain gang . . . no point in running off to live bad. They just catch you for whatever bad you doin' and back you go, understand? There's crimes that have to change a man. If the man don't change, he got to answer."

"Okay, Granny."

"Don't you 'okay' me, boy. The knowledge I give you is the oldest knowledge in the world. You don't obey, you have to pay."

Shawn nodded, waiting.

"Now look here, boy. You know, I charges people for my spells, don't you? That's the rules. It don't necessarily got to be money, but it has to cost somethin'. Now what this spell costs you is this . . . no fighting. You hear me talkin' to you? No fighting. Somebody try to take your precious shoes, you let them go. After while, they come back to you . . . one way or the other."

"I promise, Gran."

Shawn gave his Granny a kiss and went to bed, too excited to really sleep.

It took him forever to dress in the morning. He tiptoed down the stairs, watching each step carefully, maintaining the perfect newness of his sneakers as long as he could.

Mr. Bart was standing on the first floor, right near the front desk, watching. Shawn waved good morning to him. The monster waved back, not saying a word.

Rufus met him on the front steps, sporting a new lime-green leather jacket, his chest out like a peacock.

"That jacket is boss *stoopid,* Rufe."

"Thanks, homeboy. Those your new shoes, huh? Righteous!"

The two friends walked to school together. And, for one bright shining day, the whole summer's labor seemed well worth it to Shawn. Especially when Taineesha told him how much he'd grown since last year . . . he was taller than her now.

As they turned the corner to the Projects, Marcus stepped out to block their path. He had two of his boys with him, but they were just there to watch. They all watched . . . watched the black nine-millimeter automatic in his hand.

"Give it up," is all Marcus said.

Shawn put his hand in his pocket, brought out the fifty dollars he'd taken to school to impress everyone, wishing he hadn't. Rufus handed over his dough too.

"The jacket too, punk!"

Hot tears shot into Rufus's eyes, but he slowly took off the lime-green jacket and dropped it on the ground. One of Marcus's boys picked it up.

"Those look about my size," Marcus said, pointing his gun at the ground.

Shawn felt a stabbing pain in his chest as he bent to unlace his sneakers. When he let himself look up, they were gone.

Rufus went home. Shawn walked the rest of the way through the lobby in his stocking feet. Some of the older residents looked sad for him—he wasn't the first shoeless boy to walk home past them.

It was another two days before they saw Marcus again. Marcus wearing Shawn's sneakers, lounging against a streetlight pole.

"You got somethin' to say to me?" he snarled at Shawn.

Shawn and Rufus walked by, heads down.

"Maybe you gonna tell your crazy old lady, huh? Have her work some roots on me?" Marcus collapsed into laughter, his boys joining in.

Shawn and Rufus separated at the Projects door.

"I know where I can get a piece," Rufus whispered.

"No."

"No? We don't do somethin', we don't have nothin', right? Whatever we got, Marcus gonna take sooner or later."

"It'll be okay."

"You sure?"

"Sure."

"How you know?"

"I just know, Rufe."

Friday night there was a dance in the rec room. Shawn took a long time to dress . . . Chanel had told Rufus that Taineesha told her she was coming and she hoped Shawn would be there.

Everybody was there, even Mr. Bart, standing in a corner, his mountainous body moving to the music. Shawn danced with Taineesha and he didn't really miss his sneakers.

It was late when Marcus walked in with his boys. Wearing

his life-taker's jacket and Shawn's sneakers. Everyone stepped aside to give him room. Shawn prayed he wouldn't try to grab at Taineesha—he knew he couldn't keep his promise to Granny then.

The DJ was taking a break. The floor was cleared. People walked in a wide circle around the perimeter, visiting. Marcus made the circle too. Everyone he approached turned away from him. Nobody gave him back his smile, nobody responded to his challenges.

It was midnight when Marcus sauntered over to where Mr. Bart was standing. With a cobra-quick move, Marcus snatched the monster's leather bag and stepped away. He upended the bag, coins spilling out onto the floor. Nobody moved.

Mr. Bart picked up his walker, shifted it forward, slammed it down, advancing on Marcus.

Marcus grinned.

Another lift, another slam, another few inches.

"I ain't got all night for this lame to make his move. Let's book." Marcus signaled to his boys and stepped to make his exit. His foot came slowly, agonizingly off the floor, like he was pulling it from quicksand.

Another thump as Mr. Bart slammed his walker forward. Marcus pulled out his pistol and leaped forward. Heavy, ropy roots sprang from the soles of his sneakers into the floor itself. The gun went sailing into the distance as somebody in the crowd screamed.

Marcus fell to his knees, grasping for a claw hold on the floor.

Another thump, and the giant's shadow fell closer.

The rec room emptied, people walking out quietly, steadily. Nobody looked back.

The last thing Shawn heard was Marcus screaming . . . and the thump of Mr. Bart's walker.

"Vachss is in the first rank of American crime writers."
—*Cleveland Plain Dealer*

### BLOSSOM

Two things bring Burke from New York to Indiana: a frantic call from an old cell mate named Virgil and a serial sniper whose twisted passion is to pick off couples on a local lovers' lane.

Crime Fiction/0-679-77261-8

### BLUE BELLE

With a purseful of dirty money and the help of a hard-bitten stripper named Belle, Burke sets out to find the infamous Ghost Van that is cutting a lethal swath among the teenage prostitutes in the 'hood.

Crime Fiction/0-679-76168-3

### BORN BAD

*Born Bad* is a wickedly fine collection of forty-five stories that distill dread down to its essence, plunging readers into the hell that lurks just outside their bedroom windows.

Crime Fiction/0-679-75336-2

### DOWN IN THE ZERO

The haunted and hell-ridden private eye Burke, a man inured to every evil except the kind that preys on children, is investigating suicides among the teenagers of a wealthy Connecticut suburb and, along the way, discovers a sinister connection.

Crime Fiction/0-679-76066-0

### FALSE ALLEGATIONS

A professional debunker specializing in "false" allegations of child sexual abuse, has stumbled across the case of his career—the real thing. What he needs now is a man who knows how to find out the truth, a man like Burke.

Crime Fiction/0-679-77293-6

# FLOOD

## *Coming in Spring 1998*

She came into Burke's office on a steamy city morning, a small blond angel bent on revenge. Her name is Flood, and she wants Burke to find a child murderer called The Cobra—so she can kill him with her bare hands.

Crime Fiction/0-679-78129-3

## FOOTSTEPS OF THE HAWK

As Burke tries to unravel a string of sex crimes, he is caught in the crossfire of two rogue cops who are setting him up to be the next victim.

Crime Fiction/0-679-76663-4

## HARD CANDY

In *Hard Candy*, Burke is up against a soft-spoken messiah, who may be rescuing runaways or recruiting them for his own hideous purposes.

Crime Fiction/0-679-76169-1

## SACRIFICE

What—or who—could turn a gifted little boy into a murderous thing that calls itself "Satan's Child"? In search of an answer, Burke uncovers mechanisms of evil even he had not imagined.

Crime Fiction/0-679-76410-0

## SHELLA

At the heart of this story is a natural predator, Ghost, searching for a topless dancer named Shella, who has vanished somewhere in a wilderness of strip clubs, peep shows, and back alleys.

Crime Fiction/0-679-75681-7

## STREGA

The implacable Burke has a new client, a woman who calls herself "Strega" (Italian for an erotic witch)—and a new assignment that leads him into the deepest oceans of the twisted city.

Crime Fiction/0-679-76409-7

VINTAGE CRIME/BLACK LIZARD
Available at your local bookstore, or call toll-free to order:
1-800-793-2665 (credit cards only).